I0699053

GALLIVANTER
EXPEDITION

This is a work of fiction. Similarities to real people, places, or events are entirely coincidental.

SAVAGE WORLD

**First edition. February 4, 2025.**

Copyright © 2025 Cassie A. H. Moore.

ISBN: 979-8990210349

Written by Cassie A. H. Moore.

*"Man must be disciplined, for he is by nature raw and wild."*

*Immanuel Kant*

Savage World
Book Three, *The Gallivanter Saga*
By Cassie A. H. Moore

# CHAPTER 1



*Zermatt, Switzerland*
*1924*

BLOOD TRICKLED DOWN his lip as he stared at me, helpless.

In his eyes, I could see nothing but despair. He had given up the will to fight, and instead numbly accepted their torture.

"You're worthless," sneered the tall, dark-haired Italian man who grabbed him around the throat.

I winced as the man shook him, his bound hands scrabbling helplessly, trying to stop the Italian. The man shoved him to the ground, and kicked him hard in the side. Paz cried out in agony, then laid silent on the floor, breathing hard.

I couldn't watch this anymore. I squeezed my eyes shut.

The others paced around the room, speaking to each other. "Should we just kill him and move on?" one of them asked.

"He's not worth anything to us dead," another man responded. "We have to get the money first, don't you remember the plan?"

"He's a liability," the first man insisted, a cruel look on his face. "I say we cut our losses and dump him here. He's slowing us down. We can only move at night now, it's not worth it."

They spoke quickly, weighing the pros and cons.

Paz lay on the floor, listening as he panted hard. "Andi," he breathed, just loud enough that I could hear him.

I turned my eyes from the men to him, biting my lip as I saw his face. There were still fresh marks on his throat, in the shape of big fingers. The Italian man had hurt him badly. But his expression had changed from one of despair to something else.

"Andi," he whispered again, turning his face to look at me. "My family. Tell them."

I stared back mutely, biting my lip.

"You tell them," I whispered back. "You're going to make it out of here. You're going to be fine."

"Tell them," he said again, ignoring me. "Tell my family I love them. That I tried to be brave."

Tears welled up in my eyes. I blinked. I needed to be strong right now.

"And tell our team that, too," Paz murmured. "Tell them I'm sorry. I know now what a burden I've been."

He paused, and looked up at the ceiling. "Tell Cap I'm sorry."

"Stop," I whispered back. "You'll be fine. We're going to get you out of here."

He stared back at me without saying anything. I realized then what his expression was: acceptance.

"You there," one of the men shouted, noticing Paz talking to me. "Shut up! Did we tell you to open that mouth of yours, pretty boy?"

He stalked over and kicked Paz hard in the mouth. Instantly, blood and saliva streamed out and Paz moaned.

I winced, imagining the pain as if it had been me who'd been kicked. Tears rolled down Paz's face involuntarily, and he spit. Gobs of blood and spittle flew onto the ground in front of him.

The man towered over him, grinning sadistically at Paz's pain as he rolled on the ground.

"I think maybe you're right," he said over his shoulder to the others, his hand reaching for the gun he concealed under his clothes, at his back. "It's easier without him. Let's take care of him."

"No!" I shouted, as Paz stared at me with terrified eyes. "Stop!"

Suddenly, we were in a field out in the middle of nowhere. The grass gleamed up at me, brilliantly green against the sunny blue sky.

Paz was laying on the ground in front of me, blood gurgling out of his mouth. He had a bullet wound through his chest, and grabbed at it wildly with bloody hands.

I screamed as he thrashed, then went still. His eyes were glassy. Lifeless.

Wait. I've been here before. Where am I?

I looked around, and saw bodies all over the field. In the distance, smoke was rising. I cried out in fear.

*Bang.*

*Bang, bang, bang.*

I heard someone pounding at my door. "Andi?"

My eyes sprang open. My heart raced as I lay in bed in the darkness, trying to collect my thoughts.

"Andi!" Cap said urgently, through my closed door. "What's going on? What happened?"

I shook my head, clearing the sleep. It was a bad dream. Another one.

I quickly rolled out of bed, folding my arms across my chest, and opened the door. Cap stood in front of me, his blonde hair rumpled and his cheek still indented from the crinkle of his pillow.

"It was just a dream," I said quietly, willing my heart to slow down. I'd had too many of these nightmares lately.

"A bad one?" he asked, staring at me in the darkness. "You screamed out."

"I did?"

"I could hear it from the room next door."

My shoulders slumped. "I don't know what's wrong with me. I used to have these nightmares about my father's death on the battlefield in France. Now, I'm dreaming about Paz's death all the time."

Cap pushed the door open and let himself into my room. He closed the door gently behind us, then put his arms around me. "Paz isn't dead. It's just a dream, not a premonition."

"We don't know that. He may be dead."

"He's not," Cap said, stroking my hair. "They wouldn't kill him. Not yet. They need him alive to get their ransom money."

I bit my lip. "You said, 'not yet.' Meaning you think they will kill him, as soon as they get the money."

Cap pulled me over to the bed and sat down. He put his arm around me again and held me.

We sat in silence for a few minutes. I could feel his heartbeat, slow and steady, against my ear as I laid my head against his chest. Cap always knew what to say to comfort me. He was a good fiancé. But no amount of his reassurance could convince me that Paz, our kidnapped teammate, was going to be fine.

"How did we end up here?" I finally whispered. "How are we here, together, like this? Was this all a horrible mistake?"

He sighed. I felt the depth of his sorrow as he responded.

"This is life, unfortunately. Every turn is marred with triumph and tragedy. It doesn't matter what twisted, crooked path we took to end up here. If we had the chance to do it all over again, we'd screw it up somehow in a different way. We can't regret our past mistakes. All that matters now is where we go next."

"But Paz is gone," I whispered, shaking my head. "He's hurt. And we know they're bad people, the men who kidnapped him."

"We'll find him," Cap said, leaning his head on top of mine. "I have faith in us. We've been against the ropes before, and we've come out fine."

"This is different. A man's life hangs in the balance. It's a race against time."

Cap sighed again, and I felt the weight of his head droop on mine. We said nothing.

We both knew there was nothing more we *could* say. We'd said it all, already, in the last few days.

# CHAPTER 2

IT WAS FIVE DAYS AGO that our teammate, Paz, had been brutally kidnapped by a gang of four men we suspected were a part of an Italian criminal network.

He'd been pulled from the rest of the crew, targeted after the gang overheard his drunken boasting about his wealthy family at a bar in Innsbruck, Austria.

The rest of his team, the Chinook Voyageurs, had sustained serious injuries during the attack. Thankfully, they'd all survived. And Paz was the only one who had been captured. We assumed he was being kept alive for a ransom request from his family, though it hadn't come yet.

Cap and I sat together in the dark, saying nothing but holding each other. Gradually, I felt Cap's body loosen and relax.

"Lay down," I whispered, pushing him onto the bed. He groaned, but didn't resist. Nearly as quickly as his head hit the pillow, he was asleep. I curled up next to him.

I lay in bed with Cap sleeping next to me, thinking about my life. How quickly things had changed.

Was it really only a year ago that I'd stared miserably out my open bedroom window at my boarding school in France, wishing I was anywhere on earth but stuck with those prissy classmates?

Now here I was, in bed with my fiancé, a boarding school drop out who'd traveled through twelve different countries in as many months.

I sighed, slipping out of bed. I couldn't possibly sleep right now. Silently, I padded to the little desk under the window. Quietly, staring out at the moon that illuminated the snow-capped mountains outside our hotel, I slid out a piece of paper.

*"Maybe it would help to write your thoughts, Andi,"* I thought to myself. *"Take a page out of Cap's book and journal. There's been so much going on, you've hardly had time to breathe."*

But where could I possibly begin?

*"This expedition around the world, supposedly a race to beat the Chinook Voyageurs to that million dollar prize, has been nothing but a disaster,"* I scribbled.

*"If you'd known this last year, when you impulsively interviewed to join the Gallivanter team and promptly dropped out of boarding school, leaving behind everything you knew, would you have still made this choice?"*

I paused, tapping my ink pen against my hand, then thoughtfully returned to writing.

*"If you would have known that the competition between your team and the Chinooks would've gotten so ugly that the Odysseus Society, your sponsors, suspended you both and forced you to travel together—people who hated each other—would you have believed yourself ever capable of getting along with them? Could you have ever imagined coming to their aid like this, when they'd been attacked and Paz had been kidnapped, held for a ransom?"*

The twinkling stars caught my eye, and I sighed. What had been such a welcome sight as my little team of four had camped in the desert all over Africa last year, in our attempt to be the first team to travel to every country in the world in our Model T Fords, had now become an unpleasant reminder that we were running out of time to save Paz.

Every day mattered.

And today was yet another day wasted, vainly trying to figure out where the kidnappers might be holding him. Both teams, the Gallivanters and Chinook Voyageurs, had combined forces to try to find him—but with no luck so far, despite our efforts. We were sick with worry.

*"Could you ever have imagined this would be your life?"* I wrote slowly, squinting at the words in the dark.

*"Could you imagine that you'd ever be this famous? That people would stop you on the street and beg for your autograph? That you'd be this rich, as your adventures traveling the world filled the front pages of every newspaper on the globe?"*

I exhaled quietly, listening to Cap's deep breathing behind me. He was snoring lightly. I knew the burden of responsibility had been unbearable lately, as he wracked his brain to try to rescue Paz.

With the Chinook Voyageurs' team cars destroyed by the kidnappers and half their team in the hospital—including Hudson Landry, the Chinook captain—Cap had singlehandedly been shouldering the burden of both captains.

No wonder he was exhausted.

As Cap snored in my bed, my mind drifted to him. We weren't yet married, but we had lived together on this expeditionary team for a year now. I knew everything about him—and about my teammates, Chito and Bernard. Spending every hour of every day together had brought us closer than I ever knew people could become. I understood their passions and strengths, their sense of humor, knew all their bad habits and annoying quirks.

*"Could you ever imagined that you'd be this connected to a team of men—men who just a year ago, were strangers to you—who have now become your new family?"* I wrote slowly, the ink wet on my paper.

*"Could you have guessed that you'd find your fiancé here? That you'd survive the danger you already have, and willingly throw yourself into more?"*

I stared at the words I'd written, thinking slowly. So much had happened in the last year. I'd discovered who I was, in the midst of our adventures. I'd managed to survive several terrifying misfortunes, including nearly drowning in a river and getting stranded in an African jungle, alone, overnight.

I wasn't the same girl I was when I dropped out of boarding school last year.

My eyes caught a glimpse of movement outside of my window, the warmth of dawn starting to set the sky on fire. A tiny sparrow landed on my windowsill, staring in at me. It turned its head, quickly, searching all around. Just as fast as it landed, it suddenly took off.

I watched as the bird fluttered away toward the mountains, its wings beating furiously until it caught the wind and soared, effortless, out of sight.

Turning back to my paper, I wrote faster now, the words coming easily.

*"If you'd known all of this last year, would you have still made this choice?"*

I smiled, in spite of the tension that had gripped my soul for a week now, when my team and I first found out that the Chinook Voyageurs had been attacked and swiftly came to their rescue.

*"Yes, I still would have made this choice,"* I scribbled. *"I would have because it's the best thing that's ever happened to me, despite the danger and the accidents we've had to overcome. And because I know now that I'm an explorer, an adventurer. That I can never stay in one place for too long. And because I've finally found the people I want next to me on this journey."*

I lifted my pen and started to put the cap on, but then impulsively added a few more sentences.

*"I'm Andiamo Gallivanter. My story is unlike anyone else's story. And no matter what happens next, I'm going to fight to make it a good one."*

# CHAPTER 3

CAP FINALLY STIRRED as dawn was illuminating the horizon outside, the soft shades of velvety darkness melting into the warmth of daylight.

Ever since we'd slept in the desert as we traveled through Africa, we'd all found ourselves rising with the sun every morning.

"Hey," he whispered, opening his eyes. "I slept in here last night?"

"Yes," I cuddled against him. "Remember? I had a bad dream, and you heard me yell?"

"Oh, right," he said sleepily, yawning. "I shouldn't be caught in here, though."

"I know," I said. We'd agreed to keep separate hotel rooms wherever we went in order to keep up the illusion of being teammates, not lovers. We'd told the Chinooks that we were engaged, swearing them to secrecy, but we hadn't yet told anyone else. With our celebrity status, we knew any hint of impropriety—true or imagined—could turn the press against us. It could destroy our reputations as role models, and all that Cap had worked hard for many years to achieve. We tried to live above reproach, publicly and privately, knowing just how closely the world watched us both.

"I need to get out of here, then," Cap said, glancing out the window. "Can you check the hallway?"

"Yeah, hold on," I said, pulling on a robe as I padded to the door. I opened it and peeked out.

"Good morning, Andi," said Claude, who had the room across from me. Meticulous and soft-spoken, Claude was on the Chinook crew and kept track of all the supplies they required for their busy schedule. His door was open, and he was talking to Leonce, the Chinook's team cook. Leonce said little, but he had a good sense of humor that matched his good looks. Both of them were already dressed.

"You're up early?"

"Yes, I wanted to start getting supplies early," Claude responded. "You know, to be prepared. In case we start rolling unexpectedly."

"Right," I said. Inwardly, I groaned. We were in a pickle now.

"I'm going to put some shoes on," I said, ducking back into my room. Cap looked up at me from the bed.

"Claude and Leonce are right outside my door," I replied. He rolled his eyes.

"How do I get out of this now?" he said, looking toward the open window.

"Cap, no," I frowned, following his gaze.

He bounded off the bed. Leaning out the sill, he nodded. "I could make it easy, no problem."

"You're not going out my window into your room! You're ridiculous!"

"I have long legs," he responded, already starting to climb over the ledge.

"Stop it," I said crossly, watching him with worry. "You'll kill yourself, you idiot."

He grinned at me and stretched over to his window. "I love you too."

He was nearly inside when suddenly, his left foot slipped out from under him on the ledge and he crashed to the floor of his bedroom.

"Cap!" I yelled, leaning out of my window as far as I could. I couldn't see him on the floor, but I could hear him scrambling around, trying to stand up. It sounded like he'd knocked over a chair.

I hastily shoved on my shoes and flew into the hallway. I swiftly knocked on Cap's door.

"Hold on," I heard him yell, as more things thumped to the ground inside his room. Chito opened his door, sticking his head out.

"Hey," he said, frowning. "Did something happen to Cap? I hear stuff crashing in his room."

"Um, yes," I said, scrunching up my face. What was a convincing lie I could tell him?

Chito stared at me. "Was he in your room again?"

I stared back at him, guilty. I couldn't help from blushing.

"Andi," Chito said in a disapproving tone.

I shook my head. "No, he was just sleeping, I swear!"

He stared back at me skeptically.

"He was," I protested. "I had another dream."

Chito's face swiftly changed from judgment to compassion. "Another bad one?"

It had been Chito who'd beat Cap to my door a few nights earlier, when he heard me scream in my sleep after another nightmare.

I nodded. The memory of Paz's dead eyes and blood-soaked body welled up in my mind. What if my dreams weren't just dreams, but premonitions? Paz might be dead this very moment. We might be chasing a ghost.

I heard Cap swear from inside his bedroom, and I knocked lightly. "Cap?"

His feet thumped toward the door, and he opened it, rubbing his knees. "Good morning!" he said brightly, kissing me on the cheek. "Good morning, Chito!"

"He already knows," I said, as Chito glared at us.

"Chito, come on," Cap sighed. "I was just sleeping. Andi woke me with a nightmare. I went to check on her and fell asleep in her room."

Chito shook his head reprovingly. "When are you two announcing your engagement to the world? I'm getting tired of keeping your secrets."

"Soon," Cap said, stretching. "We just haven't had the right time. But it's taking a toll on me. I think I'm getting too old to be sneaking through windows."

"Anyway, what's the plan for today?" I asked, seeing Claude and Leonce walk toward us carrying a box of supplies. They stopped in front of Cap's door.

"We're leaving to visit the hospital and check on Rollie," Leonce said, setting the box down. "After that, we thought we could have a meeting of the minds with everyone? Figure out what the plan is?"

"Fine with me," Cap replied. "I'll talk to Hudson about it."

Hudson Landry was captain of the Chinook Voyageurs. Tall and handsome, with dark hair and dark eyes and a forceful personality, he was debonair and flirtatious but equally fierce. He'd grown up with his team in Quebec, hunting in the snowy woods and competing in ice canoe racing. He was just as detailed and strong-willed as Cap, and after traveling together for the last several weeks, they had newfound respect for each other.

During the robbery when the kidnappers had captured Paz, Hudson had fought back. As punishment, they stomped on his hand, fracturing his bones. He still wore bandages, but had just been discharged from the hospital.

"It's just a trifle," he had insisted, showing us his bandaged hand. "You know I'm tough as nails."

"What does that make me, then?" Patrick had groaned, leaning on his crutches.

"You got shot in the leg," Hudson grinned. "You're not tough. You're soft as a loaf of bread. That bullet went straight through you, Patty."

Hudson's teasing vastly underplayed the seriousness of the situation that had occurred. We all knew that his jokes were merely Hudson's way of coping with a terrible situation that had upended all of our lives and filled us with unrelenting worry.

"How is Rollie doing today? Anyone know yet?" Chito asked.

"Marceau went down early this morning, before dawn," Leonce said quietly. "I assume he's about the same, since we haven't heard an update."

I felt a twinge of despair. Rollie hadn't been as lucky as the other men when they'd been attacked. He and Willis, the two lead drivers for the Chinooks, had been bent over the gang's stalled out car, examining the engine, when one of the kidnappers bludgeoned them in the head from behind.

Rollie had taken the first hit—the harder hit—and had gone down cold.

He'd been battling brain swelling for the last few days, laying in his hospital bed without stirring. For the first two days, we weren't sure if he was going to survive. Now, we weren't sure if he would ever be the same happy-go-lucky, friendly man once he did finally wake up. The doctor had already told us that brain injuries were notoriously tricky to predict.

I'd grown especially close to Rollie as we traveled together, and it crushed me to see how badly he was hurt.

"I'd like to see Rollie today, too," I blurted impulsively.

Leonce and Chito unconsciously glanced at Cap, who shrugged. "Okay. I have to head out with Hudson anyway—I'll see you in a bit."

As our teams traveled together a few months ago, Rollie had flirted with me, not knowing that Cap and I were secretly together.

When Cap and Rollie had too much to drink one night, they got in a fist fight over me. Though we'd all sobered up and resolved it, I still felt a prickle of guilt when it came to Rollie. I'd made it clear to him that we were just friends—and we *were* dear friends, until he and Cap fought—but it was still a bit awkward.

Cap and I had fought bitterly over the whole situation and had finally come to a compromise, but I still didn't want to push my luck when it came to spending alone time with Rollie.

Not now, when the whole team was already so tense. It felt like we were all about to snap from the stress already.

"Let me just get dressed and I'll join you, Leonce," I said, backing into my room and closing the door. Safely alone, I exhaled in frustration.

What a mess we were in. We were all on edge, emotionally and mentally frayed, as we scrambled to figure out a way to track down Paz and waited desperately for Rollie to recover. It was if a cloud had settled on our teams, blotting out the sun. Apprehension and fear threatened to overwhelm me.

*"Something has to change,"* I thought, biting my lip. *"We can't go on living like this, trapped in indecision. We're imploding here without activity. We need to find you, Paz, before it's too late."*

# CHAPTER 4

QUICKLY, I WASHED MY face and ran a brush through my hair, braiding it to keep it out of my face. I changed into clean clothes, then slipped down to the lobby, where Claude and Leonce were sitting on the sofas, waiting for me.

"Ready?" Claude said, getting to his feet. "Hudson just left with Cap and Bernard to buy some replacement Fords for the Chinooks."

"Good," I said, tucking a loose strand of hair behind my ear. "We'll be able to get around more easily that way."

With their vehicles damaged in the attack, the Chinooks were relying on our team to get them around. Car keys were constantly switching hands as we made trips back and forth to the hospital and ran errands around town.

In the last few days, we had struggled to figure out what to do next. Cap and Hudson had immediately connected with the local police, filing reports over a missing person, violent assault, stolen property, and destroyed vehicles.

Initially, the police had scoured the area where the Chinooks had been attacked, looking for clues, but the trail went cold. No one seemed to know the men or where they were from and no one had any idea where the kidnappers had gone.

Despite Cap begging the Zermatt police department for continued help, stopping in every day to check in with the officers assigned to the case, their commitment to the case was clearly lagging.

"I think it's time to go after these kidnappers on our own," Hudson began proclaiming, even as he recovered in his hospital bed, while Cap insisted that we continue to try to work with the local police.

"We have to do this right," Cap repeated, as the team expressed their doubts. "The laws are in place for a reason. We have to trust the process, and the people in place to help us."

"Yeah, they're sure helping us, aren't they?" Willis muttered, saying what we were all starting to think: the police didn't really seem to care that much about finding Paz. Their body language and offhand remarks made it clear that they all felt that we had invaded their city and brought trouble with us.

It was increasingly obvious that we'd have to keep pushing Paz's kidnapping to the forefront of the Zermatt police department's minds, whether they wanted to pursue it further or not.

---

WE PULLED INTO THE hospital and made our way to Rollie's room. As we walked in, I saw Marceau already sitting at his bedside in the sterile room, his face tired and drawn.

"Hey," he sighed, looking utterly exhausted.

"How's he doing today?" I asked as I gazed down at Rollie's body, searching for any sign of improvement.

His face was still grotesquely swollen from the pressure his brain was putting on his skin, his features almost unrecognizable.

Rollie didn't deserve this fate.

Regret flooded my mind as I stared at Rollie's feeble form, laying lifelessly in his hospital bed. If only the Chinooks hadn't gone to a bar that night, in Austria. If only Paz hadn't gotten drunk, bragging about how rich he was to try to impress Dessie. If only the Chinooks had taken a different route that night, and hadn't wandered right into the criminals' trap. If only they would've kept going, and hadn't stopped to help the kidnappers.

I shook my head as Marceau filled us in on what the nurses had told him that morning.

"Still not much change," I heard him say, cutting through the fog of regret running through my brain. "He's breathing fine, though, and keeping down the water and medicine they're giving him. So we hold onto hope."

We sat for a while, talking quietly amongst ourselves.

"We'll discuss it later, I'm sure, but I think the plan is for us to all head to the police station together," Claude leaned forward. "Hudson told me this morning that he and Cap are really frustrated with the local police. They keep pushing them to do more, but they've pretty much given up on pursuing the kidnappers."

"So why are we all going together?" Leonce asked, his brows furrowed.

"I think they're hoping that all of us showing up will create a stronger impression," Claude replied. "An image of solidarity. To let the police know we're all desperate to find him. That we won't just walk away from this."

"They can't possibly pay any less attention to us," I responded bitterly. "If we all go in together, they'll be forced to do something. Right?"

"Right," Marceau agreed, sitting back with a sigh. "*Someone's* got to do something, anyway. Somebody needs to pay for what they've done to Rollie—and to Paz."

"*And to all of us,*" I added in my own head, fighting back a wave of worry.

# CHAPTER 5

LATER THAT DAY, WE showed up, en masse, at the police station in Zermatt. We filled the entire reception area, listening to the clack of typewriters and murmured conversation from the bullpen.

Cap and Hudson sidled up to the front desk, asking for the chief. It was clear that the police officer working the desk recognized them, and I caught him rolling his eyes as he turned to ask someone to let the chief know he had visitors.

A few minutes later, a young officer appeared. "Let me escort you back to his office," he said politely in English, nodding at us.

We trailed behind him, glancing at the busy station full of uniformed men who were smoking and cursing as they talked with each other. We reached a small office, where the young officer knocked on the open door.

"Komm herein," a deep voice boomed, and we squeezed inside the room.

Cap and Hudson took the only seats in the office, and the rest of us stood behind them, shoulder to shoulder.

"Back again, I see. And now apparently with the whole team," the chief said in English, his eyebrows lowered, leaning back in his leather chair. An abandoned cigar sat smoldering in the ashtray on top of his desk. "What exactly can I help you gentlemen with now?"

"As you know, sir, our friend has been kidnapped," Hudson said. "We've made our initial reports through your office, and we've been anxiously awaiting your next decisions about what we can do to continue searching for our friend. Per our request the other day, we understand that your officers have made contact with his family, in Spain, to share the situation?"

The police chief stood up slowly, reaching for a pile of files on top of a large metal cabinet.

"What'd you say his name is?"

"Paz De la Rosa."

He shuffled through the stack. Goodness, there were a lot of files there. Crime was good business in Zermatt, apparently. Finally, he located the file. Frowning, he opened it and scanned. He read silently for several moments.

"We already investigated the mugging and robbery and destruction of property, and found nothing conclusive. That case is now marked inactive. In regards to your friend's disappearance, it says here that our detectives made contact with Mr. De la Rosa's family yesterday, and wired the case over to their local police station in Tarragona," he said, snapping the file closed. "They'll be handling things from here on out."

"But the crime happened here, not Spain," Hudson protested, shaking his head. "The perpetrators are likely locals. Or hiding out locally. Why would you send the case off to the Spanish police already? They can't do anything to help. You, on the other hand, are located right in the center of everything."

"It's procedure. He's a Spanish citizen. It's their case now."

"I understand. But the kidnapping and assaults took place in *Zermatt*. Surely you can help us? We have the best chance of capturing this gang here, don't we?"

The chief picked up his smoldering cigar and relit it. He puffed away for a moment, a little cloud of smoke jetting up above his bald head.

"My department is limited," he finally replied. "We already did what we could for you. I'm sorry, but we don't have the resources for a wild goose chase, just to help a group of foreigners who brought trouble to our city. We need every man here."

"We're international celebrities," Cap spoke up. "We're on the front page of the newspapers all the time. Paz is internationally known. You've let the case grow cold, and you've neglected working on it after just a few days. How can you refuse to help us now? The eyes of the world are on us, and you won't even spare a single officer to assist us?"

The chief narrowed his eyes.

"*I* don't have to do anything," he replied. "I don't care if you're the Pope himself, I don't have to do a darn thing for you or anyone else. I'm in charge here, not you. And I don't have the manpower to help you with this particular case. The chances of recovering your friend alive are slim, anyway. It's a fruitless effort that my department cannot afford to indulge in—not when we have plenty of other serious, solvable cases to pursue."

"But you know as well as we do that the criminals are no doubt still hiding out in this area!" Hudson insisted. "We have the best chance of catching them and saving Paz if we get to work immediately. Right here. To do that, we need *your* help. Your men."

The chief smoked his cigar, and leaned back in his chair, studying us. It was obvious that Cap and Hudson were both trying to control their anger, but it bubbled just under the surface. I wondered if the police chief secretly liked watching them struggle with their own self-discipline.

"I can't help you," he finally breathed out, as a plume of smoke wafted out of his mouth and nostrils. "Sorry, boys."

"Please," Cap pleaded. "There must be something we can do."

"We'll go to the next town over," Hudson retorted, looking angry. "We'll ask another police department. We'll talk to anyone here who is willing to help us. We don't need you. Someone else is bound to help us, bound to care about this case. We're famous, for Pete's sake."

The chief laughed shortly. "No one else will touch it. It doesn't matter who the hell you are, in the eyes of the law. *We* have jurisdiction—not anyone else. And we don't have to release the files to any other department. If they try to take them anyway, it won't be good for them. I'll have their badges for that sort of insolence."

"Please, sir—" Cap tried again, but the chief cut him off.

"Trust me, gentlemen—nobody's going to stick their neck out and break department protocol, not even for you," he snapped. "This is a cutthroat business. You don't get to where I am by doing favors for careless celebrities who were too stupid to keep their mouths shut around the wrong people."

Cap shook his head, irritated. "We're not asking for much. Why are you so unwilling to help us? Our faces have been on the front page of every paper in the world. It'd only look good for your department to assist us right now. Think of the good publicity you'd get!"

The chief smirked. "I don't need publicity. I've done my job here. We investigated the scene and found nothing. Your friend is gone. Just face the facts."

"And what facts would those be, exactly?" Patrick interrupted.

"In my professional opinion, once someone's been kidnapped, you rarely ever see them again," the chief replied. "You need to deal with reality, boys."

"Fine," Hudson said, standing up. "If that's your attitude—that he's as good as dead to us already—we don't want you working on this case anyway. We'll handle it on our own. Thanks for nothing."

"I wouldn't do that, if I were you," the chief warned. "I advise against taking it into your own hands."

Hudson whirled around angrily. "Why not?"

"Because vigilante justice doesn't go over too well around here, like it does in your wild west," the chief said, rolling his cigar between his fingers. "We're a civilized country, Mr. Landry. We follow the law. And right now, I'm following it. I investigated your robbery and assault, and found no additional leads to follow. That case is closed. This alleged kidnapping, however, involves a Spanish citizen, and is now in the hands of the Spanish police force. But you—if you decide to bend the rules, or go after these kidnappers on your own and make them pay for their crimes—well, you wouldn't be much better than the criminals themselves, would you?"

"I didn't say we would do that," Hudson said hotly. "You're making assumptions. I merely said we'd *handle* it."

"Handle how, exactly? That's the question, isn't it?"

Hudson shook his head. "We didn't ask an unreasonable request of your department. You don't have to make this so hard for us. We've been trying to do right, to save the life of our friend. You're the one who doesn't seem to care about that at all."

The chief laughed. "Oh, this is hard for you? I thought you were the mighty explorers who could do anything."

I was outraged at this man's arrogance. He was callused beyond compassion, with no regard for Paz's life. My anger took over.

"We'll be better off without your incompetent force anyway," I blurted.

The police chief's hawklike gaze was suddenly riveted on me, and he looked me over before responding. "Right, Miss Gallivanter. If you ask me, you brought this on yourselves. Parading around the world, looking for admiration, showing off in your fancy automobiles and trotting you useless girls around, flaunting yourselves? Why are *you* even in here, anyway? This is no place for young ladies."

I refused to break his stare, but I felt my cheeks turn red with anger.

"You did this to yourselves," the chief repeated. "Your friend's blood is on your hands, not ours."

Hudson lunged for him but Cap caught him.

"Let's go," he commanded sternly, his voice low.

Hudson swore angrily in French, in response. I grimaced, thankful the chief didn't know what Hudson was calling him. We quickly filed out of his office and Hudson flung the door shut, rattling the frame.

"What do we do now?" Chito asked, pulling at his beard with a worried expression.

"Should we try another police station, in another nearby town?" Dessie asked. "Maybe if I try asking? See if I can convince anyone to help us?"

"I'm not sure even your flirting can convince someone to help us now," Hudson replied, rubbing his face. "He's right. No one else has jurisdiction. They're within their bounds to refuse an officer to help us now, if they don't have the manpower to spare. It's technically not even their case anymore. He said they already sent it off to Spain."

"Should we contact the Spanish police, then?" Cap asked.

"I don't know what use it'll do at this point," Hudson groaned. "I assume Paz's family will be contacted for a ransom. But it hasn't happened yet. So either the kidnappers are hiding out right now here in Switzerland, laying low until things settle down, or maybe they're traveling to Spain so they are near enough to the family to extort the ransom in person—or maybe rob them outright. Right?"

We stood silently, huddled together.

We'd had this debate dozens of times already over the last few days. What should we do? Pestering the local police had done nothing but waste our time. Traveling all the way to Spain would be a significant effort, requiring days of driving, and the kidnappers might already have a head start.

But what if Paz and the kidnappers were still in the area? If we left town and headed to Spain, we'd miss them entirely.

We just didn't know. We were paralyzed in our indecisiveness over what to do. Paz's life hung in the balance, and we couldn't get a clear direction to head.

"I know no one wants to hear this, but we've talked in circles around this for days now," Cap finally said. "We need to make a decision. This was our last shot, trying to get help from the police. Clearly, the door's closed with them. So that gives us at least one avenue that's not open anymore. Our choices are narrowing."

"I say we all vote on our next move," Chito spoke up. "Indecision has stalled us long enough. It's time to take action."

Hudson scratched his chin. "Seems fair."

"I agree," Cap said. "We decide tonight and act tomorrow. No more wasting time. *Our* search for Paz commences at daybreak."

# CHAPTER 6

OVER A PRIVATE DINNER at our hotel, the doors tightly sealed, the group debated our options.

"Whatever we decide, we've agreed to take action immediately in the morning," Cap reminded us. "I realize we have a lot of strong opinions in this room, but we're all well aware that Paz's life is at stake. Every hour matters at this point. We simply don't know what to do right now, but we need to do something. It's a gamble, but it's at least a step in the right direction to take some sort of action."

"As you know, we've discussed a lot of potential possibilities over the last few days," Hudson took over, counting off on his fingers as he shared his thoughts.

"One, the kidnappers have Paz hidden away somewhere in this area, around Zermatt. They're laying low, waiting for things to blow over and for the police to get distracted with other cases."

"Or they know very well the laziness of the police chief," Bernard added. "Police departments get a reputation, after all."

"Two, the kidnappers took Paz to Spain already," Hudson replied. "Paz's family lives in Tarragona, which is where Captain Gallivanter and his crew picked him up originally, when they brought him on as a local guide. Potentially, they're going to contact his family to arrange a ransom. Or maybe they're making plans to rob his family home, knowing that they're rich."

I bit my lip. I couldn't imagine his family having to deal with these evil men.

Hudson continued. "The third option? Maybe they've taken Paz somewhere else entirely. We think they're Italians, based on their accents, so maybe he's over the border in Italy right now.

Maybe they're waiting on a ransom request for a few weeks, or a few months."

"So our options are pretty narrow," Cap interjected. "We stay here and continue to search Zermatt and wait for Rollie to recover. Or, we leave Rollie here on his own and head to either Spain or Italy and try to intercept them."

"You think it's wise to have Rollie stay here in the hospital by himself?" Dessie asked. "He's thousands of miles away from his family. Who'll take care of him?"

Marceau frowned. "I agree with Dessie. I don't want to leave him on his own. If something happens during his recovery and he doesn't have any of us here to speak up for him, we'd never forgive ourselves. And what if he wakes up and finds all of us gone? He'll never forgive *us.*"

Hudson nodded. "I know. I feel the same way, I don't want to leave him behind. But what about Paz? We can't afford to wait here. It could be another week—maybe longer—until Rollie is even awake. And who knows how long until he can even get out of that hospital bed?"

"We have no idea if they're in Italy or Spain or anywhere else, for that matter," Chito sighed. "How would we even know what city to go to? They could be anywhere."

We stared at each other. He was right. It was impossible to know where they might have hidden Paz away. Assuming they hadn't already killed him.

"I hate to be the one that brings this up, but what if this is all for nothing?" Bernard said somberly, vocalizing what I had just been thinking. "What if they already murdered Paz?"

"Don't even go there," Cap said quickly. "He's alive."

"But how do we know? Maybe they'll say he's alive, just to get their ransom money, but he's already dead."

Dessie shot to her feet, her fists balled up.

"Stop it!" she yelled at Bernard, her cheeks pink with anger.

"Sorry," Bernard said hastily. "I'm just trying to be honest. He might be—"

"He's not! I'd know!" Dessie spat, looking like she wanted to punch Bernard in the face. Marceau reached over and took Dessie by the elbow, gently, and pulled her down.

"I know this is difficult to discuss," Marceau said quietly, looking at Dessie, and then staring at the group. "But we all care about Paz, and we want to help him. We're not giving up on him. No one's giving up on him."

Dessie buried her face in her hands, hunching her beautiful shoulders.

"I'd know if he was dead," she said again, her voice muffled through her fingers.

More than once, I'd wondered if Dessie was secretly in love with Paz. She certainly seemed like it, especially as I watched her now. She'd been preoccupied and distracted ever since Paz went missing. The rest of us were struggling, too, but she'd been more shell-shocked than anyone else. She'd hardly talked these last few days, and I caught her pushing her food around on her plate without eating more than once.

We all fell into silence. Suddenly, a thought came to me. "Hold on a minute," I said, frowning. "How will they get the money?"

"What?"

"The kidnappers," I replied. "How will they get the ransom money?"

Hudson frowned. "A wire transfer? Western Union?"

"Which could be traced," I responded. "They'd have to deal with a bank, then, to accept a wire transfer."

"So?"

"So, if you've kidnapped someone and are holding them ransom, are you going to gamble on working with a bank to get your money? Or are you going to do it on your own, just in case the police might be tipped off to you already, the banks might be watching out for you, and your transaction might get unwanted attention?"

Hudson nodded slowly. "So that means the only option is to get the money in person. It's the better guarantee you won't get caught."

"Right," I said. "They'll want cash. Lots of it."

Slowly, a smile spread across Hudson's face. "Andi, you really are a smart girl."

"I don't follow," Chito stared at us both, confused.

"The only surefire way they can get the cash is to retrieve it from Paz's family," Hudson explained. "They wouldn't risk dealing with bank transfers, because it'll bring in other people—other eyes. It'd be easy for the police to alert every bank in town, and for them to get arrested the moment they request the money. No, they'd want to get the ransom directly from his family, without involving anyone else. They'd probably arrange a dead drop somewhere."

"So that means..."

"That means they would want to be near Paz's family. In Tarragona."

Cap caught on.

"They'll head to Spain, not Italy," he said, pulling out his map. "Which means if we want to catch them, that's where we need to go, too."

He quickly unfolded a large map of Europe, as Claude and Chito and Patrick started stacking plates and pushing cups aside to make room for him to spread it out on the tabletop.

"We're in Zermatt," Cap said, pointing to the small city in southwestern Switzerland. "If they're heading to Tarragona, let's see..."

He traced a line through southern France and into Spain.

"Hold on, hold on," he said, grabbing for a pencil and adding distances in the margins of his map. He muttered to himself for a few moments, adding the mileage up. Finally, he looked up.

"It's just over a thousand kilometers from here to Tarragona," he said. "When we rushed here, we pushed our Fords to do nearly seventy kilometers an hour. So if my calculations are right, we could make it there in about fourteen hours."

Patrick did the math in his head, leaning on his crutches. "Calculating time for breaks and refueling and rotating drivers, I think we could safely say if we took off in the morning, we'd be there within eighteen to twenty hours at the very most. We can carry enough gasoline reserves to cover that, no problem."

"It's feasible," Claude mused. "What do you think, Hudson?"

"It seems like the only option, if I'm being honest," Hudson replied. "But we're back to square one. What about Rollie? Can we leave him?"

Patrick put his palms down flat on the table. "What if we don't leave him entirely, but we leave a few people with him? Split the team, and the majority of us go to Spain while a few hang back until he recovers?"

We turned the thought over in our minds. It made sense, I realized.

"We can't afford to wait any longer, wasting time here," Patrick continued. "But we can't leave Rollie on his own. So we leave a skeleton crew with him. Three or four people, maybe. That leaves enough for us to rotate drivers and drive straight through to Tarragona. Once Rollie is recovered enough to move him—hopefully in a few days—the second team takes off, and we all meet up in Spain."

Cap rubbed his face. "How do we decide to split the group, though?"

"We even it out," Patrick said. "Leave a mechanic, in case something happens to one of the automobiles. A navigator. A driver or two."

"Four people in a vehicle would be pushing the weight limit," Bernard reasoned. "You're better off with two in each Ford."

"So we need to leave two Fords behind, and three people," Hudson replied. "When Rollie recovers, you have two in each vehicle as you drive to Spain. That's possible. That means we'd take a team of nine to Tarragona right away."

"So how do we split it up?" Chito asked. "Any volunteers?"

"I can't drive," Dessie admitted, sounding defeated. "I know it's not a good time to admit this, but it's true. I can't be of any use to anyone right now."

"Well, that's my fault more than yours," Hudson grimaced. "It never occurred to me to teach the woman in our group."

I resisted the urge to roll my eyes. Dessie was gorgeous, but our team had long suspected that she'd only been brought onto the Chinook Voyageurs to get attention in the press, and that she couldn't even handle the vehicles. Apparently, we'd been right all along.

And now that we needed every single driver, this would pose a problem.

"So Dessie needs to go with the larger group—the first group—as a passenger," Willis said. "Hudson and Patrick can't drive yet, either. They just got out of the hospital themselves. The skeleton crew needs to be assembled of experts, those of us who know the cars inside and out. With so few people, every one of them will be immensely valuable."

Patrick glanced at Hudson.

"Captain, I think I should stay back," he admitted. "If I'm being honest, my leg could still use some time to heal up, to be strong enough to drive that far."

I glanced at his leg. Over the last few days, the bandage had gotten smaller, but I imagined he was still in considerable pain.

Patrick caught my glance, and stared at me. I stared back, confused at the expression on his face. He held my gaze and spoke again.

"And Captain Gallivanter, I think Andi should stay behind, too. I think she should be our captain."

"Andi? Why?" Hudson asked, as Cap stared at me. I was taken aback, speechless.

"She's a great driver, and she knows the cars nearly as well as Bernard, from what I can gather," he replied. "Besides that, she has grit. She's a leader. And with a skeleton crew, we'll need that quality more than anything."

Hudson turned to Cap. "What do you think? It'll be your call. It's your team."

"We'd need one more person on the team, too," Cap replied, rubbing his jaw. He was stalling.

I cringed. I knew Cap didn't want me to stay behind and be apart from him—especially not when it came to spending more time with Rollie. Rollie had flirted with me for weeks, and Cap had been rightfully angry about it. We'd patched things up, but the wounds were still uncomfortably fresh.

But I also knew there was truth to what Patrick said. I had the right qualities for the job.

"I can stay, too," Marceau offered. "I'd prefer not to leave Rollie at this point, anyway. I want to keep an eye on him. We've always been close. I keep picturing us as kids, skating on the pond behind his house. I have to make sure he's able to do that again."

The team fell silent again, their eyes traveling back and forth between Cap and me. Everyone knew we had a complicated situation on our hands. Would Cap allow me to stay back with his rival, a man who'd openly pursued me just a few weeks before? A month ago, they'd drunkenly beat each other up in a bar over me.

I didn't know if I should say something. I felt awkward, but flattered that Patrick thought so highly of me. But could I do it?

Could I lead a little group on my own, without Cap or Hudson's help?

# CHAPTER 7

THE ROOM WATCHED ME, silent, as the question hung in the air. Could I lead a crew all on my own?

*"Yes,"* I said to myself. *"A year ago, I couldn't. I would've doubted myself. But now? Now I know I can."*

Cap smoothed the map in front of him, and calmly looked up at me. "Andi, what do you want to do?"

I blinked. Cap always made the decisions for our team. He was letting me decide? I stared back at him, conflicted. The Gallivanters had never been split up before. And he'd certainly never let the crew make decisions like this before, either.

"The choice is yours," he added, staring at me with his bright blue eyes. "I trust your judgment."

He was really saying, *"I believe in you, and I trust you,"* I realized.

"I'll do it," I nodded. "I'll stay behind. With Patrick and Marceau. We'll take care of Rollie."

"Then it's decided," Cap said, looking back at his map. "We'll need supplies, and gasoline, Chito and Claude."

"We have them already," Claude nodded. "We've been ready for days now. Just waiting to move."

"We have plenty of food," Leonce pulled out his supply notebook. "We won't need to stop to restock anything for a while."

"Hudson, why don't you and I work on the route tonight?" Cap suggested. "Everyone else, prepare to leave first thing in the morning. Get some good sleep tonight. Tomorrow will be a very long day. We'll plan our rendezvous in Tarragona and telegram back here to the hotel and let you know, once we get there. Bernard, can you do a quick check over the cars before you turn in?"

"Sure thing, Captain," Bernard said, standing up. "I'll do it right now."

The other men stood up, clearly preoccupied with tasks they wanted to finish before hitting the road in the morning. I stood up, too, but I was unsettled. Shouldn't we have some sort of final word together, before we split up? One last hurrah?

Bernard left the room with Chito and Claude. Leonce and Dessie and Willis headed out behind them, talking together.

This wasn't what I imagined. Our teams had combined, but were scattering again. Did we have a clear enough picture of what was going to happen? How would I know what to do on my own? What if we got delayed or lost, and it was my fault, as captain?

I fought back against the panic I suddenly felt, my brief flash of confidence now waning. I sat back down, next to Cap and across from Hudson. They were so engrossed in the map that they didn't notice me. I realized, suddenly, that I needed to pay attention to what they were doing. This was *my* responsibility now.

"We have to go around the mountains here," Cap muttered, penciling a route. "We pick up the main road in Grenoble, that's probably the fastest route."

"Sure," Hudson said, checking the milage. "It's just under four hundred kilometers."

"Perfect," Cap said, taking notes. They continued to work, piecing the route together, Hudson writing it out longhand for the other drivers so everyone had a copy.

I leaned my head on my hand, watching them silently. The two of them complemented each other nicely, not only in looks but in personality.

Cap, clean-shaven, with his blonde hair and tall, muscular frame, was a contrast to Hudson's dark hair and stubble and lanky body. Cap was meticulous, serious, and disciplined, while Hudson was gregarious, forceful, and convincing. They didn't often work together this closely, but with their commanding personalities, it was like watching two lions circle their prey together.

"Feel good about it?" Hudson finally said, laying his completed notes on the table.

"The travel, yes," Cap said, rubbing his neck tiredly. "The rest? Not so much."

"Yeah, sounds about right," Hudson said. He glanced at me. "I'll have copies of this for you, too. Thanks for staying down here and mapping the route with us. I'm going up to bed. I'll get up early and fill everyone in on this."

"I'll be up early, too," Cap said, standing to fold his map up. "Thanks for your help."

"No problem," Hudson said, pushing his chair in. He paused to look at me. "And thank you, Andi. I wouldn't trust most people to lead a crew in a situation like this, but I *do* trust you. I know you can do it."

"Thanks," I replied quietly, giving him an appreciative smile. He glanced at Cap, then patted me on the shoulder. "I'll leave you two to talk."

I waited as Cap folded up the map and gathered his bag. Finally, he looked up at me. His eyes locked on mine.

"I know," I said quickly, before he could say anything. "You're worried about me traveling with Rollie."

He sighed.

"I promise you, there's nothing there between us," I blurted. "I don't care if he had feelings for me. I'm not doing this because of him. I'm doing it because I need to."

Cap stood there, staring at me. What did his expression mean? I couldn't tell.

"I'm sorry," I said. "I know you don't want me to do this. I won't, if you don't want me to. It's up to you. You're the captain of our crew."

"Don't be sorry," Cap said quietly. "Can't you tell what I'm feeling right now?"

"No," I admitted. "Angry?"

"No," he said, his voice soft. "I'm proud."

"Why?"

He set his bag down and sat, reaching for my hands. He held them, rubbing them gently. "I'm proud because you're the right person for the job. Because I know you're capable, and you'll do well."

"That's not all," I replied.

"No, it's not," he sighed. "I'd be a fool not to admit that I'm nervous. I worry about you traveling on your own, with a small group—especially after what happened to the Chinooks."

"I know."

"But I trust you."

"I know."

He held my hands, tracing the lines in my palms with his thumbs. "I know you want to know why I let you decide, instead of making the decision myself."

"Why did you?" I asked. "You're the captain. It was your call to make. You always make the decisions for the Gallivanters. Why let me decide, all of a sudden? Why now?"

He lifted his head and looked at me. "I didn't like the way that police chief talked about you. I'd have decked him, but then I'd be in jail right now. But it's dead wrong to talk about you like that because you are a woman. You've pulled your own weight on this team from day one—and then some. I'm tired of people looking down on you, for whatever reason, whether it's because you're female or because you're young. This was my way to validate you. Because you're smart, Andi. You can make decisions and stand by them. Even if they don't always happen to be decisions I agree with."

"So wait," I replied, staring. "You don't agree that I should be staying back?"

He sighed. "It's the most logical decision."

"But you don't agree with it?"

"Andi, stop," he said shortly. "You're asking the man that loves you to leave you behind, in a dangerous situation, after one of his teammates got kidnapped. You're asking your fiancé to let you travel alone, with only a handful of people to protect you, after a crew of *nine* just got attacked and hurt. And we're pursuing those same criminals, by the way."

He ran his hand through his hair, like he always did when he was overwhelmed with the thoughts running through his mind. "On top of all of that, you're staying behind to watch over a man that, up until a few weeks ago, I worried about."

I pursed my lips, sympathizing with his thoughts. I could understand his concern.

"It's not that I worry about your capabilities," Cap said, his expression softening as he looked at my face. "I know you're capable. It's that I'm terrified of what could happen *to* you. You're a woman, Andi. You're going to be out in remote places, traveling with only two healthy men. One, if we consider Patrick's leg injury. If Hudson's crew of eight strong men could get attacked and overpowered, how easy would it be for you to get hurt? I couldn't live with myself if something happened to you."

"We're smart, though," I protested. "We'll be fine. The trip isn't too long. You said that yourself. Just a day of travel, that's all."

"A lot can happen in a day, though," Cap said, looking up at the ceiling and sighing.

"It won't."

"But we don't know that for certain."

"Look at me," I said. He sighed again and looked into my eyes.

"This is who we are. We're risk-takers. Explorers," I replied. "We do the things that others wouldn't dare do. We push boundaries. We push each other. Even when it doesn't seem to make sense to the rest of the world. We have to trust ourselves. If anyone can do it, we can."

He shook his head ruefully.

"I created a monster," he said, leaning forward and catching my face between his hands. He kissed me.

"An adventure-loving monster," I agreed, smiling at him as he held my face.

"I know," he replied. He pulled away, and squared his shoulders. "I hate to leave you, even for a few days."

"Me too."

We sat together in the quiet room. I wasn't sure what to say now. My worry about Paz and Rollie and now Cap and the others heading into danger was rolling around in my brain. On top of that, I'd have to think as a leader for the first time. The weight of that responsibility was already weighing on me. I knew how much work it was, from watching Cap the last year.

"You'll be fine," Cap said, as if he was reading my mind. "At this point it's a toss-up what is the safer choice. Anyway, we all signed up for adventure, didn't we?"

I smiled wanly.

"I hate to say this, but I need to get to bed," Cap sighed, standing up again. "You know I want to stay. But I need to get up before dawn, and I'll be awake for probably twenty hours or so before I can sleep again."

"It's fine. I'll go to bed, too."

He put his arm around me as we walked through the silent hallways to our rooms. He stopped at my door and paused.

"You know I love you," he said quietly. "But I hope you know I believe in you, too. You'll be great as a captain."

"I do," I smiled. He grinned back at me.

"Just the two words I can't wait to hear one day soon," he joked. "When things calm down someday, we'll finally get around to getting hitched."

"Priorities," I laughed. "Let's find Paz first, and get to that when we can."

He kissed me, and I opened my door.

"Sweet dreams," I said, wishing I could fall asleep in his arms. Instead, I closed the door behind me with a thud.

I was on my own now. It was time to learn how to shoulder that burden of responsibility, as the newly-minted captain of my crew.

# CHAPTER 8

I WOKE UP WHILE IT was still dark, the faint sounds of my teammates moving around the hall stirring me from a dreamless sleep.

I quickly dressed then ducked into the hallway. Claude and Bernard were carrying out boxes together.

"Can I help?" I asked.

Bernard shook his head. "This is about it."

I followed them downstairs. The patio outside the lobby was a flurry of activity, with Cap and Hudson directing traffic as Dessie, Willis, Chito, and Leonce packed the Fords, which were lined up out front.

Feeling like I should be doing something to help but finding nothing to do, I shuffled my feet and stood off to the side, watching. When Patrick emerged a few minutes later, slowly limping toward us on his crutches, I didn't feel so alone.

"It's weird seeing them leave without us, isn't it?" I remarked.

"Yeah, it is," he replied, watching them look over the directions Hudson was handing around. "I feel like I should be doing something."

"Me too."

We watched them in silence, as they loaded the last of the bags and boxes into the back of the Fords. Bernard and Marceau alternated checking the gas tanks on each car one last time, lifting the bench seats in each Ford.

"Are we ready?" Hudson called, looking over everyone.

"Ready, Captain," Willis said, saluting playfully.

"Let's say our goodbyes, then," Hudson said, walking over to Patrick and me.

"Patty, my boy, hang in there," he said, giving him a hug and winking at me. "Keep an eye on this little renegade for me."

"Good luck, Captain Landry," I offered as Hudson pulled me into a hug.

Willis and Dessie hugged me next. Dessie looked pale this morning, with deep circles around her eyes.

"Be safe, Andi," she said, clutching my arms. "We need you with us, as soon as you can make it to Spain."

"I will," I said, smiling with courage I didn't quite feel. "You be brave. They're counting on you."

Claude and Bernard lined up to hug me, in quick succession. The quiet ones of the crew, I didn't think I'd ever get a hug from any of them. Especially not Bernard.

Sure enough, he didn't disappoint.

"I don't even know why we're hugging," he complained, as I briefly wrapped my arms around him and he stepped back. "I'll see you in a week or two, tops."

"It's a momentous occasion," I said, trying to hide my smile. "It's the first time our team's ever been separated, in over a year now. Think of that—we've spent every single day together."

"Yeah, I know," he said sourly.

Leonce laughed, behind him. "Well, I think you're right," he said, stepping in to hug me. "It is a significant moment. Be safe, Andi. I sure admire your spirit. Take good care of our boy for us."

"Thanks," I replied. What a difference this was to how we'd separated from the Chinooks only a few weeks ago. We hadn't thought we'd see each other ever again, and we had shaken hands and parted ways without a second glance, without sentiment. But now, the shared trials and stresses of the last few weeks had changed our relationships dramatically. It had made competitors into allies—into *friends.*

Chito wrapped me in a tight hug. "I don't want to say goodbye," he whispered. "I'm already worried about you."

"I'll be fine. I can handle it."

"I know," Chito said, squeezing me. "I won't say it. I won't say goodbye. I'll just say see you soon."

"See you soon, then," I replied, as Cap came up behind him and laid his hand on his broad shoulder. Chito released me, sighing.

Cap wrapped his arms around me, lowering his face to my ear so he could speak to me privately.

"I love you more than life itself," he whispered. I could feel his body clench, like he was holding himself together. "I don't want to say goodbye, either."

"I love you too," I whispered back. The rest of the team glanced our way and then kindly turned their backs, bundling into the cars.

"You have the route. And extra maps. Make sure you're prepared. And be safe."

I nodded. "You too."

"I feel like I should say more right now," Cap sighed, stroking my hair. "There's so much I want to say. About how proud I am of you. And how worried I am. How much I love you. But there isn't time."

"We have the rest of our lives to talk," I told him. "This is just a brief interruption. We'll be fine. You know me. We're going to make it through this. In a week or two, maybe three, I'll be by your side again, in Spain."

He exhaled. He was holding me so tight that I could feel his lungs deflate and then fill back up with air. "I've watched you come close to danger too many times," he said softly. "Be careful. I mean it."

"I'll be fine. You know I can do it. Trust me."

He kissed me, and Patrick awkwardly crutched a few more steps away from us.

For once, Cap and I didn't care that the entire team was there waiting. We kissed each other with all the passion of two people who weren't sure what tomorrow would bring, and didn't want to face it without each other. We stood intertwined until Hudson coughed lightly.

"Time to go," he called, his back still turned to us.

Cap pulled apart, his ears pink. "I love you."

"I love you too," I replied. "Don't worry. We'll be fine."

Cap took another long look at me, as if he was memorizing my face, and squared his shoulders. He pulled his helmet on and walked over to his car. "Load up!" he said loudly, without looking back again. Chito slid in next to him.

Patrick and Marceau and I stood on the steps of the hotel, waving as the convoy of five Fords pulled out with their nine passengers. Bernard was the only one who drove alone, at the tail end of the group.

The last time we'd traveled together, a few weeks ago, we had nine automobiles: three for the Gallivanters and six for the Chinook Voyageurs.

With the Chinook fleet destroyed by the kidnappers, we'd managed to replace four autos, an impressive feat in such a short amount of time. They'd left two for us, and they didn't have team logos on the doors.

The morning darkness soon swallowed them up as we stood on the steps, listening to the sound of their rumbling Fords grow faint. I stood watching where they'd driven away, touching the compass necklace Cap had given me weeks before.

"Every real adventurer needs a compass," he had told me as he draped it around my neck. This particular compass had a sparkling two carat diamond in the middle—the makeshift engagement ring that Cap had yet to pick out for me.

"I can't even hear them now," Marceau said, his chin lifted as he listened.

"Godspeed, team," Patrick said, leaning on his crutches. "Should we go inside? Go back to bed? It's still early."

"I can't sleep now," I replied. "Coffee?"

"I don't think I've ever said no to coffee," Marceau grinned, holding the door open for Patrick and me. We walked through, into the lobby, heading toward the small dining room.

It was just the three of us now.

# CHAPTER 9

"IT'S TOO EARLY FOR the cook to be up," Patrick said, leaning his crutches against the wall and hopping over to sit down in a chair. "We might need to wait a while for breakfast."

"We don't have anything better to do," Marceau said, glancing at the hotel clerk. "I'll go ask if there's any way we can get some coffee. Maybe they'll let me back in the kitchen to make it myself."

He walked away from the table, leaving me alone with Patrick.

It felt so different, being with these two men by myself. Like we were the last random guests at a party, stuck staring at the decorations and empty punch bowl after missing all the fun that everyone else had enjoyed.

"It's just us now," I remarked. "It feels strange, doesn't it?"

"Yeah," Patrick said, leaning back in his chair. "I guess we'll get to know each other pretty well, huh?"

"I don't think we have much choice. Can I start by asking you something, and having you answer me honestly?"

"Coming out hot right from the gate, Miss Gallivanter?" Patrick teased. "Shoot."

"Why'd you suggest for me to lead the group yesterday?"

He grinned. "I knew you'd ask me that at some point."

"And?"

He smiled, lacing his hands behind his head and reclining in his chair. "Because you're a leader."

"But so are you," I countered. "Why didn't you volunteer yourself? You could've done it. Why'd you volunteer me?"

He simply smiled back. I couldn't read him at all.

"I'm serious, Patrick. I want to know why."

"You're a leader," he repeated. "You've just never had the chance to lead. Well, this is your chance."

I blinked. "But why are you giving me the chance? Why now, with something this important?"

He shrugged. "You're capable. Why not give you the chance? I believe the right person for the job should have it. And I think that's you, in this case."

"But—I—do you think people will listen to me?"

"I do. And Cap and Hudson clearly do, too. The crews respect you. Who cares about anyone else?"

"But what about Marceau? And Rollie? What will they think, with me leading them? Will they accept the decisions I make?"

"Marceau's mother is a force to reckon with," Patrick laughed. "I've met her. Marceau wouldn't dare doubt you, you're too much like her. He'll fall in line. And Rollie? Well, let's be perfectly honest here, Andi. Rollie would follow you right off a cliff if you asked him to."

I felt my cheeks go red. I tried to ignore his comment and move on.

"I appreciate your vote of confidence," I confessed, crossing my arms across my chest. "I'm new to this, though. So I might be asking your opinion now and again."

"Of course. I'll do what I can to help," Patrick smiled. "I went to university and everything."

"Hey now," I laughed. "Just because I abandoned boarding school, you think you can rub your fancy college education in my face all the time?"

"For what I paid for it? Yes, I do."

I laughed. I appreciated Patrick's sense of humor. Despite missing Cap and Chito and Bernard, and in spite of the fear and tension we faced over Paz's kidnapping, that would make the next few weeks bearable.

"So we've spent time together already, but I haven't gotten the chance to know you that well yet," Patrick said, leaning forward. "Not on a personal level, anyway. Tell me about yourself."

"What do you want to know?"

"Start from the beginning."

"I have a mother and sister in New York," I said. "I grew up in northern New York, but my dad was Canadian. We traveled a lot, camping out in the woods, when I was little."

"No wonder I like you. You're part Canadian, like us," Patrick grinned. "Your father sounds like a man after my own heart. Does he still travel?"

I hesitated. "He died. He was in the army, a soldier in the Great War. Killed in action and buried somewhere in France."

"I'm sorry," Patrick replied, his voice soft. "Too many good men died over there. Friends of mine, too."

I nodded. I couldn't dwell on it, not now. Grief would only hamper my ability to lead. "My mother sent me to boarding school in France when I was eleven, after he passed. She was worried I was trying to fill his shoes, needed a different focus. I needed a change of scenery. I spent six years in one school, then got kicked out. I went to another school, and ended up leaving to join the Gallivanter crew."

He whistled. "You got kicked out of boarding school? For what?"

"Punching a bully. She deserved it. I should've done it earlier."

Patrick laughed. "Of course that's why. Remind me not to end up on your bad side."

"Your turn," I smiled. "What's your story?"

"Born and raised outside of Toronto, in a small town. I have a mother and little brother. My dad was an engineer, as I think I've told you before. He was successful and made good money. From the time I was little, he encouraged me to make something out of myself. Go to college, get a degree, become a rich man," Patrick explained. "Needless to say, he was a bit disappointed that I ended up doing this. But I met Hudson in college, and heard about all of this, and I couldn't help but jump at the idea of a world tour. It's the adventure of a lifetime, you know?"

"I know. I felt the same way."

"No amount of reasoning with my father worked," Patrick said, rubbing his chin, his blonde stubble rasping. "He told me this was a waste of my time and my talents. But here I am, anyway. Sometimes the people we think know us best don't really know us at all."

"True."

Marceau returned with a tray, carefully balancing three empty cups and a carafe of coffee.

"Here you go," he said, slowly placing it down in the center of the table and handing steaming cups around.

"We're just getting to know each other here," Patrick said, sipping his coffee. "Did you know Andi's dad was Canadian?"

"Who's his hockey team?" Marceau asked, adding cream to his cup. "He better not be a dirty Toronto St. Patricks fan, like this fool sitting next to us."

"Hey now," Patrick exclaimed. "We just won our second Stanley Cup. Back off."

"I don't know," I admitted. "He never told us. He passed when I was little."

"Sorry," Marceau winced, looking awkward. "The war?"

I nodded. Patrick changed the subject. "Marceau, what can you tell Andi about yourself?"

Marceau thought for a moment, holding his coffee cup up as he pondered. "I'm from Quebec, and I have sisters and brothers at home," he said. "Dad's a clockmaker. Mom's a big fan of knitting. And making bread. And we're all big fans of hockey."

I laughed. "Aren't all Canadians?"

"Pretty much," they laughed, looking at each other.

"I got into automobiles early," Marceau added, taking a sip. "I started hanging out around a neighbor who had a 1911 Model T Ford. It was a real beauty. I wasn't allowed to touch it—I was just a little kid—but I watched as he showed me all the parts. Eventually, he trusted me enough to let me tinker with it. I got good enough that I gained a little reputation around my town. Hudson and I grew up together, so he asked me right away if I'd be interested in being a mechanic on the Chinook team."

"What do you love most about all of this?" I asked, looking at both of them.

Patrick grinned. "The freedom. And the new sights and new people everywhere we go."

"Not having a real job," Marceau laughed. "If I was at home, I'd be a logger or a trapper. I didn't want to work with clocks, like my dad. I want to be in nature."

I smiled. "I love the excitement of it all. Waking up in new cities all the time? Seeing new things and trying new foods and learning about new places? It's so thrilling."

"You made out better than anyone in all of this, too," Marceau joked. "You ended up with a husband out of it."

"Well, he's not my husband yet. We're engaged."

"Same difference," Patrick laughed. "Judging by that kiss this morning, anyway. Whew."

I sipped my coffee and tried to control my blush, but I couldn't. Both the boys laughed merrily.

"It's going to be fun having a girl on the team who we can make blush, isn't it, Marceau?" Patrick teased. "We couldn't ever get under Dessie's skin like this. She just brushed us off."

"Stop," I said, trying to keep from smiling. "You're terrible."

We joked around and shared about ourselves for the next hour or so, until the kitchen finally opened and a waiter came to our table. We ordered breakfast and dined as the room slowly filled up with early morning guests. Several of them stopped by our table, asking for our autographs.

"So what do we want to do today?" I asked, feeling strange being the one asking the questions that Cap and Hudson usually asked.

"I'd like to pop over and visit Rollie in the hospital," Marceau said. "He's doing much better. The nurses said the swelling is mostly gone now, and he should be waking up fully in the next few days."

I nodded. "Let's start there, then."

# CHAPTER 10

WE MADE OUR WAY TO the Fords, piling into one.

Patrick climbed into the back with his crutches, and Marceau waited for me to slide into the driver's seat before slipping in as my passenger.

Feeling awkward, I slid into the driver's seat. Was this the new normal? They would defer to me in everything our little trio did?

Despite my unease, I felt a new sense of confidence beginning to grow. I could do this. One decision, one day at a time.

When we arrived to the hospital, Marceau led the way to Rollie's room.

"Hey, Rollie! How are you today?" he asked cheerfully as we entered his quiet hospital room.

Lowering his tone, Marceau spoke to Patrick and me.

"I've been talking to him like he can hear me. The nurse told me no one's quite sure how much he can understand, but there's been definite progress," he explained. "He's responding to stimuli now, when they take his blood or change his sheets. And he's breathing fine, too. In the last few days, his fingers have even started twitching. All in all, he's improving."

"He looks much better," I said, studying Rollie's face.

I tried not to recall how Rollie had looked when I first visited him in the hospital here, a week ago. His face had been swollen so grotesquely that even his eyelids and lips were distorted. It had been hard to look at him. Death had seemed close—almost inevitable. He'd pulled through, miraculously, to survive those horrible few days.

"The nurse told me yesterday that as soon as he wakes up and starts engaging his brain again, the recovery should come along even quicker," Marceau said, pulling a chair to Rollie's side and sitting down.

"Buddy, I'm here with Patrick and Andi today," Marceau said, leaning over his face. "They wanted to come see you. We had breakfast together this morning, and came straight over afterwards."

Patrick pulled a chair out for me, but I shook my head. "You sit," I said, nodding at his crutches. "I'll go get a chair from the hall."

I walked out, and took a deep breath to steady myself.

Seeing Rollie in such a vegetative state was depressing. It was a stark contrast to the vibrant and energetic person he'd always been. In another life, if I hadn't ever met Cap, I could see myself ending up with a man like Rollie, who loved and lived life joyfully.

*"It isn't fair that his future has been altered so cruelly by those evil men,"* I thought. Paz. Rollie. Hudson. Patrick. All of them, victims of these wicked criminals.

I shook my head, trying to clear my mind, and carried a heavy wooden chair back into the room, setting it next to Patrick.

Marceau and Patrick were mid-story, reminiscing about a hockey game they'd attended together, and I listened as they talked. They laughed as they recalled plays and hits, recounted stories of the wild crowd, and compared it to their own hockey games.

I noticed Rollie's eyelids twitching as they talked. I watched closely. Was he waking up?

Marceau glanced at me, and I pointed.

"See it?" I said quietly, nodding toward his face.

Marceau leaned in. "Rollie, are you awake?" he asked, laying his hand on Rollie's still arm.

Rollie's eyelids twitched again and he groaned.

"That's the most response I've seen from him yet!" Marceau exclaimed, standing up. "Come here, Andi. You try. He always perked up hearing your voice before."

Feeling foolish, I sat down in Marceau's seat. I took Rollie's limp hand in mind and held it. His skin was soft and warm, despite the fact that his body looked lifeless.

"Hello, Rollie," I said, squeezing his hand. "It's me, Andi. I'm here. And I want you to wake up. We all do. We miss you, Rollie. We're here, waiting for you."

"There!" Marceau exclaimed, watching as Rollie's eyelids fluttered again. "I'm going to go get a nurse. Keep talking to him."

"We're so proud of you, Rollie," I continued, feeling stupid. What could I possibly say? And could he even hear me? "You're so brave. And so strong. I know how hard it must be for you to lie here in this hospital, waiting to regain your strength. But you're very close to waking up. We have so much to tell you, when you do wake up. We need you back with us, Rollie."

Rollie sighed slightly. I stared at him.

"Do you think he can actually hear us?" I whispered to Patrick, who leaned in next to me.

"I don't know. I guess we assume that he does?"

I kept my hand around Rollie's. Suddenly, I felt his fingers move.

"Rollie!" I gasped. "Patrick, his fingers just moved!"

Patrick stood up and leaned over Rollie's face. "Hey pal, we're here. Whenever you want to open your eyes, we're here. You're not alone."

I squeezed his hand, hopeful for the first time in a long time. We'd been so worried that Rollie wouldn't come out of this.

"Good job, Rollie," I encouraged, studying his face. "You're so strong. We know you're a fighter."

Sure enough, his fingers moved again.

"Patrick!" I exclaimed, looking down at my hand.

Marceau hurried back in with a nurse. I stood up and backed away as she busied herself checking his pulse and lifting his eyelids. She reached in her pocket and pulled out a small flashlight, shining it in his eyes. Rollie groaned and recoiled his head.

"Well, hello there," the nurse chirped, smiling. "You're finally waking up, aren't you?"

Marceau and Patrick and I exchanged looks. *Thank God we stayed behind and didn't leave him here alone,* I thought.

The nurse straightened. "It appears that he's coming out of it," she said, reaching for his chart. She scribbled a few things, then looked at us.

"Keep talking to him. It's likely that he's reacting to your voices. It may take another day or two for him to come around and shake off this fog, but he's young and healthy. He's improving rapidly."

"How do you think he's going to be when he wakes up?" Patrick asked.

"It's hard to say," the nurse mused. "Sometimes these patients who have endured brain injuries take a long time to get back to normal. Many never do. Personality changes are common, you know. They can have a hard time concentrating or sleeping for months. Sometimes they struggle with dark feelings. Often, families tell us that their loved one is never quite the same person they were before the accident."

I noticed Marceau glance worriedly at Rollie, his face pale.

"You should know that one of the most common issues we see is difficulty with communication," the nurse added. "Be aware of that."

"Meaning what?" Marceau frowned.

"Think of their brains like a bowl of soup. It takes longer to fish out the pieces they want. Speech can become slower, or more labored. Sometimes patients forget words entirely and have to relearn how to speak, like a little child. You just have to be patient with them, and help them to be patient with themselves. It causes a great deal of frustration."

The three of us stood in stunned silence.

"It depends on the person, though, and the type of injury," the nurse added, looking at us with obvious pity. "There's just no way to tell at this point. All I can say is that you should be encouraged by your friend's progress so far. Like I said, he's young and healthy. He's in peak physical condition. Many patients don't survive the initial blow like he did, let alone the severe brain swelling. He's already beat the odds to make it this far."

Marceau's eyes were watery. I laid my hand on his shoulder.

"Thank you," I said. "We'll be here for a while. Should we let you know if he continues to wake up?"

"Yes, please do," she responded. "We'll need to do a complete assessment once he does wake up fully."

She started to leave, then stopped in the doorway again. "I know you're with that expedition traveling the world," she said gently. "I'm so sorry this happened to your friend. You all seem like such wonderful, brave people."

We smiled wanly.

"But being around the people he loves most?" she continued, her eyes kind. "That's the best medicine for him. Just keep talking to him, and let him hear your voices. The head and the heart are tricky things, but they both do their part to heal us."

As the nurse breezed out, we blankly sat down under the weight of crushing disappointment.

# CHAPTER 11

MARCEAU BOWED HIS HEAD and closed his eyes, overwhelmed with emotion.

"You heard her," I said quietly. "He's in peak condition. He's improving."

"Yeah, and I also heard her say he's likely to have personality changes and difficulty talking," Marceau replied softly. "She said he might not ever be the same. How could they do this? And to Rollie, of all people?"

He choked up, then added, "He's always been one of the kindest people I've ever known. You should see him with his little sisters. They absolutely adore him. He's the best big brother I know. So patient. He taught them all to play hockey, you know. And ride horses. They're a close family."

"He told me he has four little sisters," I said, remembering the conversation we'd had weeks ago. What I wouldn't give to have that lively, funny man back with me now instead of this lifeless version laying in the hospital bed in front of me.

"We haven't told them yet," Patrick spoke up. "Should someone send a telegram to his family now?"

"I don't know," I admitted. "But honestly, I don't know if we should contact them—not at this point. They can't do anything. It would take them weeks to get here, and we'll already have moved on at that point, right? And to tell them would mean telling people outside of our crew that we're hunting down the kidnappers. What if they say something? What if our plan somehow leaks out?"

Marceau shook his head. "Don't tell them. I know his family like they're my own. It'd kill them with worry. And you're right—we need this mission to save Paz to be our secret. No one can know."

"We won't contact them, then," I said. "He's going to be fine, anyway. No need to have them panic. You heard her—another day or so and he'll be waking up."

We sat silently, staring at Rollie. I wished I believed the optimism I had spoken aloud to comfort Marceau. I remembered when Cap had been in the hospital last year, and a doctor had told me the same thing about the possibility of lingering effects from his accident. I'd been petrified.

But Cap had made a full recovery. Wouldn't Rollie?

*"You know it's not the same,"* I argued with myself. *"Cap had different types of injuries. Rollie took a heavy hit to the back of the head. He's been unconscious for days. Just because Cap is fine now doesn't mean Rollie will be."*

I studied Rollie's face, thinking how odd it was to see him without a smile. When I thought of Rollie, I saw him grinning and joking around.

"I can't do this right now," Marceau suddenly said, his voice thick. "I need to get out of here. Clear my head."

Patrick laid his hand on Marceau's shoulder and reached for his crutches. "Come on. We'll go wait in the lobby for a while. Andi can sit here with him."

Marceau was already out the door as Patrick struggled to his feet. "We'll come back later."

I sighed. I felt guilty being alone with Rollie, but he was fighting for his life. Surely I wouldn't be crossing any lines if I just sat with him and held his hand.

Staring down at Rollie's white face, I frowned. What could I possibly say to him right now? I wasn't sure he could hear me or understand me. I sat down in the chair next to his bed and hesitantly took his limp hand, holding it in my own.

"Rollie, have I told you much about my childhood?" I said quietly, stroking his hand. "You'd like to know, I'm sure. You told me a bit about yours, about your sisters and your horses. I'll tell you about mine."

I started at the beginning, sharing some of my earliest memories. At first, I felt like I was babbling, but it got easier when I realized I was alone with Rollie. We'd always exchanged stories, after all.

I talked without interruption, carrying on a one-sided conversation. I told him about my mother and sister. About my father's death, and how it had torn a hole in my heart. About the loneliness I felt in grade school, and then in boarding school. What school had been like for me, how I'd struggled. How I wondered if I'd ever fit in anywhere.

I had never been one to share my emotions easily, but my words spilled out without thinking in the silence. It was as if I'd finally found my voice to be able to face the years of hurt from my childhood, here in the safety of this quiet hospital room, with a man I knew cared for me but couldn't hear me.

As I talked, I realized I was sharing things with Rollie that I'd never even had the opportunity to tell Cap.

*"We've always been so frantically busy, jumping from one adventure to another,"* I thought, as I talked to Rollie. *"Cap doesn't even know all these things about me."*

Pausing, I reflected for a moment. If my own fiancé didn't know this much about me, was it right to confide it all to Rollie? I stared at him. His eyelashes occasionally fluttered, but otherwise he wasn't moving.

*"He won't even remember this when he's awake,"* I thought, looking at his prone body. *"Cap certainly doesn't need to know about this, either. Not when he's already so tense. Oh, Rollie. This isn't fair to you."*

I held his hand, and continued rubbing it gently. I'd memorized all the creases in it now, the way his fingernails felt under my fingertips.

A nurse whirled in and smiled at me, looking chipper. "Hello there. I understand we have some improvement today?"

"I think so," I replied, as she listened to his heart through her stethoscope. She pulled up his eyelids and shined her flashlight into his dark eyes. He blinked.

"Excellent!" she said, pinching his arm. He groaned.

"Good boy," she said encouragingly. She smiled at me. "He's definitely coming around. This is major improvement."

I smiled. "I'm so glad."

"Are you his sweetheart?" she asked, taking his wrist in her strong hands and checking his pulse. "They always heal faster when a girlfriend is here, you know."

I dropped his hand quickly. "I'm not his sweetheart. But I do care about him very much. He's my dear friend."

"Well, I'm glad you're here with him," she said, dropping his wrist gently and scribbling in her notepad. "It makes such a difference when a loved one cares."

I nodded mutely.

She hurried out, and I was left alone with Rollie again. I stared down at him, noticing the intimate details of his face.

His lashes were dark and long, longer than most men's. His face was round, but lean and handsome, with a strong jaw and high cheekbones. A sprinkling of tiny freckles covered his nose, and his facial hair had grown in, and covered his upper lip and chin with dark stubble. He looked older. His hair had grown out in the last few weeks, and was curling at the ends. A small curl drooped in the middle of his forehead.

I stared at Rollie, seeing the pinkness of his lips and hearing the quiet whoosh as he exhaled. For the first time, I saw a faint scar, barely perceptible, across his eyebrow. I'd never noticed it before.

*"Because I've never been this close to his face before,"* I told myself.

Suddenly, I felt guilty. Who was I, to notice these things about Rollie? I was engaged to Cap. I sat back in my chair. I felt like I'd intruded into something private. Something not meant for me.

Impulsively, I stood up and rubbed my face. I couldn't do this anymore. Not today. I'd just kissed the man I loved goodbye this morning, and who knew what danger the coming days would bring him? And now, to look on the face of another man I cared about and wonder if he'd ever be the same? If I would ever hear his voice again? Would this be the future with Rollie—I could talk to him but *he* could never again talk to me, or anyone else?

"Goodbye for now, Rollie," I blurted. "I'll be back later."

I left hastily, heading for the lobby. The late afternoon light slid in through the blinds, making a pattern on the floor. Marceau and Patrick were sitting there, reading the newspaper. I realized I'd been in there far longer than I thought.

"Is something wrong?" Marceau cried, shooting to his feet. "What is it?"

I shrugged. "Nothing's wrong. I just need a break. I've been in there a while."

Marceau and Patrick exchanged glances, then looked at me. I sat down across from them. Marceau tucked the paper under his arm.

"I'll stay with him," he offered. "Why don't you two go back to the hotel? I'll stay the night. Keep an eye on him. I want to be here if he wakes up."

I nodded. I just wanted to get out of the hospital. It was depressing here.

Patrick stood up and balanced himself on his crutches. We walked down the hallway together, through the front lobby, out to the Ford. "I can't wait to get off these blasted things," he muttered as I walked slowly, keeping up with his pace.

Wordlessly, we strolled to the car, and I silently opened the passenger door for him. I slid into the driver's seat and turned the ignition. The car rumbled on and I pulled out, driving us past the hospital and back toward our hotel.

"What's wrong?" Patrick asked, staring at me. I didn't reply.

He leaned back in his seat, looking at the passing buildings. I was thankful he wasn't pressing the issue. I needed time to think, to clear my mind. My emotions felt scattered and uncollectible.

We reached the hotel, and I turned off the car. "I need some time on my own," I said quietly, avoiding Patrick's eyes.

"Sure. Dinner? Later? I can come get you."

"Fine," I said. I didn't feel like figuring out the details now. I pocketed the keys and made my way up to my room. In the darkness of my room, as evening started to fall, I laid on my bed. I closed my eyes, pressing my fingertips over my eyelids.

"*These are the very fingers that comforted Rollie,*" my brain said, accusingly. "*You have no right to touch him. Not after the problems your relationship caused both teams just a few weeks ago.*"

"*But I did it to help him,*" I argued back. "*The nurse said the head and the heart both work to heal us. It was innocent.*"

"*What would Cap say if he saw you now?*" my mind replied. "*What would he think, listening to you talk to Rollie like you did? Holding his hand? Sharing your past? Your feelings?*"

"*But you saw how Rollie responded to your voice, your touch,*" I thought, in response. "*Maybe there are just some things you keep to yourself from Cap. You know the truth, after all, that it's entirely innocent. You're only trying to help. Telling Cap will only bring up doubt and conflict that'll distract from the important task of finding*

*Paz. No, he doesn't need to know this. Cap has enough on his mind already. You can't be adding more stress to him—he's already exhausted and close to burning out. We all are."*

The glow of a blazing sunset burned brightly through my curtains, but soon descended into the warm darkness of early evening. I lay still in my bed, staring up at the ceiling. I didn't want to think anymore. I didn't want to see anyone.

*"It's up to you to make the right decisions, Andi,"* I thought. *"You can explain your reasoning later. Right now, you need to do what's necessary. You need to make the right calls. That's your responsibility. You're in charge now. You need to do your part to keep the team focused on rescuing Paz, without distractions."*

I tried to silence my conflicting thoughts. Never in my life had I expected to be in a position like this: choosing to conceal the truth from the man I loved, in order to use my love to help heal another man.

And now, as captain of the crew, it was up to me to make the right decisions.

I was on my own to navigate this dilemma—and all the rest of them we were sure to face in the upcoming weeks.

# CHAPTER 12

I HEARD PATRICK COMING down the hall, crutching slowly, before he even knocked on my door.

"Ready for dinner?" he called. I rolled off the bed.

"Yes," I responded, smoothing the wrinkles out of my shirt. I opened the door and joined him as we walked out into the night air. We dined together in a little cafe down the street from our hotel, where a trio of musicians played jazz music as we listened and applauded politely.

Over dessert, which Patrick insisted we have to celebrate "my promotion," as he called it, I asked him about his love life.

"You know all about mine," I teased. "It's only fair that I hear all your stories, too."

"There's not much to tell," he said, laying his fork down. "There's only ever really been one girl for me. But we're not together."

"Why not?"

He sighed. "It's complicated."

"You sound like me now," I joked. "Come on. Out with it. We're stuck together for the next few weeks, at least. I want to know."

Patrick laughed. "I see you're making me suffer for making fun of you this morning, huh? Fine. Sarah. She's beautiful, and kind, and altogether wonderful. We grew up together. We were inseparable. Everyone knew we'd end up married someday."

"What happened?"

He shrugged, pushing his fork around on the empty plate. "She fell in love with someone else. They've been married for almost three years now."

"Oh."

He sat silent for a moment, and slowly nodded. "I think we all have our own private heartaches that we hide away. But we go on living. We don't have any choice. Right?"

"Right."

"Anyway," he said, busying himself with stacking the plates up and looking for the waiter, "It led me to this moment. Being on the Chinook Voyageurs. If I would've married Sarah, my life would be completely different. So I suppose I'm grateful, in a way, that it turned out like this."

"Do you regret it? Not marrying her?" I asked quietly.

"Regret it? How can I answer that?" He laughed, rueful, then thought for a moment. "I love her. Still. But she's happy with her husband, with the decisions she's made. And I can't claim to love her if I don't want her to be happy."

He looked down, toying now with his water glass. "Like I said, it led me here. And here, I've found myself again. It's made me stronger."

"But she broke your heart," I said, staring at him. "How can you just forgive her and move on?"

"Because my heart is still capable of love, Andi," he answered. "I'll always love her, but I have room to love again. Someone else. Someday. She wounded me, yes, but she didn't break me."

I smoothed the napkin on my lap, thinking. Patrick looked at me, his dark eyes meeting mine. "Rollie will go on, too, if that's what you're really asking."

"I didn't ask that," I said quickly, alarmed that Patrick was reading my mind. I had been pondering that very question.

"You didn't have to. I can see it all over your face."

I looked down, my cheeks flaming.

"Andi, it's not your fault," Patrick said gently, as I stared at my lap and fiddled with my napkin. "You didn't do anything to lead him on or encourage him. Rollie just couldn't stop himself from falling for you, anymore than you could stop yourself from falling in love with Cap. And it's not like either of you acted inappropriately, anyway. If it hadn't been for the team getting drunk and Rollie's feelings about you coming out, it could've passed largely unnoticed."

"I don't want him to love me, though," I said in a low voice. "I didn't ask him to love me. I don't love him. And I hate to hurt his feelings like this, all over again. Who knows what state his brain is even in, anymore? What if he forgot what happened? What if he falls for me all over again, and it wounds him once more? He's been through enough."

"I know," Patrick sighed. "We'll tell him when he wakes up, if he's forgotten it somehow. He'll understand. And he'll be fine. He may need some time, but he'll be fine."

I shook my head and changed the subject. "When do you think Cap and Hudson and the rest will get to Spain?"

Patrick looked at the clock on the wall near the bar. "It's nearly eight o'clock now," he said, counting. "They left before dawn. I assume we'll hear from them in the early morning hours, at the very latest."

"That's what I was thinking, too," I replied. "Should one of us try to stay up and check with the front desk to get an update?"

"I don't know. We can just get it in the morning, right?"

I thought for a moment. "Actually, I had an idea for tomorrow. I think we should go to the scene of the attack. Look for any clues we may have missed earlier."

Patrick stared at me. I was sure he didn't want to go back to where he'd been shot and witnessed half his team violently assaulted, but I needed to see it with my own two eyes.

"Why?" he asked, his voice suddenly on edge.

"I need to see it, before we leave," I explained. "What if we missed something? A boot print? Something that fell out of their pockets? We're doing this on our own, Patrick. Without the police. We need to examine every single possibility, over and over again."

"Do you think the police missed something?"

"No," I hesitated. "But I do think we care a lot more than they do. To them, it's just another case. To us? It's personal. It's Paz. Our family."

He stared at me with troubled eyes. The table next to us erupted in laughter and for a brief moment, I wished I was them. I couldn't remember the last time I was carefree like that.

"Is this what you want to do?" he finally asked.

"Yes," I replied.

"You're the leader," he said. "It's your call."

"I'm asking you, Patrick. I'm not a dictator. I want your opinion, too."

"That's not how leadership works. You know that. You have to make the call and stand behind it, on your own. Come what may."

I stiffened. "Fine. That's the plan for tomorrow. We'll head there in the morning, and then go visit Rollie again in the hospital."

"Good girl. I knew you had it in you."

I grinned back. "Stop treating me like I'm a five year old, Patty."

He threw back his head and laughed. "You can't call me that. Hudson's the only one who does. It's always been his nickname for me, since we met in the dormitories the first day of college."

"Too bad."

"I'm trying to help you, by the way," he added, smiling. "You're vastly capable, as I've said. You just need a little practice with this leading thing. Can't make an omelet without cracking a few eggs, as they say."

"And suddenly I'm the little lady back in the kitchen, making omelets?" I raised my eyebrows playfully, teasing. "Just like that, huh?"

"Gosh, Andi," he laughed. "Your wit is wicked."

I smiled, and checked the clock on the wall. "Ready to head back to the hotel? If we're searching this site tomorrow, we probably need to make an early morning of it. Get there before we encounter other people or vehicles on the road."

"Yeah, the downside of the whole famous thing and all," he grumbled, reaching for his crutches and standing up, balanced on one leg. "At what point do you think people will realize that most of our team is gone?"

"I don't know," I admitted. "I'm surprised no one's noticed yet. We regularly make front page news. At least out of our uniforms, no one's seemed to notice the three of us yet. I mean, no one at this restaurant has noticed two celebrities sitting here in their midst."

"We'll have to thank our lucky stars, then. It'll be up to us to come up with a good cover story, won't it? Since the others are tied up?"

"Probably," I squinted. "We'll cross that bridge if we get to it. I sure hope we don't get to the point where we're inventing cover stories and lying about things. I can't even imagine."

We walked through the lobby of our hotel and headed up to our rooms. It felt odd saying goodnight, just the two of us. I was used to a dozen people around, in and out of their rooms all the time.

"I'll see you in the morning, Patty," I called. Patrick grinned cheekily at me.

"Goodnight, Captain Gallivanter," he teased, closing his door as I laughed.

# CHAPTER 13

FOR THE SECOND DAY in a row, I woke before dawn, my mind racing.

In the darkness, I bathed and put on fresh clothes, tying my hair up while it was still wet. Patrick was leaving his room when I opened my door.

"Good timing," I said as he smiled, "Good morning."

We walked down together to the lobby. Breakfast could wait, we decided, as we made our way to the Fords.

"I'm not much help to you with this leg, sorry," Patrick groaned as he eased himself up into the passenger seat. "You're going to be driving a lot more than usual."

"It's fine. You're still healing. How's it feeling?"

"Much better," he said. "I'm changing the bandages every day, like they told me, and the skin is completely closed. No swelling. It's just getting my leg used to the pressure and pain now."

I turned the automobile on, swiveling the tires on the dew-slick pavement with a practiced hand. "Think you can navigate me to the scene of the accident?"

He nodded. "It's seared into my mind, unfortunately."

We drove in silence for a while. Zermatt was a beautiful little town, nestled between grand mountains and sitting in the shadow of the majestic Matterhorn, towering high above. Every twist of the road took us farther into stunning mountain scenery.

Finally, Patrick pointed me toward some smaller roads that branched off from the main one. I followed them back into a more remote area, thick with dark forests.

"This is where they hid? Way back here?" I asked, my eyebrows raised.

Patrick nodded. "You'll see our cars, once you get up around the corner."

*"How utterly diabolical,"* I thought to myself. *"They didn't stand a chance. The Chinooks were sitting ducks out here, totally alone."*

Sure enough, I saw the Fords almost immediately after he warned me. The tires were slashed and the engines mangled on each one, pieces hanging brokenly out of the front. All six cars were burned, the blackened metal and charred wood frame folded in on itself. The Chinook logos looked sad and defeated on the damaged cars.

"They burned them? You didn't tell us that!" I exclaimed.

"Yeah, a parting gift," Patrick said, stiffening as he looked over the scene. "They flicked their lighters into the engines and laughed. Clearly, they didn't want any way for us to follow them."

I slowed and parked on the side of the road, taking my time getting out. It was quiet here, with birds chirping from the nearby grove of trees but no houses or even fields in sight.

"Why'd you go this way?"

"It was a shortcut," Patrick replied. "We were hoping to save some time."

"Why?"

"To beat your team," he answered, his forehead wrinkled. "It's a race, after all."

I stared back without speaking, feeling foolish. It seemed hard to believe that just a few weeks ago, our teams were in competition against each other. None of that even mattered anymore.

Patrick limped out and stood next to me on the road, as we surveyed the scene.

"I hate to ask you this, but do you think you can walk me through what happened here, as we look around?" I asked.

He grimaced. "Yeah."

Slowly, he crutched over to a spot up the road, near a little stand of trees.

"Their car was right here, blocking the road," he said, pointing. "The hood was up, like they were having engine problems. We wouldn't have been able to get by them, anyway. The Ford was blocking the entire road, so we stopped."

He stepped back a few steps. "It was early evening. We probably shouldn't have been on the road ourselves, but we were making good time and wanted to keep going. A man came out, limping, holding his hands up for us to stop. It wasn't clear if he'd had an accident or was injured or what, but Hudson and Rollie and Willis were in the lead cars, so they hopped out right away to help him."

"What did he look like?" I interrupted. "Would you recognize him again?"

"I don't know," Patrick shrugged. "He was dark-haired. Tan, olive skin. Muscular. Other than that, nothing stands out."

"So what happened after that?"

Patrick looked over his shoulder, staring at the dark trees. "The other three kidnappers were hiding in the woods there, waiting for us to let our guard down. Rollie and Willis walked over to look at the engine, while Hudson talked to the man. Suddenly, they ran out of the woods. The man we'd thought was injured pulled out a gun and held it to Hudson's forehead—"

Patrick stopped himself and sighed heavily. "It's awful to be here again."

"I know. But it might help. What happened next?"

"One of the other men clubbed Rollie from behind, then Willis," Patrick winced involuntarily. "They both fell down right away. I guess they passed out, because they didn't move at all during the attack. Willis had his eyes open and was moving afterwards, but

Rollie was still out cold when we got him to the hospital. He was bleeding all over the place."

"What did they hit him with? Could you see?"

"Not really. A piece of metal, maybe? A pipe?"

I bit my lip, imagining Rollie getting bashed in the back of the skull as he leaned over an engine, trying to help someone. Who would do that?

"Claude and Leonce got out when they saw Rollie and Willis get hit," Patrick continued. "Marceau and I were in the car behind them. I was already getting out to talk to Hudson."

He hesitated. "I don't know how to explain it, but I just had a sense that something was fishy. Something was wrong, somehow."

"You were right."

"A little too late," he rubbed his leg unconsciously. "I don't know what came over me. I saw Rollie and Willis drop, and rage just overpowered me. I charged right at the group. There were three of them. I don't know what I was thinking."

"That's mighty brave."

"Yeah, and stupid. I crashed right into one, took him down with me hard. I knocked his gun away, briefly. But the other shot me."

"What did the other men look like? Did you get a good look at them?" I asked.

"It all happened so fast, but I saw them. They were a blur of dark hair and dark eyes. Mustaches and beards on all but one."

"Nothing else stands out? Unique clothing? Scars?"

Patrick paused. "The one who shot me—he had a mark on his forearm. Dark. Possibly a tattoo?"

"That's quite an impressive detail to notice, considering the circumstances," I said quietly. "Could you tell what it was?"

"No," Patrick shook his head. "I was concentrating more on the gun than his arm. It just stands out because you don't see that many tattoos, you know."

We paused for a moment, staring at the scene again. The destroyed cars were a stark contrast to the beautiful scenery around us. It was hard to believe such horror had happened here.

"The one whose gun I knocked away? He kicked me," Patrick continued. "I tried grabbing his leg, but then he kicked me where they'd just shot me. It's funny, I felt the pain of the bullet but I don't know, I was in such a rage that it didn't really hurt that much. But when they kicked me? It knocked the breath out of me. I collapsed."

"I'm sorry," I winced. "I can't imagine."

He shook his head, staring at the cars. For a few moments, neither of us spoke. I began to worry if I was doing more damage making him relive the horrific event than gaining any clues to help us find Paz.

"And what happened with Dessie?" I finally asked. "Could you see that?"

Patrick's face suddenly twisted as he appeared to hold back emotions that threatened to overwhelm him.

"Andi, I—they—damn it," he stumbled over his words, then stopped himself. He took a long, ragged breath and lifted his eyes to the sky. After a long pause, he finally looked back at me. His voice was quiet.

"I saw it all. And honestly, do you know what I was thinking?"

"What?"

"I regretted having Dessie on the team," he confessed. "I didn't even think about anyone else, in that moment. All I could think was that we had a beautiful woman with us, and four men with guns. I was laying there, bleeding in the dirt, and all I could worry about was Dessie getting attacked—maybe killed—in front of me. And I would be helpless to stop it."

I stared back at him. The hair on the back of my neck rose and I shivered.

We'd danced around it, and no one had said it until now. But somehow, I knew that this had been the secret terror of every man on the Chinook crew, as they'd been ambushed. Dessie hadn't even been able to talk about what happened. They'd tried to attack her and she'd fought back.

But we all knew Dessie wouldn't have been strong enough to resist if they'd really tried to hurt her.

"It's the fear all of us had before we even brought her on," Patrick said in a voice so soft I had to lean forward to hear him. "We debated it, at length. If this expedition was simply too dangerous for a young woman, even if she was capable. No doubt it's the same fear that Cap and Chito and Bernard have for you, being on their team."

I flushed. "I can take care of myself. I'm strong."

Patrick stared at me, his eyes big. He simply shook his head.

"I *am* strong," I repeated. "You know that."

"I know," he said. "I don't know how to explain it. As men, we want to protect. We can't help but protect even the women we know are strong. We all have mothers, sisters, cousins we cherish. It was like my greatest fear coming true in front of my very eyes—to see her get attacked and to not be able to do anything about it."

He suddenly choked up. I studied him worriedly. "Patrick?"

"Give me a minute," he said, turning away and crutching awkwardly away from me. He bowed his head, his back to me, and struggled to regain control.

"I don't even love Dessie," he said, his back still to me. "I like her, as a person, but I don't have feelings for her. God help any man who'd have to see the woman he loved treated like that. He'd never be the same. Paz—poor Paz. He does have feelings for Dessie. I can't imagine what went through his mind."

I shuffled my boots in the dirt. I'd always felt protected by the men on my crew, and had always thought I could take care of myself. But if this could happen to Dessie, surrounded by her crew of eight strong men, it could happen to me, too.

Did Cap worry about these same things, when it came to me? If he did, he'd never let that fear show. Nor had he let it limit me—not even now, as I led our little trio, away from his protection.

As I kicked the dirt, I impulsively stomped my foot and felt anger. *"How can people treat each other this way? How can they attack innocent people? I couldn't stand for it. No, if I'm ever attacked, I'll fight. I'll fight to the death if I have to."*

Patrick finally turned around, and gazed at the cars again.

"They had us all at gunpoint," he continued, his voice angry. "Everyone but Paz, who was in the farthest car from them. They were making their way toward him, and he popped out. He was riding with Dessie. I think maybe he tried to hide her in there and he didn't want them to find her. He rushed to the front and grabbed Hudson's bag, distracting them. He kept yelling that we had money, we'd give it all to them, and we wouldn't tell anyone about them. He told them they could just leave, and take the money. There was no need for anyone else to get hurt."

"They took it?"

He nodded. "They grabbed the bag of money and grabbed Paz, too. The one who grabbed him said, 'Isn't this the one we want? The rich kid?'"

I grimaced. "You think he was their target all along?"

"I think so," Patrick sighed. "I think we were an easy target, in their minds. They knew where we were going, and they knew we had money and a wealthy crew member they could hold for ransom."

He pointed down the road, shielding his eyes from the glare of the morning sun. "Paz's car was down there, and I was laying back here," he said, pointing behind us. "I couldn't hear what the men were saying for a bit, but then I heard one of them ask about Dessie."

"Dessie told me that part," I replied. "She said they asked each one of you where she was. That none of you answered."

Patrick exhaled. Slowly, he said, "They beat us up. Paz and Hudson tried to fight back. They beat them the worst."

"That's when they broke Hudson's hand?"

He nodded. "I watched them stomp on it. He was right next to me. He didn't stop screaming at them the whole time. Paz, though—they beat him so much he stopped yelling."

"Poor Paz," I groaned.

"One of the men started tying him up, and shoved a gag into his mouth," Patrick continued. "Paz was struggling against them. And then they pulled out Dessie, and Paz just went insane. He spat the gag out and started shrieking at them, threatening and swearing. They beat him so much he stopped. Hudson, too."

"Dessie said she head-butted them when they came at her?"

Patrick struggled to stay calm. "Yeah. Two of them hit Dessie after she did that, then shoved her around. It was awful to see. But their leader must have told them to focus on their task and leave the woman. He was yelling something, in Italian. That's the only way they didn't—you know. They left her."

"She's recovering now," I reminded him. "At least she was spared the worst."

"Yeah, by some miracle," he retorted. His cheeks were flushed with anger.

"Anyway, they hauled Paz off and shoved him in the back of their Ford. Then they went around and tied us all up and destroyed our cars."

"Wait, how'd you get free if they tied you up?" I frowned.

Patrick's forehead wrinkled. "Dessie didn't tell you?"

"Tell me what?"

"She started carrying a knife hidden in her boot," he replied. "She cut us loose, as soon as they took off. None of the men bothered to check her for weapons. I suppose they didn't think a girl would have something like that."

My eyebrows went up, surprised. Dessie didn't strike me as the type to have a hidden knife, either. "Where'd she come up with that little trick?"

"You, I assume. Don't you carry one in your boot?"

I tried to hide my shock as I nodded. I didn't know Dessie ever noticed the knife I kept in my boot. She'd never asked about it. The thought that she'd emulated me brought me a small measure of satisfaction.

What's more, it may have saved all of their lives.

"Anyway, they disappeared into the darkness with Paz, heading that way," Patrick continued, pointing back to the main road. "They could be anywhere now."

I scanned the scene, taking it in. I tried to picture where everyone had been, when they'd been attacked. Slowly, I walked over to the trees. "Did anyone check over here, to see if they left anything?"

"I don't know," Patrick hobbled over with me. "They carried me out on a little stretcher to a farmhouse, and the farmer and his neighbors retrieved everyone from the accident scene. Hudson and Rollie and Willis and I ended up in the hospital right away. I suppose I was in shock at that point, losing blood. Things got a bit fuzzy for a while. I don't know what the others did afterwards."

We climbed down the embankment into a small grove of trees. It was a good hiding spot, impossible to see from the road. The ground was springy and soft underfoot.

Under one tree, I spotted a cigarette butt. I peered at it.

"Did any of the kidnappers smoke?" I asked Patrick, who navigated over to where I was standing, looking at the cigarette.

"I'm not sure," he said, nudging it with his foot. "Maybe."

"See any more of these? Or anything else?"

We circled the area. At the base of another tree, we saw another few cigarette butts and a crumpled piece of colorful package.

I knelt down, and grabbed the crumpled package. I unfolded it, smoothing it out. It was a tiny piece, slightly thinner than cardboard, with a few letters on it. I squinted.

Patrick leaned down next to me, balancing carefully on his good leg. "What does it say?"

"It's hard to read," I said, staring. "I can only make out one word."

"What?"

"*Prodotto.*"

"What's that mean?"

I smiled. "It means 'product.'"

"Product? Product of what? How does this possibly help us?"

"Patrick," I said, looking at him. "It's Italian. As in, *'product of Italy,'* I assume. Where the cigarettes were made."

"Italian..." he said, tipping his head.

"That's confirmation," I said. "Cigarettes made in Italy. You smoke the cigarettes easily available to you, in your own country. The kidnappers are Italian. Like we suspected."

He thumped his fist into his palm. "We were right!"

I slipped the scrap into my pocket. "We don't know where they are at this moment, but at least we're more sure of their nationality now."

The sun was warm overhead as we walked back through the ditches, carefully checking to see if the kidnappers had left anything else behind. We saw nothing, other than rocks and weeds.

We checked all along the road, above and behind where the cars had been, but still came up empty-handed.

"It wasn't like we were going to find a map to their hideout or anything, anyway," Patrick groaned, as we got back into our Ford and headed back to the hotel.

"We have one solid clue, at least," I said. "It's better than nothing."

It wasn't much we'd found, I knew, but it was something. And even the smallest clue was better than the frustrating days of nothing.

Maybe we had a chance, after all.

# CHAPTER 14

WE MADE IT BACK TO the hotel in a better mood than we'd been in for a while. The sun was shining and we'd made a little progress.

I stopped at the front desk, hoping there was a telegram update from Cap and Hudson about their arrival to Spain.

"I'm sorry, there's no telegram for you, Miss Gallivanter," the clerk said politely. "But I do have a message here for you that came on the telephone about an hour ago."

He handed me a note. On it, scrawled in dark ink, were six simple words: *"Rollie's awake. Come to hospital immediately."*

"Patrick!" I exclaimed. "He's awake!"

"Oh, thank God," Patrick smiled. "Back to the car."

We'd long memorized our path to Rollie's room and rushed straight there. The door to his room was partially open, and the lights were off.

"Rollie?" Patrick called, as we pushed our heads in.

Marceau stood up, shushing us. "He just fell asleep again," he said, directing us out to the hallway. He closed the door behind us.

"He's awake?" I asked eagerly.

Marceau nodded. "He opened his eyes earlier and looked around. He seemed to recognize me, which the nurses said is a good sign. His vitals are positive, too. It's great news."

"Did he say anything?"

He shook his head. "The doctor came in afterwards and did a bunch of tests. Said it's probably too early for him to be speaking. Remember, they told us communication would be difficult for him, at least for a while. But when I talked to him, he looked at me. He's listening, I think."

"Let's get you a cup of coffee and try again in a bit," Patrick said, slapping Marceau on the back. We walked down to the cafeteria and sat down at a round table with three steaming cups of coffee.

"What do we think we're looking at, in terms of catching up with the other team?" I asked. "It sounds like he's in better shape already than what we expected. Do you think we could leave in a few days?"

Marceau blew on his coffee, the steam curling. He looked tired. "I don't think so. The doctor said it's just impossible to give a clear timeline. He's had serious brain injury, and every case is different. Some people recover fully and bounce back just as good as new, but others take months and never quite come back the same."

"What do they think will be the outcome for him? Can they guess?" Patrick asked.

"Like everyone keeps telling us, he's young and healthy," Marceau said. "But he had serious swelling in his skull and was woozy for so long that they just can't say with certainty."

We sat making polite small talk for a while, after that, but our hearts weren't in it. I guessed that Patrick and Marceau felt the same dread I did, thinking about Rollie.

What if his recovery was only partial, and he'd be confined a hospital bed for the rest of his life? I found myself second-guessing the decision not to contact his family. Would they forgive us if he had permanent brain damage, and they didn't find out until weeks later?

"Andi?" Patrick interrupted my thoughts, staring at me with concern in his eyes.

"What?"

"I asked if you wanted to go up and see if he's awake," Patrick said, studying me. "This is the third time I've called your name."

"Sorry," I said, standing up. I dumped my remaining coffee into the waste bin and stacked the cup. "Let's go see him."

We walked back up, nurses pushing people in wheelchairs and gurneys around us. We retraced our steps to the door of his room, and Marceau took the lead and stepped in.

"Hello, sunshine," I heard him say, and Patrick and I smiled at each other.

I followed Patrick in, and Rollie stared back at us both, his eyes big in his pale face.

"Rollie!" I exclaimed, grabbing his hand. "You're awake! We're so glad to see you!"

He looked at me but his expression was unreadable. Patrick squeezed in, his shoulder pressing against mine. "Buddy, how are you feeling?"

Rollie looked up at him, then back at me. After a moment, he looked back at Patrick.

"That's right, good job," Marceau said encouragingly, from across the room. "You're doing great, Rollie. Big improvement."

I held Rollie's hand, smiling at him, and babbled to cover my nervousness. Conversation used to be so easy with Rollie. Now, even the smallest word was impossible for him to form? Could he even understand us?

"We've been here with you every day, checking on you and sitting with you and waiting for you to wake up," I smiled at him, trying to hide my apprehension. "Patrick and Marceau and I have been here the whole time. Just waiting. The weather's nice outside, too. You'll see in a few days, when you're able to get out of this hospital bed and get out there in the fresh air. The mountains are beautiful, too. So big and majestic. Why, I'd bet you'd come back here in the winter and love to see it, right?"

"Andi, you don't have to go overboard," Marceau said softly. "We're supposed to talk to him just like we used to. Not like he's a baby."

I fell silent, looking back at Rollie. He stared at me and blinked slowly.

"We're here," Marceau said, coming up on the other side of me so the three of us stood shoulder to shoulder, close to Rollie's face.

He looked back and forth at each one of us, not moving his head but moving his eyes.

"Can you understand what we're saying?" Patrick asked. Rollie's eyes turned toward Patrick's face as he spoke.

"Are you listening?" Marceau tried. Rollie's eyes found him.

Marceau smiled. "You are, aren't you?"

Rollie's eyes flickered down toward my hand, which was holding his, then back up at my face. I blushed.

"I'll go get a nurse," I said hastily, dropping his hand and slipping out of the room.

"Nurse?" I called, stepping up to the reception desk. "My friend's awake. We were told to let you know when he woke up."

"Certainly," she said, glancing at me. "Are you one of those celebrity travelers? The ones going all over the world in your automobiles?"

"Yes, ma'am. The Gallivanters and the Chinook Voyageurs."

"Where's the rest of your team? You have that good-looking captain, right? The blonde one?"

I paused. So people *were* starting to notice that we'd split up. We'd have to get in front of this, and fast. We wouldn't want to tip off the kidnappers that our crew had split up and gone searching for them. I thought quickly. What was a good excuse?

"The others are working on getting new cars," I replied smoothly. "We always upgrade to the latest models. But it takes some time, you know, to negotiate the prices and get the logos painted on them and get them outfitted for our expedition."

"Oh, of course," she nodded. "Well, we'll send someone in to check on your friend as soon as we can."

I walked back into Rollie's room, and quietly leaned toward the others. "We may have a problem. The nurse just asked me where the rest of our crew was."

"Sometimes I truly hate being famous," Patrick rolled his eyes. "So people are noticing that it's just the three of us left here?"

"Apparently."

"What did you tell her?" Marceau asked.

Rollie's eyes followed all three of us, back and forth, as we spoke quickly to each other.

"I said the others were getting new Fords and prepping them for the expedition," I replied. "But that excuse will only last for a few days. After that, we're going to have to either think of something else or get out of here. It's going to catch people's attention that the entire team is missing. We've already been off the grid for too long. All it takes is one snooping reporter, trying to get a good story, and the whole world will know that Paz has been kidnapped and we're hunting down the kidnappers."

"And we blow our chance," Patrick finished. "We'll lose the element of surprise."

Rollie stared at us, his eyes darting between our faces.

"Should we fill him in?" I asked, staring. "Can he even understand it at this point, if we try to tell him?"

Marceau's forehead wrinkled, and he leaned close to Rollie's face. "Can you blink if you understand what I'm saying right now?"

Rollie blinked.

"Okay. You can understand me? All the words make sense?" Marceau asked. Rollie blinked again.

"Well, that's encouraging," Patrick exclaimed. "Rollie, you're all there, aren't you?"

Rollie looked up at him.

"That'll be helpful," I smiled. "How about we blink once for yes, and two for no? It'll be how we communicate now, for a while. Until you get your words back."

Rollie blinked once.

Marceau sighed. "Rollie, we have a lot to catch you up on. I'm sorry. I'll tell you the whole story, from the beginning."

# CHAPTER 15

PATRICK MOTIONED ME out into the hall as Marceau started to fill Rollie in.

"We need to figure out our next step," he told me, as we heard Marceau gently explaining that Rollie had been clubbed in the back of the head and been out of it for a full week now.

"We need to reconnect with the other team," I replied. "As soon as we can. I don't want to risk hurting Rollie, but we're easy targets now. I'm afraid the kidnappers could come back here, where we're on our own, or that someone's going to connect the dots and realize our team is missing. Either way, it's bad for us."

"I agree," he said, his eyes troubled. "But we can't move Rollie. Especially not all the way to Spain. What if he needs medical attention, and we're stranded out in the middle of nowhere? It's a grueling trip, even for those of us who *are* healthy."

"We need to ask his doctor," I reasoned, wracking my brain. "Get his honest opinion, see how soon we can move him."

Patrick checked the clock on the wall behind me. "The others have to be in Tarragona by now," he said, counting in his head. "Let's check the hotel and see if they sent a telegram, and then come back and see how things with Rollie are looking?"

"Sure."

We entered the room, and listened as Marceau continued explaining the events of the last week to Rollie. "The Gallivanters came back to help us, as soon as they heard what happened," Marceau said.

Rollie looked up at me.

He explained that the others had gone on to Spain, trying to track down Paz's kidnappers, and that the three of us had stayed behind to keep an eye on him until he was stable enough to take with us.

"And now we're here," Marceau finished. "We won't leave you. We promise. I'll spend the night tonight, right here."

"We'll be back in a bit," I promised, as Patrick and I stood up to leave. "We have to head to the hotel and see if Cap and Hudson have sent word from Spain."

The two of us walked down the hallway, Patrick's crutches clicking on the floor, and climbed into the Ford. We crawled out onto the road, driving back to our hotel.

As we suspected, we had a telegram waiting for us. Patrick tore it open quickly and read out loud.

"*Made it to Tarragona without incident. Staying at el Hotel de la Puerta Azul under alias, Robinson. Send word when you are en route here. Be safe. Love you.*"

"How sweet," he remarked, smirking at me. "Cap sends his love to me."

"Stop," I laughed, secretly thrilled that Cap spent the extra money to message me that little reminder.

"At least we know they're safely there. Let's get something to eat before we head back to the hospital."

"Sure," I replied. "We can grab something for Marceau and bring it back to him. He deserves a good meal, too. He has a long night in an uncomfortable chair ahead of him."

"Good idea," Patrick agreed. "They're best friends, you know. They all grew up together, but I know those two are especially close. It has to be hard for him. To see Rollie like that."

We ate a quick dinner, and had the kitchen fix a plate for us to bring to Marceau. When we brought it to him at the hospital, Rollie was asleep.

"Thanks," Marceau replied, shoulders slumped as he ate. Patrick and I tried hard to cheer him up, but he was quiet.

I remembered how unhinged I was, as I saw Cap lay in critical care in the hospital last year. He'd nearly bled to death in front of me after his car accident. I'd been out of my mind with worry.

"Come on, mate, it's not as bad as all this," Patrick said desperately, after we told a flurry of funny jokes that didn't even put a smile on his face.

He sighed. "I'm just not in the mood."

"Rollie's improving, though," I reasoned. "Surely you see it? It's good news."

"Is it?" Marceau shot back. "You didn't know him before. Not like I did. Rollie was always the charming one, the kid always getting in trouble with the teacher because he never stopped talking. And he managed to squirm his way out of it, every time, because the teachers all adored him. And now—"

He stopped and cleared his throat.

"They've stolen Rollie from us, too. Not just Paz. What if he's never the same again?"

*"What if?"* I thought, avoiding Patrick's concerned gaze. *"What if none of us can ever be the same again?"*

# CHAPTER 16

WE SPENT THE NEXT THREE days at Rollie's bedside, valiantly fighting against a growing sense of hopelessness that he would ever actually recover.

Despite our encouragement, it was clear that Rollie could no longer speak. All three of us quietly despaired over this ugly new reality, redoubling our efforts to cheer him up.

His progress so bleak, however, that I occasionally had to excuse myself from his room so he couldn't see the tears in my eyes.

"Can you try the word 'hello' out, Rollie?" Marceau would ask him a dozen times a day. Rollie would look at him, and try to form the words with his mouth. Nothing came out.

"Good!" I'd say, choosing another simple word to say.

"Try 'lamp,'" Patrick supplied. "What about 'bathroom'?"

We went around the room like this over and over, pointing to new objects and often making them comical and silly, desperately trying to keep our spirits high.

At night, I lay in bed and tried not to despair over Rollie's slow progress. He was so terribly broken and we were on such a tight schedule. Every day mattered. How could we expect him to heal fast enough to take him to Spain with us? There was no way. But we couldn't leave him here alone.

On the fourth morning, Rollie surprised us when we came in.

"Low," he said when we walked in the door.

"Rollie!" Patrick exclaimed. "Say it again!"

"Low," Rollie said, his eyes darting back and forth between the three of us.

"Are you saying hello?" Marceau smiled.

Rollie didn't smile, but his eyes looked bright. "Low," he said again.

We grinned at him. It was a little bit of progress, but it was still progress.

On the fifth day, after consulting his nurse, we decided to try to move Rollie around the room and see if he could remember how to walk. Marceau and Patrick carefully pulled him up out of bed and eased him to his feet. I walked in front of him, smiling and clapping as he wobbled on legs that hadn't moved in nearly two weeks now.

"That's great, just like that," I said encouragingly. I could tell Patrick and Marceau were doing the bulk of the work, but we had agreed we'd do nothing but encourage Rollie at every opportunity. He had to have confidence to keep trying and not just give up.

Patrick tapped his left leg. "Put that one forward."

Rollie lurched unsteadily, but dragged his leg. Then the right leg, slowly.

We cheered like he'd just won an Olympic event.

Another few days passed the same way, and Rollie recovered his ability to walk much faster than his ability to talk. His muscles were weak from disuse, but he could soon walk down the hallways with minimal support from Patrick and Marceau. He was moving his arms, too, and we took turns helping him bend each finger and count.

One afternoon, as I sat next to Rollie and held his hand, bending each finger up and down and counting, he grasped my hand lightly, with the gentleness of a toddler holding onto his mother's hand.

"Rollie?" I asked, confused. "Do you want me to stop?"

He stared at me, struggling to form a word. I gazed at his lips. What was he trying to say?

"Stop?" I shook my head. "Or keep going?"

Rollie stared at me, his lips moving helplessly.

"What do you want?" I asked desperately, then bit my lip. Dear Lord, he couldn't tell me. Why would I ask him that?

Marceau bent down. "Do you want her to stop? Do you need something?"

Rollie stared up at him, his grasp tightening on my hand.

"I don't know what he wants," I said in a low voice, looking at Marceau. He shrugged, looking at me.

"I'll stop," I said, pulling my hand away.

Rollie closed his eyes in frustration, still moving his lips. He managed to make a guttural grunt, slightly louder than an exhale. I saw a painful expression on Marceau's face. I knew what he felt. It was the same dismay I struggled against, too, seeing how hard it was for Rollie to do such basic tasks.

"I'm going to use the bathroom," Marceau said abruptly, standing up and ducking out the door.

I sighed. Patrick was back at the hotel, sleeping, as he'd agreed to sit with Rollie overnight tonight and keep him company. He and Marceau had been taking turns every evening.

Rollie opened his eyes and watched Marceau leave, then looked back at me. His brown eyes were scared, tense. I was learning to read them, in the absence of his words.

I leaned forward, resting both my forearms on Rollie's bed.

"Listen to me," I said firmly. "You're going to beat this. No, it's not fair that this happened to you. But life has been unkind to a lot of people, Rollie. So we're not going to wallow in pity. It'll do you no good. We're going to concentrate on the small victories, every day, and celebrate every little improvement. Because this isn't your future."

He stared at me, his eyes wistful.

"Don't look at me like that," I replied. "You're not going to be stuck in this hospital room for the rest of your life. We all knew it would take some time, and it's fine. You're coming along. The doctors said this would be the hardest part—you learning to find your voice again. We all expected that it would take some time. You're not disappointing anyone, Rollie. Not me, not the boys, okay?"

He tried to mouth something, but couldn't get it out. He shook his head slightly, and let it fall back against the pillow in frustration.

*"Oh, Rollie. I've known the burden of defeat, too,"* I thought, my heart swelling as I watched him.

I hung my head, resting it on my hands. "I know you read about how I nearly died in the jungle in Africa. You've heard me talk about it, on stage at our press conferences. But you've never heard how I really *felt*. The fears that nearly consumed me."

Rollie stared at me, his brown eyes glued to mine.

"It was horrible," I continued. "It was at the beginning of the Gallivanter expedition. I was trying so hard to prove my worth, still, I think. I'd climbed onto a wild stallion, like a cocky little thing, and it had bolted. It raced us both out into the jungle, then flung me off. I landed on my neck somehow, but it didn't kill me. It stunned my body. I was paralyzed, temporarily."

I closed my eyes. I could recall the agonizing, cold fear that had dripped through my soul like ice water as I lay there, unable to move.

"I know exactly how you feel right now," I breathed, sliding back into the terror of the moment. "As hard as I willed my body to move, I couldn't. I was paralyzed. I worked and worked to lift my fingers, to wiggle my toes, and I couldn't. It was the most defeated I've ever felt. I'd never been helpless before, but suddenly, I was utterly vulnerable. The control came back, inch by painful inch, but I was still alone out there."

I exhaled slowly.

"I was afraid," I confessed to Rollie. "I've never told anyone just how afraid I was. More than afraid—I was completely overwhelmed. Because I had nowhere to hide from my feelings, all of a sudden. I was completely alone, and knew I had to save myself on my own. No one could help me. I was too far away from anyone to even scream for help. I was completely lost."

I paused to remember. "Chito told me once that I had to fight. That sometimes every day was a fight. But that sorrow and joy and love and friendship, they're mingled in all of our stories. That we can't let the hurts write our story for us. We have to fight to live a good story, in spite of our pain. And he's right. I remembered it, as I lay there paralyzed, thinking the plants and the bugs would be the last thing I ever saw."

Rollie stared at me. A lone tear escaped from his eye and sat wobbling on his cheek.

"I saw everything clearly, as I lay there and thought I was dying," I said. "My life. My real friends. Who I really was. Who I really loved. And I know you've struggled with the same emotions, probably, as you've been here in this hospital bed."

His brown eyes were wet now.

"I know it's terrifying," I continued. "I know you think you're never going to heal. I know you're angry and upset over the lack of control you have over your own body. I know you wonder if things will ever be the same. But Rollie, you're a fighter too. Don't give in to your doubts. Fight against them."

Rollie suddenly reached for my hand and grasped his fingers around it. I looked at him. It was no time to be shy, anymore, I realized. Too much time had been wasted by so many of us dancing around our feelings instead of just saying what we actually felt.

"It was out there in the jungle that I realized how much I love Cap," I said, meeting his gaze. "And I know you had feelings for me, at some point, but I say this because you need to hear it. Someday, someone will love you that same way I love Cap, and I want to be there to see it."

I paused and squeezed his hand, leaning close.

"You're my friend, and you're so very dear to me, Rollie," I told him. "I'm going to be here for you, and wait for you to recover fully, however long it takes, because this is part of *your* story. And I can't wait to see what happens in your life—in your future. But you've got to fight. And you've got to fight hard. With everything in your will, Rollie. Your life depends on it."

Rollie squeezed my fingers, and mouthed again. I squeezed his fingers back and bowed my head. It was late, and I was tired, too.

Suddenly, I heard a sound like air whooshing. I looked up, alarmed. Rollie was smiling, his expression triumphant.

"Thanks," he managed to wheeze.

I grinned back at him, squeezing his hand.

When Marceau finally came back and quietly woke me up, I realized that he'd found us both fast asleep, still holding hands.

# CHAPTER 17

WE FINALLY FELT ROLLIE was recovered enough to discuss the next step—moving him out of the hospital and taking him to Spain with us—with his doctor.

He wasn't speaking much yet, but he was able to walk with some assistance and move his arms and hands. He was still trying to form words, and could squeeze out a few short syllables here and there to say simple, one-word answers.

After waiting in the hospital room for several hours, the doctor finally breezed in.

"Doctor," I said, offering my hand as he walked in the door.

"Ah, yes," he said, shaking Patrick's hand and nodding at Marceau, who was sitting down next to Rollie. He peered at me through bifocals. "Are you the wife?"

"No," I replied. "He's not married."

"Oh," he said, consulting his clipboard. "Right, then. What can I help you with? I have here that you want to discuss the possibility of discharging him from the hospital?"

"Yes, sir," I replied. "We're in a bit of a challenging situation. We need to get to Spain, where the rest of our crew is waiting for us. We're not coming back to Switzerland, so we cannot leave our friend here in the hospital. He needs to come with us. We're wondering, in your professional opinion, if he's stable enough to discharge now?"

The doctor peered at Rollie. "Why can't you just delay a bit longer and continue to let him recover here?"

"It's complicated, and we're not really at liberty to discuss it," Patrick said. "But believe us when we say that a teammate's life hangs in the balance, and we're sorely needed."

"Hm," the doctor said, looking down at his clipboard and reading for a few moments. Finally, he looked up.

"Your friend suffered a serious hit to the back of his skull," he said. "That blow resulted in significant intracranial damage. Serious swelling of the brain. These are both dangerous conditions, even for a healthy young man like him. I know his functions are coming back, albeit slowly, but it seems like you may be rushing it."

"It's a matter of life or death, doctor," I insisted. "We wouldn't move him unless we absolutely had to. But we don't see any other choice."

"May I inquire what you're planning to do with him, once you get to Spain?" the doctor asked, taking off his glasses and looking at us with his clear blue eyes. "Will you be admitting him into a hospital there?"

"I don't know," I said helplessly. "We haven't talked about that part yet. We've been more focused on getting him to Spain."

He pursed his lips thoughtfully.

"Spain is too far to take him," he said, glancing at Rollie. "He could do a shorter trip, maybe, if it was reasonably smooth road conditions. No more than a few hours. But to jostle him all the way to Spain—I wouldn't recommend it. His brain is still healing."

"Does he need a hospital again if he leaves here?"

The doctor stared at Rollie, then looked down at his chart.

"He needs a quiet, comfortable place to recover for at least a few weeks," he offered. "I'd recommend some place with low stress but still enough opportunity for him to get mental stimulation and some exercise. He'll need to continue practicing building up his strength and speaking, of course. It's going to take some time."

"But you don't think he can travel to Spain?" Marceau asked.

The doctor shook his head. "I'm sorry, I know that's not the answer you want to hear. If there was somewhere else he could go, perhaps—some place he could get good care and quality rest—then maybe. But it sounds like you're headed into a stressful situation once you get to Spain. That won't be good for your friend. Perhaps you could instead leave him with family in the nearby area?"

Patrick and Marceau exchanged worried looks with each other. Rollie's family was in Quebec. There was no one else.

But I suddenly had an idea.

"So if we can find a quiet, calm place for him to stay for a few weeks," I said slowly, thinking aloud, "A place that won't stress him, and is only a few hours from here—that would fit the bill?"

"I think so," the doctor nodded.

"I think I know the perfect place, then," I replied, thinking rapidly. "Doctor, if I can promise you that he'll be in good hands—the best hands—in that kind of place, would you sign his discharge forms for us?"

"If you can promise that, then yes," the doctor said, putting his glasses back on. "Should I go prepare his paperwork right now?"

"Yes," I said. "Can we plan on picking him up first thing in the morning?"

"Certainly, Miss—um," he paused. "I don't think I caught your name."

I smiled. "My name is Andi."

Patrick interjected, "Captain Andi, sir."

He looked at me quizzically, but smiled. "I'll get right on it, then. Good luck, son," he said, nodding at Rollie and stepping out.

I turned to face Patrick and Marceau.

"I know where we can take him," I explained. "It's the perfect solution. You'll have to trust me on this. But he'll be in good hands,

I promise. And more importantly, he'll be safe for the weeks it'll take him to recover fully. No one would ever find him there."

Marceau squinted at me. "Where?"

I paused. "It's a bit of a detour. I'm going to have to rework our route, but it's on the way to Tarragona."

"But where are you taking him?" Patrick asked.

"Lyon, France."

"What's in Lyon?"

I hesitated.

"My past," I finally answered. "Now let's get back to the hotel. We have some packing to do."

# CHAPTER 18

IN THE MORNING, I DOUBLE-checked the map as we loaded our two cars and checked out of the hotel.

I left a note with the front desk in case Cap or Hudson called.

"Read them this if they call," I explained. The note said we'd be detouring slightly to go through Lyon, but we'd meet up with them in Tarragona in a day or two and check into their hotel.

"Certainly," the clerk said politely. "Good luck on your travels, ma'am."

"Thank you," I said, thinking we'd certainly need luck on our side. Despite what I'd told Patrick and Marceau, I wasn't sure going to Lyon was such a good idea. But we were desperate, and it was the only solution that might work for us.

It took quite a long time to get Rollie discharged and rolled out in a wheelchair to the waiting Fords.

"Can you get in on your own?" Marceau asked, as Rollie clumsily tried lifting his foot up into the passenger side of my Ford.

Rollie moved his mouth a few times, then finally breathed out, "No."

Marceau and Patrick bent over and helped lift him into the car. Rollie grimaced, and feebly tried to slide himself across the seat. I averted my eyes, knowing he was embarrassed by his helplessness, as they pushed him into place and helped pull his goggles on.

*Was I doing the right thing?* I wondered for the hundredth time, starting the engine. What if I was putting Rollie in danger by taking him out of the hospital? What if there wasn't room for him to stay in Lyon, like I planned? What if they didn't want to help us?

*"It's too late to second guess now,"* I told myself, turning to see if Marceau was ready behind me. He gave me a thumbs up as I turned.

"Here we go," I said to Rollie, pulling out and centering us on the little street that led out of Zermatt.

I was the captain now.

It was exhilarating and troubling at the same time. I had to stand behind my decisions, and trust that I'd made the best ones for our little team. Still, the nagging voice of doubt whispered in my brain as I drove, and I tried to ignore it by talking to Rollie.

"It's about five, maybe six hours from here," I said, smiling at him. "You'll see. It's some of the most beautiful countryside around, too. Pastures and quiet, shady forests. Meadows full of flowers. Farms and cows and horses everywhere. You'll love it. Did I tell you I used to ride horses around there all the time?"

Slowly, we wound our way out of the mountains of Switzerland and into central France. The landscape settled into rolling hills and farms, with fences and barns marking property lines. An occasional castle or cathedral sitting in the center of a town broke up the monotony of farmland. Stone houses, centuries old, sat guarded by cats who lounged in the sun. Each home blurred past me, a fleeting impression of domestic bliss as I drove by, a traveler just passing through.

Rollie dozed, and my mind began to wander. As I drove, I went back. Back to Lyon.

I saw a younger version of myself, carrying my bags to boarding school for the first time. Shyly meeting my roommates and navigating the difficult social dynamics of a pretentious all-girls school.

I had felt like such an outsider then. I thought I was all alone in the world. As I'd found out in the last year, it turned out that I just hadn't met others who were like me.

Not until Cap and Chito and Bernard and Paz. And now, the Chinooks.

People who felt more themselves in a foreign land than in the same living room they'd grown up in. People who wanted to see it all—even if it meant slogging through rain and snow and deserts. Explorers.

And that's who I was now. An explorer.

I took comfort knowing that I wasn't alone. That I'd found a dozen others just like me. And found several of them in the most peculiar way: as bitter rivals, who'd turned into friends.

Life was strange and unexpected and sometimes painful, but nevertheless a grand adventure.

I pulled myself out of my musings and decided it'd be a good time to pull over to refuel and eat something. We still had a few hours to go until we reached the estate outside of Lyon where Académie Sainte Thérèse de Lisieux, my childhood boarding school, dominated the surrounding area.

I waved my hand behind me, signaling Marceau that I'd be pulling over. The road around us was wide but remote, a solitary farmhouse off in the distance. The sun was shining overhead, and tiny flowers danced in the field next to where I parked my car.

"Marceau, why don't you get the gasoline and I'll get the food," Patrick said, hobbling over to Rollie's passenger door.

Rollie was awake, yawning as the sunshine illuminated his face. I realized this was the first time he'd been outside in weeks. His pale face was getting burnt. I pulled my own scarf out of my bag and draped it around his face.

"We're making good time," I said, pulling out the map and studying it. "We're right about here, which means we'll be in Lyon by early evening."

"Good," Patrick leaned over Rollie, patting his arm. "How are you feeling?"

Rollie stared at him, his lips trying to form the words he wanted to say. We waited patiently. Finally, after several tries, he bit his lip in frustration.

"It's fine," Patrick said encouragingly. "You're out here in the Fords again. Finally out of that hospital bed. That's progress, my friend. The words will come. It'll just take some time."

Rollie nodded.

"I'll help you get him out," I said, coming around the front to help Patrick, who leaned his crutches up against the front of my car as he struggled with Rollie's weight.

"How's your leg doing, by the way?" I asked Patrick, as we hooked our arms under Rollie's shoulders and helped him down.

"It's a bit sore still, but I'll live," he replied. "I just feel worthless, not being able to drive."

"It's fine," I said, watching as Rollie held onto Patrick's arm and took a few steps on the road, swaying slightly but remaining upright.

"Good, Rollie," I said brightly. "Look at that. Your first steps in France."

Rollie looked up at me and smiled crookedly. I smiled back. Every step was a victory, in our books.

After refilling the gasoline tanks and eating, we switched passengers. Marceau and Rollie drove together, and Patrick got in my car as passenger.

"We're getting close," Patrick said, staring at my map. "You grew up around here, right? Is it starting to look familiar?"

It was. The landscape had changed subtly, and I started to recognize buildings and hills. Meadows where I'd roamed on my horse, the wind blowing through my untamed hair, greeted my eyes.

Instead of heading into the heart of Lyon, we detoured around, out to the countryside. I glimpsed the sprawling grounds of

Académie Sainte Thérèse de Lisieux from afar, as we drove up slowly through the long, curling road that led to the school.

Now, more than ever, I was full of doubt about what was coming next. For so long, this place had been an anchor.

A flickering flame of hopefulness and possibility. And then disappointment.

A beacon when everything had seemed dark and my motivation to seek more from life.

Was it still?

So long has passed. I'd changed so much, too. Would I still get a warm reception?

I'd left in very different circumstances, as a girl. Now I was a woman. I was leading a team—of men, no less. And the events that led to the distance that was now here between us? I couldn't honestly say it had ended well.

Had time cooled the warmth that I was once sure would always be there for me?

Could it ever be the same as it once was? Or had we both grown apart from each other too much?

Patrick stared at me as we drove through the meandering fields, gentle with their green grains. "You're awfully quiet. Is everything okay?"

I chewed on my lip. "I hope so."

"That doesn't sound too convincing."

"I don't know, honestly."

"What's that supposed to mean?" Patrick said, looking at me.

I sighed. "It's been a long time since I've been back here. And...it didn't really end on the best terms, if I'm being honest."

"What are you saying?"

"I'm saying I'm hoping for the best. That they'll take Rollie in and take care of him."

Patrick rubbed his jaw in frustration. "We took him out of the hospital, dragged him across the border of Switzerland into France here, and *now* you're not sure if it's going to work out? Andi, we trusted you. Rollie's health depends on your judgment. On you making this work."

"I know. It's still our best shot. It's just that I'm not sure what the reception will be."

"Well, I certainly hope you're convincing enough," Patrick said, staring out at the road.

"Me too."

He looked at me again. "Couldn't you call ahead and ask, before you hauled us all out here?"

I shook my head. "They don't have telephone lines out here. Too expensive for them. The only way to do it was to actually drive here and ask in person."

"What if they won't take him?"

"I'm prepared to offer them money. A lot of money. I hope they will."

I breathed in the familiar scent of the woods as we drove through a little grove, and suddenly the massive buildings soared in front of me. It was simultaneously comforting and depressing.

Here I was, back where I'd spent six years of my life. And at one point, I thought I might move back here and stay forever. Clearly, that hadn't been how my life had turned out, after all.

After a few minutes, I eased the car to the side of the road and turned it off. The sun was low in the sky, streaming its last embers across the fields, and I shaded my eyes to look at Patrick.

"Stop," I said, holding up my hand as he started to get out.

"What?"

"I have to do this by myself," I replied, my stomach churning with nerves.

"But—"

"Trust me, Patrick. I have to do it alone. We have to talk face-to-face first, before you and Marceau and Rollie come in. I'll come get you as soon as I can."

I removed my goggles and my helmet, slowly, girding myself up for what I knew I'd encounter when I knocked on the door. Suddenly, I doubted coming here at all. What had I been thinking? I didn't want to put myself back here. But did I have any other choice?

*"It's now or never,"* I told myself. *"Our last shot to help Rollie. We need this."*

After all this time, how would I be received?

I squared my shoulders, and stood up straight as I walked to the door and knocked. Time to see for myself.

# CHAPTER 19

IT WAS DARK, STARS glowing up above, when Marceau and Patrick and I finally came back out to the cars. Wordlessly, we started them back up and got in.

Patrick climbed into the passenger seat next to me. Tiredly, I drove us toward downtown Lyon.

We'd agreed to find a small hotel there and spend the night. It'd been a long day of travel and we were worn out. We dined at the hotel, a simple meal of cheese and bread, some cold meats and vegetables on the side. We spoke little during dinner.

"Back to three," Marceau said, spearing a potato. "I already miss Rollie. I hope he'll be okay."

"He's in good hands," I replied. "I'm glad they're willing to take him in and take care of him for us."

Patrick looked at me over his plate, studying me. He'd been quiet all night, since we brought Rollie in and said our goodbyes.

We finished eating, and I pulled out the map to trace our morning route. "One more day of driving, and we'll be there. Reunited with everyone else."

"Has it really only been a little over a week since we've seen them?" Marceau said, yawning. "It feels like longer."

"We have an early morning ahead of us," I replied. Secretly, I needed time to be alone with my thoughts. The day had been emotional, and it was harder to say goodbye to Rollie than I'd imagined it would be. "Time to get to bed."

"Hold on," Patrick said sharply, as I started to get up from the table. "Look, you're not telling us everything, Andi. Who exactly were those people? And how do you know them? And why do you trust them to take care of Rollie?"

I shook my head. "He's in good hands, with someone I trust. That's all you need to know."

"That's not enough for me," Patrick replied. "You're asking me to leave one of my crew mates with strangers, and you won't tell me anything more about them? Why are you so close to them, but you insist we don't tell Cap about them? It makes no sense—"

"We already talked about this," I interrupted, giving him a hard look. "And you already agreed you wouldn't tell my crew about this stop."

"But why not?"

"I have my reasons. You have to trust me. And I want to be the one to explain it to Cap."

Patrick sighed. "Look, is it about the money? You're afraid Cap will be angry about the cost? The Chinooks can chip in, too. Rollie's really our responsibility, anyway."

"It's not about the money," I said. "Please, drop it. Just don't tell my crew. Not yet. Especially not Cap."

"I'm telling you. We have plenty of money, too. We'll split the bill."

"It's not about the money," I insisted.

"Then what's it about, then?" Patrick cried in frustration.

"It's about *me.*"

Marceau and Patrick looked at me, then looked at each other. Before Patrick could open his mouth again, I intercepted him.

"Look, it's not open for discussion. You've met them yourself, so you know he's in good hands. We've talked it over time and time again, and we all agreed this was the best option for Rollie. All I'm asking is that you keep this between the three of us for now, please. Don't tell my crew. It's a simple request. They have enough to worry about without worrying about this. I'm not going to be the one to add one more concern to the pile—not now. We're all stressed out already, as it is. Especially Cap and Hudson. We need to focus on finding Paz, without any distractions."

Patrick again started to reply, but this time Marceau put a hand on his shoulder.

"Hudson made his decisions and you didn't make him explain himself," he said quietly. "She's captain. Respect it."

I smiled at Marceau, grateful.

"You're right," Patrick said, looking at me. "I'm sorry, Andi. Or as I will henceforth address you, Captain Gallivanter."

"Stop," I laughed, glad he was teasing now.

"I am merely your humble servant," Patrick said, pretending to curtsey. "I live to serve at the beck and call of the illustrious and magnanimous Captain Gallivanter."

"Are you even speaking English?" Marceau wrinkled his nose. "Stop using your university vocabulary to impress the ladies. He does this every time there are pretty girls around, you know."

"Hey, don't tell her all my secrets!" Patrick pouted. "How am I ever going to impress girls if you tell them this every time?"

"You're better off wooing them with your French, anyway," I grinned. "Especially the American girls. They love a good-looking man with an accent."

"Ah, oui," Patrick laughed. "Bonne chose je parle couramment le français."

I smiled. "C'est parfait."

"I don't know much more beyond that," Patrick confessed, his eyes twinkling. "Marceau, it's your native language. You have one up on me with the ladies, I guess."

Marceau grinned and tossed his dark curls. "I have that *and* this head of hair working in my favor."

We went to our rooms still laughing as we said our goodnights. As I lay in bed, I hoped I'd made the right decision about Rollie.

*"It's too late now to second guess it,"* I told myself, rolling over. *"You know it was the only thing you could do. You're in a desperate situation. Every minute wasted is a minute that could've been better spent looking for Paz. There's no sense in causing Cap to lose his focus. He needs it all for the search for Paz."*

I just hoped Cap and the others would see it that way, once they finally found out what I'd done—and that I'd decided to keep it to myself, for now.

# CHAPTER 20

WE TRAVELED THROUGH France and into Spain, the sky huge above us as we cut through fields and sloping hills of green and amber.

We slowed as we inched through villages of all sizes, some ancient with all the buildings and churches made with old rounded stones, some more modern with colorful wood and timber construction. In the wide expanses of open farmland and forests, however, we sped along.

When we made it to bustling Barcelona, an unmistakably eclectic and vibrant old city, my spirits rose. We were close to Tarragona now.

The topography had changed and become hotter, more arid. As we rolled into Tarragona, I held Cap's handwritten directions in one hand and navigated my Ford toward el Hotel de la Puerta Azul, the address he'd telegrammed to me.

A butterscotch-colored inn with planters of flowers beckoned us warmly, after the hours of exhaustive travel we'd endured. I was ready for a hot bath and a change of clothing to remove the dust that had caked on from the journey. Even my mouth felt gritty, like I'd breathed in sand kicked up from the road.

"This is it," I called. "We made it!"

Patrick and Marceau and I slapped each other on the back as we climbed out of the cars and made our way inside to the front desk.

"Hello, we're checking in under the last name Robinson?" I asked the receptionist. "We should have several rooms."

"Si, the family reunion!" the young clerk smiled, looking for our keys. "How nice that you are all able to connect together as one big family."

"Yes, the family reunion," Patrick grinned, catching my eye. I hid my smile. That had to be Hudson's humor. Cap wouldn't dare tell a fib that cheeky. We unloaded our bags and trunks into our rooms, washed up and changed clothes, and reconvened in the hotel lobby.

"Where do you think they are right now?" I asked, as we sat down.

"Who knows?" Patrick replied. "We'll have to wait here for them to come back. In the meantime, I say we celebrate with a drink while we wait. For once, I'd like to sit mindlessly and sip something strong. The last few weeks have been pure hell."

"Oh, I'd give anything for a glass of Rupert's ice wine right now," Marceau groaned. "He made the best stuff in Quebec. You'd die if you had a glass."

"Allow me," Patrick said, turning to the bar. "I'll put an order in for us."

"You can't carry a glass with those crutches!" Marceau shoved him back down. "I'll bring them over."

Patrick settled into a big chair in front of the decorative fireplace in the hotel lobby while Marceau stood with his back to us, talking to the bartender.

"Well, Captain Gallivanter, now I can congratulate you on a finished expedition. You did it," he smiled.

"*We* did it," I corrected him. "And you better drop that 'Captain Gallivanter' nonsense when Cap shows up."

"He's not here yet," he laughed. "Honestly, you did well. I know you had some doubts but you're a natural leader."

"Thank you," I smiled. "I really didn't do much, though."

He leaned forward. "On paper, you're the first girl who's ever led an expedition like this," he winked. "Even if it was only for a week or two, it still counts."

"I...am?" I said, frowning. "I hadn't thought of that."

"I know," Patrick smiled. "*I* did, though. I suppose one might argue that Joan of Arc beat you to this sort of thing a few centuries ago, but you're not exactly leading an army against England—right?"

"But I didn't feel like this was anything special," I complained.

Patrick laughed. "You don't exactly feel it when you're breaking barriers, I suppose. All you feel is the complaining from others who are grumbling about what you're doing. Look at Henry Ford—everyone complained about those Model Ts when he first invented them. But he pushed the world forward. And eventually, everyone accepted it. Imagine what would've happened if he gave up when he hit a little resistance? If he would've listened to all those people who criticized him?"

"We wouldn't be here, driving our own Fords," I mused. "I suppose you're right."

"First woman to captain an automobile expedition," Patrick's smile was wide. "I'm glad I got to witness history being made with my own two eyes. Add this to your resume, when you take over Cap's job someday."

"I'm not taking over his job," I laughed.

"Fine, you're right. Go for Hudson's instead."

"You sure have a progressive view of women."

"You know, I met plenty of smart women in college," he replied. "It seems a shame to me that our society puts more emphasis on women like that to get married and do their husband's laundry than to use their brains. I mean, sure—if that's what they really want to do. But what if some of them want to become engineers? Or surgeons? Or professors? Or explorers? Why is it that only men can do those jobs? The world is big enough for all of us, right? Besides, my mother is the smartest person I know. I have a high opinion of women's brains."

"I don't disagree," I said, as Marceau came back with a tray of small glasses and handed them around.

"Here's to pushing the needle forward, then," Patrick said, lifting a glass to me.

"Together," I added, clinking my glass to his.

The liquid burned when I took a sip. "What is this? It's horrible!"

"I don't really know," Marceau grinned. "I told the bartender we were celebrating. He responded in Spanish so I just nodded."

"Let's get another round after this," Patrick sipped, trying not to choke. "We need it. We've been stressed for too long."

"But the others—"

"They can catch up when they get here," Patrick finished for me. "Come on, relax. You earned it. We can't do a thing but sit here and wait for them, anyway."

# CHAPTER 21

WE WERE WELL INTO OUR third round when I heard the sounds of motors outside.

Doors slammed and boots clicked on the ground, and I heard familiar voices. A thrill raced through me when I heard Cap's voice amongst the others. I put my drink on the table and raced out into the lobby.

"Cap!" I yelled happily, as I saw him come in behind Bernard and Willis.

"Andi!" he said, smiling and catching me in his arms as I launched myself at him. "You made it! How was the trip?"

"Good," I replied, kissing him.

He wrinkled his nose and grinned at me. "It must've been good. Been drinking?"

"Been *celebrating*," Patrick supplied, leaning on his crutches behind me. "She did well, Captain. She's a good leader."

"I knew she would be," Cap replied, his arm around me.

"She's coming for your job next," Patrick added, winking at me. "Watch out, world, there are two Captain Gallivanters now."

I blushed, but Cap just laughed.

"She can have it," he groaned. "It gets old making decisions all the time. Especially after the last few days."

Chito grabbed me in a big hug, pulling me away from Cap. "Glad you made it, Andi."

We exchanged hugs all around, and settled into a cozy group in the lobby, everyone busy talking and catching up. Hudson and Dessie ordered drinks, but Cap glanced around. "Where's Rollie?"

"He's doing much better," I said hastily, as Marceau and Bernard and Willis listened. "We were able to check him out from the hospital, but the doctor cautioned us about bringing him into a high stress situation here. They advised we have him stay somewhere calm, with low stimulation, for a few more weeks. He needs more time to recover, to learn to speak again and move his body better. So we left him with some friends outside of Lyon."

"Friends?" Cap raised his eyebrow. "You have friends in Lyon?"

"I went to school there, remember? Of course I do," I replied, praying Marceau and Patrick wouldn't spill any additional information. "Anyway, we're paying them to take care of Rollie, but he's in really good hands. The setting is perfect, too. Simple, healthy, country living. Fresh air. Just what he needs."

"He'll be happy there," Marceau added. "It was a good call, on Andi's part."

"So who are these friends?" Cap pressed, but I quickly interrupted to change the subject.

"Rollie's really struggling to speak," I said. "He can say a few words. But it's going to take a lot more effort on his part to control his speech. The doctor said he's made great progress already, and it should come a lot faster now that he's getting the basics down."

Hudson had returned, and he and Dessie were standing and listening.

"Poor Rollie," Hudson sighed. "He's such a brave soul. I have no doubt he's fighting hard, but it has to be maddening."

"It is," Marceau replied, staring down at his drink. I wondered if he responded for Rollie or for himself.

"So what have you guys been doing?" Patrick said, sipping what had to be his fourth or fifth drink. He was in a better mood than I'd seen him in the last few weeks. So was I, for that matter. Alcohol had dulled our worry.

"That's a story for a different time," Cap replied, shooting Hudson a look.

"Come on!" Patrick said, cuffing Cap on the back, clearly buzzed. "We're all a part of the team now. You owe us."

"We'll talk about it when we're in private," Hudson replied, exchanging looks with Cap.

*"We all had secrets now, didn't we?"* I thought, feeling better about my own.

"Let's just forget about all the stress and enjoy ourselves tonight, shall we?" Willis leaned in, and lifted his glass. "We have time tomorrow to catch up with our troubles. Tonight, let's just celebrate. To the Chinook Voyageurs and the Gallivanters! We all made it here in one piece!"

"Don't you mean the Robinson family reunion?" I teased.

Hudson bent over laughing. "I knew you'd like that. Imagine what the hotel clerks must think, seeing all these young single men and two beautiful girls together, trying to figure out what kind of family we are."

We spent the evening laughing and teasing each other, trading stories and inside jokes from the time we'd spent together. Snuggled into Cap's arm and warm from the alcohol, I felt happy for the first time in weeks. Despite my worries about Rollie and Paz, I was glad that we'd found new friends in the Chinook Voyageurs, however strange the road was to end up here together.

Cap and Chito walked up to our rooms with me later, as the numbing drinks did their work to make us all sleepy.

"Goodnight, Andi," Chito smiled at me, ruffling my hair as he went into his room. "It's good to have you back with us."

"It's good to be back," I replied, leaning against my own hotel door.

Cap reached out and took my hand in his. "I hate to admit it, but I worried about you every single day. I know you're capable, but it was torture being separated."

"I know," I replied, feeling the familiar thrill as I felt his warm hand interlacing with mine. "I missed you."

"So tell me honestly," Cap said, leaning against the door frame next to me. "Rollie?"

"What about him?"

"How was he?"

"He's in rough shape. It's disheartening," I replied truthfully. "Being around him every day was depressing. It's hard to see him so broken. He's trying so hard, too. I'm not sure that he'll ever be quite the same man."

Cap stared back at me, leaning his head against my door frame. "I missed you, Andi. And I worried terribly about you—especially as you handled the mantle of leadership for the first time. That's hard enough, but the things we've been dealing with lately are heavy—it's taking a toll on me, at least. Are *you* okay?"

"Not really," I admitted. "I'm discouraged. And angry. I can't believe someone did this to them. It was an act of selfishness. Of pure evil. Cap, we have to find these men and make them pay for what they did. We have to save Paz."

He pulled me to him, holding me tightly. "We will. We'll find him. And we'll take care of them, too."

# CHAPTER 22

CAP AND HUDSON CALLED everyone together for a team meeting the next morning in a small conference room in the back of the hotel.

Seeing them for the first time in a few weeks gave me fresh clarity, a chance to observe them with sharper eyes. I knew that Cap had been on edge, handling the stress of Paz's kidnapping, but now Hudson seemed like he'd already fallen off that edge.

Hudson's dark eyes smoldered with intensity, and his hair and beard had both started to grow out in the last few weeks. His sense of humor had become dangerous—perhaps even reckless. If he wasn't laughing, he was brooding and angry. There was no emotion in between anymore.

Patrick and Marceau sat down next to Chito and me. Chito leaned over and patted Marceau on the back. "Good to see you back with us, friend."

"It's good to be back," Marceau responded. "Have you guys managed to make any progress in tracking the kidnappers?"

Chito glanced at me. "What has Cap told you about it?"

"Nothing, really," I responded. "Every time I ask, he just pushes it off and says we'll talk about it soon enough."

"Well—he's the boss. He and Hudson have a plan, but they're keeping it pretty private right now, I think."

Patrick leaned over on the other side of me. "Cap won't even tell you?"

"I guess not."

Patrick and Marceau raised their eyebrows and looked at each other. I wondered what Cap and Hudson had cooked up that was so closely guarded that they wouldn't tell the rest of us. What did they plan to do, now that we were all in Spain?

Hudson and Willis were in deep discussion with Cap, and the three of them continued talking as the rest of us settled in expectantly. Dessie pulled a chair behind me.

"Hey," she whispered. "Do you know anything yet?"

I tried not to roll my eyes. If Dessie couldn't worm a secret out of a man, how did she expect me to?

"No," I replied. "I just got here, remember? You know more than me at this point."

"At this point?" she whispered, grinning. "I'd like to think I'm altogether wiser and more experienced than you, Andi."

Now I did roll my eyes.

Willis finally sat down, and Hudson and Cap faced the group. At Cap's signal, Hudson walked across the small room and closed the door. He sat down on the top of a table, propping his long legs up against a chair. Cap stood, his hat in his hand.

"What we're going to share here today has been a closely guarded secret," Hudson began, leaning forward and talking in a low tone of voice. "As you know, Cap and I have been discussing our options for the last few weeks, and we've explored a variety of avenues as we search for Paz."

He rubbed his beard as he shook his head.

"We've obviously been working with the police, both in Switzerland and now here. The Swiss police initially interviewed the bartender, but they sent the reports straight to the Spanish police department here in Tarragona, as they transferred the case over."

Cap cut in, his face etched with frustration. "Patrick, Andi, and Marceau, you don't know this yet because you were still with Rollie at the hospital, but we went back to the bar where Paz first encountered the gang. We talked to the bartender, who indicated that he had quite a lot of details about the kidnappers, but he refused to tell us anything."

"It was incredibly frustrating," Hudson added. "He insisted that he'd already done his duty, and told everything to the police. 'I don't want any trouble, I just serve everyone,' he kept telling us. I assume he probably has criminals in there all the time, and doesn't want to spook any of his regulars."

"Did you offer him money?" Patrick interrupted. "We have plenty. Surely that should factor in?"

"Trust me, we tried everything," Hudson replied. "We offered money. A lot of money. He wasn't interested. We appealed to his sense of duty, asked him to do the right thing, told him Paz's life was on the line. Hell, we even threw Dessie at him to tempt him—he wouldn't budge."

"Just doing my duty," Dessie winked at me.

"Anyway, we know the bartender has details about the kidnappers that he shared with the police, and that the police already sent the file off to the local police department in Tarragona," Hudson continued.

"We've been in contact already with the police department here in Tarragona. They're small, and don't have much experience handling cases like this. We appealed for a detective from Barcelona, to help us work this missing persons situation, but they can't spare anyone and the chief at the Tarragona station was quite offended that we didn't seem to think his department up to the challenge. Paz's family has already been working with them, since they heard word about his kidnapping, but I can't say that I hold out much hope that they'll crack the case."

"Why not?" Chito asked. "Even if they've had limited experience, they still have more experience than us. They have the resources to deal with this."

Cap spoke up. "That's true. But we realized that we have another issue on our hands, as we started dealing more closely with them. We've spent countless hours in there at this point, after all—we learned a lot. And it's not good."

"What?" Patrick asked.

"We're pretty sure the local police are dirty," Hudson admitted. "Let's just say that we've noticed some odd things. Quite frankly, we're not sure how much we can trust them to handle this case. Who knows? Maybe they're even conspiring with the criminals themselves. Organized crime and small police departments have a long history, after all."

"There's no way," I protested. "An entire police department? Unable to be trusted? I don't buy it."

"I know it's hard to believe, but we've talked to them dozens of times," Hudson said. "They shuffle a lot of papers around and offer a lot of excuses, but they're not willing to actually do anything. Their answers don't always make sense."

"So you really think we can't trust them?" Chito asked incredulously.

Cap and Hudson both nodded.

"I don't trust them at all," Hudson replied. "Not anymore. Not when they've been unwilling to help us with a serious case, even though we're international celebrities."

"We've tried everything," Cap added. "We've offered to pay. We've begged to hire a detective on our own dime, at triple what his salary would be with the police department. We've pleaded. We've said we'll go to the press and reveal their ineptitude to the world. Nothing's changed their mind. They just flat out refuse to help us."

"This is the problem with some of these countries," Patrick shrugged. "You hear about it all the time, even in the United States, right? Gangs and mobs controlling the local government and police department? I just can't believe we're facing it now, here in Spain, when we need them."

"And after the Zermatt police were so lazy and unwilling to help?" Marceau frowned. "Why can't we get anyone to actually take this seriously?"

"I don't know," Cap admitted. "It's disheartening. I don't know if it's the case itself that's the problem, or maybe our fame makes us unpopular. It could be that these police departments are worried about us blowing this into an ugly, highly public affair if they fail to find Paz, and maybe they don't want to risk their reputations and touch the case at all because of that. Either way, we seem to be on our own here."

"But they're the police!" Leonce squinted, his face worried. "What can we possibly do if we can't utilize them? We're not cops!"

Hudson leaned forward. "That's why we've been keeping this to ourselves so far. Cap and I have discussed a thousand different options for trying to find Paz. And the two of us have secretly met with Paz's father about all of this, since we got here. The three of us have carefully weighed all the pros and cons of what we're thinking about doing, and we're in agreement about what to do next."

He paused and glanced at Cap. His dark eyes glittered as he leaned toward us. "We're finally ready to loop the rest of you in."

Cap crossed his arms and sighed. "But before we go any farther, we need to be clear. This is a very dangerous situation we're walking into."

He hesitated, rubbing his jaw, before adding, "And not only that, but what we're planning to do is against the law."

# CHAPTER 23

"WHAT?" BERNARD SCOFFED. "You wouldn't break the law, Cap! No way!"

Cap stared back at him grimly. "I don't want to. But I promise you, it's my last resort. We've tried every other avenue. Exhausted every possibility. This is the only way forward, at this point, to try to find Paz."

"You still haven't told us what you want to do, though," Dessie pointed out.

"Right," Hudson replied, standing up and starting to pace. "We want to give everyone the chance to decide on their own, right now, if they're in or out."

"But we don't know what you're planning!" Chito exclaimed, shaking his head. "How can we decide if we want to be a part of it or not before we even know?"

"It's for your own protection," Cap replied. "For *everyone's* protection. If you decide you're out, then you can walk away without question, and without any knowledge of anything we're planning to do. You can talk to the police or the media and honestly say you didn't know a thing. You'll be entirely innocent."

He sighed. "Most importantly, if we get in trouble, you'll walk away without any repercussions."

"But if you decide you're in, you're committed," Hudson cut in. "We'll tell you the plan, but you're in. And if you're in, you'll be on the hook if we get caught. No backing out, once you've heard the plan. You face the music and deal with the consequences if we get caught."

"This is an impossible situation!" Patrick exclaimed, a hint of anger in his voice. "How can we agree to a plan that we have no details for? You won't tell us anything!"

"I know it seems like a challenging choice," Cap admitted. "Without knowing the plan, it'll be hard to judge for yourselves. I understand how difficult this is for each of you, I do. And I swear, we've tried every option. I'd be angry if I was faced with this choice, too."

"Then why do you insist that we make it?" I said, feeling as frustrated as Patrick. "How can we trust that we're making the right decision, without knowing all the facts?"

Cap turned his eyes to me. His blue eyes bored a hole into my soul. "What it really comes down to is whether or not you trust the two of us."

"That's not fair," Dessie said angrily. "Of course we trust you. But you're asking us to blindly follow you into something illegal, without knowing any facts!"

"Yes," Cap nodded. "But I'll ask this of my crew—Gallivanters, have I ever knowingly led you into danger?"

"No," came the immediate response from Bernard, Chito, and me.

"Have I always tried my best to involve you in decisions? To fill you in on all the facts before we face something, so we can decide together, as a team?"

"Yes, but this isn't the same thing," Chito said, shaking his head. "We weren't doing anything illegal before."

"I know that," Cap replied. "But we've never had a teammate kidnapped before, either. We've been thrust into a situation we never expected to find ourselves in, but we're here. There's no playbook for how to handle this. No statistics or facts that can help us now. We're figuring it out as best we can, the only way that seems to be open to us. Unfortunately, it involves breaking the law."

He hesitated, the stress evident in his bearing as he faced us.

"While we certainly won't be asking anyone to commit murder or anything, we still could end up in jail for our actions," he said, his face tight. "We want to be crystal clear with you now about the very real possibility of danger and consequences, before anyone hears anything else."

I stared at Cap. I was entrusting this man with my love—my life, my entire future—and he was asking me to break the law with him? I had no choice and no hesitation.

"Yes," I said resolutely, getting to my feet. "I'm in."

"Thank you," Cap said, his eyes briefly warm as he looked at me and held my gaze.

"It's decision time for everyone else," Hudson announced. "There's no shame if you want to walk away. We completely understand, and we support your choice. And your choice now has no bearing on your position with the expedition."

The rest of the group exchanged looks. Patrick stood up. "I'm in, too."

"And me," Chito said, as Marccau and Willis also stood up.

Claude, then Leonce stood up. "We're in it until the end," Leonce said.

Bernard and Dessie still sat, staring at each other.

"What was it that Ben Franklin said?" Bernard drawled.

"Huh?" Cap frowned.

"Wasn't he the one who said that we must hang together or we'll all hang separately?" He stood up. "Guess we'll all hang together, right?"

Now only Dessie remained seated, her face unreadable except for her eyes, which blazed. She looked fiercely beautiful, her slender neck lifting her small white face as she glared around the room at the rest of us, her long blonde hair unpinned and streaming down her back.

"Dessie, my dear, there's no shame in walking away," Hudson said gently, walking over to her and putting his hand on her back. "We'll get you some money for your trip home, of course—"

"Stop," Dessie said, jerking away from his hand. "I'm in."

"What?"

"I'm in," Dessie repeated, staring up at Hudson. Her voice was hard. "I'm committed, of course. But I want everyone here to promise me—to swear right now—that you're willing to do whatever it takes to get him back. And I do mean *whatever* it takes. We stop at nothing until we find him."

"I think we're all on board with that, aren't we?" Hudson said, looking around as the rest of us nodded.

"Right, then, let's get down to business," Cap said, pulling a chair in and inviting all of us to sit in a tight circle. I sat wedged in, shoulder to shoulder between Chito and Marceau.

"As we've already shared, Hudson and I have attempted to work with the police here already, but they're unwilling to help us," he started, speaking quietly as we leaned in to hear him.

"We're in agreement with Paz's father, who's also been extremely frustrated by the local police's response to all of this. He also tried to pay for a private investigator or a detective, but as we told you, the Tarragona police have been absolutely unwilling to share their files or any information with us or anyone else."

He rubbed his face as he looked around the circle. "We *know* the police have information we need, at that station. That's where the bartender's report is."

Cap glanced at Hudson. "We've already quietly offered cash—a lot of cash—to several different officers, trying to get that file with information from the bartender, but we've had no bites yet. They simply won't share any information with us at all. They won't let us look at it, won't share any details from it, nothing."

"So what can we do? Can't we get that information some other way? Surely there's someone above the local police?" Willis asked.

"We've tried," Hudson groaned. "I appealed to the Spanish government and the Swiss government, but neither of them wants to create a major issue out of it. We all know how a small political incident can flare up into a world war, right?"

"I can't believe this," Patrick muttered.

"They're highly aware that we're famous," Hudson continued. "They know that if people find out that if celebrities of our caliber were attacked, or are experiencing trouble with kidnappers, it'll drastically hurt tourism in their countries. They wouldn't come out and say it, but they're just stalling us, hoping we go away. They won't help us."

Cap crossed his legs, smoothing his pants. "I went to the American ambassador in Barcelona and tried him, too. He took my report and expressed his regret for the situation we're in, but told me that it'll take months to get across the right desks in Washington. Unfortunately, we don't have that kind of time."

"What we're saying is that we're out of options for following the law," Hudson summarized, his thick eyebrows knit together in frustration.

"What about the Odysseus Society?" I asked. "Can we ask them for help?"

"I did," Cap sighed. "They were one of my first calls. They told me to work with the local police. When I telephoned them again, to share that the police have been unhelpful, they suggested the American ambassador. Since I struck out with both of them already, we're back to square one."

"Wait, what about the British embassy, then? Mother England has quite the pull over here in Europe, doesn't she?" Willis asked. "We *are* Canadian. We should get something from the damn crown, just once in our lives."

"I tried them, too," Hudson said. "Same issue Cap had. Government moves too slowly to be of any use, in pretty much any situation."

"Ain't that the truth," Chito muttered.

"But wait, did you tell the Odysseus Society that the police and the ambassador hadn't actually helped you?" I replied, circling back. "Maybe they just didn't realize the trouble you're having?"

"No, I've kept them updated at every step," Cap replied. "They told me in no uncertain terms that they can't offer any help. They're a privately funded, international goodwill organization, 'not a detective agency,' as they told me. They don't have the resources. Furthermore, they asked me to keep this out of the newspapers. They don't want their names dragged through the mud again, and they don't want future expeditions to be tainted by this unfortunate kidnapping. They're afraid no one would ever sign up for a competition again, based on what's happened to us."

"Nice, huh?" Hudson added, slapping his knee with a hollow laugh. "Our own sponsors aren't really there for us. Hard to believe, I know."

"There has to be someone else," Patrick protested. "What about if we hire a private investigator? Find someone that'll work on our behalf, without our names attached to him?"

"We've talked about that," Hudson said. "The problem is that they're going to run into the same obstacles we are. As soon as the police connect the dots and find that they want that file with the bartender's information, any private investigator will come up against a brick wall, just like us."

Unconsciously, he dug his fingernails into his knee. *"Hudson is furious,"* I thought, watching him quietly. *"He looks like he's about to snap."*

"Ultimately, we need that file that the police have. And they won't give it to anyone," Hudson's forehead wrinkled. "The government certainly isn't going to come to our aid and force them to hand sensitive files over. It would become a complex international incident overnight."

"Right," Cap added. "It already involves team members from three different countries, while the kidnappers hail from a fourth country and are operating in a fifth country. We could very well start another world war if we strained diplomatic relations over this issue. Especially with our celebrity status."

"Isn't it worth a try, though?" Chito asked. "It's Paz. We have to try everything."

Cap and Hudson again looked at each other.

"We told you, we've tried everything we can think of already," Cap responded. "Like Hudson said earlier, we're out of options for following the law."

"I caught that when he said it the first time," I responded, tilting my head and trying to figure out what the two of them were dancing around. "What exactly does it mean?"

Cap was a stickler. He'd never actually break the law...would he?

"Isn't it obvious yet?" Hudson asked, looking at Cap. In response, Cap sighed and motioned to Hudson.

Hudson grinned wickedly. "How do you feel about stealing from the police?"

The rest of us stared at him, and then uneasily at each other. For several beats, no one said anything. Finally, Dessie broke the silence.

"You *are* joking, right? What's the real plan?"

"That's the plan," Hudson said, his teeth flashing white against his dark beard.

*"He's far too cavalier right now about something so serious,"* I thought worriedly. *"Just moments ago, I saw his rage. And now he's kidding around?"*

Apparently, Patrick thought so, too.

"This isn't funny, Hudson," he cried. "Why do you have that stupid grin on your face? We're not talking about a lark here. This is serious. You're talking about breaking into a police station!"

"Oh, trust me, I know," Hudson said, still smiling. "Why do you think we gave you all the option of backing out?"

"This is insane!" Chito blurted, throwing up his hands. "You can't possibly ask us to walk into a police station and take that file. There's no way. We'll never be able to get away with it."

"There has to be a better plan," Patrick shook his head. "We have to think of something else."

Willis frowned, too. "No way, guys. It wouldn't work."

"Surely we can think of something less risky?" Marceau said, looking back and forth between Cap and Hudson.

"We've tried everything already," Hudson said, the smile still tugging at his mouth. I wondered if he was still of sound mind. Had his brush with the kidnappers and the loss of Paz unhinged him? His attitude verged on complete recklessness.

"We can't possibly do this," Patrick insisted. "They'll catch us. We'll never be able to pull it off."

"You're right, we can't," Cap replied, then nodded toward Dessie and me. "But *they* can."

# CHAPTER 24

I FELT LIKE THE WIND had been knocked out of me.

"What?" I gasped, staring at Cap. I must have misunderstood. He'd never willingly put me in a compromising situation like this.

"What on earth are you talking about?" Dessie said, her voice shocked. "We could get arrested! We could end up in jail!"

"Hear me out," Cap implored, holding up his hands. "You're two beautiful, famous women. Anyone who meets you will be dazzled—starstruck. And on top of that, few men think that women are capable of something as bold as stealing in the middle of a police station. They all think you're fragile, delicate little daisies. But we know differently. We've seen just how determined and capable you both are."

"They'll never see it coming," Hudson jumped in. "If it was one of the boys, maybe. But you? The two prized beauties? They wouldn't suspect you. And best yet, they wouldn't dare search you for the file."

"Like hell they wouldn't!" I exclaimed angrily. "Why wouldn't they search us, if they suspect anything at all? Of course they would! We can't do this! Do you want us to end up strip-searched, naked in a jail cell?"

"You can just play modest and coy, can't you?" Hudson responded. "Or you can faint if they do try to search you?"

"I've never fainted in my life," I protested.

Dessie turned to me. "Oh, I've fainted lots of times. It's easy. I can show you how."

"I don't need to know how!" I said irritably, glaring at her. "Have some self-respect, Dessie. Fainting shouldn't be a toy in your little playbook of manipulation."

"It's not a toy," she pouted. "It's more like a tool. A highly effective tool, I might add."

"Cap, come on," I pleaded, turning to him. "You have to think of something else. You can't possibly expect the two of us girls to waltz in there and steal a file from the police. How would we even know which one it is?"

"We'll have to search for it," Cap replied. "We have a plan in mind. And I'm sorry. We have no other options. Believe me—if I could spare you from this, you know I would."

Patrick's face was concerned. "This is a huge risk for them to take, guys. What happens if they get arrested? They'll have been caught red-handed. There's no way we can bail them out. They'll be tried and charged. They'll do time in prison."

"Then don't get caught, dolls," Hudson laughed.

I noticed Chito and Marceau both frowned, staring at Hudson. They, too, must be noticing his odd attitude.

"We gave you each the option to back out, and you choose to participate in this," Cap reminded us. "We're a team. And you could've walked away, but you didn't. So now we're asking you to trust us. To do this. We need you, to pull this off. You're the only ones who can."

I glared at him. Hudson stood up, and walked over to me and Dessie, draping his arms over our shoulders.

"Chin up, girls," he grinned. "If you end up in jail, we'll probably all end up there, too. So we'll suffer together. A little prison party, so to speak."

"What is wrong with you?" I said sharply, jerking away. He merely laughed.

Cap wearily ran his hand through his hair and sighed. "We've been under immense stress. Believe me, this isn't our first choice. I'd never ask someone else to do something I could do myself. But the fact is that our best chance of success in finding Paz is getting that file. And with the police unwilling to work with us, our only shot is to *steal* the file. And to do that, we need you two. Like we already said, they'll never suspect two beautiful women to be capable of pulling off this heist."

"I don't know," I said, staring uncertainly into Cap's eyes. He held my gaze. I could see the conflict in his face as he looked back at me. His eyes silently implored me.

"Trust me, Andi," he said softly. "Trust that I've played out every possible scenario to save you from doing this. But it's our only option right now. And we have a plan."

"Fine. I'm not happy about it. But I trust you. *Both* of you," I added, looking at Hudson. "Don't screw this up for us, though."

"Me? Screw up? Never!" Hudson laughed, clapping like a showman in the center ring of a circus. "Let's sit down and talk through the details of the plan. We're going to be here a while, folks. Settle in."

# CHAPTER 25

I KNOCKED ON DESSIE'S hotel door, waiting for her to answer. She opened the door and frowned.

"No," she said, taking one look at me.

"Good morning to you, too," I grumbled, pushing my way in.

A strange contraption sat on her desk. It had a long electrical plug, a rounded metal barrel about five inches long, and a pair of wooden handles tipped with metal sticking out the end. The entire thing rested on a small metal plate, where two electrical plugs connected under where the barrel rested.

"What is that?" I asked, as Dessie still stood at the door, frowning at me.

"It's an electric curling iron," she snapped, walking toward me and pointing her hairbrush accusingly. "And no. Go back and change into something else. Something more feminine."

"You use this on your hair?" I replied, ignoring her and squinting at the little machine. It looked like an instrument of torture.

"Of course I do. It heats up, like curling tongs, but it's much faster because it's electric."

"Interesting."

She glared at me. "I know exactly what you're doing. You're hoping that if you distract me and get me talking about myself, that'll I'll forget about your outfit and that I've asked you to change."

"What? No."

Dessie sighed, throwing her head back. "Andi, you look like you *always* do. Frumpy and boring."

"I'd prefer the term 'practical.'"

She shook her head. "You can't wear a shirt and pants and a bare face and expect to walk into a police station and have them treat you like a damsel in distress. You have to look the part. Elicit some sort of protective emotion from them, with your female wiles. And walking in with trousers on is *not* going to draw that out of them, I guarantee you that."

"But this is how I look," I said, staring down at my clothes. They weren't so bad, were they? "Besides, it's all I have."

"Yeah, that's the problem," Dessie said, digging through her bag. "Don't you have something with lace? Satin? Little bows, maybe?"

"Um....no."

Dessie exhaled, digging through her clothes. "I don't know if I have anything that'll fit you, you're so tall."

Her long blonde hair fell in front of her face and she brushed it aside, distracted. "Don't you have a single skirt you could wear?"

"No," I said. "I'm on an expedition around the world, where I have to haul boxes and crawl under the automobiles and change the gasoline and oil. Why would I need a skirt for any of that?"

"How on earth you managed to hook a man like Cap, I'll never understand," Dessie grumbled, pulling out a length of silky black fabric. "Here, try this. It's the longest skirt I have."

She tossed it to me, and I wiggled out of my pants and slipped the skirt on. Even before I zipped it, I could tell it was much too short.

"This won't work," I said, at the exact moment Dessie crowed and clapped her hands, saying, "It's perfect!"

Out of the comfortable protection of my trousers, my bare legs felt exposed. The cool breeze felt foreign on my legs. Dessie was petite, and the skirt must be modest on her. But with my long legs and tall, lean frame, it rose alarmingly high on my knees.

"I can't wear this," I grimaced as I looked at myself in her mirror.

"Sure you can," she said, coming up behind me and zipping up the back. She tugged the skirt up on my waist, exposing even more of my leg. "There."

"No, this isn't staying on," I said, reaching for the zipper. Dessie's hand grabbed mine and twisted it, pinning it behind my back.

"Don't you dare touch that skirt," she threatened. "Cap and Hudson told me in no uncertain terms to style you for this heist, and I take my work seriously."

"They did not say that," I sputtered hotly, wrestling my arm away. Dessie held it in a tight grip. She was so much shorter than me that I leaned forward painfully, my arm trapped. Goodness, she was much stronger than she looked.

"They most certainly did," she said, her tone commanding. "And I swear to God, I won't let your arm go until you agree to let me do my job in peace. I'm in charge here. This is my kingdom, and I rule with an iron fist."

"I don't want to wear it, Dessie," I said, then gasped as she twisted my arm. "Ouch! Stop!"

"No. Not until you agree to play by my rules. And that means you wear what I tell you to wear. And let me at least *attempt* to fix your face."

"Fine," I winced as she released my arm from behind my back. I massaged my sore wrist. "What's wrong with you? Normal people don't go pinning their friends' arms behind their backs like that, you know."

"Oh, we're friends now, are we?" she grumbled, going back over to her bag and digging around. Articles of clothing piled up on the floor around her.

"What are you still looking for?" I said, staring at her outfit. She was wearing a form-fitting dress, cut low in the front. She looked sensational—as she usually did.

"Some sort of top that'll fit you," she replied, studying a gauzy fabric in her hand. "This might work."

I looked over her shoulder. "It's transparent."

"Exactly," she grinned. "You have a camisole on, right?"

"Yes, but that's completely sheer. Everyone would see my undergarments."

"Obviously. We're trying to distract them, muddle their heads, Andi. What part of this are you not understanding?"

"I don't care what we're trying to do, I'm not going to go prancing around half-naked in public like this," I said angrily.

"Being a little provocative with your outfits can be empowering, too, you know," she said, pulling hair ribbon out of her bag. "You don't aways have to dress like a man to prove yourself."

"I dress how I like. I don't care if I look like a man. It's comfortable for me."

"What if you wear this top but I let you put a coat over it?" Dessie said, tilting her head and holding up the shirt.

I paused, chewing on my lip. "Fine. If I can wear a jacket over it."

"Good," she said brightly, tossing it to me. "Take off that ugly shirt and see if this blouse fits. Don't ruin it. It's one of my favorites."

I unbuttoned my simple cotton shirt and slipped it off, folding it neatly and laying it on the foot of her bed, next to my pants. Carefully, I pulled the shirt on over my head, praying I wouldn't accidentally tear the delicate fabric.

The sheer white fabric was edged with lace and tiny shimmering beads woven into the center of the lace. It was beautiful. And showed off way more of my chest than I was comfortable with.

I started to tug it up to take it off, and Dessie snapped at me. "Leave it on!"

My arms dropped to my sides, defeated. I couldn't fight her on everything.

"Now, shoes and stockings," she said, studying me with clinical precision. "My stockings would never fit you. But surely you have some nice pairs?"

"Um, I think I have a pair."

"Just one?"

"I usually wear pants."

"Nuts, Andi!" Dessie exclaimed. "Well, you'll have to wear yours, I guess. Can you at least roll them?"

"Am I supposed to?" I asked, confused.

She brushed her hair back from her face and threw up her hands. "I feel like I'm dealing with a child. How are you so absolutely clueless about fashion?"

I shrugged. She hitched up her skirt, the fabric already tight against her body, and showed me her polka dot pattern stockings. With a practiced hand, she pulled them up and then rolled them down, so the rolled top rested right below her knee.

"You're not wearing garters?" I replied, raising my eyebrows.

"Welcome to freedom," she replied, rolling the other stocking down on her opposite leg. She glanced up at me.

"Now here's a real trick, one that I wouldn't show anybody but you," she said, reaching for her blusher. She dipped her brush in, and dabbed it onto her kneecaps.

"Why?" I asked, staring at her. She stretched her legs out in front of her, admiring her knees.

"Because men aren't used to seeing our legs at all," she responded. "This ensures they stare. Linger with their gaze a little bit. All the fashionable girls are doing it, especially when they're going out dancing."

She wiggled her toes happily. "Now I slink into some cute shoes, and we start on hair and makeup."

I sighed, knowing Dessie would criticize my shoes next.

Sure enough, after she slipped on her own dainty black heels, she asked, "And what are you putting on those feet?"

"These," I said, holding up a pair of plain mary janes with a low heel. "Don't even start on them, either. My choices are limited—I have only these and my boots."

"Golly. You are a hopeless case, aren't you? Well, they'll be looking at me more, anyway."

I sat quietly on Dessie's bed while she applied her makeup for the next few minutes. As she colored in her eyebrows with a small colored pencil, she released a barrage of unhelpful advice.

"Don't walk like a hulking giant. Try to make your movements graceful, light, and gliding. Carry a small bag—there's no way you have one, I already know. You can borrow one of mine. For heaven's sake, don't speak your mind. We're there to fool them into thinking we're silly, flighty little helpless things who can't think for ourselves. Laugh at whatever the men around you say, even if it isn't funny."

"Oh, dear Lord," I groaned. She whirled around, still holding her mascara in one hand.

"Don't utter exclamations like that, either," she said, frowning. "Basically, you probably need to fight every natural instinct you have. Can you cry on demand?"

"Cry on demand?"

"Yes, muster up a little tear to roll down your cheek at your own urging?" she said, dotting a bit of blush on the center of each cheek. *"No wonder her face was always so delicately rosy,"* I thought.

"Sadly, that's not one of my skills," I replied. "But if you're looking for someone to tighten wing nuts or replace the fuel line on a Ford, I'm your girl."

"Again, you and Cap make no sense," Dessie sighed, drawing a cupid's bow with her lipstick and filling in her lips. She blotted her lips with a tissue and turned. "Get over here. It's your turn."

I slunk over and sat down in her desk chair. She tugged at my eyelids painfully, dragging her charcoal pencil across my lash line.

"Careful!" I cried, my eyes watering.

"Don't be a baby," she commanded, smudging the color into my eyelashes. Next, she skillfully applied mascara, lipstick, and blush. All the while, she offered a running commentary of unsolicited counsel.

"I'd tell you to tip your chin down and look up through your eyes so a man can watch you bat your eyelashes up at him, but you're ten feet tall," she said. "You look every man in the eye. It's unsettling."

"I'm barely six feet tall, actually," I replied. I'd always been tall. Thankfully, a lifetime's worth of teasing had hardened me to any insults about it.

"We're playing helpless, don't forget," she said. "Speak in a soft voice. Don't use that direct, bossy attitude of yours. Hem and haw more. Lots of 'oh, I don't know, sir,' and 'I'm just a little lady, I couldn't possibly,' if they ask any questions."

"Me? Bossy?" I exclaimed. "I think my direct, no-nonsense brain has been an asset as we've traveled through dangerous situations, you moron. It's certainly saved *your* rear."

"Listen, Andi," Dessie cried, sounding like she was losing her patience with me. "Cap and Hudson told me to teach you all my tricks. We both know it's an act. It's not who either of us really are. We're curating an image—crafting a persona, in order to convince these policemen to trust us. We don't want them to think we're capable, smart women. They have to think we're simpering idiots!"

Glaring at me, she continued. "Of all the women on this planet, you're probably the worst possible girl to play along with me and try to keep up. You wouldn't know how to simper if your life depended on it. But a life *does* depend on it—Paz's life. And God help me, I can't live with myself if something happens to him—"

She choked up suddenly, and fell quiet.

I wondered again if Dessie was secretly in love with Paz. She was certainly emotional, every time we brought him up. And hadn't she been the one to make us promise that we'd do whatever it took to save him? I stopped fighting.

"I'm sorry," I said, staring at Dessie in the mirror. She blinked rapidly, hiding the sheen of tears I'd already noticed, and frowned at me.

"We need to fix that mess you call a hairdo," she said, turning and grabbing her hairbrush. She tugged it through my hair, more harshly than I deserved, then spent several moments curling and arranging my hair.

"Well, I think I've finally outdone myself," Dessie said, stepping back. I stared into the mirror, glimpsing myself for the first time since she started applying my makeup. "What do you think?"

A stranger stared back at me.

My eyes stood out, framed with long lashes and dark liner. My hair fell in soft waves across my shoulders, contrasting with the delicate sheer white fabric of my shirt. My lips were bright red, drawing the eye.

For the first time in my life, I felt pretty.

I stood up, still chagrined at the short skirt and immodest top, but feeling more confident now that I'd been thoroughly primped. *"I can play this role,"* I thought. *"It's like an actor, wearing a costume. I can pretend to be silly and shallow and helpless, if it'll help Paz."*

I swished my skirt, watching it hug my slender legs. Impulsively, I grinned at Dessie. I wanted to hate it, but I couldn't. I felt great.

"Thank you," I said, squeezing her shoulder. I was so pleased with the results that I was clean out of sarcastic comebacks for her.

Dessie wasn't lost for words, though. She never gave up the chance to needle me.

"My, my, Andi, you can almost look like a proper girl when we slap all this makeup on you," she said. "Now if only we can find a way to shorten you by a foot or so, and change the way you walk and talk, you might even pass for a delicate little beauty."

"We all work with what we have," I said cheerfully, ignoring her comments. I realized now that Dessie's catty remarks were covering up the nervousness she felt, but didn't want to reveal to me. "You've done a good job, Dessie. This should fool them."

"Well, I think any man's eyes will linger on you now, at least," Dessie replied. "Keep in mind, we'll have to hide a file on your body somewhere once we get it."

"*My* body?" I exclaimed. "You dressed me in a sheer lace top! Where am I supposed to hide a file?"

Dessie nodded at my skirt. "Right there. They won't look there. They'll be too busy staring at your décolletage."

"Why don't you hide it in your dress?"

"Because I need this tight little dress to show off my swaying hips," she said, swinging her lithe body to demonstrate the movement. "And we both know I'm the only hope we have for distracting them with my hips. If you tried, you'd end up looking like you're attempting to play golf."

"Fair enough," I said, looking at myself in the mirror again. Dessie came up behind me, silently. She looked astonishingly beautiful, all dolled up in her dress and heels, not a single hair out of place.

We stared into the mirror together. In that instant, as I saw the same grim determination reflected in both our faces, I recognized an unexpected comrade.

Dessie and I were different in the way we dressed and interacted with the men around us, but at our core, we both had inner strength and rebellious hearts. Neither of us liked to be told by society what we should be doing with our lives, and we both had the courage to flaunt the staid examples set by all the other women we knew and blaze our own trails.

I met Dessie's eyes in the mirror. "Ready?"

She nodded.

"I know I already asked you," she said quietly, staring into my eyes with an intensity that unsettled me. "But I'm asking you again, Andi. Do *whatever* it takes, because I will. We have to save him."

"I promise," I replied.

She held my gaze for a moment and sighed. Her shoulders slumped, but then she squared them again. "Let's do this, then."

# CHAPTER 26

I GRABBED MY JACKET and we walked out the door together, heading toward the lobby. Hudson, Cap, Leonce, Chito, and Bernard already sat there, waiting.

All five of the men stared at us, spellbound, as we approached. Cap stood up as we neared, running his hand through his hair while his mouth hung open.

"Andi, wow. You look...um..."

"Naughty," Hudson filled in, grinning.

"That's my fiancée you're talking about," Cap warned, glaring at him. Still, his gaze wandered back to me, like he couldn't drag his eyes away.

Hudson winked at me and playfully slung his arm around Cap's neck. "I know. You're a damn lucky man, you know that?"

"You definitely look like a couple of hotsy-totsy ladies," Leonce grinned. "It'll do the trick, distracting those policemen."

"I agree," Chito smiled kindly. "You both look lovely."

Bernard was openly staring at my face, wearing a perplexed expression. "Did you put something around your eyes?"

"Yes, it's makeup," I replied.

"You don't even look like you," he shook his head. "You look like—I don't know—"

"Beautiful? Stunningly gorgeous?" Hudson offered flirtatiously, as Cap frowned at him.

"No, not quite," Bernard replied, searching for the right word. "I had a little dog once. A little runt, cute but raggedy. But one day, my mom gave it a bath and trimmed it up, and it looked real nice. That's how it is with you, Andi."

"Gee, thanks."

"No, but I mean you look like you're trying hard to look nice," Bernard added. "Like how Dessie always tries hard."

Now Dessie was offended, too.

"Why's he always opening his mouth and ruining the moment?" she exclaimed, glaring at him.

"Strange, I've always had the same thought about you and your mouth," Bernard shot back.

"Look, this is exactly what we're going for," Cap said, still staring at me. "You both look incredible—the eyes of every man in that police station will be on you. It's just what we need. They'll be so distracted by you that we'll be able to sneak in, pull off our plan, get the file, and hide the file on one of you."

I pulled on my jacket, watching as Hudson and Leonce and Cap all stared at my every move, clearly mesmerized by how different I looked all dolled up.

"I'll be hiding the file," I said, nodding at Dessie. "Her dress won't work to conceal it. It's too tight."

"I'll say," Hudson remarked, whistling as he watched Dessie spin playfully and smirk.

"We all have our valuable assets in this mission," Dessie grinned, winking at me.

"*Assets*, doll?" Hudson repeated, raising one eyebrow suggestively. "More like as—"

"Just stick to the plan and we'll be fine," Cap interrupted. "Remember, everyone follow what we talked about."

"And don't get strip-searched," Hudson chuckled.

Cap glared at him again. "Captain Landry, do you need a moment to get control of yourself?"

Hudson smirked. "There he is, folks. Good ol' Cap, making an appearance as the stalwart commander, the fearless leader who always has his troops under control. Stand up straight, everyone. Don't forget to salute."

"Hudson," Leonce groaned, shaking his head. "Stop joking around. This is serious."

Looking at Cap, he nodded. "We know what to do. We're ready."

We filed out to the Fords, Cap climbing into the driver's seat and Chito crawling into the back bench. Slowly, I eased myself up into the passenger's side, trying to hold my skirt down and protect my modesty in the breeze outside.

Hudson, Dessie, and Leonce crammed into the other automobile, behind us. Bernard stood on the front porch, arms crossed as he watched us.

"Careful!" he called as we started our engines.

"We will be," Chito hollered back.

"Don't get arrested!"

"Who'd have ever thought we'd be getting such helpful advice from Bernard?" Cap grumbled, as he navigated the car onto the road and headed toward the police station.

# CHAPTER 27

AS WE DROVE, I TOOK advantage of the moment to have a heart-to-heart with Chito and Cap. I leaned toward them as the wind whistled around us.

"What do you make of Hudson's attitude lately?" I asked. "Does he seem like he's weird?"

Chito shrugged. "He's always been a bit devilish. He has a good heart, though."

Cap glanced at me and nodded. "I've felt like he's been off for a few weeks now. It's like this business with Paz has made him loopy. I know he's worried—we are too—but he's taking it too hard."

He sighed, gripping the steering wheel. "It was sure easier when it was just the four of us Gallivanters."

"Now we're just having twice the fun with a bigger crew," I replied.

Cap rolled his eyes. "You mean twice the people to bail out of jail, if this goes south?"

A few minutes later, we pulled up to the police station and neatly parked the Fords out front in the visitor parking spaces.

"Showtime," Cap said under his breath, as he turned off the car. He hopped out of the Ford and came around to open the door for me, making a show of giving me his hand and helping me down.

We'd agreed that our performance had to start in the parking lot in order to be convincing. If anyone happened to glance out the windows and watch us approach, they couldn't see us conferring in the parking lot together.

Dessie already had a worried expression on her face, as we'd planned. She stepped carefully around the puddles in the parking lot, taking small steps on her spindly high heels.

I took her arm, and she suddenly stopped.

"Oh, one more thing," she said, pulling my jacket off and handing it to Chito. "Hold this for her."

I felt exposed, standing in front of the men in my sheer lace top. I groaned. "Dessie."

Hudson held the door to the station open and we stepped in. It was busy inside, a smoky room filled with electric fans whirling and papers shuffling. But the entire room of men stopped what they were doing and watched as Dessie and I sauntered in, trying our best to look helpless and overwhelmed.

Immediately, a young officer sprang to his feet and rushed over to us. "Buenas tardes, chicas," he said eagerly.

Dessie clutched her chest and the officer's eyes followed her hand, as I'm sure she intended.

"Oh, dear, we don't speak Spanish," she exclaimed. "But please, we do need some help."

"You are very lucky then, because most of us speak English here," the officer grinned, unconsciously straightening his uniform jacket. He smiled broadly at both of us and invited us to sit down.

Chito, Cap, Hudson, and Leonce loomed behind us, looking surly.

"We've been here already," Cap said irritably to the young officer, acting the part of a long-suffering, short-tempered team leader. "She just realized that something else was stolen, along with our money, and she needs to make a police report so she can make an insurance claim."

"Yes, of course," the officer said smoothly, not taking his eyes off Dessie. She sat perched on the edge of her seat, skirt hitched up and her legs stretched out in front of her, nearly touching his.

Right on cue, Leonce spoke up.

"Do you have some water here?" he asked, holding up his empty canteen. "We've been on the road all day. My bottle's dry. Do you mind?"

"Sure, it's down that hall," the officer said, taking out a piece of paper to write down Dessie's information. Without hesitation, Leonce wandered away, slowly meandering through the desks and making his way toward the back hall. He was looking for the file, I knew.

Dessie leaned forward, laying her hand on the desk near the policeman's hand.

"Don't you need to start with my name and contact information?" she purred. "I'm staying at a hotel right now, you know. With a room all to myself."

"Yes, oh, let me write this down," he said enthusiastically, as Hudson scowled and started pacing behind her. Dessie intentionally strung out her answers as long as possible, to give Leonce time to snoop.

"My name is Dessie, which is just the sweetest story, actually," she said, her throaty laugh causing the surrounding officers to look up with interest. "My grandmother—she was French, you know—told my mother that I just had to be named Dessie. My mother had in mind to call me Margaret, after my father's sister, but Granny said no. 'She's too exceptional,' my Gran said. 'She needs a name with character, a name that fits her.'"

"Um, hm," the officer said, fidgeting with his pen. "So what's been—"

"What do you think of it, anyway?" Dessie interrupted, batting her eyes.

"Of what?"

"My name," she teased. "Do you like my name?"

"Yes, of course," he said quickly.

"Do you think my Gran was right?" she continued, smiling at him. I felt almost sorry for him as he gazed into her eyes.

*"This was too easy,"* I thought. He'd played right into her hands.

"Right?"

"That I'm exceptional?"

"Oh, um, yes..." he stumbled over his words, looking down at his paper. "About your stolen item, miss..."

"I'm good at a lot of things, you know," she said, coiling a strand of her hair around her finger. "A *lot* of things."

The officer turned bright red, as Hudson exhaled loudly and said, "Dessie!"

"Sorry, honey," she said, turning to look over her shoulder at Hudson. "I'm just being friendly to this nice officer, I swear."

As she turned back to me, Dessie said quietly—but loud enough that the officer could clearly hear it—"It's just that this officer is *so* handsome, my goodness. I do *love* Spanish men."

The officer blushed even deeper red, the flush extending all the way down his neck. Dessie grinned as he stared down at his paper and scribbled nonsense.

I saw Leonce wandering slowly back through the room, taking a different route, and watched his eyes flicker across every desk. He was quiet and unobtrusive by nature, and with the bustle going on in the smoke-filled room, officers standing up and darting to and fro, hardly anyone gave him a second glance.

Over the officer's shoulder, I saw him stop suddenly and stare. He looked up, catching my eyes, and nodded slightly, shifting his water bottle into his left hand.

That was it. Our signal for where the file was.

I marked the spot, noting its location in the room. It was near a back wall, thankfully, but still in plain view of all the other desks. Drat. I'd hoped it would be a more private location. We'd have to think on our feet.

"So the jewelry I'm missing," Dessie had started to explain. "It's a ring. A gold ring, to be precise. Not an engagement ring, I'm not married yet, but I'd love to be. Wouldn't you? I'm just waiting for the right man to come along and sweep me off my feet...you never know when you might meet him..."

The officer blinked, staring at her. "A ring," he repeated as he wrote it down, his cheeks still flushed.

I waited until his eyes were averted, and tapped Dessie discreetly on the thigh.

She grinned at me, and immediately screamed at the top of her lungs.

# CHAPTER 28

EVERY FACE IN THE STATION instantly swiveled toward us. I fixed a look of confusion on my face, to match everyone else.

In a flash, Dessie had bolted out of her chair and clung to the officer, sobbing as she practically lay in his lap, screaming.

"I saw it! It was right there on my leg! Help me! Get it off! Help!"

Several other officers rushed over, and Hudson and Chito and Cap charged toward Dessie.

"What's going on?" I screamed, pulling away in mock fear. "What is it?"

"A spider!" Dessie shrieked, clawing at her leg. She pulled her skirt up even higher, and yanked at the officer's hands. "It was a huge one! Is it on me? Help! I can feel it on my leg!"

Hudson roared with rage, lunging at the officer.

"How dare you touch my woman like that!" he screamed as the officer tried to stand up.

"Stop it, Hudson!" Cap yelled, wrapping his arms around Hudson and trying to pull him away from the poor officer, who was still trapped under Dessie's desperate flailing.

"Don't you dare touch her!" Hudson screamed, his face red with rage. The veins in his neck stood out as he strained against Cap, twisting and kicking. "She's mine! Don't you touch her!"

Three officers stepped in, trying to help Cap. They blurted a confused mixture of Spanish and English back and forth, trying to figure out what was going on while they attempted to de-escalate the situation.

"That's it, I can't do this anymore!" Dessie yelped, now standing on top of the officer's chair, clutching both sides of her face. "I'm not in love with you, Hudson! I'm in love with Chito! We've been keeping it from you this whole time, but I can't hide it anymore! I love him, I can't possibly be with you!"

"*What?*" Hudson screamed, turning to Chito in a rage. "How could you? With my woman, Chito? You lying, two-faced skunk!"

Chito exploded, charging toward Hudson, swinging his large fists. Another several officers rushed in, restraining Chito, who screamed back at Hudson so violently that spittle flew from his mouth.

"I can't take this!" Dessie screamed, tears springing to her eyes. "How can they break my heart like this? Oh, I need to be alone!"

She leapt off the chair and rushed through the desks toward the back hall.

I sprinted after her, catching up with her easily. I wrapped my arms around her, feigning comfort, and guided her toward the desk where Leonce had spotted the file.

"Dessie, calm down!" I said, over and over again.

"Calm down? My heart is broken, Andi! It's shattered into a million pieces!" she wailed, pretending to stumble.

"No, it's not, sweetie," I said soothingly, listening as the men continued to all scream at each other in the front of the room. *"We're so close to the desk,"* I thought. *"A few more steps and we'll make it there."*

"How can you say that, Andi?" Dessie cried, the tears spilling out of her eyes and down her cheeks. "My life is ruined! It's all over! I've been humiliated! Oh, how can this have happened to me? I just wanted to be with him! I just wanted a good man! And now look at the mess I'm in!"

I guided her over, my arms around her, and whispered in her ear, "This one."

"I just can't go on, I can't!" she sobbed loudly, collapsing without warning across the top of the desk.

She threw her face down into her arms, her back heaving with her turbulent crying. Her long blonde curls streamed out all over the desk, covering the files.

"Dessie, dear, it'll be alright," I cried, leaning over her. Under the cover of my broad back and arms, while Dessie pretended to sob, she scanned the desk and inched the right file toward her, concealing it in her arms.

My heart was beating a million miles a minute as I listened to the men continue to scream and curse each other. We had only a few seconds until someone noticed us here.

"Dessie, look at me!" I commanded, and she lifted her head quickly. I stared over her shoulders and she stared over mine, both of us quickly scanning the room to see if anyone was watching us. As we'd expected, the few men that were still near their desks were all staring at the fight up front.

"Now!" she whispered, shoving the file from under her arm into my lap.

I crouched down quickly, pretending to soothe her. She leaned forward so that her long hair became a shield in front of me. I deftly slid the file up my skirt and held my hand to my thigh, desperately hoping the papers wouldn't slip out somehow.

Just then, I heard a man's voice behind me. "Can I help you ladies with something?"

I swiveled my head, praying he hadn't seen me slide the file up my skirt.

"I'm sorry, what did you say?" I replied, frantically trying to think of how to respond.

"Can I help you with something?" he repeated, his Spanish accent thick. He stared at us, his head cocked. "What are you doing back here, anyway?"

I froze. My stomach dropped hollowly. I didn't know how to talk our way out of this. We'd been caught red-handed, stealing a confidential file.

"I'm sorry, sir," Dessie said as she blotted her eyes, blinking her long eyelashes. She stared up at him pitifully. "We're just so upset. We had to get away from them—they're so angry—"

"I'm sorry, you can't be back here," the man interrupted, his voice stern. "This is a police station. We can't have people just sitting down at desks. We have private information here, young lady."

I rose slowly, my arm still holding the file to my side. Curse this silky skirt, the whole thing could slide out at any moment and land on the floor right in front of this man. I felt dizzy with worry.

Dessie kept talking to cover my silence.

"I'm so sorry, sir, we're just so upset that we're not thinking clearly at all," she said, blinking away her tears as she stood up and offered him her hand, smiling gently. "Who do I have the pleasure of meeting?"

"Lieutenant Ramos," he replied curtly, studying her face. "And you are?"

"Dessie," she replied, looking up at him through her long lashes. "You're a lieutenant here? My, how impressive."

I cringed, realizing we'd just been caught by the man who was likely the most senior official in the building. Which probably meant he was the hardest to fool. Oh, dear Lord. We'd never get away with this now.

Lieutenant Ramos looked cooly at me. "What exactly are you two doing back here?" he said, his eyes traveling up and down my body. I tried to relax, and keep the panic out of my expression. I knew the police were trained to spot liars by their body language.

We were doomed.

*"I'm going to jail,"* I thought despondently. *"My mother will be so ashamed of me. She'll die."*

Dessie bit her lip. "I'm sorry, Lieutenant Ramos, but I can't tell you. It's a terrible secret that we've been trying to wrap our poor little heads around. You know us girls, we just needed to have a good cry and get it out. It's been *so* hard."

"But why are you back here, at a desk?" Lieutenant Ramos said, his voice tinged with suspicion.

"Oh, gosh," Dessie said, her voice cracking. "Andi, we need to tell him. It's time to let it out. Come on. He's such a nice man, I'm sure we can trust him with it."

"What?" I said, staring fearfully at her.

"Come on, Andi," she repeated. I shook my head, my eyes wide. Oh, no. Dessie was going to blow it.

# CHAPTER 29

IN MUTE HORROR, I WATCHED as Dessie turned to Lieutenant Ramos. "Sir, I don't know exactly how to say this, but my friend here is just beside herself with worry."

Unexpectedly, she wrapped her arm around me and leaned up against my body, pulling me in close.

I didn't remove my hand, but Dessie's pressing up against me so tightly pinned my hand in place, still holding the file under my skirt.

"You see, we've been processing some terrible news together," Dessie continued, her arm around me. "My friend here is awfully afraid. She doesn't know what to do."

"What are you talking about?" Lieutenant Ramos said, narrowing his eyes.

"She doesn't want to talk about it, not even with me. But I told her that we *have* to talk about it. That I'll be here for her, no matter what," Dessie said, staring at me with a pitiful glance. "She just found out she's pregnant, sir."

"*What?*" I exclaimed, as Dessie squeezed me even tighter.

"I told you, Andi, you can trust me," she said, her eyes twinkling as she lied. "I'll be there for you, and your baby, too. Don't worry. It'll be fine."

Lieutenant Ramos took a step back. "You're expecting?"

"I—I didn't want anyone to know," I stumbled over my words, my cheeks pink.

Dessie lowered her voice. "She's not sure who the father is," she whispered to Lieutenant Ramos, nodding up to Hudson and Cap, who were still screaming at each other. "And she's beside herself with worry, because obviously there's tension there already between them. And they don't even know about the baby yet! We're petrified what they're going to do when they discover that one of them is the father."

"Why would you say this to him?" I choked out, as Dessie shook her head warningly.

"Andi, dear one, they're the police," she said, stroking my shoulder. "Who can we trust, if we can't trust these fine gentlemen with this secret?"

Lieutenant Ramos stared at us both.

"You can't be back here," he repeated. "I'm sorry for your troubles, miss, but you need to work this out with the men. And be safe about it," he added, looking up at the crew.

"I will," I said, not sure how to respond. Goodness gracious, were we going to get away with it after all?

"Lieutenant Ramos, sir, could you please direct us to the restroom?" Dessie simpered.

"Yes, I need to use it," I jumped in, catching on to what she was setting up. "Right away. It's urgent."

"That's the problem with these babies, right?" Dessie said, giving me a friendly squeeze. "They just wreck your whole body, don't they?"

"Down the hallway and to the right," Lieutenant Ramos replied, taking another step back. "But please, use it and then go back up to the front, where the reception area is. You're not allowed back here."

"Thank you, Lieutenant," I called, as Dessie kept her body pressed up against mine as we walked slowly to the restroom.

We cleared the hallway, and made it to the bathroom. Dessie opened the door for both of us, and we collapsed inside. I held my finger to my mouth and checked to make sure we were alone.

"What was that?" I hissed furiously, as I stepped into a stall and yanked the file out of my skirt. I removed the papers inside and rolled them up, tucking them under the secure elastic of my knickers.

"Oh, the pregnancy bit?" Dessie grinned at me. "I came up with it on the spot. I was afraid he saw us take the file, and would insist on searching us."

"But telling him I'm *pregnant*? Are you insane? Why would you say something like that? You know that I'm not!"

"Because men have no idea what to do with pregnancy, Andi! Didn't you see his face? No man knows how to handle that emotional blow. They instinctively reel back. Just like he did."

"You made me look like a floozy!" I whispered. "You told him I didn't know who the father was! You pointed at Cap and Hudson!"

"Oh, come on," she snapped. "Half the world probably speculates about that, anyway. Who cares? Besides, I needed your reaction to be genuine shock and dismay in order to be believable. You're a horrible actress, you know."

"You make me so angry," I fumed, as I carefully tore the cardboard file up into tiny pieces and flushed it down the toilet.

There. Now the file didn't even exist, so if the police went looking for it later, they'd hopefully just assume that someone misplaced it. And we were all pretty sure that they wouldn't go looking for it, anyway. We had no plans to come back here and pursue the case.

Dessie rolled her eyes. "We can fight about it later," she said. "Right now, we have to get out of here, and fast. We don't want them to stop and start asking questions. Ready for a quick exit?"

"Ready," I said, smoothing my skirt.

"Look upset," she whispered, pushing out through the bathroom door, holding my hand.

# CHAPTER 30

LIEUTENANT RAMOS WAS waiting for us in the hallway. "I'll escort you ladies back to the front," he said, turning on his polished heels and marching us toward the reception hall.

I fervently hoped that the lieutenant would walk us to the lobby and go back to his office, but we had no such luck. Lieutenant Ramos followed right behind us, ushering us to the front of the station. I prayed that the thin silky fabric of my skirt wouldn't show the roll of papers I'd stuffed into my knickers. Hopefully he was staring at Dessie's rear, in her tight dress, and not mine.

We walked up to Hudson and Chito, who were still being held back by a combination of Leonce and Cap and the police officers. Lieutenant Ramos stopped and held up his hand.

"Gentlemen, stop this nonsense and listen to me," he said sternly, and Chito and Hudson both glared at him, straining against the others.

"I don't know what's been going on with your crew here, but apparently there have been some major problems," Lieutenant Ramos said, his voice firm. "You two are fighting, the two young ladies are dealing with—with some, um, *issues* of their own—and this whole operation here is clearly struggling."

Cap and Hudson stared at me, questioning with their eyes. I nodded slightly. *We have it,* I hoped my look communicated.

"I recall reading about your fighting in the newspapers, some months ago," Lieutenant Ramos continued. "Perhaps you should consider taking different paths now, and going along in your own separate teams. I don't want to see you in here again, fighting like this. It's not good for your image, and it's going to get you all in trouble. You're lucky we aren't pressing charges for this little fight today."

"You heard him—get lost," Hudson snarled at Chito. "We don't need you hanging around us, you worthless sack of garbage!"

"Hold on, lieutenant," the young officer said, holding up his half-completed form. "We were interviewing the young lady here about a missing item?"

*"No,"* I thought desperately. *"We have to get out of here. The longer we sit here, the more suspicious they might get. And what if that officer goes back to his desk and notices the file missing, and we're still here?"*

We had to get out. As soon as possible.

Time to lean into Dessie's lie. She was right: the topic of pregnancy clearly made men uncomfortable. I needed to use it to my advantage and get us out of here, and fast.

I clutched Dessie's arm, swaying on my feet. She glanced at me, confused.

"Dessie, I think something might be wrong," I said, loud enough that Lieutenant Ramos could hear.

Cap stared at me, concern in his eyes. "What is it?"

"I can't tell you," I replied, hoping my voice sounded convincingly desperate.

"What? Why not?" Cap asked, stepping toward me. "I'm your captain."

Dessie put her arm around my waist. "Is it—*the baby*?" she mouthed, her eyes wide. Cap's eyes bugged out.

"What?" he gasped, staring at Dessie. "What did you just say?"

"I didn't want you to find out this way," I exclaimed, covering my mouth with my hand.

Dessie clutched my waist. "Come on, Andi, we need to get you to a hospital," she said, pulling me toward the door.

"But miss, what about your ring?" the young officer stood up, the form still in his hand. "You haven't finished the report? We can't file it unless you finish."

"You know what, it's not that big of a deal after all," Dessie shrugged, inching us toward the door.

Lieutenant Ramos stared at us. "Ma'am, you came here to make a police report. Don't tell me you wasted this officer's time? Are you filing a claim with your insurance company or not?"

Oh, no. A stickler.

Impulsively, I clutched my stomach and swayed again. "Dessie, I think I might be sick."

Now Chito and Hudson were staring at me, too, frozen in place as the police still stood between them.

"What's wrong?" Chito asked, his voice worried.

"We can't tell you," Dessie said desperately, still clinging to me. "It's—it's personal. Life changing. For Andi, anyway. And maybe for one—um, two—of you."

Hudson blinked. "What? What does that mean?"

Lieutenant Ramos crossed his arms, watching us closely.

"*Better put on a good show*," I thought desperately. I spoke up.

"Cap, Hudson, I'm *so* sorry," I said, biting my lip and staring back and forth at them. "I didn't know how to tell you...you're going to hate me for this..."

Dessie played along, lying with expert ease.

"Come on, Andi, you can do it," she encouraged, smoothing my hair. "I'm right here. I'm here for you. And your little one."

"Hold on, *what*?" Hudson replied, bewilderment etched all over his brow.

"I'm expecting," I said, touching my stomach. "And I'm not sure which one of you is the father."

In a flash, I saw a twinkle appear in Hudson's eye and then rapidly disappear as he arranged his face into a suitable mask of rage. I had a feeling this was just the kind of elaborate lie that Hudson had been waiting his whole life to throw himself into.

"How can you tell me like this?" Hudson roared, slapping his hand over his mouth in shock. "I thought what we had was special!"

"I'm sorry," I replied, still holding my stomach. "I didn't want to tell you like this. I just—I don't know what to do."

"What do you mean, you don't know who the father is?" Chito shouted, staring at me wildly. "You're having a baby?"

Cap reeled back like he'd been punched. "What are you talking about? You can't be!"

"Yes," I said quickly. "Cap, I'm sorry. I don't know what to say."

The policemen stood staring at us, gripped by the human drama unfolding in front of them. One of them spoke up.

"But wait, I thought the blonde girl here was um—uh—with you two?" he said, swiveling toward Hudson and Chito and looking back at Dessie.

Dessie jumped in before either of them could say anything.

"I am!" she wailed, throwing her head back in despair. "Dear me, we just can't keep our hands off each other! I knew we never should've traveled together—we should've known it would end up like this—"

I swayed again, pretending to be overcome with emotion.

"Dessie, the hospital," I groaned dramatically. "I think it's all this stress. I need to get to the hospital."

Dessie gasped. "Boys, we need to go!" she yelled, half-dragging me toward the door. "Hudson, Cap, you can figure this out later. Right now, you need to step up and be there for your baby—it could be either of yours, so you both have a responsibility here to help. Step up and be men. We need to go to the hospital *now*."

"Hold on a minute," Lieutenant Ramos snapped curtly, stepping in front of Cap and Hudson. He glared at them.

"Gentlemen, this is no way to act toward these ladies. I expect more from you. How dare you? I never want to see you in this building again. I was right about you all along, I see. You're just a bunch of despicable, fame-hungry renegades with loose morals."

He turned to us, his voice gentler but still stern. "Ladies, are you sure you're safe? The gentlemen you're traveling with are unsavory characters. You need to protect yourselves against these cads."

"Yes, of course, sir," Dessie replied as I nodded. "It's our fault, too. These things *do* happen, when you're around a bunch of attractive people, all on your own."

*"Goodness gracious, we must look like a traveling harem to this entire station,"* I thought. I prayed they wouldn't leak this story to the press. Our future would be absolutely doomed if they did.

Apparently, Cap had the same thought.

"Gentlemen, I'd appreciate if you kept everything you've seen and heard here private," Cap beseeched, holding his hat in his hands. "Obviously, our teams have been going through some difficult situations. We'd hate to see this story end up in the newspapers, and have to file a civil suit against you for libel."

Lieutenant Ramos glared at him.

"If you don't want your lives and secrets out in public, perhaps you should live them better in private," he chided. "You've chosen to go on this adventure of immorality and impropriety, and I promise you, one day it will all come to light. But I assure you, we are professionals, bound by confidentiality. Your debauchery won't leak to the papers. Not from this office, anyway. Not because we respect you, or your team, but because we respect *our* jobs and *our* office."

He paused, lifting his head arrogantly. "Good luck trying to hide an infant from the prying eyes of the newspapers, when you lust after fame and glory. And a whole lot of other things, apparently."

"Thank you," Cap replied, turning toward the door.

*"We're almost out,"* I thought desperately. *"We're so close to actually pulling it off."*

"Hospital," I groaned again, leaning against Dessie.

"Dear Lord, she looks terrible!" Hudson exclaimed, coming up to the other side of me. He slipped his arm around my shoulders and helped Dessie drag me out the front door. "Come on, darling. Let's get you to the doctor."

The two of them helped me into Cap's Ford, and Cap stood at the passenger side with Hudson.

"The show's not over yet—they're still watching out the window," I whispered. "Hudson, get in the back. Cap, you drive."

"I have a lot of questions," Cap replied, his eyes narrowed, as he slipped in and started the car.

Hudson climbed into the back and leaned forward, draping his arms over me and hugging me. His breath tickled my ear as he whispered, "Did you get it?"

"Yes," I breathed, leaning my head back like I was overwhelmed with emotion. "It's in my skirt."

"Good girl," he whispered back, trying to hide his smile.

Cap glared at Hudson from the driver's seat. Hudson leaned back and settled into his seat with a grin.

"Congratulations, daddy," he said to Cap, as we pulled away slowly. "How should we three decide on a name? Roll the dice? Or do both of you like Hudson Junior?"

As soon as we were out of sight of the police station, I whirled around to Hudson. "You know I'm not—we're not—it's not possible," I sputtered, my cheeks flaming. "My fiancé is an honorable man, and I'm—we don't—"

Hudson crossed his arms and grinned, his smile splitting his face. "Whatever you say, Miss Gallivanter."

"You got the file?" Cap asked quickly, changing the subject. His cheeks were red, too.

I reached behind me and touched my skirt, feeling the roll of papers. "We got them. They're in my skirt."

"Don't take them out yet," Cap commanded. "We'll wait until we get back to the hotel. I don't want to risk them blowing away in the breeze. Not after all we went through to get them."

Hudson leaned forward again. "You and Dessie sure went off script there at the end, didn't you? We certainly didn't plan *that*."

"We were desperate," I sighed. "Lieutenant Ramos caught us, red-handed, just as we had taken the file. He was suspicious. We needed to find a way to get away from him, and quickly. It was Dessie's idea to pretend I was pregnant. She said it makes men uncomfortable."

"Well, she was right," Hudson laughed. "It's very clever."

"It was probably the best way to extricate ourselves," Cap admitted. "I fear that if we would've lingered there much longer, they would've started asking questions that would've caused problems. And who knows? Someone might have noticed the missing file. They might have searched us."

"I tore up the folder and flushed it down the drain," I said, exhaling slowly. I couldn't believe we'd gotten away with it.

"It went off without a hitch," Cap replied, glancing at me. "Except for the fact that Dessie singlehandedly destroyed all our reputations. Let's hope those officers honor their promise and don't tell anyone about this. It would cause irreparable international embarrassment. For all of us."

Hudson slapped Cap on the back. "Cheer up. If the world explorer thing doesn't work out, now we know that we can go on the road as a traveling troop of thespians!"

Cap groaned, clenching the steering wheel. "Andi, can we agree on one thing?"

"What?"

"This is another story we never tell your mother, okay?"

I smiled, feeling the papers tucked into my waistband and the wind in my hair. "Agreed."

# CHAPTER 31

WE ARRIVED BACK TO our hotel and quickly ducked into our rooms, changing as fast as we could into different outfits.

Part of the plan that Cap and Hudson had devised now called for us to disguise ourselves, so that people wouldn't recognize us as the celebrities we were. We were changing hotels and calling ourselves by different names, too, to make sure the police couldn't track us down now.

The Gallivanters and the Chinook Voyageurs were officially disappearing from society, without warning and without anyone in the world knowing.

Safely in my room, I pulled off Dessie's clothing and carefully placed the papers we'd stolen from the file on top of my bed. I unrolled them and scanned, reading quickly. I sucked in my breath as I read. The bartender had noticed a lot about the kidnappers, and had relayed it all here. On top of that, the police had their own notes.

This file was gold. It was absolutely worth the risk of stealing from the cops.

A knock sounded at my door.

"Andi, I need the file," Cap's voice said. I opened the door and handed it to him.

Chito stood next to him. "We leave in five minutes."

"I'll be ready," I promised, dashing to the bathroom. I turned the water on in my sink and waited until it was warm, then scrubbed my face free of the thick makeup Dessie had applied that morning. I didn't want to stand out anymore. We couldn't be noticed, now that we were going into hiding.

Between Cap and Hudson's meticulous planning, we were going to elaborate lengths to protect our identities. They'd decided that while we spoke to each other in public—something we'd try to avoid—we needed to use fake names. Cap wisely suggested that we use a close variation of our name in case we forgot at some point and accidentally called each other by our real names, alerting strangers to the familiar names they'd seen in the newspapers for months.

"That way, if your false name is close enough to your real one, you can stumble through it," Cap had explained to all of us the night before. "You know, cough and smile and grin, play it off."

"I'm going to go by Humphrey," Hudson announced, with a grin. "I did always wonder what a boring name would feel like."

"And I'm going by Carter," Cap said.

"Oh, I'll be Deanna!" Dessie exclaimed happily.

Chito elected for Chip, Claude opted for Clint, and Leonce shortened his name to Lee. Marceau hemmed and hawed, finally landing on Marv.

"I've always wondered what a short name sounded like," he laughed. "It's so much less of a mouthful."

Patrick chose the name Paul, while Willis became Winston.

"It sounds regal, doesn't it?" Willis said, twirling an invisible mustache. "I feel like I should start drinking tea with my pinky up with a name like Winston."

I decided to go with Alicia, but Bernard refused to choose a different name.

"I'm Bernard," he said flatly. "It's the name I was born with, and it's the name I'll die with. I'm not going to play around with some other fool's name."

"What if we call you Barrett?" Chito suggested. Bernard shook his head.

"Bergen?" Marceau suggested.

"What? No, I hate that name."

"It's my brother's name," Marceau said quietly, under his breath.

"What if you go by Berkeley?" Patrick offered. "Or Barry?"

"I'm Bernard," came the stubborn reply.

Cap jumped in. "Can't you at least go by something slightly different? Bertram? Bertie? Bernie?"

Bernard paused and studied Cap. "Can't I just go by Bernard?"

"No."

"Is that an order?"

Cap sighed. "Bernard, yes. I'm *ordering* you to choose a different name. Everyone else did. You're part of this team, too. You have to follow the same rules that everyone does."

"Fine," Bernard grumbled. "I'll go by Burt."

"Burt it is," Cap had announced. "Remember, we're only using these names if we have to address each other in public. So practice using them when we're alone, so it sounds natural."

I practiced running through everyone's new name as I washed my face, staring at myself as I tried my own alias out.

"Alicia," I said, the name sounding foreign and odd on my tongue. I looked in the mirror as I scrubbed off my lipstick.

"Hello, I'm Alicia," I repeated, over and over until it sounded more normal.

After washing my face, I pulled on a new skirt and blouse that Willis, Claude, and Marceau had picked out for me at a nearby store. While we'd gone to the police station, they'd gone shopping for new outfits for all of us, searching for clothing that would make us blend in seamlessly as residents of Tarragona.

I buttoned my blouse rapidly, dumping my boots into my travel bag alongside my Gallivanter uniform. I wouldn't need any of it for a while. On top, I put Dessie's folded shirt and skirt.

Glancing around the room one last time to see if I'd missed anything, I stopped short as I glimpsed myself in the mirror. I stepped forward and stared at my reflection.

I'd just stolen. From the police, of all people.

I hadn't hesitated, when it came down to the actual theft. My hands hadn't been shaking, I hadn't lost my nerve, and I hadn't frozen. I calmly executed every detail of our plan to perfection and improvised quickly, thinking on my feet alongside Dessie, when we'd nearly been caught red-handed.

*"Just who have you become?"* I thought, staring at my face in the mirror.

# CHAPTER 32

I HAD NO TIME TO REFLECT on my behavior. It was time to act.

Turning around, I grabbed my bag and left my room. Down in the lobby, Cap was already checking out with the clerk. He nodded toward the cars, still collecting receipts.

I ducked outside. Chito sat in my car, holding the keys. I strapped my bag into the back and slid in. "Ready?"

We'd talked about this part, too. Dessie and I would no longer drive the vehicles, as most women didn't drive automobiles. Instead, we'd let the boys do all the driving.

Bernard had painted over our Gallivanter logos, covering them with black paint this morning. They looked like every other Model T Ford on the road now.

The night before, Cap had put Patrick in charge of sorting through a vast stack of photographs from both of our teams, telling him to find images that didn't show specifics of where we were but were rather generic. Cap had already compiled a fake itinerary that took both teams around Europe, in separate directions, and he planned to divvy out photographs in the press every few days to keep our cover story going.

It would appear to the rest of the world that we were still engrossed with our expeditions. That we had parted ways, and were competing against each other once again.

Only we weren't splitting up and we weren't traveling around Europe. We were going after the kidnappers. Together.

With our new clothes and false identities, our generic cars, and the fake story of the journeys we were on, we were suddenly incognito.

For all intents and purposes, the Odysseus Society Around-The-World Expedition had ceased to exist...and no one knew it but the eleven of us.

Dessie climbed into the passenger seat of the Ford in front of us. She turned around and waggled her left hand at me, grinning.

"How does it feel?" she shouted to me, showing off her wedding ring.

I glanced down. The gold band on my ring finger gleamed in the bright sunlight.

"Pretty good," I smiled, holding up my own hand.

Hudson finished strapping boxes into the back and leaned over Dessie's passenger side. He gave her a hearty kiss on the cheek. "I sure adore you, my lovely little wife. Have I told you how utterly ravishing you look today, doll face?"

"Oh, I can get used to this," Dessie grinned, swatting Hudson on the arm.

"I'm just playing the part," Hudson winked.

The men who'd gone shopping had gotten four modest wedding rings. Dessie and Hudson were pretending to be a married couple, as were Cap and I. Hudson and Dessie had taken to the role with surprising enthusiasm.

"Those are two people who sure love the spotlight," I whispered to Cap, as we'd all met and worked through the plan.

Upon announcing that the four of us were going to pretend to be married, Hudson had stood up, thrown his arm around Dessie and tipped her back, pretending to go in for a long, romantic kiss. She'd giggled, her long curls streaming over his shoulder as he held her in a tight embrace.

We'd decided as a group that the best cover story we could come up with was that we were a group of old friends, reuniting for another pal's wedding here in Spain.

"Pretending to be in town for a wedding will allow the eleven of us to mingle together freely and keep odd hours," Cap had announced. "It'll give us a reason to be at the same hotel together, too."

As we prepared to leave this hotel and step into our new false identities, I felt a sudden rush of excitement.

We were embarking on a whole new adventure—this one, perhaps, the most dangerous we'd experienced yet.

Cap jumped into the back seat, a pile of receipts in his hand. He set his bag down on the seat next to him, and pulled out a city map.

"Chito, we're headed here," he said, leaning over the front and pointing to the outskirts of town, on the far side of Tarragona.

"Got it," Chito nodded, turning to look at all the other Fords. "Everyone ready?"

"Say goodbye to life as we've known it," Cap sighed as we pulled out, Chito taking the lead to drive us to our new hotel.

"We're ready for it," I replied. "You and Hudson have really outdone yourselves, planning all of this."

"I just hope it's enough," Cap muttered, watching as we drove through a winding street of colorful homes, potted lemon and lime trees sitting in front of small porches.

"It will be," I said, turning in my seat to look at him. "We're going to find him. I scanned the file we stole, before I gave it to you. You saw how much is in there. You were right. It was worth the risk."

"Yes," Cap admitted. "I'm relieved. I've been worried that maybe we took a huge gamble, stealing that from the police station, and it wouldn't pay off."

"From what I saw, I think it'll help us. We'll discuss it at the new hotel, right?"

"Yes," Cap closed his eyes and leaned back. His shoulders slumped as he exhaled tiredly. "You cannot imagine how I felt sending you into that station to steal the file."

I reached over the seat and with some difficulty, grabbed his hand and squeezed. He opened his eyes and stared at me.

"I'm in it with you until the bitter end, Cap. You know that. No matter what happens, I'm along for the ride."

"Let's hope the end isn't too bitter."

Chito grinned at me, taking his eyes off the road for a moment. "Look at you two, talking like an old married couple already," he joked. "We throw a ring on your fingers and suddenly you get mushy, huh?"

We drove the rest of the way to the hotel in silence. I imagined the two of them were worrying about the next part of the plan, just like I was.

As we traveled along, I watched people walk around with baskets, shopping for groceries and smiling at each other. A young girl walked arm-in-arm with a handsome man, chatting. A woman pushed a baby carriage and walked a small white dog next to her on a leash.

*"How ordinary their lives are,"* I thought. *"They have their routines, every day. They wake up and know what their day holds. Not us. We have no idea what to expect. Or what might happen to us."*

I glanced at Cap and Chito out of the corner of my eye, suddenly sobered by the situation we found ourselves in: we were hunting down criminals. *Criminals.*

And now *we* were criminals, too.

# CHAPTER 33

WE PULLED UP TO THE hotel, a smaller and shabbier establishment than we would normally stay in, given our celebrity status.

It was painted a cheerful yellow, but paint peeled off the window frames and the lettering of the hotel name, La Posada del Sol, was in need of a touch-up.

"Welcome to our new base of operation," Cap announced, as Chito eased us into an empty spot on the street in front of the building.

The other Fords had stopped and pulled off a block away, each car agreeing to stagger its arrival so we didn't all appear to arrive together. We were taking every possible precaution to disguise ourselves.

Chito and Cap and I grabbed our bags of clothing and walked inside. Cap held the door for me, then put his arm around my waist as we walked to the receptionist.

"Buenas tardes, señor," Cap said in a friendly tone. "We're checking in. We're town for a wedding, and a bunch of our dear friends are coming to stay here, too."

"Ah, si, you must be the party that called earlier. We have your rooms ready," the man replied, reaching for a pen. "Who are you?"

"The Gal—the Williams," Cap said, catching himself as he had started to respond reflexively.

"And how many rooms for you three?"

"Two rooms," Cap responded, pulling me tight against him. I could feel his tension. Though we'd traveled together for the last year, slept side-by-side outside under the stars, and had frequently shared close quarters on our expedition, we'd never had a hotel room to ourselves.

Cap and I had always been sticklers for decorum. We'd decided long ago not to let our love life make anyone on the team feel uncomfortable. But now, we'd have to set that to the side and pretend to be married already.

"Here you go," the clerk said, sliding us two skeleton keys and giving us our room numbers. Chito grabbed one and Cap took the other.

"Thank you," we said politely, turning to leave. Just then, Dessie and Hudson swept into the lobby.

Dessie squealed, and rushed toward me like we were best friends and we hadn't seen each other in years. "Alicia! Carter! Oh, sweetie, look at you two! My goodness! You look *fantastic!* Married life suits you!"

I hugged Dessie back and she held me at arm's length, studying me.

"Oh, gracious me, just *look* at you!" she exclaimed, touching my cheek. I resisted the urge to swat her hand away. "You're a sight for sore eyes, honey! Oh, goodness, baby, look at Alicia here! Doesn't she just look marvelous? It's been *too* long, sweetie."

"It has," I replied, wincing as Dessie threw herself at me again and hugged me enthusiastically.

Chito and Cap suppressed their grins as they shook hands with Hudson. "Good to see you again, Humphrey."

"How was your trip over?" I asked conversationally, watching as Hudson put his arm around Dessie.

"Oh, it was wonderful," Dessie gushed. "So many exciting things to see on the trip here. I don't know if we'll ever be able to go back home again, will we, honey?"

Hudson grinned and kissed the top of her head. "Maybe we'll just have to stay here, darling."

I bit my lip. We'd only driven across town.

"Shall we get our room?" Dessie asked, smiling at the clerk. "Oh, I'm so excited to be here! I just can't wait to see the others!"

"Our oldest friends, in town for the wedding," Chito explained to the clerk. "Such a wonderful occasion."

"Very nice," the clerk replied, opening his guestbook. "So is that a room for one, sir?"

"Yes," Hudson replied, pulling Dessie up to the reception desk with him. He winked at Cap. "Do you happen to have a honeymoon suite?"

"Oh, no, we don't have any suites here, I'm sorry," the clerk replied.

Dessie put her hand on Hudson's chest. "It's fine, honey. A bed's a bed, right?"

They laughed, looking at each other flirtatiously. Cap and I blushed, but Dessie and Hudson had no such shame. They were having the time of their lives, apparently, playing the part of two lovestruck newlyweds.

*"Boy, give them a part to play and they sure embrace it,"* I thought.

Cap cleared his throat. "Humphrey, you old devil, it seems like you're enjoying life?"

"Why, of course I am. Just look at this foxy wife of mine," Hudson said, pulling Dessie in for a kiss. She laughed and pushed him away.

"No kisses for you, Mister," she giggled. She tugged at his beard gently, turning to Cap. "Just look at this face of his. With this beard, it's like kissing a wild animal."

Before Hudson could make an unsavory remark about animal instincts, I stepped in.

"Let's get changed and go get a drink together," I said, linking arms with Dessie and dragging her toward my room.

Hudson chuckled and checked them in, while we walked away. Cap carried Dessie's bag upstairs with us, and set it down in the hall.

"Holy cats, Dessie," I whispered as Cap opened our door. "Don't you think you're taking this acting a little too far?"

"What? We're in love, Andi," Dessie said, her eyes wide. "He's my husband. How dare you say this is an act?"

Hudson arrived in our room a few moments later, and dropped his bag unceremoniously on the floor.

"Well, here we all are again," Hudson joked. "And aren't we the amorous ones of the crew, too, according to that little scene in the police station? Can we even be around each other without tearing our clothes off?"

"We all know we can put that lie behind us now," Cap frowned, as he unpacked his bag and put his clothes in the dresser.

"Listen, Cap, I've been meaning to talk to you," Hudson said, coming up behind him and removing his hat. He looked serious.

"What?"

"It's about Andi's baby," he said, looking at me with mock concern in his eyes.

"Cut it out," I shook my head.

"I just want you to know I'll be a good father to your baby," Hudson continued, now smirking at me. "And I'm willing to take my fair share of responsibility, of course. I won't let you down. But I *do* draw the line at changing dirty diapers. Cap, you can take that job."

"Hudson, it's not funny," Cap sighed, as Dessie and Hudson giggled together.

"It *is* pretty funny," Dessie laughed, flipping her hair over her shoulder. "Of all the people to have a scandalous love triangle with an illegitimate baby, you three—it just kills me."

"Please, drop it," I said, glaring at them. "Clearly, it's not humorous to anyone but you two."

"Fine," Dessie said, changing topics. She turned to Hudson. "Which side of the bed do you sleep on?"

"The middle," Hudson replied.

"You mean the right side," Dessie said. "I sleep on the left side of the bed, always."

"Well, I hope you'll be comfortable with me rolling over and squashing you in the middle of the night, then," Hudson wrinkled his nose.

"You don't snore, do you? If I find out you snore in your sleep, I'll divorce you," Dessie threatened.

"Oh, honey, do I ever snore," Hudson boasted. "It's alright, though. I have plenty of other redeeming qualities. Like not screaming in horror when I wake up next to you tomorrow morning."

"You're the worst husband I've ever had," Dessie laughed, slapping him on the arm.

"Well, I've never been so proud in my life. I must say, you're a terrible wife, as well."

"Thank you," Dessie curtsied.

Chito stared at them. "You two should never get married in real life, you know that? You're awful together."

"We must be doing it right then," Dessie said slyly, shooting a look at me. "We're just taking a cue from Andi and Cap, after all."

"What? We do not act like this," Cap replied hotly. "We may be engaged, but we're not the insufferable lovestruck fools that you two are pretending to be. Don't insult us. If you want to play at love, be my guest. But don't insinuate that Andi and I are anything like you two idiots."

"Lighten up," Dessie smirked as Hudson chuckled. "It's a joke. You're too tense, you know that?"

"Let's go to our own room, baby," Hudson remarked, picking up their bags. "I think these two need some time alone."

"Oh, good idea," Chito awkwardly stood up from the desk chair he was sitting in, following them out of the room and closing the door behind him.

"They're insane," I said, starting to unpack my own bag. "What's wrong with Hudson lately?"

"It's nerves. People handle stress in different ways," Cap replied, pulling his maps and travel guides out and putting them in the bottom drawer. "I know the worry about Paz is eating him alive. He feels a greater responsibility for what happened, because Paz was on his crew, under his care, when he was kidnapped."

"But it wasn't his fault."

"It doesn't matter. He still feels the weight of responsibility. It's a heavy burden on his shoulders, and it'll be there until we get Paz back."

"So he's been like this the whole time that Patrick and Marceau and I were gone?"

Cap sighed. "He's gotten worse lately. It's like being with a teenager sometimes, he's so irreverent. But I get it. I can overlook his behavior, as long as he continues to make good decisions. And so far, he is. So don't let his jokes get to you, Andi. It's his way of coping."

I pulled my clothes out of my bag. My Gallivanter uniform was at the very bottom. I lifted my new blouses and skirts out, staring at the unfamiliar and colorful fabrics. It was an odd thing to be out of the familiar uniform I'd been wearing for so long, and having to wear items that someone else had picked out for me.

The last few weeks had been unexpected. Who'd have ever thought we'd end up here, pretending to be different people, hiding from the police and from a gang of criminals? The thought of what was ahead filled me with dread.

I glanced at Cap, who had finished putting his belongings away and was sitting down at the small desk under the window. I had given him the police file, and he sat reading it, already scribbling notes in his journal.

*"Bless his meticulous little heart,"* I thought. The one constant in all of this was my team. They were reliable, through it all. Especially Cap.

"What side of the bed do you sleep on, anyway?" I asked, my question lingering in the silence of our room.

Cap looked up at me. Slowly, a smile spread on his face. "The middle."

"Me too."

"Well, this will be fun," he replied, grinning at me.

# CHAPTER 34

THE OTHER SEVEN CREW members arrived in small shifts over the next few hours. By sunset, we were all checked in and settled into our rooms.

Normally, we all had a block of rooms together, as was fitting for our celebrity status. Hotels would often put us in our own hallway, away from other guests, to afford us more privacy from the crowds that gathered around us.

Here at La Posada del Sol, though, we'd let the hotel place us all over the property. That way, if the police managed to track down one of our rooms, the others could hopefully still escape.

We'd agreed in advance to stage a reunion down in the lobby, for the benefit of our fellow hotel guests and staff.

Dessie clutched Hudson's hand as Cap and I made our way with them down to the lobby.

"Tone the romance down, you two," I warned, as Hudson pecked Dessie on the cheek. "It's not believable if you're working this hard to sell it."

"But it's my only chance to kiss her!" Hudson said, looking mischievously at Dessie. "Right? Or...maybe...do I have other chances in my future?"

Dessie smiled slyly and squeezed his hand. "Let's just enjoy each day as it comes, honey."

Hudson groaned. "You drive me wild, sweetheart."

Cap and I rolled our eyes at each other as they walked in front of us. I fervently hoped our teammates had never felt this way about us.

We met in the lobby, and a flurry of handshaking and hugs ensued. We pretended like we hadn't seen each other in years, enthusiastically catching up on each other's lives and looks.

"Look at that handsome beard!" I exclaimed, hugging Leonce like I hadn't seen him in ages. "It looks good on you!"

It was convenient that most of the men had grown out their facial hair over the last few weeks. Out of uniform and sporting beards and longer hair, they looked nothing like the clean-shaven men whose faces had graced the front page of the newspapers for months.

Even Bernard played along, begrudgingly shaking my hand.

"Hello, good to see you," he said flatly.

I tried to pull him into a hug. "It's been so long, Burt!"

He refused, ducking under my outstretched arms. "I don't care if we're acting or not, I'm not going to hug you," he scowled quietly.

I tried not to laugh. Some things never changed.

We broke into two mixed groups, a combination of Gallivanters and Chinook Voyageurs, to head to dinner in different locations.

"We don't know what the next few days will hold," Cap told us, his forehead wrinkled. "We've been tense for days, eating sporadically. We need to take care of ourselves now and stay healthy, for what we're going to be doing. Enjoy a good meal tonight. It might be the last one for quite some time."

He was right. None of us had eaten all day. I felt faint from hunger.

"Better go in small groups, too," Patrick piped up. "We'll attract far less attention."

"And in mixed groups, the Chinooks and Gallivanters split up," Hudson nodded. "In our plain outfits, with different combinations of individuals, we shouldn't even be recognized."

Patrick, Willis, Cap, and Bernard and I choose to go to a small seafood restaurant near the seaside. We were seated at a round table overlooking the golden beach, and I could smell the salty air as I inhaled. In the background of the quiet murmur of conversation from the tables around us, waves crashed against the shore.

"Isn't it nice to sit down in a restaurant and not have people staring at us because they recognize us from the newspapers?" Patrick asked, glancing around. "I feel positively anonymous."

"I love it," Bernard sighed. "I wish it was always like this."

"I can't believe we haven't been recognized by anyone," I replied. "Our faces have been on the front page of newspapers on and off for a year now. It's hard to believe people don't see who's sitting right in front of them, simply with us being out of our uniforms."

"It's affirmation that we've done a good job disguising ourselves, at least," Cap said, holding his menu.

A waiter arrived at our table, a small towel folded over his arm. "Buenas tardes, caballeros y señoritas. Tonight's special is the cassola de romesco and the seafood paella. Both are excellent."

"What's cassola de romesco?" I asked with interest. Chito would expect a full report about the cuisine we enjoyed here. He lived for trying different foods in every city.

"It's a local casserole, made with a rich nut sauce," the waiter replied. "I also highly recommend the arròs negre, if you're wanting to try something we specialize in."

"And what's that?"

"Rice cooked in squid ink."

"Oh. In that case, I think I'll try something else."

We ordered and chatted as we waited for the food to arrive. When it did, we sniffed deeply at the delicious aromas wafting up, passing around our dishes for everyone to try. For a brief moment, I forgot about the perilous situation we found ourselves in.

When I remembered, I suddenly felt guilty. How could I enjoy a meal while Paz was still in danger? My dinner was no longer appetizing as my stomach lurched. I swallowed a few bites, then pushed the food around on my plate. My thoughts wandered to the contents of the file. I'd tried hard to keep them out of my mind but I couldn't. It haunted me.

Patrick noticed my silence and lack of appetite.

"What's wrong?" he asked softly, from where he sat next to me.

"I read the police report," I replied quietly. Cap and Willis and Bernard were engaged in conversation about the best bait for local fish and wouldn't overhear us.

"And?"

I pushed my leftover food around in my plate. There was no sense to lie about it now. He'd find out tonight, anyway, at our team meeting. Glancing up, I met his eyes.

"It's bad," I replied. "The police matched them to other kidnappings, based on the description the bartender gave and the way the crimes were carried out."

"So they've done it before," Patrick whispered. "What happened?"

"Andi—sorry, Alicia—what do you think?" Willis interrupted, staring at us from across the table. His eyes danced as he and Cap looked at me.

"I'm sorry, what?"

"Fishing. Is it boring or relaxing?"

I glanced at Patrick. He exhaled slowly.

"Boring," I replied.

Cap laughed as Bernard and Willis groaned. "I told you she'd say boring," Cap grinned. "She's a girl who loves action. I knew she wouldn't want to sit still and wait for a fish."

"But it's so solitary," Bernard said, shaking his head. "It was my favorite thing to do, growing up."

"Your favorite thing, sure," Cap laughed. "But not hers. Come on, you know she lives for adventure."

I smiled automatically, but my smile didn't reach my eyes. Cap and Willis and Bernard continued their good-natured argument. I waited until they were suitably distracted, and turned my gaze back to Patrick.

"I don't know if we'll be able to find him," I continued, my voice low. "They're experienced professionals. The notes from the police say that they suspect they have ties to one of the big crime families in Rome, but they haven't been able to prove it yet."

"They're from Rome?" Patrick asked. "Then we were right. *You* were right. They were speaking Italian, after all."

"Why do you two look so serious?" Willis interrupted us again.

Cap studied me and I looked down quickly, avoiding his gaze. He set his napkin on the table. "Let's get going. We still have a meeting tonight. The others must be done with dinner by now."

As we stood to leave, I met Cap's eyes. Only the two of us—and Hudson and Patrick, now—knew how much worse it was going to get when the others heard what was in that file.

The team would need to be able to shoulder even more bad news.

What we were up against were men far more evil than we even imagined.

# CHAPTER 35

WE MADE OUR WAY BACK to our rundown hotel, walking near the ocean under a moonlit sky.

The waves gleamed, reflecting the faint glow of the starry sky overhead. Cap and Patrick walked on either side of me, quiet as Willis chatted mindlessly with Bernard about squirrel traps and beaver dams.

The five of us entered the little lobby, sitting down in the worn leather chairs and sagging sofa to wait for the others. Cigarette smoke filled the air, as the clerk behind the reception desk lazily puffed away.

I leaned into the chair, fiddling with the gold ring around my finger. I wasn't used to it yet. I wondered idly if I'd ever get used to wearing an engagement ring.

It seemed like a lifetime ago that Cap and I were discussing our future. And somehow, we'd come up with a plan to use our wedding planning as a scheme to hunt for Paz. We'd blown right by that plan, fumbling around in a different direction.

*"Looking ahead too far is tricky,"* I realized, exhaling slowly. *"Sometimes you can't plan ahead. You can only do the best you can, in the moment, and hope that it works out somehow."*

Soon, we heard laughter from the street outside. Dessie and Hudson strode through the lobby door, arm in arm, with Chito and Marceau chatting behind them. Leonce and Claude trailed up the rear, walking quietly.

"How was dinner?" Chito asked, plopping down in the empty seat next to me. "What'd you eat?"

I smiled. As I suspected, Chito wanted to interrogate me about food. "Paella. Remember? You're the one who first introduced me to it, last year."

"Oh, yes. So good," Chito groaned, patting his ample stomach. "I ate so much tonight. The food here is exquisite."

Cap was swiftly counting everyone.

"We're all here," he announced. "We'll meet in Chito and Bernard's room this evening. Please take a few moments to prepare yourself and take care of business. It's going to be a long meeting. Probably a late night for all of us."

He pulled out his pocket watch and consulted it. "Let's plan to meet there in ten minutes, everyone. Room four one seven."

Cap and I headed up to our room so he could change out of his tie and dinner jacket into something more casual. He waited until I closed the door, and then asked, "You told Patrick about the file, I assume?"

*"He never misses a beat,"* I thought. Cap was uncannily observant.

"I told him a little," I confessed. "He could tell I was upset. He asked why, and I told him I'd read the police report and the description matched other kidnappings. That they suspect they have ties to an organized crime ring, in Italy."

Cap nodded, unbuttoning his shirt as he stood on the other side of the room. "Did you tell him what happened in those other cases?"

"No," I said, biting my lip.

He sighed as he slipped his shirt off. I glimpsed his toned chest as he grabbed a different shirt, and turned away to sit down on the bed, suddenly bashful. I'd seen all the men on my crew shirtless plenty of times, but somehow it was different, now that we were alone in a hotel room together.

"How am I going to tell them?" Cap said after a moment, as he folded his dinner jacket.

"I don't know."

I looked up. Cap was nearly done buttoning his fresh shirt, a simple blue linen that matched the intense blue of his eyes. He met my gaze.

"We can't keep secrets," I replied. "The truth is better than a lie, however disheartening it may be."

Cap considered, putting his clothes away in the dresser drawers. "And maybe it's better to prepare everyone now, in case—"

"We'll find him," I cut him off. "We're smart. And we have a good lead now."

"Yes. But if we don't—"

"We will."

Cap threw his head back and sank down next to me on the bed. For a moment, he hung his head down in despair. Then, he lifted it and looked at me again.

"I can't let them sense my doubt," he said, meeting my gaze. "You're the only one I can be completely honest with. And I have to be honest with you now, Andi, having read that file from the police station—I'm riddled with doubts. I'm afraid they'll have too much fear when they hear it. They won't be able to face what's ahead of us."

"I know."

"I don't know how we can possibly outsmart them," Cap said quietly. "They're professional criminals. They've done this before and gotten away with it, many times. What's facing us—I don't know how we can even muddle through it without falling apart. I don't want it to destroy this team but I fear it will."

Cap pursed his lips and looked at the door. My heart swelled at the thought of the burden he'd been shouldering.

"You have me, at the end of all of this," I said, my voice concerned as I studied him. "No matter what you face, no matter how terrible your day may be, you'll always have me here for you, at the end of each day."

He smiled, but I could tell he was already distracted. No doubt he was running through his speech to the team in his mind.

"Ready?" he asked, standing up and grabbing his small satchel with the police report and his notes in it.

"Yes," I replied, walking to the door. We went up two flights to Chito and Bernard's room and knocked softly.

# CHAPTER 36

"COME ON IN," CHITO said. We ducked inside, Chito offering me the desk chair. I declined.

"Dessie can sit there," I said, sitting crosslegged on the floor, leaning against the wall.

Cap leaned against the wall next to me, standing. I knew he preferred to pace while he spoke to the group.

Dessie and Hudson knocked and entered. Chito gave her the chair, while Hudson sat down on top of the desk and propped his feet on the back of Dessie's chair.

"Don't get your dirty shoes on my hair," Dessie said, pulling her locks away from him.

"Gosh, wives are so demanding," Hudson joked, winking at Cap. "Nag, nag, nag."

The rest of the team slowly trickled in, finding their own space in the small room.

"Like I said, settle in for a long night," Cap said, diving in without his usual preamble of thanking everyone for coming and showing up on time.

Patrick nudged me. "He's getting straight to the point tonight. The news is that bad?"

I nodded silently.

Cap held up the papers from the file. "It took every person in this room, working together, to pull this off. Thank you, everyone."

He looked across the room, making eye contact with Leonce, then Dessie, then me.

"A special thank you to you three," he added. "Leonce, you brilliantly managed to find the right file. I don't know how you did it. And Dessie and Andi—you two are fearless. As the two that actually pulled off the heist, we owe you the biggest thanks."

We nodded, and Cap continued.

"As we suspected, the bartender in Switzerland had a ton of information he shared with the detectives that he refused to share with us. A lot of it is going to be very helpful as we continue to track down Paz."

He began pacing in the small room. "You're welcome to read the file yourselves, but for the sake of urgency, let me summarize."

He glanced at Dessie. "The bartender described four men who interacted primarily with Paz, and a bit with Dessie. Sound right, Dess?"

"I mean, they flirted with me a bit," she confessed. "I was sitting next to Paz at the bar. One of them tried to buy me a drink, but I just smiled and waved him off."

"Well, they grumbled among themselves about it, apparently," Cap replied. "The bartender told the detectives that they complained about you being a tease."

Dessie tossed her hair. "So what if I am? That's my right."

"Hey, that's my wife you're talking about!" Hudson exclaimed, a smirk on his face.

"Hudson," Patrick and Willis groaned at the exact same time.

He grinned and waved his hands. "Sorry, just trying to lighten the mood a little."

Cap ignored Hudson and pressed on. "The bartender had talked to the men before Paz and Dessie showed up, I guess, and they mentioned that they were traveling and were only in Zermatt for a short time. When he asked where they were from, conversationally, they told him they were from Italy. Then, lucky for us, one of them clarified that they were visiting from Rome."

"Rome?" Willis repeated. "What were they doing in Zermatt, then? That's pretty far away from home."

"We'll get to that," Cap grimaced, his shoulders tense. "Now, I want to be sensitive here. The bartender shared their descriptions with the Swiss detectives, and they recorded it all here. I realize you were attacked, and that things happened fast?"

He looked around at the Chinook team members.

"They were all a blur," Patrick said, from his seat on the floor next to me. "Dark hair and eyes. Mean-looking."

"Right," Cap nodded. "But one of you *did* get a closer look at them. And I hate to dredge this up again, and make you relive it. But we need to make sure the descriptions match."

I watched as Cap turned to Dessie. She was already slowly paling under her rosy makeup.

"Dessie?" Cap said gently. "I know they attacked you. I hate to bring this up. But when they shoved you around—you got the closest look at them of anyone. You were face-to-face with them."

Dessie's hand subconsciously went to her throat. I remembered that she'd told us, sobbing, how she'd head-butted them. They pushed her down and strangled her, for her impudence. Luckily, they hadn't done more than bruise her face, as their leader had stepped in and told them they needed to leave.

"Dess," Hudson said, putting his hands on her shoulders from behind. "You're safe now. We're all here."

Even Dessie's lips were white as she pursed them together and closed her eyes. "The tallest one had dark hair that was curly at the end," she recounted, her eyes shut. "He had a scar on his chin, like he'd split it a long time ago."

Cap scanned the file. "Yes. That matches."

"The other two, the ones with the guns, were shorter. They had dark hair, too, but not as curly. One of them had a big nose, but it was crooked, like maybe it'd been broken and wasn't reset."

"The bartender doesn't have specifics on them, he just mentioned dark-haired men," Cap read from his notes. He looked up. "Do you remember anything about the fourth man?"

"Yes," Dessie said, breathing hard through her nose. "He was savage. He was the one who clubbed Rollie and Willis in the back of the head."

"What can you tell us about him?"

"He had dark eyebrows. Really thick, like big caterpillars on his face. His hair was darker, almost black. It was longer than the others. He was shorter, and thicker—more muscular. His hands were huge, though."

"His hands?" Bernard frowned.

"He wrapped them around my throat," Dessie replied, opening her eyes and staring at him. "He was the one who hurt me. After he knocked me down, and dragged me back up, he put his hands around my throat and throttled me. I'd remember those hands again if I ever saw them. He had dirt under his fingernails. Freckles across the top of his hands."

"Sounds right, but there's something missing," Cap frowned. "He had—"

"A tattoo, I remember!" she filled in. "A tattoo of a horse shoe. On his forearm."

Cap looked up sharply. "Yes. Exactly."

Dessie held his gaze, an intensity on her face. The effort to remember was costing her, but still she pushed on.

"I had noticed his tattoo in the bar, actually, because I've never seen a tattoo so close up in real life before," she continued. "I think he mistook my staring at his tattoo as a sign of interest, that I wanted him to talk to me. But I could tell even then that he seemed dangerous. That's why I made my excuses and slipped away."

"Your instincts probably saved your life, Dessie," Cap said quietly. "Not just your instincts at the bar, but that instinct to fight back against him."

Dessie shook her head. "Paz stayed up there at the bar with them, though. He was drunk. He kept talking about how wealthy his family was, and how they had a whole collection of paintings and relics, and that they had servants and gold. If only he'd kept his mouth shut. If only—"

"The one with the tattoo," Cap interrupted, staring at her over the papers.

"Yes?"

"He's the only one the police identified, for certain. Because of the tattoo. Tattoos are pretty rare, we all know."

Willis got to his feet, crossing his arms. "What do we know about him?"

Cap read from his notes. "Enzo Gabriele Trimboli. He's thirty-eight years old. He's an ex-convict, has served a good amount of time in prison in his life. His criminal activities begin when he was a teenager, and ramp up from there. He first was picked up by police in Rome for petty theft when he was eleven years old."

"Eleven!" Chito exclaimed. "Why, that's nearly my niece's age!"

"He graduated to stealing horses within a year, but it looks like the horses were returned and the victims didn't press charges," Cap continued to scan. "For a while, there was no criminal activity recorded, but eventually he was picked up for disorderly conduct—I'm guessing he spent the night in jail. After that, he started breaking into homes and has a burglary charge. He was caught red-handed at age fourteen, by a butler, with the homeowner's watch and the wife's jewelry in his pockets."

"Bold little rat," Willis whistled.

"When he was seventeen, he again got picked up for burglary, but had a new charge this time: a misdemeanor, for killing the family dog."

"A dog?" Patrick reacted angrily. "How could he?"

"I told you he was evil!" Dessie declared. "What a horrible man."

"Just wait. It gets worse," Cap sighed. "In 1906, he served time. Weapon offenses, burglary, assault, obstructing the police...and an assault charge, after an incident in Milan. It looks like he was sentenced and served time for that."

"An incident?" Claude frowned.

Cap kept his eyes on the file. "With a woman."

The room fell silent. For several moments, we stared down at the ground. *"Dessie could have been—it could have been her, too,"* I thought. I glanced at Dessie to see her holding Hudson's hand, her face pale.

Finally, Cap cleared his throat and rattled the papers. "Trimboli went away to prison for a long time. Ten years, to be precise. He was twenty years old when he was sentenced, and when he finally got released, we were in the middle of the war."

Cap held up a large black and white mugshot.

"Here's what he looks like," he said, passing it around the room.

Trimboli's face was wide and could've been considered handsome, except for the crooked and flattened nose that looked like he'd been in more than a few fights. He had high cheekbones, dark eyes and dark, wavy hair. He scowled at the camera, a vivid scar running across his right cheekbone, up through his eyebrow to his hairline.

"How nice, he got out of war service, too," Patrick muttered. "He's a coward *and* a brute."

"There's a bit of a gap, then, at least in the police records," Cap said. "But there's a note from his prison records that he fell in with a gang while he served time, and they suspected he'd be working with them after he got released. They're seriously bad, this gang. A dirty history of drug trafficking, bootlegging, burglary, armed robbery, and homicide."

"Nice friends," Willis said in disgust.

"I have a list here of some known associates, according to what the police dug up," Cap said, leafing through the papers. "There are about a dozen names. So he could be working with any of the men on this list, or others entirely new."

He flipped a few papers, and held out a few more photographs. "Here are mugshots of a few of the known associates he's worked with in the past."

We examined the photos with interest as they were passed around the room. The men were varying ages, ranging from what looked like older teenagers to middle-aged men. One man, a curly-haired Italian with deeply tanned skin, caught my eye. While the others stared at the camera with angry expressions, his face looked surprised, like he didn't know why he was there.

"Here's where it gets pertinent, when it comes to our situation," Cap continued. "This gang also has a history of kidnapping—usually high-profile businessmen or mid-level government employees. People that have money, but won't cause an international scandal with their absence."

"You don't say?" Patrick leaned forward. "So what did they do? Kidnap and then demand a ransom?"

"Precisely. Some of the victims have been kidnapped from their homes or workplaces, but some have been assaulted in public, too. Either way, they're kidnapped and hidden away for a few weeks—I assume long enough for the police to start working other cases—and then the ransom demands start."

"I'd be willing to bet it was just dumb luck that they happened to be at the bar that night, and Paz was bragging about his family's wealth," Willis groaned. "They probably didn't even target us. They just happened to notice Dessie and then started listening to Paz brag about his family. From there, they realized who we were and what we had to offer, and made a plan to attack us and take Paz to collect a ransom."

Cap nodded. "That's what I think, too."

"So what happened, with the other kidnapped victims?" Dessie asked, her voice strained. She twirled her hair in her fingers nervously.

I watched Cap. His eyes flickered to me for a split second, then back to the paper. I knew what was coming.

We were getting to the worst part now.

"The gang's apparently kidnapped and extorted money from somewhere between five and seven different people," Cap said slowly.

"In every case, they held their victim for a few weeks, waiting for attention to die down over the kidnapping, and then they sent in a ransom request to the families. That's why it's hard to pinpoint whether it's been five or seven victims, because in at least five cases, they told the family not to go to the police and just pay. But in those five cases, every family *did* go to the police. That's why we have record of it."

"But when they received the ransom, what did they do?" Dessie said, jumping in before Cap had the chance to take a breath. "Were they okay, in the end?"

Cap paused. I stiffened my own shoulders and bit my lip.

"In all five cases where the families included the police, the outcome was the same," Cap finally replied, his words soft. "The gang murdered their kidnapped victim, after receiving the ransom."

# CHAPTER 37

"NO!" DESSIE CRIED OUT, her voice strangled.

Hudson reached forward and wrapped his arms around her. "I'm sorry, Dess," he said so quietly that I barely heard him.

She buried her face in her hands and cried into his shoulder as he stroked her back.

"They murdered them?" Chito repeated incredulously. "*All* of them? So it didn't matter what the families did?"

"I'm afraid so," Cap admitted, his shoulders hanging. "In the other two cases, they also found the bodies of victims who had been reported missing by friends or business partners. The police had no record of their families paying ransoms, however, because the families had elected not to involve them."

He glanced at Dessie, then added, "But we don't know that they'll do that to Paz. Criminals aren't always predictable. They don't always follow patterns. Even now, with you guys, they didn't follow a pattern—they just acted impulsively, to take advantage of a situation that presented itself. You were simply a good target at the right time."

Willis stood up and clutched for the papers from Cap. "Let me see this."

The room filled with the sound of Willis flipping parchment, his eyes darting back and forth across the pages.

He finished reading and swore violently.

"Seven people, murdered in cold blood," he said, throwing the papers down on the bed in anger. He swore again, his face beet red. "How can this be? Why the hell couldn't Paz just keep his mouth shut?"

Dessie had been sitting silently, Hudson's arms still wrapped around her. Suddenly, she bolted to her feet, knocking Hudson backwards.

"I need some air," she cried, rushing toward the door. She reached the handle and yanked it open, then stopped abruptly. The dim light from the hallway streamed into our room, illuminating Dessie as she stood with her back to us, her small body heaving with emotion.

Her head still bowed, something changed. As I watched, Dessie squared her shoulders, lifted her chin, and slowly turned.

"No, I don't need air," she said clearly, her voice trembling with suppressed rage. "What I need is for us to find these beasts and make them pay."

She slammed the door behind her and crossed the room toward Cap, stopping inches from his face.

She was a whole head shorter than Cap, but she was a force even as her petite body shook with anger. Her fists balled up, she spat her words with such ferocity that Marceau, who was sitting nearest to them, actually shrank back.

"I swear on all that is holy, we are going to find these men and hunt them down like the black-hearted, revolting dirtbags they are," Dessie said hotly. "I won't rest until we find them and make them pay. No—not pay. I want them to *suffer* for what they've done to all these families, including Paz and his parents. And to us. To *all* of us, because Paz is part of our family."

She turned and marched toward Hudson. She grabbed his hand and raised it in the air, showing the room. He winced, his fingers still clearly hurting him.

"They shattered this," she said, through gritted teeth. "Do you remember, Hudson? Do you remember that moment when he stomped on your fingers? That moment when you felt the bones crack? The pain it caused? It felt like your hand was on fire, you told me at the hospital. Can you remember that feeling?"

"Yes," Hudson replied, his voice hard.

Dessie dropped his hand swiftly and rushed across the room, pointing to Patrick's leg.

"They shot you," she exclaimed. "How did it feel, Patrick? To see someone aim a gun at you, and watch them pull the trigger? What was it like to see that? To hear the sound of a bullet leaving a gun and go through your *body*? You might have died. Did you think about that, as you lay there in the road, bleeding?"

Patrick sighed. "Of course I did."

She spun around angrily. "And Rollie! Poor Rollie, who's never said an unkind thing about anyone in the world," she exclaimed. "How did you all feel, watching him lay there in the hospital, his head swollen up like a melon? What went through your brains, listening to the doctor say he probably wouldn't make it? And then when he did pull through, to hear the doctor say he might never be able to talk and walk and be himself, ever again? God knows what will ever become of Rollie, at this point."

Marceau sucked in a breath like he'd been punched in the stomach. I looked at him, in sympathy.

"And Andi! What about you, Andi?" Dessie said, turning to me with glinting eyes. "Knowing what happened to me, will you ever feel safe again? Will the worry of being attacked ever leave your mind completely, or will it always be there, lurking, causing you to see shadows everywhere you go for the rest of your life?"

"No," I admitted.

She stepped up to Cap again. "And you? You'll never be able to lead your team without fearing this could happen to you, too. It's changed you. It's changed the way you'll lead."

"Yes, it has," Cap admitted, running his hand through his hair.

Dessie whirled around, challenging each person in the room, her hair streaming out behind her. I'd never seen her in such a fury. I didn't even know she was capable of such passion.

"They've marked all of us with their crimes," Dessie said, her face blazing. "This isn't just about Paz. It's about *all* of us. About the damage they've done to every one of us here. We're different people now than we were a few weeks ago. And we'll sure as hell never be the same as we were, before this."

She stepped in front of Cap as we watched her, transfixed.

"We can't go back and change time," she continued. "We can only move forward, and that means finding Paz. Whatever it takes."

Slowly, she laid her hand on her heart. Her chest heaved with anger.

"We channel all this," she said, thumping her heart, her eyes steely. "All these thoughts. The rage. The anger. This is what fuels us now. They will not win. They cannot win. We cannot let them win."

In that moment, I saw Dessie's unrelenting courage on full display. *This* was the girl who'd faced a gang of criminals, certain they were going to attack her, and had the audacity to fight back.

I spoke up. "She's right. We channel it. Whatever it takes."

Dessie nodded at me, an ally, her cheeks flushed.

"*Whatever* it takes," she repeated, staring around the room.

# CHAPTER 38

"BUT HOW?" PATRICK ASKED, throwing up his hands next to me. "So we have a name now, and a criminal record. What do we do with it? We can't go back to the police and ask for help."

"Isn't there some way we can track a name?" Willis said. "What if we bribed someone at a public records office? Or maybe a church has records—you know, a home address, a family member's name, something that might be useful?"

"But what use is that kind of information going to be to us?" I protested. "Even if we get a home address, he won't be there. He'll be on the road somewhere, headed here to Tarragona to collect the ransom cash."

"So we hunt for them here, in Tarragona," Hudson replied.

"But how?" Chito asked. "We have no idea where they'll go. I mean, to Paz's home, possibly. But maybe not. And they'll be on high alert, either way, when they go there."

"We don't know when they'll show up, either," Marceau added. "Maybe they're already here. Or maybe they're coming next week, or in two weeks. In all the other cases, they waited weeks before asking for the ransom. What are we going to do—camp out in the streets and watch for them?"

We fell silent, thinking about the possibilities. Finally, Chito spoke up. "So what's the plan, Cap?"

Cap hesitated. "I don't have one. Not yet."

"But you always have a plan!" Dessie said, echoing the surprise I felt. I'd figured he'd have an idea, too. His mind was always racing ahead of the rest of us.

Even Hudson reeled, but then recovered. "Well, that's what we're here to do. We'll figure one out together."

Silence reigned again as we screwed up our faces and thought. What could we do next, if we couldn't rely on the police or government?

"What if we manage to track down one of Trimboli's family members and lean on them?" Willis reasoned aloud. "You know, his mother. Or a sibling. Even a cousin or friend could give us some useful information."

"What do you mean, 'lean on them'?" Chito asked. "You don't mean torture, do you?"

"Why not? Look at the pain he's caused dozens of family members already," Willis retorted. "It'd be justice. And who cares? No doubt his family is low-level street scum, just like him."

"But maybe they're not," Chito shot back. "We can't start torturing innocent people. The ends don't justify the means."

"Why can't we?" Dessie said hotly. "I think Willis is right. The people who raised him to be such an evil human being deserve some of the blame, too."

"Yeah, I agree, too," Leonce spoke up. "Think how long Trimboli's been rotten. What'd you say, Cap? He was picked up for his first offense when he was eleven years old? He didn't learn that on his own. No doubt someone in his family was teaching him to pick pockets at a tender young age. They deserve to be dragged through the mud for raising such a criminal. Who cares if they get a little dirty, in the process?"

"But that's a huge assumption," Chito protested. "What if we're wrong, and the kid was just a scoundrel from the moment he was born? Or maybe something happened to him during his childhood that caused him to fall off the path and turn to crime? We don't know."

"Who cares?" Willis snorted. "It'll send a message to Mr. Trimboli, either way."

I saw Hudson and Cap exchanging glances. Cap's face was expressionless—he was a master at hiding his emotions—but Hudson's face was pained. Hudson shrugged, indicating he didn't know what to say.

Unexpectedly, Marceau stood up from the bed.

"Do you hear yourselves?" he said angrily, his neck flushed. "You're seriously considering hunting down Trimboli's family and torturing them, just to get information? We don't know if they'd have any information, or if it would even be useful for us!"

"Why not?" Willis said, shaking his head. "Look what they've done to us. You saw what they did to Paz. And to each of our faces. And Rollie? Come on, they deserve it."

"Who cares if they deserve it or not?" Marceau snapped. "It's not about them. It's about *us*."

"And we're out for revenge," Dessie replied evenly.

"But we're not like them!" Marceau insisted. "We're good people. We don't go around hurting innocent people. If we did—why, we'd be like them. Laying in wait to attack an innocent caravan of travelers. Is that who you want to be, Dess? Willis?"

"I'll be whatever I need to be, in order to bring Paz back," Dessie said, whipping onto her feet and glaring at Marceau. "Maybe the real issue is that you don't care enough about him to get your hands dirty?"

From the floor next to me, Patrick drawled, "Just think how pleased Trimboli and his gang would be to hear us all arguing like this?"

Cap positioned himself between Dessie and Marceau, who were still glaring at each other angrily.

"Enough," he said, holding out his hands. "Patrick's right. We can't let an argument tear this team apart now. We all need to be on the same page. This is what they want—for us to fall apart and stop thinking clearly. But we have to reason this out. Logic must prevail, not our anger."

Hudson spoke up, his long legs now propped on the window sill. "Instead of tracking down Trimboli's family, what if we can somehow capture him here, in Tarragona? It's not a very big town. And we're reasonably sure he'll be coming here, where Paz's family lives, to pick up the ransom."

"But how can we possibly track him down?" I spoke up, thinking. "We have no idea where he might go. He could stay with friends, check into a hotel, or stay out of the city completely and hide in the countryside."

"What if we hide out somewhere, and keep a constant lookout?" Willis suggested. "We could get binoculars to watch for him and all take different shifts. There are some high points in the city that might make good lookout posts."

"It's a good thought, but it'll look suspicious right away when people keep showing up to watch from the same spot, over and over," Cap replied, thinking hard. "Someone might get concerned and report us to the police, and we obviously have to keep our distance from them now. And then what happens if we do spot him, but he ducks into a building or under cover of trees? We'd have no way to follow him, being all the way up at a lookout spot."

"Maybe we just get a long-range rifle and put a bullet in his head, then," Willis said darkly.

"We need to take him alive in order to find Paz," Hudson interrupted, before Cap could respond. "What if Paz is hidden somewhere? What if there's a combination to a lock that we can't open, and Paz starves to death inside a room because you just killed the only person with the information we need?"

Willis swore under his breath, his face swarthy.

"You bring up a good point, though," Patrick replied. "Should we get some weapons? We've already been attacked once. We should be able to defend ourselves, if we ever find ourselves in the position to do so."

"The Gallivanter crew has two rifles," Cap replied. "We all carry a knife in our boots, even Andi. But yes, it wouldn't be a bad idea to stock up on some additional items."

"Even you could get a little handgun, Dessie," Chito joked. "We'll teach you how to shoot."

"You think I haven't shot a pistol before?" she scoffed, lifting her chin. "Please. It's one of the most common ways a man tries to show off to a girl."

She stood up and reached over Bernard, who was sitting on the edge of the bed near her, pretending to hold a gun in her hands.

"Here, little lady, let me show you how to use this big, powerful weapon," she crooned, resting her chin on Bernard's shoulder. "Let me lean in *real close* now, and put my arms around you and show you—"

"Jumpin' Jehosophat, get off me!" Bernard cried, ducking out under her arms. "What do you think you're doing?"

Dessie smirked and sat back down.

"Teach me to shoot," she muttered. "I'm a good shot already."

Bernard glared at her warily and stood up. He crossed over to the door and sat down on the floor, his back against it. *"He couldn't have possibly gotten farther away from Dessie unless he was in the hall,"* I thought wryly.

Cap absentmindedly ran his hand through his blonde hair. He stared up at the ceiling, lost in thought.

"What if we manage to track him while he's doing something here in town?" he asked, still staring at the ceiling above our heads.

"It's a possibility, but where?" Hudson replied. "We have no idea where he'll go."

"Right. But what if we could narrow down a place he *might* go?"

"Like what?" Hudson frowned. "There are a million restaurants and hotels and inns around here."

Cap rubbed his chin, thinking. "What about a market? They have to eat."

Chito spoke up. "I've already seen some of the markets, with Claude and Leonce. They've been to more of them, though."

"There are many markets in town," Claude jumped in. "Actually, almost every neighborhood has a different one. Some are tiny, just a stall or two, but others are quite large. They're scattered all over. On top of that, you have butchers and bakeries in storefronts. And of course, the docks for fresh fish and vegetables."

"In other words, it'd be hard to predict where Trimboli and his boys might go, to get food," Patrick cut in. "What about clothing? Or some other supply they might need?"

"I can't imagine that a gang of men on the run, holding a hostage, will stop and shop for clothing," Hudson said, shaking his head.

"What about medical supplies?" I suggested. "Could we stake out some place where they'd have to stop and replenish items?"

"That's hard to say," Claude replied. "When we restock before another leg of our trips, we usually go to a pharmacy or market. But they could go to just about any store, or even to a hospital or clinic to buy items, too."

I bit my lip, wracking my brain. Where else could we find Trimboli?

Patrick jiggled his leg next to me nervously, tapping his toes on the ground. The room fell quiet again. We were at a loss.

"We're *so* close," Chito said suddenly. "We have his name, for Pete's sake. His photograph. How can we not think of some way to find him?"

Cap shook his head mutely.

We sat silently, the tension in the air palpable. For several long, painful moments, no one spoke. It was agony, having such a critical piece of information but not having any idea what to do with it.

And we'd risked so much to get it, too.

# CHAPTER 39

OUT OF THE BLUE, BERNARD blurted, "Hold on!"

We all stared at him. He held his finger up, his face suddenly animated. The wrinkles in his thin face disappeared, and he looked like a happy little boy who'd just caught his first trophy fish.

"Marceau, where do we always go first when we get into a new town?" Bernard asked, his eyes bright.

Marceau was the Chinook Voyageur's mechanic. He and Bernard were frequently tinkering with the Fords on their own, just the two of them. Screwing up his face in concentration, Marceau stared back at Bernard through squinting eyes.

"Jeepers, I don't know," Marceau said. "Depends on the day. Sometimes we need to find a garage, to replace something. Or maybe to pick up more oil. Sometimes we have to track down a new tire, at a shop..."

"But where do we go *first*?" Bernard asked, barely containing his excitement.

Marceau sucked in his lower lip, thinking. Suddenly, he inhaled a sharp breath as it dawned on him. "Bernard, you genius!"

"What?" Hudson said, leaning forward as we stared at the two of them.

"Gasoline!" Marceau exclaimed, as Bernard nodded excitedly.

"Gas stations!" I cried, immediately understanding where they were going with this. "They're right! There aren't ever very many gas stations in town, and they're usually on the outskirts of downtown, everywhere we go. We could easily stake out all the gas stations here in Tarragona and watch for Trimboli and his men!"

"Bernard, that's brilliant," Cap blurted. "By gosh, it could *work.*"

Bernard counted aloud on his fingers. "I'm pretty sure there are only three or four gas stations in town. We stopped at one on the northeast side of town, when we first arrived several days ago. There are two others I noticed on the south side, as we drove around picking up supplies those first days."

"We can do some reconnaissance work and see where they all are," Hudson jumped in. "We can position ourselves at all the stations, to watch and see who comes through."

"But how?" Willis asked, looking around. "We're all international celebrities. People recognize us wherever we go, asking us for autographs and shaking our hands. Trimboli and the other three men attacked us already and got a good look at our faces as they beat the living daylights out of half of us. They'd recognize us in a heartbeat."

"He's right," Hudson sighed, deflated. "Curse the newspapers for making us famous. It's brought us no end of trouble lately."

"Hold on, though—they don't know us," Chito said slowly. "I mean, the world knows the Gallivanter crew. But the kidnappers haven't interacted with us."

"How would that possibly work?" Marceau frowned. "You're probably more famous than us, to be honest. Andi is, for sure. Everyone recognizes her."

"You're too tall," Dessie remarked unhelpfully.

"Yeah, I know," I rolled my eyes.

"So we wear disguises," Chito suggested. "With beards and ragged clothes, a bottle of rum in our hands, no one would look twice at us. We can pretend to be homeless bums, sleeping on the sidewalks and in the corner of the stations."

"Hiding in plain sight," Cap said, drumming his fingers against the file. "What would we do when we spot Trimboli, though? We can't run inside a hotel or bank and make a phone call to the others. No decent establishment would let a homeless bum inside. We'd lose them again."

"What if we get bicycles?" Patrick offered. "When you spot Trimboli, you can stagger off and get on your bicycle, and follow him to see where they're going. Tarragona is small enough, with all these tiny, winding medieval streets, that you can't speed around too quickly in your automobile anyway. You could easily keep up with them."

"That could work," Cap mused. "We'll need raggedy clothes. Bicycles. Rum, maybe a couple of old newspapers and hats, if we need to hide our faces."

"You need hair dye," Dessie said, staring at Cap. "You're so blonde. You don't look like you're a Spaniard, and you need to look Spanish in order to be a bum here. Your blue eyes are bad enough, but the hair is a beacon that you're American."

"It's easy enough to dye it black," Cap said. "And if I wear a hat and keep my face down, no one will notice my eyes."

"So that's three homeless bums," Hudson counted. "We'll have to look, but you think there may be a fourth gasoline station?"

"I'd guess so," Bernard replied. "Tarragona is very old, so it won't be in the middle of town. Usually, these older cities only have room for new construction in the outskirts, and there's usually a station on every side of town—north, south, east, and west."

"Right. Tarragona actually has a fascinating Roman history, of all things—" Cap started to say, slipping into lecture mode. I shushed him.

"So we need at least one more person to stake out the fourth station," Hudson said, frowning. "We don't have enough people to cover it."

Willis raised his hand.

"I'll do it, too," he said. "They didn't get much of a look at my face, right? You told me they whacked me in the back of the head. So they don't know what I look like. I can still fool them."

Hudson raised his eyebrows. "I appreciate the offer, Willis, but they could've killed you. You were in the hospital from what they did to you. I mean, look at Rollie. Are you sure you're comfortable with this?"

"All I remember is standing over that engine, then everything going black and waking up in a hospital bed," Willis declared. "I'd rather be in the middle of the action, anyway, and not stuck waiting somewhere for Cap and the others to report back. No offense, Cap."

"None taken," Cap replied. "I understand. And we'd welcome your help, Willis."

"Are we going to sleep on the streets then?" Chito asked, rubbing his beard thoughtfully. "And how will we get food? And how will we, um, use the facilities?"

"Couldn't you still sneak back into the hotel rooms here, late at night, and sneak out before sunrise?" I asked. "We could let you in through a window. Post a lookout guard, on different shifts, so we can sneak you in without anyone noticing."

"Right. What if we pretend to be smoking cigarettes?" Dessie asked. "That way, one or even two or three of us could be standing around, at odd hours, with a valid reason to be standing outside socializing, or even walking around the building and chatting."

"That's a good idea," I replied. "That way, it can be any combination of us, too."

Hudson clasped his hands together, but his body betrayed his inner excitement.

"The more I think about this, the better it gets," he exclaimed, appearing for all the world like a troublesome kid planning to prank his teacher.

"We can drop food off for you, too," Patrick suggested. "We can leave it at a predetermined spot or take turns giving it to you in person, like we're strangers giving you a handout."

We continued talking late into the night, making lists of supplies we needed to pick up and locations we needed to scout first thing in the morning. By the time we finished talking, it was the middle of the night.

Cap and I returned to our hotel room, tiredly changing into our pajamas with our backs to each other. As I slipped my skirt off and slid into pajamas, I thought how scandalous it would be if my mother or sister found out I was sharing a bed with Cap before we were married. Feeling a twinge of guilt, I crawled into bed.

The bed bowed as Cap sat down on it and groaned. "The first time I get to share an actual mattress with you, you beautiful creature, and I'm so exhausted that I can barely keep my eyes open," he said, laying his head on his pillow and looking at me.

I smiled. "We have a lifetime of this. What's one night? Besides, my mother would murder me if she ever found out I was sharing a hotel room with you."

He nodded, his eyes already fluttering.

"Don't want her to murder you," he said softly. "Or me, either."

I watched him pull the blankets up around his neck, and heard his breathing start to deepen and slow.

"Cap, this is going to work, right?" I whispered, pulling the blankets up on myself and rolling over toward him.

He was already asleep.

# CHAPTER 40

I WOKE UP ABRUPTLY, conscious that someone else was in the room.

Opening my eyes and squinting in the morning sun peeking through the cracks in the curtains, I remembered that Cap was in bed with me.

I breathed a sigh of relief and turned over to look at him. He usually woke up early, out of a never-ending sense of duty to be the first one up, making plans or stoking the fire or starting the coffee. I could only remember a few times where he'd slept in later than me.

In the dim light of the room, I stared at Cap's face. It was strange to see him asleep, at peace. His eyelashes were long. Above his forehead, he was starting to get wrinkles where he frowned every time he concentrated. Along his jaw, small blonde stubble was starting to grow in from lack of regular shaving.

Cap snored softly and twitched. I smiled into my pillow. I already knew he snored at night, from sleeping under the open stars and sharing paper-thin hotel walls with my team.

A few minutes later, Cap stirred again. I watched him open his eyes, squinting slowly, and he turned his head to look at me.

"Why are you staring at me like that?" he whispered, rubbing the sleep from his eyes.

"I was just watching you sleep."

"That's creepy," he whispered back. "You're not one of those unhinged women who's secretly been plotting my murder all this time, are you?"

A laugh bubbled to my lips. "Don't you think you'd know already if I was crazy?"

He grinned. "Maybe you've been hiding it all this time. Until this exact moment. And now that everything is perfectly aligned, just according to your wicked plan, you're going to strike me dead!"

He rolled over and pinned me down with his arm, his chest resting on mine.

"Cap, get off!" I laughed, trying to push him up.

"No," he said sternly. "Not until I check to see if you have a knife hidden under those blankets, young lady. I'm not about to get murdered in my own bed."

"Stop it!" I squealed, as he pulled the covers off me. A blast of cold air sent a shiver down my spine and brought goosebumps to my bare arms. "Give me that blanket back! It's freezing in here!"

He smirked, replacing the blankets and draping his arm over me. Slowly, he leaned his face in, close to mine. I closed my eyes, anticipating his kiss.

When it didn't come, I snapped my eyes back open, confused. Cap grinned at me, his face inches from mine. "Did I snore last night?"

I grinned back. "Like you do every night."

"Still want to marry me? Or have you decided you've had enough?"

"I think I'll keep you. But rip those blankets off me one more time and I might just change my mind."

Cap laughed, and leaned down to kiss me tenderly. For a few moments, we lay together, enveloped in a warm cocoon of love and security.

"It feels like we're living two different lives right now, doesn't it?" I said quietly, feeling Cap's chest rise and fall as he held me in his arms, his cheek next to mine on the pillow.

"How so?"

"By day, we're ruthless, cunning vigilantes, hunting down murderers. By night, we're—this. Soft-hearted romantics."

"I would never call you soft-hearted, Andi," Cap smiled. "I'm not sure ice doesn't flow through those veins sometimes."

"Well, that's the pot calling the kettle black."

"I do wonder one thing, though," Cap said, his drowsy breath tickling my ear.

"What?"

"Will you still lay here with me like this when I've become a dirty, smelly homeless drunk panhandling in the streets of Tarragona?"

"You're not going to be allowed into this bed if you're dirty and smelly when you get in it."

"And you just called yourself a romantic," he teased. "You sure know the way to my heart."

"Through humor?"

"Through honesty," he said, smiling. "Of all the qualities I respect in a person, being truthful is the most important to me."

I struggled to keep a smile on my face, lest he see the guilt that immediately swept over me like a tidal wave. If Cap found out what I was concealing from him, he'd no longer call me honest. He'd be furious.

*"He can't find out,"* I told myself. *"He won't find out. I'll tell him when the time is right. And the timing is all wrong, right now. He has too much on his plate already. He doesn't need to be distracted by this, too."*

"We better get up and get going," Cap said, cutting through my silent worry.

Relieved, I jumped to agree. "Right. We have a lot to do this morning."

I watched him stand up and stretch, and start digging through his bag for fresh clothes. Staring at his back, I bit my lip.

How had this unraveled so quickly? I'd only tried to come up with the best solution for all of us. I couldn't possibly tell him the truth—not now. Not with all the stress we were dealing with here. Not when Cap was clearly exhausted, at his breaking point already.

He couldn't ever find out I was lying about this. Even though it had been the right choice, I wasn't sure he would ever trust me in the same way again.

I resolved to sneak away and find an opportunity to dash a telegram off today, just in case.

# CHAPTER 41

EACH OF US HAD A TASK this morning, and we dashed in and out of the hotel without comment to each other, carrying out our roles.

Bernard and Marceau had gone out at first light to track down all the gasoline stations in town and were already back, working on their notes.

"We were right, there are four stations around town," Marceau showed us, pointing to their locations on a hand-drawn map. "I think it makes sense for Cap to stay at this one, as it's at the base of a steep hill. No offense to anyone else, but I think he's probably the most athletic one out of the four of you—he could tackle that hill on a bicycle, if he had to follow Trimboli's car up it."

"I always knew being muscular had drawbacks," Bernard quipped. "I'm content being a twig."

Chito patted his stomach. "Are any of them at the top of a hill, by any chance?"

"No," Marceau laughed. "But I suggest you and Willis take these two. And Bernard takes the one up here," he said, pointing to his map.

"We'll drive the routes together, the four of us, and explore the area around each gas station," Cap said, jingling the Ford keys in his hand. "We'll see you later, everyone."

Hudson and Patrick were out looking for small weapons that each of the men could easily conceal within their homeless costumes.

"Just what I love most," Hudson had said, rubbing his hands together. "Shopping for bean-shooters."

"Knives are best," Cap had told them. "We don't want to draw attention with gunshots."

"I don't mind gunshots," Bernard had grumbled as they left. "I also don't think I'd mind shooting people."

Leonce and Claude were picking up cigarettes for the team, along with bottles of rum and food for our "Hobo Quartet," as Hudson had started calling them. We'd also taken photographs of the black and white mug shots of Trimboli and his suspected associates with the Gallivanter camera, and they were going to get the film developed so that our four watchers could each have a set of identifying photos on hand, if they needed to check faces.

Dessie and I had been tasked with finding clothes for the four men who were pretending to be homeless. We walked rather than drove to the stores and markets in order to avoid attention.

"We'll tell them that we're teachers, looking for costumes for a school play!" Dessie exclaimed as we headed toward a small shop at the end of the street. Shawls and jackets were draped on a display out front, moving slowly in the breeze.

"You don't look at all like a teacher," I said, staring at her. Even in her simple clothes, she was stunning. She looked more like a movie star than someone who dedicated her life to children.

She frowned, looking down at herself. "You're right. In this frumpy dress? We'll say we're from a church instead."

I rolled my eyes and pushed into the shop with her. We explained to the shopkeeper that we needed costumes for our play, and asked if she had any old, ragged items that she'd mind selling to us. She emerged from the back room with several patched shirts and pants.

"These are perfect!" I replied, looking at the bundle. We paid her, and she smiled her thanks.

"Where can we find hair dye?" I asked, carrying the bag. Dessie twirled her hair around her finger with her gloved hand, smirking as two boys walked by and winked at her.

"I'd try a barber first," she replied, looking back over her shoulder. I frowned.

"Well, I hope you're prepared to walk," I said, picking up the pace. She couldn't keep up with my long strides and immediately started pouting.

"Slow down," she panted, scurrying behind me. "Why are you always rushing?"

"Dessie, we have to get back as soon as possible."

"Is this about me smiling those boys? Andi, *slow down.*"

I slowed, but kept us hurrying at a fast clip. "Why do you feel the urge to flirt with every man you see? It's aggravating. Especially when we're in a hurry, like now."

"I don't always mean to. It's just habit. And it causes no harm to anyone. It's just a little fun, what's the big deal?"

I pursed my lips and watched her out of the corner of my eye. "But what about Paz?"

As I expected, my words hit her with a blow. She stiffened and started fiddling with her gloves. After a moment, she replied, "What about him?"

We passed by a small bakery, the aroma of sweet bread filling the air. I glanced in the windows, and saw an old man wearing an apron busy behind the counter, stacking loaves.

"Would you still flirt with all the other boys if Paz was with us?"

Dessie looked at me suspiciously. "What are you trying to say?"

"Nothing. I'm just trying to figure out what you and Paz are," I replied evenly, my tone matter-of-fact. "You get heated every time his name is brought up. I know you two were close—at least, as close as I've seen you get with any man. And he'd nearly outdone himself trying to impress you, even though you dismissed him time and time again. That's what he was doing in the bar in front of Trimboli and the other men, right? He was trying to get your attention? Impress you?"

As I watched my words land, I realized I'd gone too far. I was a bonafide expert at putting my foot in my mouth. Dessie was pale, and stared ahead at the sidewalk without looking at me.

"Look, I'm sorry," I winced, embarrassed at my insensitive questions. "It's just that I hate not knowing what's going on. And we're the only girls on the team. I don't know. It's hard to talk about all this stuff with guys sometimes, and I know we aren't close but—but maybe we could be."

Dessie stared ahead, breathing hard, continuing to keep up with me. I slowed my pace, watching her. Was she about to cry?

"Hey," I said, putting my hand on her shoulder and stopping. A cat yawned at our feet, peeking out from underneath a cart of lemons sitting in front of a shop. "Dessie, I went too far. I'm sorry."

She glared at me, blinking away a sheen of tears in her eyes. "You don't have friends, do you, Andi?"

"No, not really," I replied honestly. "Just my teammates."

"Yeah, I can tell," she tossed back.

"Do you?"

She paused and stared at me. She started to speak, but then bit back her words.

"No," she admitted, after a moment. We stood in the middle of the sidewalk, looking at each other.

"Are you in love with Paz?" I prodded, my voice low. Dessie sighed.

"I might be," she said, her shoulders slumping. "I don't know. It's possible."

She paused again, tilting her head back and looking at the sky in exasperation. "Fine, yes. Yes, I think I am."

I smiled. She glared at me. "What? Don't look at me like that!"

I shook my head, but my smile grew. I *knew* she had feelings for him. I'd thought it for weeks now. And I already knew he had feelings for her.

"Sorry," I replied, feeling giddy as I grinned. "But really, that's good. Isn't it?"

"Stop!" Dessie commanded. "This is why I didn't want to tell you!"

"Sorry," I said, trying to hide my smile but failing.

Dessie groaned and glared at me. "I swear to all that's holy, Andi, if you tell this to anyone else on our teams—I swear I'll make you pay."

"Mum's the word," I said, pretending to button my mouth. "I'm happy for you. That's the last thing I'm going to say."

"Thank God," she said, walking briskly away from me. I smiled and hurried to catch up with her.

We passed through a courtyard, the buildings green with hanging vines around us. Women pushed their strollers, small children running around, as men swept the sidewalks in front of their stores and stopped to chat. As we walked, I considered if I should tell Dessie that Paz had fallen for her, too.

She solved it for me, running her hands through the vines creeping up a tall building as we passed it.

"So what's Paz said about me?" Dessie said, glancing at me. "Don't play dumb and tell me you've never talked about me. I know he confided in you."

"I don't want to get in the middle of you two," I teased. "I think we outgrew this behavior in elementary school, didn't we?"

Dessie pulled up short and stooped over. Swiftly, she pulled out a short knife and pointed it at me.

"Hey!" I said, taking a step back. "That's not funny."

"I'm just informing you, in a calm manner, that I do have a knife hidden away in my boots now. Like you do," she said, still holding it.

"Put it away," I said quickly, stepping in to shield her. "We're not supposed to draw attention to ourselves, remember?"

She tucked it into her boot and smoothed her skirt. "Why can't you just tell me what he said about me? Or do you just prefer to constantly rile me up and upset me for no good reason?"

"Fine. He likes you, okay?"

Dessie's face lit up. "He does?"

"Yes. He's liked you for a long time."

"Of course he has!" Dessie exclaimed happily. "I thought so. I just—I knew it. But he told you? Really?"

"My goodness. This *is* elementary school, all over again," I complained, while my eyes crinkled in a smile. Dessie deserved this moment of happiness after the emotional torment of the last few weeks.

Dessie smiled, frozen in place. In that moment, I felt a genuine fondness for her. Despite the teasing and sarcasm, perhaps we could actually be friends.

We started walking again. Dessie's face was aglow with excitement, her cheeks flushed. A maintenance man washing windows at a bank put down his rag and whistled at her, but she didn't even glance his way. As we walked, though, Dessie's joy ebbed away. By the time we'd reached the end of the block, her shoulders drooped again.

"What is it?" I asked. I'd been watching her closely, out of the corner of my eye, and she looked like she might be getting ill. She shook her head, closing her eyes briefly.

"Dessie?" I asked again.

"I don't know, Andi. I just don't know."

"Don't know what?"

"About him! About us!" she exclaimed, the color rising in her neck. "I don't know if there will ever be an *us*, with Paz."

"Don't go there. There will be. I know it."

"No, you don't," Dessie retorted. "You weren't there, Andi. You didn't see how vicious they were, when Trimboli and his crew attacked us. Damn it, you didn't see the look in Paz's eyes when he told me to get down, when he tried to hide me from them. He was so brave. And what did he get for it?"

Her voice broke as she shook her head, reliving the horror. "They beat him within an inch of his life. He wasn't even able to stand on his own two feet when they dragged him into their car, he was hurt so badly. Do you know what it was like for me to hear them beat him senseless like that? Knowing the man I love was at the mercy of pure evil?"

Dessie strode away from me angrily.

With her back to me, she added, "That's why I attacked them. I mean, it was to save myself—but it was also because I was just so angry about what they'd done to Paz. I would've killed them with my bare hands in that moment if I could have."

"I understand. I'd feel the same, if it was Cap."

"And I can't help but feel that somehow, this is all my fault," she continued, turning to face me. "I flirted with him, but with everyone else, too. I didn't want Paz to know how I felt about him. Not really. So I intentionally drove him wild. And you're right—he was showing off at that bar in Innsbruck because of me. Because I was playing hard-to-get."

Instead of the tears I expected, Dessie was only growing angrier.

"What if I'd just been honest and told him how I felt about him, Andi? He never would've sat there, getting drunk, bragging about his wealth to total strangers if he knew that I loved him. And we never would've been attacked like we were. Paz would be safe and sound, Rollie wouldn't have massive brain damage, Patrick wouldn't be limping around..."

"Dessie, it's not your fault," I protested, reaching for her arm. She brushed me off, furious.

"Why does the world tell us women that we need to play these stupid games with boys?" she cried. "Why can't we just speak our minds and be direct? Why do we have to be coquettish and drop hints and waste time? Why is it somehow womanly to hide our passions and opinions, instead of just being honest about who we are and what we want in life?"

Blindly, I reached for her hand. She frowned and yanked it away.

"Don't coddle me," she exclaimed. "You're the only equal I have here. You're the only one who might possibly understand how strong I have to be. Even if I don't want to be, and even if I don't feel like it, I *have* to be."

I nodded. "I know."

She stared at me, and we shared a moment of silent solidarity. After a beat, she frowned.

"We need to keep moving," she said. "We're looking for dye. Let's look around. I'm not sure a barber will have anything, but we can try a pharmacy, too. We're not done yet."

# CHAPTER 42

WE MANAGED TO FIND hair dye and some old hats and scarves after visiting nearly a dozen different stores. Our excursion took a few hours, and we walked back to the hotel with our arms full of bags and sore feet.

"You two were gone forever!" Patrick exclaimed, rushing to lift the bags from our arms as we entered the lobby. "I was worried. I was thinking about getting a Ford out to go look for you downtown."

"It was hard to find everything," Dessie said. "We walked all over this blasted town. My feet are about ready to fall off."

"Did you ladies at least have a nice time together?" Chito asked, taking the last bag from my arms.

Dessie looked at me. "No," she smiled cheekily.

We traipsed to Chito's room, which we had decided would be the staging area for dressing the boys. It was on the ground level of the hotel, facing the alley, and they could climb in and out of the window when it came time for their shifts. Cap and Bernard entered behind us, and Willis arrived a few minutes later. Dessie and I started laying out the clothes we had purchased.

"Ah, the Hobo Quartet is already here," Hudson said, stepping in a few minutes later with a briefcase. "Excellent."

"If we ever form a jazz quartet, that'd be a great name," Willis joked.

"What'd you get?" Cap said, eyeing the briefcase Hudson carefully laid on the foot of the bed. Hudson smiled and snapped open the case.

"Oh," Cap and Chito exclaimed at the same moment, staring inside.

I craned my neck to look. Inside, six pistols were lined up neatly in rows, cushioned against velvet fabric.

"What are they?" Cap said, reaching for one. He held it in his hand, weighing it against his palm. The dark metal gleamed ominously.

"These beauties are brand new Browning 1922s," Hudson replied, picking one up. "Semi-automatics. Ever shoot a Browning 1910? These are much the same, but a little different. It has the same sights and the ribbed slide sides, but the barrel's a bit longer. Most importantly, the magazine capacity is larger—this baby can fire eight rounds."

Chito reached in and picked one up. "It's heavy."

"The safety is here, in the rear," Hudson said, showing him. "It should be even more accurate than any other pistol you've ever shot, with that long barrel."

"Where'd you get these?" Willis asked, holding one up and checking the empty chamber. "I imagine it's a bit harder to get this many handguns over here in Europe. You can't just order them out of a magazine like you can in America."

"Don't ask," Patrick replied, as Hudson grimaced. "I thought we were going to get shot in the process. Let's just say it's a good thing Hudson has a smooth tongue. This man can talk his way out of anything."

"Wait, are these hot?" Cap asked, staring at Hudson.

He shrugged. "I didn't ask. I don't want to know. But judging by the seedy little gremlin who sold them to us, probably."

"Hot?" I asked, confused. "What does that mean?"

"Stolen," Dessie filled in. "Probably used in a crime, so if the police catch us with them, we'll look like we committed the crime."

Chito groaned. "Dessie, how do you know such things? Young ladies shouldn't. I don't think I like the type of men you hang out with."

Cap furrowed his brow, reaching for the bullets that Hudson was pouring onto the bed. He loaded eight rounds into his Browning, then slid the magazine into place with a click. He checked the safety, then tucked the pistol into the small of his back and pulled on a jacket. "We'll have to make sure we don't get caught with these."

"Wait, we still need to dye your hair," I said, staring at Cap's bright blonde locks. "We have hats, but your hair's still too light. If the hat slips off your head somehow and your hair peeks through, you're going to look out of place."

"Fine," Cap said, pulling off the jacket and grabbing the desk chair.

I opened the box and frowned as I read the instructions. "This looks complicated."

Dessie snatched it out of my hands. "Haven't you ever dyed your hair before?" she said, popping out a bottle and a pair of gloves.

"Not really," I said. "But I guess I'll figure it out now—"

"I'll do it," Dessie interrupted, winking at Cap. "I've always wanted to run my hands through that head of hair."

She rolled up her sleeves quickly, pulling on the gloves. "Though, to be honest, this isn't *quite* the way I imagined it might go."

"Dess," Hudson laughed as Cap coughed, his ears turning pink with embarrassment. I rolled my eyes. If I hadn't heard Dessie tell me that she loved Paz, I'd be upset. But now I knew that her flirting was merely an amusement, and didn't mean anything.

"You need to take that shirt off," Dessie commanded, standing in front of Cap with the bottle of dye in her hands. "If I spill, it'll stain your shirt."

"You just want my shirt off," Cap grumbled, unbuttoning his shirt and tossing it to me. He sat still, in his white undershirt, while Dessie started rubbing the solution into his hair.

"It smells terrible," Willis complained, pinching his nose. "Women actually use this stuff?"

"Yes," I replied, watching as Dessie massaged Cap's head, working the dye into his roots and down along each shaft of hair. "The price of beauty is steep, when you're a girl."

"It burns," Cap complained, shifting in his seat. "It's itchy and hot and painful, all at the same time."

Dessie elbowed him in the neck, her hands dark with dye.

"Stop moving, you big baby," she ordered. "Gosh, you wimps would never make it in this world as a woman. This is the easy part. Try wearing a corset or high heels, or plucking your eyebrows. That's *real* pain."

"Plucking your eyebrows?" Marceau repeated, sounding scandalized. "Girls do that?"

"You innocent simpleton," Dessie sighed. "You have so much to learn about women."

Marceau stared at me, his face confused. I wondered if he was trying to discern if I plucked my eyebrows. I couldn't help but laugh.

After several minutes of application, and then what felt like an eternity for Cap, who squirmed in his chair and complained about the "burning hellfire on his scalp," Dessie and Cap headed for the bathroom to rinse out the dye.

When they returned, the entire room froze. Cap looked like an entirely different person with black hair. He looked older. More serious.

I hated it.

"You'll pass for Spanish, alright," Hudson said, putting his arm around Cap and leaning his dark hair next to Cap's newly blackened locks. "Look, we look like we could be brothers now!"

Chito and Bernard and Willis were already dressed in their ragged outfits, having torn various sleeves and holes to make them even more disheveled. Cap pulled on his clothes, and they lined up to show the room.

"What do you think?" Willis said, spinning around. A half-drunk bottle of rum peeked out of their pockets, the pistols tucked away in their waistbands.

"No one will want to come near you," Patrick replied, nodding. "You look perfect."

We decided that the men should sleep in their costumes, in order to rumple them up, and leave before dawn. We'd help usher them out, and they'd climb onto their newly acquired bicycles, hidden safely in Leonce's room, and pedal to their assigned gas stations.

"This is it, team," Cap said, as we packed up and prepared to turn in for the night. "We're ready. And whatever happens next, we're in it together. For Paz. Sleep well, everyone. We have a long few days—maybe even weeks—ahead of us."

⸻ ◉ ⸻

CAP AND I TIPTOED BACK to our room, climbing into bed. I stared at Cap's dark hair, shockingly black against the white pillow that cradled his head, and whispered, "I'm worried about you being out there all day, every day, all by yourself."

"I'll be fine," he whispered back, his voice reassuring in the darkness of the room. "I have a gun. And a knife. And my fists, too."

"But what if Trimboli recognizes you somehow?" I asked, trying in vain to keep my fear at bay. We were international superstars. Even with his dyed hair and costume, Cap's face had still been splashed across the newspapers for months. What if he was noticed?

"Andi, you forget that I was a soldier once," he reminded me. "I can take care of myself just fine. I'm a strong man."

"Did you ever kill someone?" I blurted without thinking, suddenly curious.

Cap never talked about his time in the military, as a young man. He'd grown up dirt poor in Poland, and had joined the Polish army to feed himself as a teenager. Orphaned at a young age, it was there that he'd developed his hunger for travel and adventure, and first started dreaming of becoming an explorer. After finishing his enlistment, he used his paychecks to book passage on a ship to the United States, where he'd started a whole new life in New Orleans. I'd always sensed that he wanted to forget the painful beginnings he'd experienced.

"No," he replied.

"Do you think you could kill someone?"

He paused and studied my face in the darkness.

"Yes," he said quietly. "I know I could. And I wouldn't hesitate to, if I needed to protect the people I love."

I stared at him, silently, wondering if I could kill as easily as he could. I wasn't sure. I'd never been faced with a decision like that, and I hoped I never would. Was I ruthless enough to murder someone, in order to save others?

"If it was me who'd been kidnapped, instead of Paz?" I asked. "Would you kill them?"

"There's no end to what I would do for you," Cap said darkly. He rolled over onto his back. "Let's hope I'm never faced with that kind of decision."

I rolled over, too, facing the ceiling. What would any of us find ourselves doing, if we were faced with choices like that?

# CHAPTER 43

CAP AND I WOKE UP IN the darkness to the shrill jangle of the alarm clock on the nightstand. He sat up quickly, pulling his boots on in the gloom. He was already dressed in his shabby clothes from the night before.

I rose, wrapping a blanket around me. A chill went through me, knowing that this was the last moment that Cap and the other men were safe.

They were willingly putting themselves in danger, with their choices.

"Be careful," I said quietly, watching as Cap stood up and tucked the gun into his waist, pulling his clothes over it. He sat down again, slipping his knife into the tall shaft of his boot. With his newly darkened hair and oversized, baggy outfit, he looked like a stranger.

"I will," Cap said, tucking the photographs of the mug shots into the pocket inside his jacket. He had grabbed an old newspaper the night before, and stuck that inside his pocket along with a bottle of alcohol.

He stood up again and patted himself.

"Weapons, rum, paper, mug shots," he listed absently, touching each one.

"Can I help with anything?" I asked, curled up in my blanket. We had already planned that Marceau and Hudson would be the sentries to help Bernard, Chito, and Willis sneak out the window with Cap and get to their posts before the sun rose.

"Just be waiting for me here when I get back tonight."

"Don't forget, I'll walk by at some point today and check on you," I reminded him.

"Don't come talk to me, though," Cap said. "Well-bred ladies would never stop to talk to a homeless man on the streets."

"I know," I frowned. "Please be careful, okay?"

Cap leaned over me, kissing me on the forehead.

"I'm always careful," he said, gazing into my eyes. "I don't take stupid risks. You know that about me."

"I love you," I replied. "Even when you look like a tramp."

He smiled, and bent down to kiss my lips. "I love you, too." Walking quietly to the door, he opened it slowly and peeked out, gave me a wink, and slipped away.

I laid back down, sure I wouldn't be able to go back to sleep. *"I hope this works,"* I thought to myself, staring up at the dark ceiling. *"What if Trimboli and his men don't stop at a gas station? What if our boys don't recognize them because the kidnappers are wearing disguises? What if someone else hurts them or runs them off or calls the police on them, thinking they're actually homeless?"*

Tossing and turning for another hour, I welcomed the first light of dawn. I got up and quickly got ready for the day, putting on a demure floral dress and sensible hat. Marceau and I had already planned to go out walking to check on Cap and Bernard today.

I waited impatiently in the lobby for the others to wake up, sipping a cup of coffee. I had no hope of enjoying anything else for breakfast, as my stomach was tied up in knots. Somehow, today seemed like it had brought us one step closer to danger.

Patrick appeared with Hudson, and ruffled my hair playfully. "Why the face?" he asked, sitting down next to me.

I jiggled my foot, watching the last remnants of my dark coffee dance in the delicate porcelain cup.

"Just thinking about how evil Trimboli is," I replied, lifting my eyes to his. "What are we doing, Patrick? We're throwing ourselves into danger, interacting with a murderer. Good gravy, he's killed seven people. *Seven.*"

Patrick's forehead puckered.

"But it's our best chance to catch them," he said. "And besides, you know Cap and Willis and Chito can handle themselves. Bernard, well, I think he's probably been itching to shoot someone in the face his entire life."

"It's not funny."

"And I'm not laughing," he replied, his face serious. "Look, they're armed. We'll be checking on them, all day. They'll be coming back here to sleep a little every night. They're intelligent men who are used to thinking on their feet. They'll be fine. You need to trust them."

I sighed. *"I just want this nightmare to be over,"* I thought to myself, staring into my cup.

# CHAPTER 44

THE NEXT FEW DAYS BECAME an exhausting drain, pushing each of us to our breaking points as we worked furiously to keep our schemes in operation.

If we weren't actively surveilling Trimboli and his men in pairs, we were shopping for food items, or walking and driving around town to check on Cap, Chito, Willis, and Bernard as they sat near their respective gas stations.

Leonce had cleverly fashioned a board in his hotel room where we moved our names frequently around into various roles, indicating to the others where we happened to be at every hour of the day. We rotated different outfits and accessories, as well as different partners, throughout the day in order to avoid attention from casual bystanders.

I intentionally walked around Cap's stop the most often.

The gas station where he had positioned himself looked almost like a house, compared to the tin-roofed shacks that Chito and Willis sat under. With its pitched roof and double pumps out front, covered with a green canopy, it appeared to be a clean and modern facility.

Each time I walked by, Cap was slumped over or appeared to be sleeping, a huddled mass with a bottle of booze peeking out from his dirty clothes.

Willis had adopted the same strategy at his small station on the other side of town, and had apparently been liberal in sprinkling himself with alcohol each day. I could smell the tang of his alcohol-soaked clothes from several feet away.

Bernard's gasoline station had a large service bay for car repair and maintenance, and I noticed that he shifted closer and closer to the building, as if to watch what the mechanics were doing to the automobiles inside. At some point, they must've kicked him out, because he ended up pouting on the sidewalk a few days later, a scowl on his face as I passed by, carefully avoiding his eyes.

Chito had apparently craved human interaction, and had set out a dirty old cap in front of his spot on the edge of the gasoline station's property. At one point, as Marceau and I walked by, carrying a bag of groceries, I dropped a coin in. To my surprise, there were already several coins in the hat.

"Are you doing alright?" Marceau asked in a low voice, as I fished a sandwich and a drink out of my grocery bag and handed it to him.

"Well, it's not the most fun I've ever had, but at least I'm making money," Chito joked, carefully taking the sandwich from my hands. "At least it's been nice to find out that there are some good people in the world."

After a few long days, we finally had some action.

Hudson and Dessie were just climbing into a Ford in anticipation of their afternoon rounds to check on the Hobo Quartet when Chito pedaled his way back to the hotel in the middle of the day, breathless.

"Chito!" I exclaimed, standing out front waiting for Marceau to drive us the opposite direction the hour after Hudson and Dessie made their rounds. "What's wrong? What are you doing here?"

He waved with one hand, indicating for us to pause, as he nearly fell off his bicycle. His face was red and streaked with sweat, and he was sucking gulps of air in so vigorously that for a moment, he couldn't speak.

"Are they okay?" I cried, fearing something that happened to them.

"Yes...okay..." he panted, bent over with his hands on his knees. "Guys...*we got them.*"

"What do you mean?" Hudson said, his eyes wide. "Trimboli?"

Chito nodded, wiping sweat out of his eyes. "They pulled in. Got gas where Willis was stationed. Four of them, one matching a mug shot we have. And Trimboli, too. Willis even saw the horse shoe tattoo on Trimboli, plain as day. It's them. He's sure of it."

"Yes!" Hudson yelled, throwing his hat in the air. It landed ten feet away from the Ford, on the road. "Please tell me he followed them?"

"He did," Chito said, still breathing heavily. "Hopped on his bicycle and followed behind them when they pulled out. He took the sidewalk, mostly, so they didn't see him. Nearly killed a man walking his dog, he told me."

He paused, and mopped his face with his sleeve.

"Sorry, I pedaled as fast as I could to get back here. Willis followed them all the way to a small house in the outskirts of the city. They parked there and went inside. Still there. Willis circled around the block and settled in to watch them, just to make sure they were staying there. He saw them go out again and come back with bags, like they'd been at the market. He's pretty sure it's their home base. As soon as he saw them come back with groceries, he took off and pedaled over to me and told me to come back here and find you guys and tell you."

"I'd be willing to bet they rented a house so they can have some privacy," Hudson said, his eyes gleaming. "I bet they have Paz in there, tied up and gagged."

Chito nodded, still dabbing his brow. "Hudson, let me drive. We'll go over there. I'll show you where he told me they are."

"I want to come!" I cried, reaching for the passenger door to climb into the back. "Dessie, tell Marceau what happened. We'll be back later."

Dessie's eyes were big. "I can't believe this plan worked," she said, shaking her head in shock.

The three of us scrambled to pile into the Ford. Dessie grabbed Chito by the arm as he slid into the driver's seat.

"Your outfit!" she hissed. "You still look like a bum! People will think you stole this car!"

"Oh, good call," Chito breathed, wiggling out of his dirty jacket and hat, tossing them to her.

Without warning, Chito abruptly gunned the Ford and shot us out into the street.

"Chito, calm down," Hudson yelled, grabbing his arm. "I know you're excited, but we have to blend in and look like we're just three everyday people, out for a relaxing afternoon drive."

Chito exhaled, and whipped us around a corner with lightning speed. I skidded along the back seat, bracing myself against the side. "Chito!"

We raced through the streets until we reached the northern outskirts, decidedly less maintained than the quaint downtown streets. Here, houses needed a fresh coat of paint and weeds grew up in the cracks in the sidewalk. A couple of children playing marbles in the street stared at us as Chito finally slowed to a crawl, passing by them.

"Not much farther," Chito said, navigating through several short streets. "Let's see. Willis should be sitting somewhere around the next corner."

Sure enough, a bundle of clothes was laying on the sidewalk, curled up with an empty rum bottle next to his head. He didn't move as we passed by.

"See that little tan house there, with the Ford parked out front?" Chito said to us. "That's it. That's where Trimboli and his men are camped out."

The house was small, with a knee-high fence around the front yard. It looked cared for, but tired. A solitary flowerpot sat outside the front door, drooping yellow flowers inside. The shades were all drawn, I noticed.

"Who's the other man that Willis managed to identify?" Hudson asked, as we drove down the next block. I already knew Chito was taking us to the gas station where Cap was, so we could tell him the good news.

"Massimiliano Rua, known to his friends as Masso," Chito replied. "He's younger. Early twenties, as I recall."

Hudson chewed his lip, thinking.

"He's the one who did time for armed robbery and arson," he said. "Not long. Just a year or two. He was in the same prison as Trimboli, which I'm sure is how they met. But he was suspected of several burglaries and arsons, according to the police file."

"Nice guy," I said, disgusted. I prayed there was one decent fellow in the gang, or poor Paz had no hope of being taken care of while he was being held captive.

I recognized the office buildings and storefronts as we approached the gasoline station where Cap was camped out. We pulled in, a few moments later, and my eyes searched rapidly for Cap.

Sure enough, he was hunched over a newspaper on the side of the station, his head down. With his oversized jacket and torn pants, a scarf draped around the back of his neck to protect him from the sun, Cap looked pitiful.

Chito eased the Ford up to the pump and climbed out first, to fill up with gasoline.

Hudson made a show of getting out and stretching his arms, then stretching his legs. He casually dug through his pocket, pretending to notice Cap out of the corner of his eye, and walked toward him. I stayed in the car, as a proper lady would while sitting at a gas station like this.

"Hey there, amigo," I heard Hudson drawl, approaching him. Cap looked up, his face darkened by the hat pulled down low on his head. I couldn't even see his eyes.

Hudson flipped him a coin and Cap neatly caught it, his hands blackened with dirt from laying on the ground. I knew Hudson was telling him to meet us in the alley two blocks away, so we could take him back to the hotel.

Turning on his heels, Hudson sauntered back to the car and swung open the passenger door. "You still want to marry that bum?"

"Yes."

He whistled irreverently.

"There's no accounting for taste, apparently." He ran a hand through his dark hair and glanced at me. "Do you like Cap's hair black like that?"

"No, not really," I replied, grimacing.

Hudson laughed. "Ouch. Guess Miss Gallivanter only has a thing for blondes. Dreams don't always come true."

Chito finished pumping gas, wiped his hands on his pants, and started the car. He circled around the corner and zipped down to the alley two streets down. He pulled us slowly behind a large pile of boxes, and we waited.

A few minutes later, Cap shuffled down the alley. With his head still down, he looked furtively left and right, before approaching our automobile.

"Good news," Hudson said, without even greeting him. Cap looked up sharply. "We found them."

"What? Where? How many are there? Where are they staying?" Cap cried, pulling off his hat and jacket so he could climb into the Ford. I scooted over, so he could sit in the back next to me.

"You reek of alcohol, you know that?" Hudson complained as Cap climbed in over him without even waiting for him to open the door.

"Yeah, I know," Cap replied, tossing his discarded clothing next to my feet. "I figured it'd be more convincing if I stank like a drunk, so I splashed the bottle all over my clothes."

"What a waste of rum," Hudson grumbled.

Chito was already pulling out to show Cap the house. We scissored through the neighborhoods again, and Chito pulled over a few blocks away.

"Andi and Hudson, you better get out and wait here," he said. "Cap, you drive, and I'll guide. We have to be as cautious as possible, anticipating that they're watching everyone and everything, too. We don't want them to notice that our car's gone by the house twice in the last hour."

"Good idea," I replied, as Hudson climbed out and held the door open for me. Cap hopped into the front seat, taking the wheel.

"Wait here," Chito called as they pulled away. Hudson leaned against the house behind us, fishing in his pockets for a pack of cigarettes to use as cover for lingering in the alley.

"Good thing I carry these now," he said, offering one to me. "I wonder if this will become a habit?"

"Not for me, it won't," I wrinkled my nose as the acrid scent of tobacco wafted up in a cloud around us. He offered me a light, and I dipped the end of the cigarette in and held it in my hand, watching the tip burn red.

We stood there, waiting, until Chito finally pulled around again a few minutes later and picked us up.

Hudson climbed into the back with me and put his arm across the back of the seat.

"Well, we did it," he grinned. "Can you believe that harebrained scheme of ours actually worked?"

"No," Cap admitted, his cheeks flush with excitement. "I can't. But thank God it did. We actually have a shot now to find Paz."

"We'll have to arrange surveillance around here now," I pointed out. "New disguises, maybe."

"The homeless thing would still work over here," Chito replied, looking around. "But if you've noticed, bums tend to move on after a few days. We'll need a different ruse."

"We can talk about it back at the hotel, with the whole team," Cap beamed. "Good golly, I just can't believe our plan actually *worked.*"

# CHAPTER 45

WHILE WILLIS PRETENDED to sleep across the street from Trimboli's rental house, the rest of us rapidly came up with a new plan, new surveillance roles, and new costumes.

"We need to watch them for a few days, at least," Cap said, pacing around the room like a caged tiger. "We need to learn as much as we can about each man. Who is he? What does he like? What captures his attention? What are his potential weaknesses? How can we take advantage of him, and have the upper hand in a fight?"

Hudson looked at Dessie. "Dess, darling, I'm afraid you're going to have to sit this one out."

"Why?" she replied, her eyes snapping. "I want to help!"

"They know your face, though," Patrick jumped in. "Three of them saw your face close up, remember? One of them was even head-butted by you."

"So?"

"So they'll recognize you in a heartbeat," Hudson replied. "Besides, you're pretty enough that you stop men in their tracks. What happens if you attract their attention and they stare at you just a little too long, and remember you?"

"No fair," she whined, glaring at Hudson.

"Andi, I want you paired up with a man at all times," Cap said. "After what they tried to do to Dessie, we can't be too careful."

"I can handle myself," I replied. "Especially if you let me have a pistol."

Cap shot me a look.

"If you think I'm going to let you walk around by yourself around these men, you're delusional," he said sternly. "They're the worst of the worst criminals, Andi. They've killed seven people, and those are only the ones we know about. You absolutely will not go over there by yourself. If you can't agree to working with a partner, I'll happily tie you up and leave you here."

"Fine," I grumbled.

Hudson winked at me. "I'll go with you. I'll even let you have a gun, if you want one."

"Good," I replied, feeling validated while I saw Cap make a face at Hudson. At least I wasn't sitting out of the action completely, like Dessie.

"You still trying to convince Andi to join the Chinook Voyageurs after all this settles down, Hudson?" Marceau joked.

"Don't say it in front of her!" Hudson laughed, punching Marceau in the arm.

"Stop horsing around. This is serious," Chito said, sounding so much like Cap that the entire room smiled, in spite of ourselves.

Cap flew through a flurry of instructions as we listened. We'd keep Trimboli's house under surveillance, twenty-four hours a day. We were to make careful mental notes on every detail we noticed about them, no matter how small. Every time we came back to the hotel, we'd add our details to an ongoing list compiled from everyone's observations.

"Be smart," Cap advised, as we picked through the pile of costume clothing and grabbed what we needed. "Pay attention, be safe, and above all—don't get noticed."

Chito was taking the first surveillance shift, then Leonce. Hudson and I slotted in behind them, for the afternoon block.

When it came time for our shift, Marceau drove us partway into town and then dropped us off in a narrow alley behind a restaurant.

"Have fun, kids," he called as he drove away. "Don't forget to be home in time for dinner."

We walked arm-in-arm toward the house, pretending to be a couple out on a romantic stroll through the neighborhood. As we walked, I smiled at him.

"Thanks for volunteering to take me," I said. "I would've gone crazy being cooped up in a hotel room while you boys were having all the fun."

"I know," Hudson glanced at me with a grin. "You don't hide your feelings, you know. Subtlety is not your gift, doll."

I rolled my eyes at him, swatting him with my gloved hand. "Nor is it yours."

The buildings around us hummed with afternoon activity, as women watered plants on their stoops and men arranged their wares in shop windows and stopped to catch up. Children zigzagged in front of us on the sidewalk as school ended for the day.

We strolled slowly, chatting about the places we wanted to travel to next. "I can't wait to go to Egypt," I told him. "Seeing the pyramids? Riding a camel through the sand? Seeing the markets and the spices and the people?"

"I've always wanted to go to Iceland," Hudson said.

"Iceland? What's there?"

"A lot of lava fields, apparently," Hudson replied. "Hot springs. Mountains. And fermented shark, their national delicacy."

I cringed. "Fermented shark?"

"Yeah. I read about it. They gut the shark and bury it in the ground, pressing it down with stones. Then after a few weeks, they dig it up and eat it. Supposedly most people can't even swallow it, it's so gross."

"That sounds awful. You'd actually try it?"

"Sure, why not?"

We ambled amiably, rounding a corner. About a hundred yards ahead, two men walked toward us on the sidewalk, their hats pulled low.

Hudson squeezed my arm suddenly, whispering. "Is that them?"

I peeked.

"Oh, no," I inhaled. It was Trimboli and another man. They were both wearing large, dark coats and had their heads down, like they didn't want to be recognized. Perhaps they were walking toward the liquor store we'd passed a few buildings back?

"Damn it," Hudson whispered under his breath.

We were both shaken by the unexpected encounter. Seeing Trimboli's face so close sent a jolt of electricity down my spine. What if he saw us and recognized us? We'd blow the whole operation. We'd barely even gotten it off the ground yet.

"Cripes," I breathed. We couldn't stop without drawing attention to ourselves, and Trimboli and his partner were approaching rapidly, walking at their fast clip.

Thinking fast, I reached for Hudson's free hand and swiveled my body toward him.

"Kiss me," I commanded breathlessly, and Hudson reeled back in surprise. Instantly, however, understanding flashed in his eyes.

He pulled me in for a kiss, whipping his hat off his head and covering our faces. I leaned into him, wrapping my arms around him as he wrapped his arms around me, his left hand holding the hat up to shield us.

I prayed we looked like a couple, kissing irreverently on the sidewalk, and that Trimboli wouldn't think twice about it.

It was a strange sensation to be kissing Hudson platonically, without any passion. His beard tickled my face, but his lips were surprisingly soft. Even though we locked lips unexpectedly, I couldn't help but notice, guiltily, that he was a good kisser.

We kissed, waiting with pounding hearts until we heard their footsteps pass by. I glanced toward them through squinting eyes, my lips still locked with Hudson's. Swiftly, I pulled away. I continued to keep my arms wrapped around Hudson, waiting to see if they'd turn around.

They didn't. Sure enough, they looked to be heading toward the liquor store.

"We need to get out of here before they see us again," I breathed, grabbing Hudson's hand and inching toward an alley between apartment buildings. "That was too close."

Hudson held my hand as we quickly cut through the alley and popped out the other side. We walked several blocks, until we came to a small city park lined with trees. Finally, we slowed our frantic pace. Still, my heart hammered inside my chest.

"Dear Lord, they could've seen us," Hudson groaned. "You don't think they did, right?"

"I don't think so," I replied. "We noticed them before they noticed us. And you were hiding our faces that whole time. Good move with the hat, by the way."

I massaged my shoulders. My back was tied up in knots from the tension of the moment.

"Good thinking with the kiss," Hudson replied, then suddenly grimaced. "Oh, golly—"

"What?"

"Cap's going to murder me," he moaned. "Oh, why'd it have to be you? Literally, any other girl would've been enjoyable to kiss."

"Hey now," I said, offended. "Don't be so insulting."

"Heavens, no," he said, his cheeks pink with embarrassment. "No, you're delightful to kiss. I enjoyed it, trust me. It's that—no, wait. That's not what I meant—"

I pursed my lips, my own cheeks turning pink now. "Just stop talking."

"I can't," Hudson groaned. "It's like my mouth has a mind of its own sometimes. It runs along ahead of my brain, I swear. No, I meant—it's not enjoyable *now* because I know Cap is going to kill me, so it—but it was—no—"

"Just shut up already," I said, shielding my eyes with my hands. I didn't know whether to be flattered or humiliated, or both.

Hudson wisely buttoned his lips and kept walking next to me. After a few awkward moments of silence, he glanced my way with mirthful eyes. I stared back at him, shaking my head, but I couldn't keep the laughter out of my eyes, either.

"I never thought I'd say this, but apparently the great Captain Landry needs lessons in how to talk to women," I smirked. "Lesson one involves never kissing a girl and then saying, '*oh, if only it wasn't you I just kissed,*' sir."

He sighed in mock despair. "I don't need lessons. It's just that this was so unexpected and you caught me off guard...and Cap. I mean, he's not the kind of man I want as an enemy, you know?"

"Well, we have to tell him. It was necessary. He'll understand."

Hudson cringed. "I don't know if we *have* to tell him."

"I do. I don't want secrets between us."

"Oh, to be that naive again," he laughed, glancing at me. Slowly, his smile faded. "You're serious?"

"What?" I said defensively, needled at his derision.

"I forgot, you're so young," Hudson said. "How old are you now, anyway?"

"Nearly twenty," I replied, tossing my head. "You're not that much older than me, so stop pretending like you're some ancient sage doling out jewels of wisdom."

"First boyfriend, though, isn't it?"

"So?"

He winked at me. "You'll learn, Andi. You don't tell them every thought in your head, if you're smart. You learn what to keep inside your own mind, when to hold your tongue, for the sake of peace in your relationship."

"Maybe that works for you. It's not how I plan to operate."

"Good luck with that," he said. "People are never totally honest with each other, little lady. Not even married couples. You can't truthfully tell me that you hold *nothing* back from Cap, can you?"

I started to argue, but suddenly clammed up. In fact, I *was* lying to Cap. About something I knew would upset him very much. Instead, I changed the subject.

"We need to circle back around to a pick up spot," I said. Cap had cleverly mapped out four different pick up spots that we could all rotate around to, in order to get picked up in the Ford and have the next pairing dropped off for the next shift.

He looked at his pocket watch and nodded.

"Let's head toward the government plaza," he said, turning us toward the busy roundabout in front of a local government building, where cars and carriages constantly pulled in and out. We'd decided that'd be an easy place for our Fords to blend in, with all the commotion.

We walked for a few minutes and made it to the plaza. Hudson checked his watch and motioned us to sit down on the edge of the fountain, bubbling happily in the middle of the concrete plaza.

"There he is," Hudson said a few minutes later, shielding his eyes as he spotted our Ford pulling in. "Oh, great. It's Cap picking us up. Of course."

We reached the car, and Hudson opened the door and slid into the back. I climbed in the front and closed it.

"How'd it go?" Cap asked, pulling out smoothly and pointing the Ford back toward the hotel.

"Well," I replied, my forehead wrinkled. "We need to come clean about something."

"What's that supposed to mean?" Cap said, glancing at me with concern.

"We were strolling along, and we came around a corner and spotted Trimboli and one of his men walking toward the liquor store," I explained. "We didn't have time to duck away without catching their attention, so we had to improvise."

Hudson broke in, leaning forward. "I swear to you, Cap, it meant nothing—"

I shoved him back with one hand. "We embraced like lovers, and hid our faces behind Hudson's hat. They walked right by us—didn't even notice us," I said, alarmed at how easily the lie rolled off my tongue. Maybe I'd been hanging around Dessie too much.

Or maybe Hudson's advice had rattled me more than I wanted it to.

"You're sure they didn't see your faces?" Cap asked with concern. How typical of him, to focus on the plan and miss the human melodrama playing out right under his nose.

"They didn't, we're sure of it," I replied.

Hudson leaned forward again. "Listen, Cap—"

I pushed him back again.

"But now we know which liquor store they'll walk to, next time," I said, shooting a quick glare at Hudson.

Cap nodded, rubbing the stubble on his face thoughtfully.

"I wonder if they'd all walk to the store together, at some point," he mused. "Maybe while they're all out, we could sneak into the house and rescue Paz..."

Behind me, Hudson yanked my hair. I spun in my seat.

"Cap, we kissed," Hudson said curtly.

*"What?"* Cap cried, turning to me.

"There's no way they saw our faces," Hudson continued. "We were facing each other completely, and our faces were hidden with my hat."

Cap's eyes bored into mine. "What do you mean, you kissed? For how long? What kind of kiss?"

"It was out of necessity," I replied quickly, shooting Hudson a look. "Trust me, it meant nothing. It was all we could think of, in a pinch. We had to hide our faces, and the best way to do it was to face each other and kiss."

Hudson sank back into his seat, crossing his arms. I glared at him again, and settled into the front seat with my arms crossed, too.

"I told you to take care of her, to keep her safe, not *kiss* her," Cap said irritably, shaking his head.

"I did," Hudson protested. "Really, I did."

He paused, sincerity creeping into his voice. "Honestly, Cap, you're a lucky man. And I meant what promised you earlier, that I would protect her at all costs. I know how much Andi means to you."

Cap shook his head, but I sensed that his anger was fading at Hudson's words.

"Don't make it a habit," he said gruffly.

We drove in silence back to the hotel, and got out as Cap parked the car. I hung back as Cap walked into the lobby, grabbing Hudson by the arm.

"You told me not to tell him about the kiss!" I hissed at him, glaring. "Why did you decide to tell him like that?"

Hudson grimaced. "Maybe you're right. Maybe honesty is best in relationships."

"Oh, now you're changing your mind? Convenient timing."

He stared at me. "You're the one who wanted to be honest in the first place. I don't know. Maybe that's why you're the one getting married, not me."

I dropped his arm and he brushed past me into the lobby. I stood outside the hotel doors, suddenly uncertain. I couldn't be honest about everything. Not yet.

*"I'll tell him some other time,"* I thought, guilt rising again as I thought of Cap. *"Right now, we have too many other things to worry about. The timing isn't right. You can't distract him, not now."*

But my brain wouldn't leave it alone.

*"If he finds out you went behind his back, he'll never forgive you,"* it whispered. *"You know that honesty matters more to him than anything else. And you're not being honest about what you did."*

I brushed it away, trying to push it down. It was too late now, anyway.

# CHAPTER 46

THE NEXT MORNING, CAP escorted me out to walk around town while the others did their surveillance shifts, watching Trimboli's house.

"I thought we could use some time to talk," he said, as we walked down the sidewalk in front of our hotel. "It seems like we haven't done a whole lot of that lately."

"Sure," I replied, slipping my arm into his. Now that we were in disguises and wouldn't be recognized as the famous Captain and Andi Gallivanter, we could more easily show some affection in public.

We traipsed through the streets, and Cap gazed around in appreciation. "Tarragona was quite the epicenter of Roman gladiator games, did you know that? That old colosseum near the water used to house thirty thousand spectators, in its heyday."

"Fascinating," I replied, glancing at the tall palms and old stucco buildings around us. Tarragona was a gem of a seaside town, one whole side of the city bordered by sparkling waters and golden, sandy beaches blending into pine forests that sighed when the sea breeze swept through.

The crumbling, old city walls, dating from the third century, rose high above a melting pot of buildings from different architectural eras.

We walked slowly toward the old church in the center of town. It soared in front of us, a sandstone cathedral carved in elaborate Gothic and Romanesque architecture. I stared up at the large rose window, and smiled when I heard the bells start to ring, their loud booms echoing through the city.

Cap glanced at me as the bells pealed out, watching my face. When they stopped, he put his arm around me.

"Can we sit down and talk?" he asked. "I mean, *really* talk."

"Yes," I said, a small lump of fear settling in my stomach. He led us over to a bench in the open plaza in front of the church, and we sat down. For a moment, we watched people walk through the plaza, carrying bags of groceries and pushing strollers.

"That kiss with Hudson yesterday," Cap began, looking at me out of the corner of his eye. "We need to talk about it."

"There's nothing to talk about. I told you, it was out of necessity. We had to hide our faces, and we didn't have time to dart away."

"I know," Cap pursed his lips. "I understand that. But—why didn't *you* tell me about it? Why did Hudson tell me?"

I sighed. "I didn't know how you'd react. I knew it would bother you, understandably, but I wasn't sure how to bring it up. I thought maybe I should wait and tell you another time, when you weren't under such stress."

Cap thought silently for a moment, crossing his leg. "Do you always selectively decide when I should hear the truth?"

I tried not to squirm.

"I don't always think it through," I admitted.

"So that's a yes, I take it?"

"Sometimes."

He sighed. "I just want you to be honest with me, Andi. I need to know that you're completely open about what's going on, even if it makes me upset. I'd always rather hear the truth from you. You know how much Milly wounded me with her lies—she upended my life by not telling me the truth. And yes, sometimes I get angry. But anger and frustration are very reasonable reactions to a lot of the things I have to deal with, as the leader of this expedition. I can handle whatever you tell me, I promise—as long as you actually *tell* me about it."

I bit my lip. Was now the time to tell him?

Cap interrupted my thoughts.

"It's not that I'm worried about Hudson," he said, watching two toddlers dip their hands in a fountain in front of us and shriek with joy.

"I mean, I don't think he's quite your type, with that devil-may-care attitude of his," he continued. "But I was worried about you falling for Rollie earlier this year. The two of you spent so much time together, and everyone—including me—could see the bond that was growing between you. And I realize now that we never did this—we never sat down and talked about what was really going on. So I'm trying now, Andi."

He exhaled. "I want things to be good between us. And I want to head into our marriage with things ironed out between us. Our relationship has always existed in the middle of the throes of danger, do you realize that?"

I nodded. "Ever since we met, we've been teetering on the edge of one adventure after another."

"Exactly."

We sat in silence again. In front of us, birds strolled across the plaza, searching for crumbs.

"I know I love you," Cap said quietly. "But I'm concerned what our relationship will look like, if things ever settle down. We've only known each other as partners, desperately clinging together to survive near-disasters. Can we exist in the mundane?"

"I hope so," I said, reaching for his hand. "I can tell you that there's no one else I'd rather have by my side than you, no matter if I'm facing the mundane or the perilous."

I wove my fingers in between Cap's and squeezed. He squeezed back.

"Look, there's something else," Cap sighed. "I feel terrible that I haven't gotten you a real engagement ring yet, and that we haven't announced to your family or mine or anyone publicly that we're engaged. I know you wanted to write a letter to your mother, but then everything happened and—I keep thinking we should make it official, you know, but with everything that's been going on with Paz and Trimboli—"

"I'm not going anywhere," I interrupted.

I patted the compass necklace he'd given me, embedded with its diamond, and smiled. "This works for now. I don't need a ring yet. I told you that already. And the people that matter in our lives all know about us being engaged. The rest? Well, they'll find out when we're ready."

"I feel bad about it, though," Cap muttered. "Believe me, I'd like to shout it from the rooftops and have the world's biggest press conference to declare my love for you. I can't believe I haven't had the chance to do it yet."

I laughed. "Well, we'll plan on it after we rescue Paz, then."

Cap glanced at his pocket watch. "As much as I hate to leave this rare moment alone with you, we need to get back to the hotel. I'm scheduled to do surveillance next."

# CHAPTER 47

WE WALKED BACK TO THE hotel, where Cap changed into a suit.

He picked up a briefcase and a newspaper and pulled a hat down low onto his head. With his dark hair and outfit, he looked like one of a dozen nameless businessmen we'd seen at the park, reading newspapers on a bench in the afternoon sun.

He kissed me goodbye, then headed out for his surveillance shift. I listlessly wandered down to the lobby, where I found Marceau sitting by himself, drinking a cup of coffee.

"Mind if I join you?" I asked.

"Be my guest," he said, waving at the chair next to him. I sat down, tucking one leg underneath me.

"Have you heard from Rollie at all?" I asked, as he waved the waiter down and ordered me a cup of coffee.

"No, not lately. The last telegram we had was a few days ago, right?"

"Right," I said, lowering my voice. "I need to make sure that you didn't tell anyone."

He shook his head. "I promised you I wouldn't, and I'm a man of my word. But Cap is bound to find out at some point. When are you going to tell him?"

"I don't know," I replied. "It's just been so chaotic. I don't know how I can possibly tell him this while he's in this state. Hudson's stressed out, too, but he doesn't absorb the tension like Cap does, you know? I'm afraid this will snap Cap completely. Look at how the situation with Rollie played out—it ended in a bar brawl. I don't want him to lose focus on this operation to find Paz. He's

259

managing a thousand details, all at once. I could never do it. I don't know how he's even functioning."

Marceau sipped his coffee and frowned, lines appearing on his forehead. "I have to be honest, I think you're playing with fire here. You need to just tell him. The longer you hide it from him, the bigger the problem will be when you do finally confess."

"I will tell him. When the time is right."

He sighed. "I wish we never would've walked into that bar that night in Innsbruck. It threw our lives into chaos. Yours, too. And Rollie...I just hope he recovers."

We sipped our coffee in silence. My stomach twisted in knots, thinking about Rollie. I pushed the feelings down and tried to focus on something else.

"Now that we know where Trimboli and the gang are hiding out, what are we going to do?" I asked. "They have to have Paz hidden in that house, tied up. We've got to get in there and get him."

"Hudson said we'd need to find a way to break in, somehow," Marceau replied. "I expect he's working on a plan with Cap."

"How, I wonder?" I asked. "Trimboli's an experienced criminal. He's not going to leave Paz unguarded. They'll be on high alert."

"We'll think of something."

Marceau and I were soon joined by Chito, Patrick, Hudson, and Willis. As they ordered breakfast, we chatted.

"So I know we're still sending out those fake press releases to make it look like we're traveling in other parts of the world," Willis said, stirring sugar into his coffee. "Where are we supposedly traveling through right now, Patrick?"

Patrick felt for the small notepad in his pocket and pulled it out.

"Let me see," he said, scanning the page. "Three days ago, I sent photographs to newspapers in Romania and London. The

Gallivanter crew is supposedly traveling through the countryside in Romania. I used one of your candid shots of Andi behind the wheel, and a team photo with an indistinct hill behind you."

He continued reading. "Right now, the Chinook Voyageurs are pretending to be in Libya. I sent a photograph of Hudson and Leonce fixing a flat tire, and added a line about how the post offices are few and far between in this region of northern Africa, so they probably won't have updates in the newspapers for several weeks."

"Clever," Chito nodded. "That buys us some time."

"Should we submit it to the local newspaper, too?" Marceau suggested. "On the off chance that Trimboli and Masso or the others read the local news, it might cause them to drop their guard even more if they think we're all out of town."

"Good idea," Patrick said, nodding. "I'll do that today."

I hung around the hotel with the crew the rest of the day, chatting until Leonce headed out to replace Cap. Our team sat huddled together at a small table, looking up expectantly as Cap joined us.

# CHAPTER 48

"HOW'D IT GO?" CHITO asked, as Cap walked into the lobby, his hat in his hands.

He sighed, shrugging off his overcoat and setting the briefcase down next to the chair he dropped into.

"Fine," Cap frowned. "They sure don't ever leave that house unattended. Actually, they barely leave the house at all. It seems like one, maybe two men at a time duck out to get food or liquor, and then they go back in."

"They must have Paz in there, if they're guarding it that closely," Patrick spoke up. "It's the only explanation."

"Or maybe they're seasoned criminals and they know they're wanted by the police, so they're laying low," Chito replied. "I mean, we have mugshots for two of them. They're on the police's wanted lists."

"Or perhaps they just don't go out much," Marceau shrugged. "We don't know."

"That's why we're studying them," Cap replied. "I actually wonder if they're quietly watching and waiting to see if things have died down enough to issue the ransom for Paz. It's certainly odd that they haven't contacted his family for a ransom yet, but I suppose it fits their pattern. In every other case, they kidnapped their victim and waited several weeks before they asked the family for a ransom."

"You don't think that means Paz is—is—you know," Dessie faltered off.

"Dead?" Bernard filled in.

Chito whacked him as Dessie winced.

"I don't think so," Patrick jumped in, before Cap could respond. "They need him alive, in order to collect the money. I mean, if they ki—they silence him, they won't have any way to track down his family and know where to get the cash."

"Unless they tortured his family's whereabouts out of him already," Bernard said.

Now Cap frowned at Bernard. "The most logical explanation, and the one that follows the pattern with their other victims, is that they have Paz tied up, and are hiding him in that house until things die down and the police move on to other cases. Then they'll use Paz's personal information to contact his family and ask for the ransom money."

"But isn't it about time that they'd ask? It's been a few weeks already," I pointed out.

"I think they will soon," Cap replied. "We're still at an advantage here. They think we're split up, traveling in different countries far away from here. They don't know that we know who they are, that we have their photographs and names. I also wonder if they realized Paz was part of a celebrity crew after they nabbed him, and have been waiting longer than normal to ask for the ransom, knowing the police might have more desire to work the case for longer."

"True," I pondered. "So if they follow their pattern, they'll ask for the ransom sometime soon, and then collect it. And after that—"

"They kill him," Patrick supplied, shrugging as Dessie shot him an angry look. "Sorry, Dess. But we have to face reality here. The clock's ticking to rescue Paz as soon as they ask for the ransom."

"Yeah, I'm well aware," she retorted, her voice laced with anger.

"How are we going to get into that house, though?" Hudson asked, leaning forward in his chair. We sat alone in the lobby, the clerk whistling to himself as he filed papers in the back office.

"I meant to ask the team that," Cap said, drumming his fingers on his chair. "Anyone have any bright ideas?"

We sat staring at each other, mute, for a few minutes. Finally, Patrick spoke up. "What if we break a pipe and knock on the door, posing as repairmen, and ask to go inside to fix it?"

"But what if they want to stand there behind you and watch you repair it?" Bernard replied. "I would, if it was my home. Or my car."

"They frequent the liquor store," Hudson mused. "What if we use that somehow to lure them out?"

"They only seem to go anywhere in pairs, at the most," Chito pointed out. "It's like they're taking turns guarding Paz."

"What if we print up some fake flyers, advertising free drinks at a local bar?" I suggested. "You first met them in a bar, right? So maybe that'd be enough to entice them out of the house for an evening."

"Maybe," Hudson nodded. "We'd have to prepay a bartender to keep the ruse going long enough for them to sit down and have a few drinks. But what happens if they ask the bartender about the free drinks? Or if they start talking to other patrons, and realize they're the only ones who got a flyer?"

"They wouldn't talk to other people in a bar," Willis scoffed.

"They talked to you guys in a bar," I pointed out. "Or, at least, they listened to Paz bragging about his money in one."

"Yes, but they just committed a violent crime and have a hostage hiding in their home," Cap interjected. "They're obviously cagey, and on edge. Their behavior is different now. Any little thing could spook them."

We fell silent again, each of us screwing up our faces as we thought hard.

"How about we show up in the middle of the night wearing masks and just put a gun in their faces when they come to the door?" Willis said darkly.

"Yeah, no," Marceau replied. "You want to get into a shootout with known murderers? They'll have guns, too."

"We have to flush them out somehow. What about if we light their house on fire?" Willis countered. "As they come running out, we can run in the back door."

"Willis! It's not even their house, it's a rental!" Patrick cried.

"So?"

"So? You want to ruin innocent people's lives just to flush some criminals out of hiding? Besides, what if Paz is inside, hidden away, and we can't find him fast enough? What if the house burns down around him? What if the fire spreads and burns down the surrounding houses? It could kill people, Willis. It could kill Paz."

Cap held up his hand, shaking his head. "Listen, I know we're all desperate to get Paz back, but that's not who we are. We won't destroy the lives of strangers who have nothing to do with this. Patrick is right, Willis. We can't risk injuring people."

Goosebumps suddenly raced down my arm.

But what if that's what it took to save Paz? Could any of us do that? How far were we willing to go, exactly?

Looking around at the faces of the people I'd come to trust, I knew it wouldn't be possible.

*"That's not who we are,"* I told myself. *"We would never cross that line. We're not bad people. We're just desperate."*

Still, the goosebumps prickled.

# CHAPTER 49

THE ROOM WAS TENSE, our faces pinched with worry as we wracked our brains trying to brainstorm some way to get into the gang's house.

"I have an idea," Hudson drawled slowly, after a few moments of silence. "What if we could be sure that we didn't hurt anyone, but we merely hurt some of Trimboli's property?"

"What exactly do you mean?" Cap asked, raising one eyebrow.

"If we could ensure that something that *belonged* to Trimboli and his men could get damaged, but nothing else would be—and no one would get hurt—that would work."

"But how?"

Hudson started to smile, knowingly, at Willis. Willis smirked in response.

Slowly, Marceau's eyebrows raised. He glared at Willis and Hudson. "Mr. Hanson's shed?"

Smiling guiltily, they both nodded.

"What?" Marceau exclaimed. "Why? He was such a nice man! What'd he ever do to you?"

"Nothing. But that shed was ancient. He didn't miss it," Willis responded quickly. "He got the insurance money for it."

"So? His father built it by hand! It was part of his home. Do your mothers know that *you* were the ones that burned it down?" Marceau retorted angrily.

Hudson laughed. "Lord, no. My mother would've skinned me alive."

"She should have!" Marceau replied, the color rising in his cheeks. "I have half a mind to write to her and tell her. I can't believe you two!"

"What's going on here?" Dessie interrupted, glaring at all three of them. "Is this another stupid story from your childhood?"

"Yes," Marceau said angrily. "Our neighbor, Mr. Hanson, had an old shed on his property. One night, it mysteriously burned down. He was sick over it. He suspected some kids lit it on fire, but he didn't know who. And he fretted about why somebody apparently hated him. I had to go help him clean it up, then build a new one. It took weeks."

Hudson patted him on the back playfully. "Even as a kid, Marceau was the responsible one."

"Yeah, I didn't know it was my best friends who burned it to the ground," Marceau crossed his arms. "That was rotten. And to hide it from everyone? Even me? Why?"

"Because twelve year old boys aren't supposed to be experimenting with petrol bombs, are they?" Willis shot back. "Come on, Marceau. Just because you were the goody-goody golden boy with Rollie doesn't mean the rest of us were perfect all the time."

"You were *twelve*?" Chito asked, his face a mask of shock.

"Yeah, but I still remember how to make the bombs," Willis replied.

I knew Chito wasn't commenting on the length of time it'd been since they last made the explosives, but rather connecting the dots that his own niece was around that age now—the age where Hudson and Willis had apparently committed arson.

"Enough of this walk down memory lane. What exactly are you thinking of doing?" Patrick interrupted.

"We make a petrol bomb, and throw it in Trimboli's Ford," Hudson said. "It solves a few problems for us, actually. One, it'll be sure to lure them all out of the house, giving us time to sneak in. Two, it'll disable them from leaving Tarragona...at least, until they can get a new car."

"It's a serious crime, though, to set someone's car on fire," I exclaimed. "Are we sure that we want to go down this path?"

"And before you answer, let me tell you that if you throw a fire bomb in that car, the whole Ford will probably explode," Marceau interjected. "We could be dealing with shrapnel. Broken glass. We'd need to make sure no one's around when you throw the bomb in. Or that it's not close enough to burn down any nearby buildings."

"Their Ford's parked right in front of their house," Cap pointed out. "It wouldn't give us an opportunity to sneak someone in. They'd be standing right there, out front."

"Unless we steal the car and drive it down the street, maybe to an empty lot?" Willis suggested. "We could send someone to pound on their door and tell them their car's on fire, down the street. Hell, we could make it look like kids took it for a joyride or something."

"So now we're stealing a car *and* committing arson?" Chito asked. "This is pretty grave crime we're talking about."

"If I could get away with it as a twelve year old, I'm pretty sure I can now, too," Willis replied, his voice low.

We fell quiet. I glanced around the room. Everyone's face was serious, thoughtful. Even Hudson, who made jokes at all the wrong times, was quietly contemplating. Just how far would we go to save Paz? Would we commit serious crimes, with no guarantee that he'd even survive this kidnapping?

"How would we even move the car, anyway?" Chito said, thinking aloud. "We don't have their keys."

"Oh, that's easy," Bernard said. "You just hotwire the car."

"Bernard!" Chito exclaimed. "Tell me you don't know how to do that?"

"Of course I do," Bernard sniffed. "I bet Marceau does, too. You forget, the two of us know these cars inside and out."

"He's right," Marceau replied. "I can hotwire, too. Most mechanics can. But that doesn't mean I would do it to aid in stealing a car."

"Goody-goody," Willis grumbled.

Marceau turned to Willis, still obviously steamed about finding out about Mr. Hanson's shed.

"Shut up," he glared. "Just because I have reservations about *breaking the law* doesn't mean I'm worthless. Are we really willing to cross these lines? To become criminals ourselves?"

"Listen, we already walked into a police station and stole from the police," Willis responded hotly. "Any line you're worrying about crossing now is long gone. We've already committed a crime that could land us all in jail. And we did it to help Paz."

"He's right," Dessie jumped in. "The time to have this conversation was a week ago, when we took that file. It's too late now. We've already crossed the line."

"So, what, we're outlaws now?" I asked, looking around the group. "We're just going to do whatever we deem necessary, no matter how illegal it is?"

"We're more like vigilantes, aren't we?" Hudson replied. "Paz's life is at stake. And Trimboli and his men have committed murder. Many times. They're criminals, and the worst kind of criminals—the kind that prey on good people for selfish reasons. Bad people deserve bad things happening to them."

"Like their Ford getting blown up," Willis added.

"But what you're wanting to do, it takes us to a whole different level," Chito argued. "We're not bad people. We're good guys."

"We're good guys who had bad guys *attack* us, brutally," Dessie replied, her expression hard. "They're vicious. They deserve whatever we decide to do to them. I wouldn't feel bad if we killed them, personally."

Cap and Patrick raised eyebrows simultaneously at Dessie's harsh words. I blinked in surprise, and glanced at Marceau and Chito. Both of them were staring, shocked, at Dessie.

I understood she was struggling with the loss of the man she loved, but who'd have thought delicate little Dessie could be so heartless?

"We're not killing anyone," Cap interjected, shaking his head. "But what we're talking about is very serious. I'm not sure I'm comfortable with it, to be honest."

"It's our only option, though," Hudson replied, his face taut. "We can't think of anything better, can we? Can anyone here offer up a better plan?"

I bit my lip. He was right—we hadn't come up with anything better.

"We just need more time," Cap said finally, after a moment. "Let's sleep on it, at least. Trimboli hasn't issued a ransom yet. We can continue thinking about plans tomorrow. For now, let's do dinner. In small groups and pairs, of course. We'll meet and go through this again tomorrow."

Rising to our feet, the group paired off to make dinner plans. I glanced at Patrick and Marceau, as Cap reached down to get his briefcase and jacket. "Want to get something together?"

"Yeah, I do," Marceau said quickly, shaking his head. "I can't believe them. Mr. Hanson was always so kind to all of us. He let us sled in his backyard all the time. Every winter."

Patrick put his arm around him. "If it makes you feel any better, Hudson wasn't much better behaved at university, either."

We walked out the front of the hotel together, Chito and Bernard trailing behind us.

"Bernard's on duty next, so we're going to grab a quick bite at the market," Chito called as they peeled off across the street.

Cap, Marceau, and Patrick and I walked slowly down the street. It was dusk, and lamps were just being lit in rooms and restaurants all over town. I breathed in, inhaling the faint salty tang that could only be found in the air of seaside cities. Palms swayed distantly, their dead leaves rattling overhead.

Tarragona was beautiful. If only we weren't all more tense than we'd ever been in our lives, we might actually enjoy the city.

We dined at a large restaurant, attempting to talk about anything but the worries that weighed us each down. Patrick and I worked hard to create interesting topics of discussion, but Marceau and Cap were both quiet tonight, lost in their own thoughts.

I hung back with Patrick as we paid and exited. "What do you think, honestly?" I asked, my voice low. "Should we really torch their car?"

"I don't know," he replied. "I can only speak for myself, and I see both sides of it. We're desperate, and we can't think of anything else. And we need to draw them out of the house, if Paz is in there and we have a chance at rescuing him. But—I don't know that it's who I am, to do something like that."

"I know," I muttered. "I hate this whole situation."

"Well, we'll sleep on it, like they said," Patrick replied. "Maybe we'll have an epiphany overnight, and have a brilliant plan in the morning."

"Fingers crossed," I sighed.

# CHAPTER 50

UNFORTUNATELY, BAD news found us before dawn. Cap and I woke up in the middle of the night to an urgent knock at our door.

"What on earth?" Cap grumbled, sitting up. His chest was bare, and reflected the light of the lamp he lit on the bedside table. He swung his feet off the side of the bed and darted toward the door. I sat up, rubbing my eyes.

Hudson stood in the hallway, and pushed into the room as soon as Cap cracked the door.

"Sorry, lovebirds, but we can't have this conversation in the hall," Hudson said quickly, sitting down in the desk chair in our room.

Cap sat down on the bed, instantly alert. "What's going on?"

Hudson was still in his pajamas with his dark hair unkempt, I noticed. He looked like he'd just woken up himself.

"The ransom came in," Hudson replied. "I just got the phone call from Paz's father. I'd given him the phone number of this hotel, and the fake name I registered under. I told him to call me, anytime, day or night, and tell the staff it was life-or-death news so they would find me immediately, even if I was sleeping."

"So Paz's father called?" I asked.

"The hotel clerk woke me up a few minutes ago," Hudson nodded. "I rushed down to take the phone call in the lobby. It was Paz's father, saying the kidnappers had called and demanded money. They put Paz on the line, even—proof of life. His father said he sounded weak, but it was definitely him."

"Oh, thank God!" I exclaimed. "He's still alive!"

Hudson ran his hand through his hair. "I know. I told Dessie. She's in her room right now, crying her eyes out. I think she's been close to snapping for a long time."

"So what do they want?" Cap asked impatiently. "How much money?"

Hudson grimaced. "They're demanding a hundred thousand dollars for Paz's safe return."

Cap clapped his hands to his head. "A hundred thousand?" he repeated, then let out a barrage of angry curses.

"A hundred thousand dollars?" I swore alongside Cap. "That's insane!"

I calculated the math swiftly in my head. Our cars cost nearly four hundred each. Even if we sold all six Fords, we'd need more than forty times that to meet the ransom demand.

I knew the Gallivanters had a fortune in savings, after donations had poured in from excited fans all over the world, but I wasn't sure how quickly we could pull money out. The Chinook Voyageurs were fairly rich, too, I remembered—and what about if Paz's family pooled their wealth in, too?

"How much can we pull out, Cap?" I asked, turning to look at him. He was on his feet now, pacing, already shaking his head.

"It's not that easy, Andi," he replied, his forehead wrinkled. "The whole world thinks we're still traveling through Romania. If I try to go to a bank here and withdraw money from our savings account, they might think I'm an imposter. I might end up right back in that police station we just robbed. And how do I possibly explain myself? I can't admit that we're a part of this. What if they noticed the missing file and connect the dots, realizing we took it and have been working the case?"

"Drat," I said, chewing on my lip. "Okay. What about Paz's family?"

"They're already scrambling to collect the money," Hudson replied. "The kidnappers gave them forty-eight hours until they need to leave it at a drop site. If they don't leave it there in two days, they said they'll kill him."

"Dear Lord!" I exclaimed, clapping my hands over my mouth. "But if they stick to the pattern, they'll get the money and then kill their kidnapped victim anyway, right? So either way, Paz only has forty-eight hours left to live!"

"So his family can pay for the ransom on their own, then?" Cap said, his arms crossed tight across his chest as he paced the room.

"Apparently."

Cap shook his head. "Paz wasn't exaggerating, then. They *are* very rich."

Hudson stared hard at Cap. "What do we do?"

Cap looked up at the ceiling, his frustration visible. "Forty-eight hours. I didn't think they'd give us that little time. I thought we'd have maybe a week. All I can think is that they know Paz's family is incredibly wealthy and has quick access to that amount of money."

"His mouth always gets him in trouble," Hudson groaned.

Cap paced back and forth, his steps clipped with stress. After a few moments of silence, he stopped in front of Hudson. "Fine. We do it your way. Wake Willis up, and go get the supplies for the petrol bomb."

I could see the knots in his shoulders, with his shirt still off. He didn't agree with this decision, I could tell, but he felt backed into a corner. Still, he continued talking, coming up with a plan on the spot.

"We'll wake up the rest of the team and fill them in. Andi can help with that. I'll wake up Chito first and tell him. He's Hispanic, so he's the only one of us who'll really pass for Spanish. He'll have to knock on Trimboli's door and tell them that their car is on fire."

"He doesn't know much Spanish," I interjected, worried. "They'll know he's not local!"

Cap was already a step ahead of me. "That's why I'm waking him first. He'll go straight down and practice a short Spanish phrase with the desk clerk. All he needs to really learn is, *'Sorry, sirs, but I believe your car is on fire down the street.'* We'll pay the clerk off to keep quiet."

"When are we doing this?" Hudson asked, standing.

"It has to be immediately," Cap replied. "We'll make it look like a teenager stole the car in the early hours of morning and bombed it for a cheap thrill. Maybe we scrawl some graffiti across it or something, to throw them off our trail."

"That lessens our chance of people seeing us steal it, too," I said, comprehension dawning on my face. "It'll still be dark out."

"Exactly."

"But who's going in? And how?" Hudson asked. "That's the most dangerous part of this whole plan. We haven't even discussed it."

"Wait," I said, thinking quickly. "Send me in."

"You?" Cap barked. "No. No way."

"It *has* to be me. They know the faces of all the Chinook crew, Chito is knocking on their door to tell them about the car, and you're too recognizable, as the famous face of the Gallivanter team," I said. "I can go in wearing a disguise. No one will look twice at a woman entering a house. I'm the least threatening one of everyone."

"She's absolutely right," Hudson breathed. "She can go in dressed as a cleaning lady. If she gets caught, she can just beg her way out and say there was a miscommunication—that she cleans the house the third Monday of every month or something, and duck away. It's a rental house—they won't think twice."

"Yes," I replied, nodding. "No one will even pay attention to me if I go up to the house calmly, with a broom and a bucket of rags. I can sneak in somehow and find Paz and get him out while Trimboli and the men are down at the car fire."

Hudson plopped down on the bed next to me. "You'll need to learn Spanish phrases, too, in case they come back early and ask you what you're doing in there."

I nodded. "I can do that. I'm fluent in French and I have passable Italian already. Spanish is just another Romantic language, and those come easy to me."

"How are you possibly going to get in?" Cap interrupted, his arms still tight across his chest. "You can't just walk in the front door. You can't be seen."

"Luckily, I bet a whole lot of cleaning ladies go in the back door anyway," I replied. "I'll find a way in. Even if I have to break a window."

"Andi, no," Cap said shortly. "We can't send you in all by yourself into a den of murderers! It's too dangerous!"

"And stealing a file from the police wasn't?" I replied, raising my voice. "Stealing a car and firebombing it isn't? Chito walking up to a door in the middle of the night and having a conversation with murderers *isn't*? Cap, I know you want to protect me, but everything we've done has the potential to be dangerous! We can't just not do it because it *might* be dangerous. We have to risk it, and you know it."

"Forty-eight hours, Cap," Hudson reminded him, his forehead creased with worry.

"Let me do it," I begged, turning to Cap. "Please. I can do it. I *want* to do it."

"Andi, no," Cap stalled. "Let's get the rest of the team together and vote on who should go in."

"No!" I exclaimed, frustrated with him. "Not everything can be a democratic decision, Cap! You know that. Sometimes, as a leader, you have to make a call and stick with it, come hell or high water. It's my life, and ultimately, my vote is the only one that matters. And my vote is *me*."

"Andi," Cap started, but I waved him off.

"Trust me. I'm smart, and I can think on my feet. I'm a survivor. And I'll carry a gun, too. I can do this, Cap. You know I can."

"Golly, I love her," Hudson interjected, looking at me with admiration. "What do you say you ditch this wet blanket and marry me instead, sweetheart?"

"Shut up, Hudson," I muttered. "Cap?"

"Why is it always you and me having these conversations?" Cap said, glaring at me. "Why does it always have to be you, headed into danger?"

"Because I can handle it," I replied. "And if we're capable of the job, we should have the job. With ability comes duty."

Hudson took both my hands in his and clasped them. "You want to do this? You're sure?"

"Yes. I *can* do it."

Hudson squared his shoulders and looked Cap in the eye, straightening his back. "I'm co-leader of this expedition, Captain Gallivanter. We're equals here in making decisions. And my decision is that Andi should go into that house, disguised as a cleaning lady."

"Fine," Cap said, throwing up his arms. "I can't fight both of you. And we don't have time to argue."

Without another word, Cap walked toward the door. "Hudson, go wake up Willis. Start working on the petrol bomb."

Hudson grinned.

"I never thought I'd hear you tell me to make a bomb, old boy," he said, winking at me as he closed the door.

# CHAPTER 51

CAP GROANED AS HE TURNED to me. I was already scrambling for clothes, balancing on one foot as I shoved my feet into shoes.

"Andi, wake up the others and tell them what's going on. Have Dessie assemble a maid's uniform for you, but go straight down and practice your Spanish with Chito and the desk clerk."

"Wait, one more thing," I said, pulling a sweater over my pajamas.

"We don't have time to argue about it. The clock is ticking."

"No, not that. I meant your shirt," I said, pointing at his bare chest.

"Oh, yeah," he said, looking down. He strode quickly to his bag and threw on a shirt, then shoved his feet in his boots. "Go."

I hurried out of the room and started waking the team. They were befuddled with sleep, but their eyes became wide as I swiftly filled them in. Dessie was already up, the lights in her room blazing, and she started pulling a costume out for me before I even finished explaining what I needed.

"Leave it to me," she said grimly, gritting her teeth.

Chito was in the lobby already, standing at the reception desk with the clerk.

"Buenos dias señorita," the clerk greeted me, looking at the clock. "You are all up at some odd hours tonight."

"Yes, we are," Chito said, looking at me with desperation. "This kind gentleman was just asking what we're doing. Want to tell him?"

"Oh, well, yes," I replied slowly, wracking my brain for a convincing lie. "Well, we are going to a very unusual sort of surprise party. We're pretending to dress up as different people and surprise our friends. And that's why we need your help."

"Interesting," the clerk smiled. "Well, I'm happy to help. What can I do? I understand from your friend here that you need to learn some phrases in Spanish?"

"Yes," I replied, swallowing hard. "We need to learn how to say, *'I'm sorry to wake you, but I think your car is on fire.'*"

"Uh, hmmm," the clerk said, his eyebrows raised nearly to his hairline. "That's a very strange phrase to want to learn."

"Yes," Chito said, his forehead puckered. "But it's just a joke. Surely you understand."

The clerk stared at him, then looked at me. "Is that all you need from me?"

"Not exactly," I said, grimacing. "I also need to learn how to say, *'I'm the cleaning lady. I come on this day every month, to clean the house.'*"

The clerk stared at us.

"Are you trying to buy drugs?" he leaned forward, his voice barely a whisper. "Because if that's what this is about, I know people who can help you. You don't need to go to strangers in the street, mis amigos."

"No, not that!" Chito replied, horrified. "We're surprising a friend, that's all!"

I pulled a twenty dollar bill out of my pocket and slid it across the desk.

"Do you take American currency?" I asked hopefully.

The clerk grinned wide.

"Of course we do," he said sweetly, whipping the bill off the table and tucking it into his interior jacket pocket. "Now, what can I help you with? Anything you want, my friends."

# CHAPTER 52

IN JUST UNDER AN HOUR, we'd slapped together disguises for Chito and me, along with enough material for three petrol bombs.

Willis had them carefully packed in a wooden crate, and peeled back the sheet hiding them from view to show me. "There they are," he said, his eyes glinting with suppressed excitement.

*"He must be a bit of a firebug,"* I thought to myself. The little glass milk jugs inside were filled to the brim with fuel, a dirty fuel-soaked rag shoved into the top of each one.

"We light them here, and throw," Willis said. "Guaranteed fire, every time."

"Every time?" Chito asked sharply. "How many times have you made these, exactly?"

Willis just grinned, and pulled the sheet back over his box.

Dessie had outfitted me in a plain black skirt and top, with a large apron and gloves sticking out of the pockets. She helped me pin my hair up under a handkerchief, and filled a large bucket with rags and cleaning solution. We borrowed a broom and mop from the helpful desk clerk, who waved at us as we packed ourselves into the Fords out front.

"Have fun at your party!" he smiled.

"Some party," Hudson grinned, as Willis carefully eased himself into the passenger seat, the box of petrol bombs cradled on his lap. "You might even say it's going to be a *dynamite* time."

"Explosive fun for all," Willis cracked, laughing with Hudson.

Patrick scowled at me from the front seat, and Hudson grinned at me from the back seat where he was crammed in next to

Marceau. Patrick had volunteered to go along with them as they stole the car and set it on fire.

I suspected he felt he had to supervise Hudson and Willis.

Cap was driving Chito and me, and planned to watch from a nearby spot as Chito and I went to the gang's house. Chito would go first and tell them about the car, and I would go in immediately after they left.

I noticed that Cap had brought his pistol and his rifle along, just in case. He'd scanned my body as I appeared in my new outfit. "Where are you hiding your gun?"

"Right here," I said, patting my apron pocket. It was heavy and pulled my apron down, but I had nowhere else to store it for easy accessibility.

We were all silent as we drove slowly through the empty streets. It was a cloudy night, and the moon and stars were blotted out with the heavy blackness that lay over the city. Patrick drove slowly, looking out for the occasional cat that darted across the road, and we followed right behind him.

As we approached the blocks surrounding Trimboli's house, we turned off our headlights and drove in the pitch black. About a block away, Patrick and Cap parked in a small alley and we slid out, not daring to slam the doors shut.

"This is it," Cap whispered in the darkness. "Remember, if you get caught, ask for your ambassador. Don't talk to the police about this. State that you're American—or Canadian—and insist that you must speak first with your ambassador. Or a diplomat. That it's a matter of life or death."

"We won't get caught," Willis replied. Cap and Patrick both sighed.

"Let's go!" Hudson whispered, slapping Cap on the back and tiptoeing away.

The seven of us moved swiftly down the alley, Hudson and Willis carefully carrying the box of petrol bombs together. We reached the house within a few minutes, and ducked down under a nearby hedge of bushes.

"Looks quiet," Marceau breathed, as we stared at the gang's hideout. As it always was, their Ford was parked out front on the street directly in front of the house.

"Showtime, guys," Willis whispered, ducking across the street. Hudson went with him, and they carefully climbed over the door of the Ford and silently hoisted themselves in.

"Oh gosh," Marceau exclaimed softly, uttering a curse, then followed them.

In the darkness, only the faintest light streaking across the sky, we could barely see Marceau. I could hear the soft pop of the engine lid being opened, however. We strained to hear what he was doing, but could only hear the occasional snip and screech of metal.

Suddenly, the car rumbled to life.

"Good boy," I whispered, crouched down under the bushes. In the silence of the early morning, the engine sounded deafening.

Marceau quickly whipped the car down the street, headed toward the empty lot. The lot was half a block away, still visible from the house, but far enough away from any other homes that we hoped it wouldn't do damage to anyone.

The sun was just starting to warm the dark night, the faint purple of morning glowing overhead. I glanced at Cap, who had his lips compressed in a tight line. He was watching for the eventual blaze that we'd see down the street.

The moments felt endless as we waited in the dark. The Ford must be down there by now, right? What was taking so long?

"Come on, come on," Chito whispered, watching next to me. "What's the hold up?"

"Did something happen?" Cap whispered, so close to my ear that I could feel his hot breath on the side of my head. "What if they got caught?"

Suddenly, we saw one, then two rags light up with flame at the end of the street.

"There!" Chito exclaimed, as we watched the flames soar through the air, a dazzling orange blur, and crash loudly in the car. Instantly, a column of fire blazed up several feet, and settled into the upholstery, burning brightly.

Another rag was lit and tossed, the sound of shattering glass in the air. They must have popped open the engine and thrown the last one there, because the Ford shot flames into the air, illuminating two sprinting figures running away.

We heard tires squeal as Patrick whipped them down the street, speeding away from the scene of the crime.

*"We actually did it. We just committed arson,"* I thought wildly. *"And automobile theft, too."*

This couldn't really be my life, could it?

# CHAPTER 53

"GO!" CAP WHISPERED, and Chito took off without another word, running across the street. A few seconds later, we could hear him pounding wildly on the door.

"¡Despierta!" he yelled. "¡Tu auto está en llamas!"

*Wake up, your car is on fire!*

No one came to the door.

Chito kept pounding, repeating his urgent yells. "¡Tu auto está en llamas!"

I watched, my heart in my throat. What if they asked Chito something else? He didn't know any other phrase except this one. This would never work. I waited with bated breath, concern written on my face.

Abruptly, the door was wrenched open.

"Cosa sta succedendo?" yelled a dark-haired man in rumpled pajamas. It was Italian.

"He asked 'what's going on?'" I whispered for Cap.

"¡Tu auto está en llamas!" Chito yelled again. He shifted and suddenly, I saw the man's pistol, pointed at Chito's gut.

My mouth went dry.

In desperation, Chito repeated the only Spanish phrase he knew. "¡Tu auto está en llamas!" he screamed, pointing at the blaze down the block. Then I heard him yell, "Ford! On fire!"

The man screamed over his shoulder in Italian, and Trimboli came sprinting out, cursing. Another man pushed out the door, and Masso emerged a second later.

Cap and I watched breathlessly. Chito was now face-to-face with four hardened criminals. What would they do?

Trimboli took one look at the car and went sprinting down the street, swearing loudly. The other three went running after him, headed toward the burning wreckage.

Chito started to run after them, but suddenly took a hard right and sprinted quickly toward the alley where we'd hidden the car. He would be circling around to pick me up in just a few minutes.

I didn't wait for Cap to tell me. I was already standing up, my bucket in one hand and my broom and mop in the other. I cut across the street, and climbed onto the porch.

I balanced the broom and mop under one arm, carrying a large bucket filled with cleaning supplies in the other hand.

*"No one will look twice at the cleaning lady,"* I thought, forcing myself to relax. *"I can make an excuse and let myself out quickly if someone catches me."*

Still, my heart was racing.

I walked toward the house, head down, trying to look like I'd done this a thousand times before. I hummed to myself as I climbed up the sagging wooden porch and set my bucket down, searching my pockets for the keys.

Naturally, I didn't actually have keys to the house. But just in case any neighbors were watching, I wanted to put on a good show.

I knocked on the door, knowing the four men were at the scene of the car fire already. But just in case there was someone else inside—someone we didn't know about—I could pretend it was the wrong house and move on.

No one answered.

I tried the door handle. It was locked, even though the men had sprinted away in a panic. Maybe Trimboli was the type who slept with the key around his neck.

I quickly leaned my broom and mop against the house, next to the front door. Vainly, I hoped that if the men came back and caught me inside, they'd see them and assume I was just the cleaning lady. If they went in, expecting someone to be in the house as they walked in the door, there was less of a chance they'd shoot me—or so I told myself.

Still carrying my bucket full of rags, I carried it around back and set it next to a small door at the rear of the house. There was a window here, also with curtains drawn.

Looking around to make sure no one was watching, I put my ear up to the door. I listened for a few moments, but it was quiet inside.

*"Try the easiest way first,"* I thought, trying the handle of the back door. It was locked.

Drat. Well, we hadn't expected it to be open. I was prepared for another attempt.

Quickly, I searched around to see if there was a key hidden anywhere. With a rental house, I'd expect the owners to hide a spare under a rock or flower pot.

Unfortunately, the yard was completely bare, and with the exception of the one flower pot on the front porch—now full of dead flowers—there wasn't even a place to hide anything.

Sighing, I returned to the back porch and examined the door. It was an exterior door, so probably solid wood instead of the hollow wood that interior doors usually had. However, the hinges weren't visible, which meant I could try to kick it in.

The lock was mounted just above the door handle. I knew that this was likely the weakest spot in the door.

Willis had warned me I might have to kick a door in, if I couldn't find another way inside.

"Be careful, Andi," Willis had cautioned me. "You can break your foot if you kick the lock or the handle itself. Keep your feet flat, and don't strike with the ball of your foot—use your heel. Make sure your knees are bent, too, otherwise you'll hurt yourself."

I stood in front of the door and breathed in, summoning my strength. I planted myself, hoping I didn't get injured. Swiftly, I kicked as hard as I could, aiming my heel right above the lock.

I nearly jumped at the loud crack it made, the entire door shuddering under the force. It didn't open, though, and I nearly fell backwards off the small stoop as I stumbled to regain my balance.

Surely the neighbors had heard me now. My eyes darted around in fear and I held my breath, waiting for someone to yell at me.

I glanced around at the surrounding houses, then the apartment complex across the street. Should I go over to a neighbor's house and see if they had a key? I could pretend to be a new housekeeper who'd lost the keys, and who was terrified of losing her new client.

Even as I thought of it, I frowned. My Spanish wasn't that good, and the neighbors might recognize my face from the newspapers.

They'd be sure to do a double take, anyway, over seeing such a tall woman at their door. I didn't want anyone to become suspicious and mention me later, either. And frankly, I didn't have that kind of time.

I had a few minutes, at the most.

I had to try the door again. If I couldn't get in the door, I'd have to break the window. That was my last option, but my least favorite because it'd be loud, time-consuming, and I'd likely cut myself on the broken glass.

Positioning myself in front of the door, I again kicked as hard as I could. The door popped open with a loud bang, the heavy wood crashing hard against the wall inside.

I didn't even have time to congratulate myself before I was ducking through the door, my cleaning bucket still in my hand.

"Hola, estoy aquí para limpiar la casa!" I called, then switched to what I hoped passed for heavily accented English. "Hello, I am here to clean the house!"

What I'd do if I encountered one of Trimboli's men was beyond me, at this point. What cleaning lady kicked in the door of a client's home?

I moved quickly through the dark rooms, listening to see if I heard creaks or shuffles that indicated anyone was inside. The back door opened to the kitchen, where bottles of alcohol and a few bags of food sat on the counters and the small wooden table in the center. Trash was littered across the floor.

The kitchen was separated from a small room with a closed door. With bated breath, I eased open the door. Inside, a small desk and dresser sat empty, the curtains in the room drawn shut.

Easing my way over the wooden floor, I passed the living room. A couch and two sagging armchairs sat in the room, a tiny coffee table and a stack of magazines in the center of the space. Half a dozen empty beer bottles sat on the coffee table, smelling like stale, warm malt. With the curtains drawn, the whole house was dark inside.

The front door opened to the living room, but the bedrooms were across the way. All four rooms had their doors shut. I gulped, still holding my bucket in front of me.

I eased open the first door, and jumped. Someone was staring back at me. I stifled a scream, feeling like my heart was going to burst open. A second later, I realized I was staring at my own reflection in a large mirror above a pedestal sink.

It was the bathroom.

I bit my lip. I didn't have time to panic. I had only moments until Trimboli and Masso and the others might come back.

Quickly, I closed the bathroom door and opened the next door. It was a small bedroom, with two beds inside. The sheets were rumpled and untidy, and clothes were strewn across the floor at the foot of both beds.

I tiptoed inside and swiftly searched the clothes, looking for any notes or maps that might indicate where they were planning to go next. There was nothing.

I dropped down to my knees, and searched under both beds, then pulled out the lining of the pair of boots sitting next to the nightstand. There was nothing tucked inside.

Sitting up, I scanned the room. I couldn't see anywhere else to hide anything, so I stood up and walked to the next room.

Feeling braver now, I swung open the door and slipped inside. There was a larger bed here, and the clothes were stacked in piles on a chair. A large map of central Europe sat folded next to the clothes.

I bet this was Trimboli's room.

There were two large bags sitting on the floor. I opened one, and found that it was full of ammunition. I squinted at it. It looked like something for a pistol, but I wasn't sure. I grabbed a box and shoved it in my apron pocket. Cap and Hudson might find it useful to know what kind of weapons the gang had.

I opened the second bag, and found wigs, hats, glasses, and a few other random accessories inside. Clearly, they were prepared to disguise themselves, just like we were doing.

Again, I dropped to my knees and looked under the bed. Finding nothing, I then slipped my hand under the mattress and felt around. Nothing there, either.

*"Where's Paz?"* I thought to myself frantically. He had to be in here.

Pushing myself up, I darted to the next room. This one had a single bed, too, and a small closet.

*"Finally,"* I breathed a sigh of relief. Paz must be stashed away in there, in the darkness. I swung the door open, a smile ready.

It was empty.

"No!" I exclaimed quietly, cursing. Where could he be? Was he not here? Had they hidden Paz somewhere else entirely?

I spun around in the room. Whoever this was, he was a slob, too, his clothes tossed across his bed. I searched, but couldn't find anything. Had I missed anywhere else?

Maybe they'd left a clue in the trash?

I darted back to the kitchen, carrying my bucket. I dumped the trash bin over, looking for anything that might be evidence, but all that was inside were discarded receipts, a few tissues, and remains of the meals they'd eaten.

Oh, gosh. I would have to return to the team empty-handed. I didn't have a single scrap of useful information for us.

I groaned. I knew I was out of time, and had to get out of the house. Cap had told me I had two, maybe three minutes to get in and out. I had no idea how long I'd been inside already. I had to go.

Grabbing my bucket, I hustled through the kitchen and out the back door. I pulled the door closed behind me. The wood was busted near the lock, and the door didn't close all the way. They were sure to notice it.

But we only had forty-eight hours to find Paz. We didn't have time for a foolproof plan.

Not anymore.

# CHAPTER 54

HOLDING MY BUCKET, I walked around to the front of the house, resuming my humming. I grabbed my broom and mop and tucked them under my arm, trudging down the street at what I hoped was a reasonable pace.

I kept my head low, but my eyes darted frantically all around me, watching people.

When I heard a car come up behind me, I turned to look. Chito was driving, Cap sitting in the back seat.

"Thank God," Cap breathed, standing to open the door for me. Chito didn't even slow the car to a complete stop as I launched myself in and he drove away.

"He's not there," I shook my head. "No sign of him."

"Damn it," Cap exclaimed, slapping the seat in frustration.

Chito merely sighed, driving us a few blocks away into an alley. Cap was already untying my apron and throwing it into the bottom of the car floor. As we pulled up next to a large dumpster, Cap swiftly grabbed the broom and mop and threw them in the trash.

I pulled the handkerchief off my head and reached for an elaborate hat that was sitting on the passenger seat, waiting for me. With Chito and Cap both wearing proper hats, we'd look like different people now, if anyone spotted us.

"Good?" Chito asked, starting to pull away.

"Yes," Cap said, leaning back against the seat. "Get us home. And make sure Trimboli doesn't follow us back."

Chito pulled through the alley, popping out on a pedestrian street on the other side. He swiftly drove us back to our new hotel, on the other side of town.

Now that we were putting ourselves in the dangerous position of interfering with Trimboli and Masso in person, we wanted to take every possible precaution. While I was breaking into the house, Dessie had rented rooms at a second hotel, several blocks from the first. Half the team—the ones who'd been involved in the illegal activity this morning—would be spending the night there tonight just in case Trimboli managed to track us to the first hotel.

"So Paz wasn't in there at all?" Cap asked, when we finally got a few blocks farther from the house. The veins in his neck stood out from tension. "Was there any indication they were holding him there?"

"None," I said desperately. "I looked everywhere. And I checked for hiding spots. No ropes, no restraints, nothing. I thought maybe there'd be a map or an address or something, but I couldn't find anything."

Chito groaned, throwing his head back in frustration. "Nothing?"

"No."

He turned in his seat and looked at me again. "How did you get in?"

"I had to kick in the door."

Cap's forehead wrinkled, worried. "Did you hurt yourself at all?"

"No," I replied. "I'm just mad that I didn't find anything. Well, I grabbed a box of bullets, so we at least can tell what kind of weapons they have."

"That's better than nothing," Cap sighed, but I knew he was as disappointed as I was. We'd all hoped Paz was bound and gagged inside the house, and that I'd be able to get him out.

Chito whipped us into the new hotel. Dessie shot out of the lobby doors before we even finished parking.

"He wasn't there?" she cried, her face crestfallen.

"No," I replied, hopping out. "I'm sorry. I looked all over. There was no indication they'd kept him in the house. They must have him at a secondary location."

Dessie moaned. "Paz....where on earth are they hiding you?"

"Are the others back?" Cap asked, removing his hat and raking his hand through his hair.

"Willis and Hudson and Marceau went up to change clothes. Patrick is in the lobby, with Bernard and Leonce and me," Dessie replied. "Claude is on surveillance duty."

I followed her in, Cap and Chito on my heels. Patrick stood up, anxious, as we entered the lobby. "How did it go?"

"He wasn't there," I replied quietly. "Cap, where do we want to talk about this?"

"Our room," he replied. "Dessie, where'd you put us? Can you lead us there?"

She pulled a key out of her pocket and nodded, leading us down the hall. Patrick walked with me, while the others trailed behind. She reached a room at the very end of the hall, and opened the door.

"I asked for the quietest hall, without other guests," she told us as she swung open the door. "There's no one booked on this floor but us, apparently."

"I'll wait for the other three," Leonce volunteered, stepping out. The rest of us settled in, waiting anxiously for the others. A few moments later, the door swung open and Leonce, Hudson, Willis, and Marceau piled in.

"Well hey there, fellow fugitives!" Willis crowed, grinning at me where I sat next to Chito. "How did it go? I assume he wasn't in there, judging by the fact that we're all sitting here crammed into a hotel room?"

"No," I replied. Quickly, I recounted my story of searching the rooms. "I looked everywhere. No sign of him, no clues where they might be holding him. They must be holding him hostage in a different location."

"How'd you get into the house?" Marceau asked.

"I had to kick open the door," I replied. "It took two tries, but I got in."

Hudson winked at Cap. "Did you ever think you'd be marrying the kind of girl that kicked in doors?"

Cap rolled his eyes. "Not exactly."

"Oh, did it change your mind about her?" Hudson asked, his eyebrows raised. He turned to me and grinned cheekily. "What do you say? If Cap isn't interested, I am. Don't you think 'Mrs. Andiamo Landry' has a certain ring to it?"

"In your dreams, Hudson," I replied irritably. "Can't you ever be serious when you need to be?"

"Hudson, tell us what happened," Chito interrupted, as Cap sighed loudly in frustration. "Did the petrol bombs go according to plan?"

"Worked like a charm," Hudson smiled, elbowing Willis. "The boy here has the magic touch when it comes to flammable objects."

"Hey, we all have our talents," Willis shrugged. The manner of their joking gave me a glimpse of how they must've been as troublesome little boys.

"What happened to the car?" Cap asked. "Did you disable it?"

"Oh, we disabled it alright," Willis smiled wickedly. "We hit it with all three bombs—two in the body of the car, and one in the engine. When it hit that fuel line, it just blazed. It went up in minutes. It's an empty black shell now. There's no way they'll ever be able to drive that car again."

Bernard groaned. "What a loss."

"A loss?" Willis snapped. "Did you forget they did the same thing to all six of our Fords? I call it payback, plain and simple."

"Enough, you two. This buys us time. In order to go anywhere, they'll have to get a new automobile," Cap said, tapping his chin absently. "That'll buy us a day or two, at least."

"Unless they steal one," Patrick pointed out. "I wouldn't put it past them. They're criminals, after all."

"True," Cap said, thinking hard. "Claude's watching them now. I'll be curious what he observes today. They can't make a police report on that car, because the police will recognize them from their mug shots. That means they can't fill out an insurance report. So they'll either have to buy a car with cash, or steal one."

"I didn't see a bag of cash," I supplied. "I bet they steal one."

"Which means they'll have to find one and come up with a plan of their own, to steal it," Cap filled in. "Hopefully, that slows them down and gives us more time to find Paz."

"What's next, then?" Hudson said, propping his feet up on the desk. "No Paz, no idea where he is, no clues in the house, and a ticking clock on the ransom delivery. What do we do now?"

Bernard checked his watch. "Do you want hour-by-hour updates on the time, as the clock runs down on the deadline?"

"No," Marceau blurted, as Dessie bent over and put her head in her hands, her long blonde hair falling forward around her face. She sat there, motionless. Marceau patted her back, looking concerned.

For several moments, the room was silent. We wracked our brains, thinking. I reflected desperately that it had seemed like this was all we did lately, huddled together in tiny hotel rooms trying to come up with schemes to save Paz.

I was tired of it. We needed more action.

# CHAPTER 55

"LET'S KIDNAP ONE OF them," Leonce said quietly, sending shockwaves through the room.

Chito was the first to respond, as the rest of us stared in horror at Leonce.

"I don't know what kind of crackpot idea that is, but it's not happening," he exclaimed. "I looked the other way when there was the suggestion to steal the police file, even though it was breaking the law. I justified stealing their car and setting it on fire, even though we're risking prison ourselves if anyone finds out about that. But kidnapping? I draw the line there!"

"They're criminals, though," Willis jumped in. "What other option do we have? We can capture one of them and force him to tell us where they're hiding Paz."

"I say we go back to the police and tell them the whole thing," Chito said stubbornly, his jaw tense. "We admit that we took the file because we were desperate to find him. Face the punishment they decide to dole out, but we get them to help us."

"And what if they *don't* help us?" Hudson asked, raising one eyebrow. "They didn't help us before. Who says they will now? They're even less likely to want to, if they know we stole from them."

"I won't do it," Chito replied, shaking his head. "I won't become like them and commit the same crimes they do."

"It's Paz's life we're talking about!" Dessie exclaimed, lifting her head. Her face was white and strained. "Can't you suspend your morality for a day in order to save his life? What kind of selfish monster *are* you?"

"He's not selfish," Marceau said quickly, coming to Chito's defense. "I can't say that I'm comfortable with the thought of kidnapping them, either. I mean, what are we going to do with them if we even manage to kidnap one of their men? It's not like he's going to tell us where they have Paz hidden, and then go about his merry way."

"Easy," Willis replied, a hard look in his eyes. "We torture it out of him."

"Hold on a minute," Cap lifted his hands. "Let's think this through—"

"Don't be a baby, Grant," Willis snapped, glaring at him. "You know this is our only real shot. It's our *last* shot, probably. We have to kidnap one of Trimboli's men and force him to give up the location of where they're hiding Paz."

It didn't escape my notice that Willis had addressed him by his first name, not his title. Judging by Cap's frown, he took note of it, too.

"I won't do it," Chito proclaimed, folding his arms across his chest. "I don't care what you say to try to convince me. You can't change my mind. I won't sink to that level. We aren't those people."

"I agree," Marceau said. "I won't have a hand in this, either."

Hudson looked around the room. "Should we take a vote?"

I stared at Cap, who glanced at me. I wasn't sure where he stood. I guess I was about to find out.

"All in favor of kidnapping one of Trimboli's gang and getting the information out of him—whatever it takes?" Hudson asked, slowly raising his hand in the air.

Willis and Dessie shot their hands up immediately. After a moment, Leonce slowly lifted his hand.

"All opposed to a kidnapping?" Hudson continued.

Marceau, Cap, and Chito raised their hands.

"You actually have to pick a side, you know," Dessie growled at me, noticing that I didn't vote one way or another.

"Patrick and Bernard didn't vote, either," I replied, squinting in embarrassment.

"It's four in favor of the kidnapping, three opposed to it," Hudson said, staring in turn at each of us who hadn't yet voted. "You three will be the tiebreakers. So what will it be?"

Bernard spoke up. "I don't want to go to prison over this. We don't even know if they would tell us the truth about where they've hidden Paz. My vote is no."

"So then that's four to four," Hudson replied, staring me down.

I hesitated, glancing at Patrick. He was lost in his own thoughts, a grimace on his face.

"Vote already," Willis complained. I shook my head.

"I'm sorry," I said, glancing at Cap. "I think we should kidnap them. Paz's life is on the line. It's not my first choice, but it's the most viable option for us right now."

"I agree," Patrick said, nodding. "It's wrong, and it's a huge risk. We could go away for a long time if we get caught. But if it gets a violent criminal off the streets and saves a good man from death, it's worth it."

Cap avoided my eyes.

"Good," Hudson replied, rubbing his hands together. "We've made a decision, and we can move forward. How will we kidnap him?"

The group started tossing around ideas, but I sat silently, watching Cap. He and Chito both studiously avoided making eye contact with me. I felt awful. For the first time, I'd sided against the entire Gallivanter team. Would they hold it against me?

I had my answer as Cap interrupted the brainstorming to give everyone a short break to use the restroom and get something to eat.

"Eat fast," he commanded, his eyes sweeping the room. "Hudson, Patrick, you're up for surveillance duty next. The rest of you, we'll continue brainstorming ideas here as soon as you've gotten a meal. Fill up. It might be a while until we eat again."

I stood up, hoping to talk to him privately. Instead, he shrugged me off, ducking away from me every time I tried to speak with him. Hurt, I stood in the middle of the room, staring at his back.

Patrick came up beside me.

"He's mad at you, isn't he?" he observed quietly, looking toward Cap.

"He and Chito both are. I've never sided with the Chinooks before. I think they feel betrayed."

Patrick sighed. "I'm scheduled to go out on surveillance with Hudson. Want to tag along? They can brainstorm without you for a while. And it'll get you out of the hot seat for a bit. Get your mind off your misery."

"Yeah, that sounds great," I replied, smiling gratefully. "Thanks."

Patrick checked his pocket watch. "We leave in half an hour," he said. "Why don't you eat, change, and meet me in the lobby in twenty-five minutes or so?"

"Perfect."

I waited until all the others left our room, hoping to chat with Cap, but he slipped out with Marceau. Gritting my teeth, I changed quickly and slammed the door behind me, without leaving a note to tell him I was planning to do surveillance with Patrick and Hudson.

I'd let him figure out on his own that I was headed out for the night.

# CHAPTER 56

PATRICK WAS WAITING for me in the lobby when I came down. "Any luck talking it over with Cap?"

"Nope," I replied. "He ducked away before I could catch him. I don't know where he went. He's clearly avoiding me."

"Well, it's his loss," Patrick said, nodding as Hudson walked toward us. "Let's forget about it. We'll just enjoy our time, the three of us."

"She is ditching that wet blanket, after all!" Hudson greeted me, a wicked grin on his face. "Welcome to the Chinook Voyageurs, mademoiselle. We have great fun here. You'll get along with us splendidly."

"It's just for a while," I smiled in spite of myself. "I'm still a Gallivanter. You know that."

"Yes, but do they?" Hudson smirked.

Patrick rolled his eyes and cleared his throat. "Enough shop talk, Hudson. Give her a break. She's coming with to get her mind off of things."

"Oh, good," Hudson replied. "We can get your mind on all sorts of other interesting topics, can't we, Patty?"

"We'll start with discussing your university pranks," Patrick said, shooting me an amused glance. "Has he ever told you that he nearly got expelled? We had to write a letter to the dean, talking him out of it."

I laughed as the three of us climbed into a Ford and jetted across town. We planned to do a few laps, driving around to look at Trimboli's house, then park and stroll through the neighborhood.

Hudson and Patrick regaled me with wild tales of their time at university together as we drove. Patrick had clearly been the studious, steady fellow who kept Hudson from getting himself in serious trouble. They were in the middle of telling me a story about their friends gutting a deer in the boiler room in their dormitory, when suddenly Patrick hushed us.

"Is that Masso leaving the house?" he asked, pointing toward the front door of the rental. In the descending gloom of early evening, it was hard to tell.

"Get out, get out!" Hudson cried, quickly pulling over and nearly pushing me out of the car. We tumbled out. "We'll follow him on foot!"

"What?" Patrick exclaimed, stopping in his tracks. "Follow him?"

I hesitated, but only for a fraction of a second. Impulsively, I followed along right behind Hudson.

Patrick gaped at us, frozen in place.

"Stop!" he whispered furtively, before rushing to catch up with me. He shook his head, lightly catching my wrist.

"We shouldn't be doing this," he hissed. "What if he sees us? Their car was destroyed today, and their home broken into and searched. They know someone's messing with them. They're bound to be on high alert, watching for trouble. He'll see us!"

"Be quiet!" Hudson commanded under his breath, his eyes locked on Masso's back. He was several lengths ahead of us, walking in the middle of the sidewalk with his head down.

"What if this is a trap?" Patrick continued, staring at Masso. "What if they were hoping we'd be watching them, and they're trying to draw us out?"

"I think he's walking toward the liquor store," I said quietly, trying to figure out what he was doing.

"It makes sense, doesn't it? They've walked to this liquor store before," Hudson whispered back. "And of all the days to want to drown your sorrows in booze, it'd be a day like today."

We continued to walk quickly behind him, darting around oblivious strangers selling fruit and chatting together on the sidewalk. Sure enough, he glanced up ahead and I saw his eyes linger on the small wooden sign above the door that proclaimed, in Spanish, "Alcohol y Licores Finos."

"What are we doing?" I breathed, as Masso turned and let himself in the door of the liquor store. The bell chimed as he walked inside.

The three of us crashed into each other with our sudden stop as we stood there, several feet away from the door, clutching each other with uncertainty.

"What are we going to do?" I repeated, my eyes on the door. We couldn't see into the windows, but I assumed that Masso was loading up on more beer, like I'd noticed in their kitchen and living room earlier that morning.

"I'm going in after him," Hudson said grimly, springing forward.

"Wait! Why? Stop!" Patrick and I both fumbled, grabbing wildly for him. "Hold on!"

But he was already too far ahead of us, moving purposefully toward the door of the liquor store and wrenching it open. Without a backward glance, he hurried through it and disappeared.

"No!" Patrick gasped, rushing to follow after him.

Oh no. We'd been seen. He'd be sure to recognize Hudson in that tiny store. All those weeks of our careful surveillance would come to an end in this exact moment, as Masso saw him. He'd blow our chance of kidnapping one of the men.

Unless...

No. We weren't ready.

*"Hold on!"* My brain screamed. *"He couldn't be trying to kidnap him right now, could he?"*

I scrambled inside after them.

# CHAPTER 57

THE LIQUOR SHOP WAS small, simple wooden shelves lined with hundreds of bottles of beer, wine, and other spirits.

A long wooden counter with a cash register separated us from the more expensive bottles of wine, their glassy jewel tones reflected in the electric lights overhead.

A glass-doored case of cigarettes sat in the middle of the room, and Masso stood leaning in front of it, both hands pressed to the glass, looking inside. Hudson was at the counter already and Patrick stood next to him, their backs to Masso.

Masso continued to peruse the contents of the cigarette case, obviously looking for something.

"Buenas tardes, caballeros," the owner chirped, a rotund man in a white shirt, tie, and a large apron. He stood behind the counter, beaming at the four people suddenly all inside his little shop.

"He was next," Hudson murmured, jerking his head behind him toward Masso, his back still facing him.

The store owner leaned over to Masso.

"Welcome back, señor," he said cheerfully. "Is there something I can help you with?"

"Yes, do you have any more of these cigarettes?" Masso asked in English, holding up a small red and white box. "I need a few more boxes."

Instantly, I recognized the coloring from the tiny scrap we'd found outside the crime scene where the Chinook Voyageurs had been attacked. They were cigarettes made exclusively in Italy, I knew from the tiny print on the back of the label. It had been the only clue we had to go on that they were Italian, until we saw that police file.

"Oh, you may have purchased the last box last time, but I'll go check," the man said, ducking into the back room.

As if in a dream, suddenly everything was happening in slow motion.

Hudson whirled around, reaching behind his jacket for the pistol he kept hidden in his waistband. Masso looked up in surprise, sudden recognition flashing in his dark eyes.

In a flash, Hudson had his gun out and pointed at Masso's head.

"I'll blow your brains out right here," Hudson growled quietly, his face a mask of murderous rage. "Just give me a reason."

Masso froze, his jaw twitching as he stared at Hudson. His hands were held out in front of him, as if to stop Hudson. As I stood watching in horror, Masso's right hand flinched, as if he was thinking about reaching for his own gun.

"Don't you dare," Patrick said, stepping out smoothly behind Hudson, his pistol now pointed at Masso's forehead. Holding the gun on him, he reached into Masso's waistband and pulled out a small pistol, tucking it into his own belt.

I could hear the sounds of the liquor store owner moving around in the back, his heavy footsteps dragging across the floor. "I think I have a few more packs of those cigarettes," he called, as I heard a crate being shoved around. "Give me just one more minute here."

Here in the main store, the four of us stood frozen in mid-action—Masso with his hands up, Patrick and Hudson with their guns to his head.

"What do you want?" Masso asked, his deep voice husky and heavily influenced by his Italian accent.

"You know what we want, you bastard," Hudson snarled. "Keep your hands where we can see them. We're going outside."

Just then, the shopkeeper emerged from the back, holding three packs of cigarettes.

"¡Duerido Dios!" he exclaimed, pulling up short and staring at us, confused.

"Outside," Hudson repeated, grabbing Masso by the collar and pushing him toward the door.

Masso stumbled forward, his hat falling off his head, but Hudson merely shoved his gun into Masso's shoulder blades and continued to push him out to the sidewalk. Patrick followed along, next to Masso, his gun now trained directly on Masso's heart.

This couldn't be happening. Not right now. We hadn't prepared for this.

But it was.

I stared at the store owner, who gaped at me, his mouth open in an expression of shock.

"I apologize," I said, the words pouring out of my mouth before I even had time to think of them. "We're here on behalf of the United States of America's government. You've heard of the Bureau of Investigation, right?"

He nodded, his eyes big.

"Well, we're here as undercover agents. We've been tracking this man for weeks. And this was our operation to get him, and take him back to justice for the crimes he's committed," I said, hoping I sounded convincingly confident as I lied through my teeth.

I reached into my own waistband and pulled out my pistol. "That's why we all have these," I said, showing him. "Standard issue for all BI agents, of course."

"Oh my," the man said, putting the cigarettes on the counter and wiping his hands nervously on his apron. "I didn't know they employed women as agents for the government?"

Goodness gracious. Did this man really have the audacity to ask me something like that, when we were in the middle of kidnapping a hardened criminal from his shop?

"Of course they do," I snapped. "Women make the best field agents. No one ever suspects us."

"Right," he blinked, still staring. I backed toward the door, tucking my gun back in my pants.

"Thank you, sir," I said, starting to open the door.

"Wait a minute," he called, still staring at me from behind the counter. "I sold that man a lot of cigarettes. And a lot of beer. Am I going to be in some sort of trouble here?"

I thought quickly.

"You won't be in any trouble, as long as you don't tell a soul about this," I said, my voice stern. "This is an active investigation. If you so much dare to tell your wife, or your neighbor, or your next customer about what happened here, we'll come back and shut this place down. And then I'll personally drag you through the American court systems for impeding an international investigation. You'll lose everything that matters to you. And you might even face jail time."

"Oh," he replied, the color draining from his cheeks. His jowls sagged as he opened and closed his mouth. "I won't say anything to anyone. Don't worry."

"I never worry," I replied, pushing my way through the door. "I'm packing heat."

# CHAPTER 58

OUTSIDE, HUDSON AND Patrick both had Masso's arms pinned behind him, guns trained on him as they walked down the street.

They were several yards in front of me already, moving fast. Hudson was leading him back to the car. I hurried to catch up, hoping my tall frame would block anyone's view of the two men holding their pistols on Masso.

"This is madness!" I sputtered as I reached them. "There are dozens of people out here to witness this!"

"So?" Hudson spat, marching Masso down the middle of the sidewalk.

We reached a cluster of men, their hats tilted back on their heads as they chatted. One leaned over a broom. They glanced at us curiously for a moment, suspending their conversation, but then shrugged and moved slightly to the left, giving us space to pass them. They resumed talking without a second glance.

I risked a glance over my shoulder as we passed them, sure they'd raise the alarm after seeing Hudson and Patrick with their guns to Masso's back. But they didn't even look at us.

Were we going to get away with this bold action?

The car was parked haphazardly on the side of the street where we'd left it, abruptly, when we jumped out in pursuit of Masso a few moments before.

When we reached it, Hudson spoke.

"Andi, reach into my left pocket and pull out the keys," he commanded, his tone unflinching and hard. "You're driving. We're going to keep a close eye on our friend Mr. Rua here."

Without hesitation, I stepped up to Hudson. As I did, Masso studied me for the first time, his eyes narrowing with coldness.

Unexpectedly, he swore and spit at me. I felt the warm glob land on my neck.

"Hey!" Patrick roared, shoving Masso into the side of the Ford with a loud crash. He yelped as he collided with the metal door.

Patrick yanked him back, nearly pulling him off his feet. Masso looked like an oversized rag doll, being tossed around by Hudson and Patrick.

I reached into Hudson's pocket quickly, fishing out the keys. I wiped Masso's spit from my neck with the back of my hand as Hudson climbed into the back seat, twisting Masso's arm painfully as he ascended into the back.

Masso swore angrily in Italian. Patrick kept a firm grasp on his other arm, hopping up into the back. As he was securely sandwiched between them, their guns held low and against either side of his pelvis, I cranked the engine on.

I guided the Ford down the dark street quickly, heading toward the hotel. Behind me, I heard Patrick ask in French, "Shouldn't we blindfold him or something, so he doesn't see where we're going?"

Clever, I thought. Masso could apparently understand English, but hopefully he didn't speak French.

If we spoke French in front of him, most of the team—including me—could converse together without him understanding us.

I heard the sounds of Hudson pulling off his jacket. Glancing back, I saw Hudson wrapping it tightly around Masso's face, covering his head.

Once the knot was tied behind his head, using the sleeves, Hudson shoved him down, face first, toward the floorboards. Masso groaned, the sound muffled by the thick fabric. Hudson kept his left hand wrapped around Masso's arm, which was still pinned behind him, and had the gun pressed to the base of his skull.

"What are we going to do when we get to the hotel?" I asked in French.

"I don't know," Hudson sighed. "You'll have to go in and get Cap. And Willis."

A few minutes later, I glimpsed the hotel. I guided the car to the closest alley to the hotel, backing us into the shadows.

"Wait here," I said, jumping out and running to the lobby doors.

# CHAPTER 59

I THREW OPEN THE HOTEL doors, but none of the team were sitting in the lobby.

Frantically, I checked the clock on the mantle. Drat, we'd hardly been gone at all. They must still be eating. That meant they'd spread out at restaurants around the area, together. There was no telling when they'd get back.

Thinking on the fly, I ran up to my room. I grabbed my belt and dug through my bag, finding a gauzy yellow shirt. I held it up—it could work as a gag.

I searched Cap's bag and found a couple of old handkerchiefs that he kept on hand to keep the dust off his face when we traveled through the desert. I grabbed one and dashed downstairs again.

Dessie, Leonce, and Marceau were just coming in together. "Hey, you're back already?" Marceau asked, surprised. "Aren't you supposed to be on the surveillance shift still?"

Clutching my armful of clothing under one arm, I grabbed his elbow with my free hand. "Where's Cap?" I asked, my tone urgent.

"I think he went out to dinner with the rest of your team," he said. "I saw Bernard and Chito down here earlier, and Chito was talking about some new place he spotted—"

"Where?" I asked desperately.

"I don't know," he replied, staring at me. "What's wrong?"

Dessie and Leonce were a few steps away, also staring at me. I looked at them wildly. "We got Masso."

"What?" Marceau uttered, his body visibly reacting. "What do you mean? You saw him?"

"No. He's in the car *right now*."

"What?" Dessie said, taking a step forward. "You captured him?"

I nodded, my eyes wide.

"How? When?" Marceau cried, shaking his head. "What on earth? How did this happen? You just left!"

"No!" Leonce gasped, his face white. "Where are we going to put him? We're not ready for this. We didn't plan anything yet!"

Dessie was the only one not frozen at the news. She sprang through the lobby doors out into the darkness. In the glow of the lamp, I could see her hair flying as she spun her head from side to side, looking for the car.

I ran out after her. "That way!" I pointed, jogging toward the alley.

Dessie followed me as I sprinted toward the car. Hudson and Patrick were still where I left them, Masso pinned down in the seat.

"Let me see him!" she hissed.

"Hold on now," Patrick hesitated, as Hudson hauled Masso up by the collar.

"Let me see his face," Dessie cried, her face contorted in an ugly mask of anger.

Hudson grimly yanked the jacket up off his face, as Masso recoiled. His eyes darted around, taking in the surroundings, glancing at Hudson and Patrick and me, and then landing on Dessie. I saw him flinch with recognition.

Without invitation, Dessie wrenched open the passenger door and climbed up into the front seat of the Ford, balancing on her knees. "Remember me?" she said, glaring at Masso.

He said nothing, but gave her a derisive half-smile.

Quick as lightning, Dessie's fist snaked out and crunched hard against his nose. His head flung back, and Hudson and Patrick braced against his body's movement. He howled in pain, the blood already spurting out. With his hands still pinned behind his back, he could do nothing to ebb the flow that dripped down his mouth and chin. I could tell that his nose was broken.

Dessie swore at him.

"That's for slapping me to the ground!" she shrieked, and pulled her fist back before any of us could utter a word. She popped him hard in the right eye, and he cried out.

"Stop!" I said, racing up to hold Dessie back. "We have to get him inside! We can't let people hear him!"

"Jeepers, I can't believe this," Marceau uttered, staring in shock having followed us to the car. He and Leonce stood next to the rear of the car, looking up. "What are we going to do? We can't take him into our hotel room?"

"Speak French," I said hastily. "He can't understand it. He knows English, apparently."

"We have to get him into a room, at least temporarily," Hudson responded quickly, switching to French. "We don't have anywhere else to put him tonight, and it's getting late. We need to get him out of the car and out of view of any witnesses."

"Where the hell is Cap?" Patrick asked, looking around. "We need him!"

"He's still at dinner," Marceau responded. "He and Chito and Bernard went out on their own. We don't know where."

I handed Patrick my belt. "This should work for temporary handcuffs, right?" I asked, unfolding the handkerchief to make a large square. Deftly, I rolled it into a long rectangular shape and reached up to tie it around Masso's eyes.

He glared at me, his right eye already swelling after Dessie's punch. I didn't bother to be delicate as I slapped the handkerchief over his eyes, pulling the ends tight and yanking a firm knot in it.

While I worked, Patrick and Hudson laced the belt through his arms several times and cinched them together, clasping the belt behind his back.

I picked up the gauzy yellow shirt and crumpled it up into a small ball, shoving it into Masso's mouth and tying the ends of the sleeves together, behind his head.

"There," I said, staring grimly at him. "Now he's bound and gagged, at the very least."

"How are we going to get him inside?" Marceau asked, still speaking French.

Dessie, the only one of us who wasn't fluent, was spinning her head back and forth, furiously trying to understand what we were discussing. I stared at her. Even in the dim light from the street lights, with no makeup on, she was beautiful.

"We use Dessie as a distraction," I said, studying her. She whipped her head toward me, catching her name as I spoke rapid-fire French. "We send her in first, and have her flirt with the desk clerk. Get his attention away from the lobby door. Then we sneak him into the first room we can reach."

"That'd be mine," Leonce interjected. "I'm the first room when you come up the stairs."

"Perfect," I replied. "We throw Hudson's jacket over his head and pretend like he's just passed out drunk, if anyone asks."

I turned to Dessie. "Dess, can you distract the desk clerk somehow? We need to sneak him in."

"Oh, sure," she said enthusiastically. "I have loads of routines. I can use the old 'something bit me' trick."

"What's that?" Patrick asked, wrinkling his nose.

"I've used this one with the boys since I was a kid," she said, grinning. She bent over, pulling her skirt scandalously high on her thigh, exposing her legs.

"I ask him to kneel down and check and see if something bit me on the thigh," she said, winking. Her shapely curves were on full display as she bent over, and I couldn't help but notice Patrick and Hudson both glance down her blouse. "I don't even have to specify what kind of bug. He'll be staring. Trust me, his attention will be fully occupied."

Judging by the boys' stares, she was exactly right.

"Yeah, that'll work," I said, as Marceau visibly shook his head like he was trying to clear his brain of cobwebs.

"Give me just a minute," Dessie said, smoothing her hair and unbuttoning the top button of her blouse.

*"She's unbelievable,"* I thought to myself. But if she got the results we needed right now, I'd overlook it...this time.

Dessie entered the lobby, and I counted slowly to twenty. When I reached it, I nodded. Patrick slid out first, pulling Masso with him. Hudson followed behind, the pistol still pinned against Masso's back.

Leonce reached in and grabbed Hudson's jacket, draping it over Masso's head to conceal his face. Marceau positioned himself in front of the three, and Leonce behind, making a tight formation. I crept to the lobby window and peered in.

Sure enough, Dessie had her skirt pulled up nearly to her knickers, and the hotel clerk was on his knees, examining the back of her thighs with interest.

"Go now!" I whispered, waving them on. Leonce slipped in the door first, and I ducked in behind him, holding the lobby doors open for the others to creep in.

"I swear, it feels like a little pinch right there on the back of my leg," I heard Dessie purr. I glanced over, and saw Dessie bend down a little bit lower, her rear inches from the clerk's face. "Do you see it? Look carefully, please, it really hurts."

Hudson and Patrick shoved Masso forward as he tried to brace himself against the lobby floor, his feet skidding and scrabbling against the tiles. They nearly picked him up, quickly dragging him up the stairs and disappearing into the hallway.

I followed behind them, watching for other people who might be witnessing us manhandle our hostage. Luckily, the hotel was shabby and seemed to be unpopular. We'd barely seen anyone but a few hotel staff here.

Leonce pulled his key out and slipped it into the lock, turning the handle and swinging open the door. He waved them in.

Patrick, Masso, and Hudson squeezed through the door. Marceau and I followed on their heels, closing the door behind us and turning the deadbolt to lock us in.

Marceau grabbed the desk chair, pulling it to the middle of the room, in between the two short twin beds. Hudson slammed Masso into it, his head wobbling from the sudden shove.

"Go out to the Fords and get some ropes from the trunk," Hudson said, speaking again in French and looking at Leonce. "Get the tire repair kit, too, and any medical supplies you can wrangle up. Marceau, get Willis. Send him straight here."

"Tire repair kit?" Leonce asked in confusion.

"Yes," Hudson said, clenching his jaw. "Matches, too. Bring matches."

"Wait—matches?" Patrick said, shaking his head. "Hudson..."

"Go," Hudson commanded, and Leonce turned and left. I stood in the corner, not sure what to do. We hadn't planned this out yet. How were we going to get him to talk? Hudson wasn't actually going to torture him, was he?

A quiet knock sounded at the door.

"It's me," Dessie's voice called out softly.

I crossed the room and let her in, closing the door behind her.

"He didn't even know you came in," she announced, tossing her hair. "You're lucky you have a girl as pretty as me on the team, you know."

"Trust me, we appreciate you, Dessie," Hudson said. "Can you be a doll, though, and wait in the lobby for Cap and Bernard and

Chito? We need to grab them as soon as they come in, and tell them what's going on."

"Why can't Andi do it?" Dessie asked, glancing at me. "I want to be in here with him. If he tries to escape, I want to be the one to kill him with my bare hands."

I blinked. I couldn't tell if Dessie was joking or not, but her face was alarmingly cold.

"Fine, I'll go," I replied, walking to the door. Before I stepped out, I stopped.

"Don't hurt him," I said to Hudson and Patrick, in French. "You know the whole team wasn't on board with this kidnapping in the first place. They'll never be able to look at you the same way if you torture him. We're not like them, even though we're desperate. Don't bring us down to their level."

Hudson stared back at me evenly, without expression. Patrick winced, clearly feeling guilty already.

"Cap," Hudson finally replied, staring at me.

"I'm going," I grumbled, walking out the door.

# CHAPTER 60

I WALKED DOWN THE STAIRS to the lobby and sat down in the chair closest to the door, crossing one leg over the other. I jingled my foot nervously, twisting my hands together, waiting for my team to come in.

What was taking them so long?

What might Hudson be doing to Masso right now, upstairs, without my influence?

What were we going to do?

Would he actually tell us anything?

What if we'd just committed a serious crime for absolutely nothing?

I debated going back upstairs and checking on what Hudson might be doing to Masso, but I hoped that Patrick would be the voice of reason.

Hudson wouldn't go too far, would he? We weren't bad people, after all. We were just trying to save Paz's life.

Where was Cap? It wasn't like him to be away from the rest of the team this long, when he knew we were in a time crunch with the ransom. What could he possibly be doing?

After nearly twenty minutes, I heard Chito's voice outside. I shot to my feet, rushing toward the door. Bernard walked in first, Chito and Cap behind him. He nodded, but Cap and Chito ignored me.

"Where have you been?" I asked frantically, blocking their path.

"If you must know, we were coming up with an alternate plan," Cap sniffed, clearly still chafed with me. "We figured it out. We don't have to kidnap anyone after all. That was a foolish and risky plan, anyway. We'll write an anonymous letter to the police, and—"

"It's too late for that!" I hissed. "We have Masso upstairs!"

"What?" Cap uttered, stopping dead in his tracks, frozen.

"Masso! He's upstairs, right now. We ran into him on the street and Hudson just snapped. He held a gun to him and dragged him outside and threw him in the car."

"What do you mean, he's upstairs?" Chito asked, his voice an octave higher than normal. "They went through with it? They actually kidnapped someone?"

"Yes! We've been waiting for you, to get you upstairs to talk about what we're going to do!"

Cap swore under his breath. "Show us."

We hurried upstairs to Leonce's room. Cap rapped impatiently at the door and called out, "It's Cap. Let me in. Now."

The door cracked open, and the blood drained from Cap's face. He swiftly pushed into the room, and Bernard and Chito and I piled in behind him. I closed the door behind us and locked it.

The small room was crowded with people. Dessie and Patrick stood together next to the desk, and Willis sat on top of the desk, glowering at Masso. Claude and Leonce were sitting on one bed, fiddling with the contents of the first aid and tire kits, which they had laid out on the bedsheet.

"Took you long enough," Hudson drawled, looking up from his seat on the bed next to Marceau. He held a mug in his hand. From the smell of it, it was whiskey. "Where have you three been?"

"We were planning—some other option, rather than this," Cap faltered, staring at Masso. He was now bound to the desk chair with thick rope, his eyes still covered with the handkerchief and his mouth still gagged with my shirt.

"What happened?" Chito asked, his eyes fixed fearfully on Masso. I could already see regret and guilt in his face.

"Hold on, we're only speaking French in front of him," Hudson interrupted, standing up. "He can't understand it. Go down the hall and talk in Patrick's room. He'll fill you in. We'll wait here."

Patrick nodded toward the door. We followed him to the room he was sharing with Marceau, who also ducked out with us.

As soon as the door closed, Cap demanded answers.

"What happened?" he said accusingly. "We didn't even plan this out yet. Why did you decide to kidnap him? And what the hell are we going to do with him now?"

Patrick filled him in on how we'd noticed him walking down the sidewalk on our surveillance rounds, and impulsively decided to follow him into the liquor store and nab him when the owner stepped into the back room to check for cigarettes.

"We didn't really think it through," Patrick admitted, staring at Cap apologetically. "And Cap, I swear to you, it was Hudson. Andi and I tried to stop him, but he was like a man possessed. I've been trying to manage this the best I can, ever since he drew that gun and put it to Masso's head in the liquor store."

"He's telling the truth," I said quietly. "Hudson didn't even tell us what he was thinking. He just blindly followed him in and took advantage of the moment. I don't know how we possibly got away with it, but we did."

Cap thought for a moment, his lips pursed. "Okay. We're in a huge mess now. There's no sense in dwelling on the stupidity that got us here. We have to think about how to manage this, moving forward."

He tapped his chin, looking at Marceau.

"I need you to level with me," he said, looking him in the eyes. "How violent can Hudson be? You've known him your whole life."

Marceau screwed up his face.

"He's not a bad guy," he said slowly. "But does he have a bad temper? Sometimes. Can he lash out and hurt someone, if he's upset? I suppose so."

"But how bad is he?"

"He's been in a bunch of fist fights," Marceau admitted. "I don't know. He roughed people up, playing hockey. I've never seen him under the sort of stress he's been under lately, since we got attacked and Paz has been held hostage. I've felt like he's a totally different person lately, to be honest."

"What about Willis?" Cap asked. "He seems capable of hurting someone."

"Yes, I could see that," Marceau replied. "He was always a troublemaker in school. Beat up a few kids, played hooky, snuck alcohol into the punch bowl at school dances. Between us, my mother never wanted me to be friends with him. I mean, he set a shed on fire. That says something about him, doesn't it?"

"Can you see them torturing Masso?"

Marceau hesitated. "I suppose so. I know they're both good men—but aren't we all capable of some pretty dark things, depending on what we're faced with?"

"What are they going to do to him?" I asked. "We didn't talk about anything at all. We didn't plan this out."

"No kidding," Chito said, shaking his head. "And I'm sorry, I don't feel comfortable leaving Masso alone in there with Hudson and Willis. I think we need to be in there with them, making sure they don't do something foolish."

"That's a good point," Cap sighed, rubbing his chin. "Let's get back in there."

# CHAPTER 61

THE SIX OF US HEADED back to Leonce's room. Chito knocked lightly on the door, but there was no response.

Inside, we heard a low muffled moan, then furtive whispering. Patrick frowned, looking at Marceau. "You don't think—"

"What?" Cap said, stepping up to them.

"They had some pliers and scissors out earlier, from the mechanic's kit," Patrick started, then stopped. "But—they wouldn't. Right?"

Chito knocked again, harder this time. The sound of whispering persisted, and we heard the noise of a chair being scraped across the floor.

"Hey, guys, let us in," Patrick called, leaning his head against the door. He frowned. "It sounds like they're opening the window?"

"Just a minute!" called Hudson's voice. Cap glanced at me, and then Patrick.

"What are they doing in there that they don't want us to see?" he asked, his tone angry.

Finally, the door eased open.

"Hold on," Hudson said, pulling blankets away from the foot of the door. Cap and Patrick pushed in ahead of me, blocking my view of the room. I stepped over a pile of blankets and pillows that someone had pulled off the bed and piled around the door. There were blankets draped at the base of the window, too, which was open. Were they trying to soundproof the door?

As I entered the room, I wrinkled my nose. It smelled terrible inside.

Masso was still sitting in the chair in the middle of the room, but now he was covered with a white bedsheet. His head hung down, swiveling toward the door as Bernard closed it.

Dessie and Willis were both standing in front of Masso, hands behind their backs. They stared at us. Dessie looked like she was ready to unleash her fury.

I hung back by the door, next to Bernard and Chito, as Patrick and Cap blocked my view, staring at Hudson and the others. I sniffed the air again, trying to figure out the strange smell. It smelled like tobacco and burnt matches, but something else that was sickly sweet.

"What's going on in here?" Cap demanded. Willis and Dessie stared at him, defiant, but Hudson avoided his eyes.

Patrick swiftly stepped forward and pulled the bedsheet off of Masso. I gasped involuntarily.

Masso's eye was swollen shut and his nose crooked and crusted with blackened blood that ran over his lips and down his chin, the product of Dessie's punches. But his shirt had been ripped open, too, and there was a small and angry red, oozing spot on his bare chest.

Chito clapped his hand over his mouth as he cried out in shock. "You burned him?"

Masso lifted his head and stared at Chito with his good eye.

I stood in front of the door, unable to move. That explained the strange smell in the room, and the open window—it was the unmistakable scent of burning human flesh. They'd been trying to air out the room before we came back in.

I felt like I might be sick. I knew we were desperate, but this? This wasn't who we were.

Cap stood motionless, staring hard at Hudson. For a long moment, they glared at each other with the intensity of two wrecking balls ready to collide with each other and cause utter destruction to everything around them.

"Why?" Cap snarled.

Hudson stared at him. "We *had* to. And we knew you'd stop us."

Willis spoke up. "You seem to forget that the majority of the team voted for this, Cap," he said, furtively sliding the box of cigarettes into his pocket. "You knew what this was and where it would go. Don't play dumb."

"He had the choice," Hudson spat. "We told him we could do it the easy way or the hard way. He chose the hard way."

"This isn't what we talked about!" Patrick said, standing next to Cap. "We didn't plan *this*! We didn't agree to *this*!"

"Not everything can be a carefully planned activity!" Hudson exclaimed. "We're not all Mr. Perfect Grant Gallivanter, researching every single step for days on end before actually doing anything at all. Sometimes you just have to act and figure it out on the fly."

"Yeah, and you're doing so well at figuring this out on the fly," Cap shot back, his face red with anger. "What are you going to do now? Did he tell you where they're holding Paz? Or do you need to torture him a bit longer in order to get it out of him?"

Dessie and Willis looked at each other, behind Hudson's back.

"I take that as a no," Cap said, his voice rising. "He didn't tell you, did he?"

Masso's one good eye was darting back and forth, watching Cap and Hudson and Patrick.

"What did you think we were going to do, when we said we were going to kidnap him?" Willis exclaimed, crossing his arms in front of him. "Did you think we were going to buy him a beer and talk him into confessing it to us? You sound like a damn idiot right now, Cap."

"Better an idiot than a criminal," Cap retorted. He stepped forward so he was face-to-face with Hudson, his rage palpable.

"Call it off, Captain Landry," he spat. "These are your men doing this. Call it off."

"I can't," Hudson replied, holding Cap's gaze.

"Why not?"

Hudson glared back at him, defiant. "Because I told them to do it. I believe it's necessary. And sometimes we're forced to choose between a bad decision and a bad decision. But we still have to choose one."

"No," Cap replied. He leaned into Hudson's face and poked him hard, in the chest. "You don't have to choose. You can choose a third option—to do what's right."

"What's right?" Hudson shot back, holding his ground. "He's a *murderer*, Cap. Did you know he spit in Andi's face when we kidnapped him? Do you remember that he's one of the men who punched me in the face? Who shoved Dessie to the ground, hitting her? What's right is that this dirtbag should pay for his crimes. And if the police aren't going to do it, then someone has to. Justice must be served."

"Not by us," Patrick said, from behind Cap. "This isn't our role. We're rescuers, not criminals."

"Sometimes even the good guys have to get a little dirty," Willis replied, his voice cold.

"This is wrong and you know it," Chito spoke up. "That's why you waited until we were all out of the room to torture him. That's why you tried to muffle the sounds with these blankets at the door. Because you know we wouldn't approve. That we would stop you."

"No, because we knew you wouldn't have the stomach for it," Willis retorted. "You're all high and mighty. You think everyone sees the world the way you do. Well, wake up, pal. Sometimes you have to fight fire with fire."

"Besides, sometimes being smacked around makes you stronger," Hudson growled, a distant look in his eyes. "Let him suffer."

At his words, Claude and Leonce and Marceau exchanged meaningful glances. Were they worried about what Hudson and Willis might do?

As the boys argued, I saw Dessie's eyes slide to Masso's face. She was staring at him with open fury.

"Call it off, Hudson," Cap repeated, still in Hudson's face. "Don't turn us into one of them. We're not. By doing this, you're tainting every single person on this team. *Both* teams."

"So?" Willis said, stepping up next to Hudson. "He's not forcing us to do this. We want to do it. And don't forget, the clock is running on Paz. He only has what, a day left until they get the ransom and then kill him?"

I heard Dessie inhale softly, and she silently slipped across the room toward the bed where all the supplies from the mechanic and first aid kits were laid out.

"He's not going to tell you anything," Cap raged, throwing up his hands in frustration. "You just kidnapped him and burned his body, and he didn't say anything? What makes you think he'll tell you anything at all?"

"We'll keep pushing him," Willis replied, his eyes hard. "I have no problem with turning up the pain."

Dessie was running her hands softly over the tools on the bed. Was I the only one watching her? Frowning, she picked up a large pair of scissors in one hand, and a wicked-looking metal clamping instrument. She held one in each hand, looking back and forth at them.

"I don't feel comfortable with this at all," Cap exclaimed. "Look around the room. Look at the faces of everyone in here. At least half the group is furious right now, Willis. You need to stop. None of us want this."

"I do," Dessie said, her voice ugly but clear. Swiftly, she stepped toward Masso, the large scissors gleaming brightly in her hand.

# CHAPTER 62

BEFORE ANYONE COULD stop her, Dessie shoved the pointed end of the scissors at the base of Masso's throat.

He flinched, his body stiffening as he stared up at her wildly with his one good eye.

"I don't even know what these are called," Dessie said, her voice deadly. "But they look like they could do some damage, don't they?"

From behind me, Bernard spoke up.

"They're tinsnips," he said. "We use them for cutting metal."

"Thanks, sweetie," Dessie purred, pushing them harder into the hollow of tender flesh on Masso's throat. A red spot was already appearing from the pressure.

"Dessie," Cap warned, stepping toward her. She glanced up at him.

"One more step and I push it in farther," she spat vehemently.

Cap froze. We all stared at Dessie, unsure of where she was going with this.

Dessie turned her attention back to Masso's face.

"I remember you, you know," she said, pressing the scissors a little bit deeper in.

Masso shuddered.

"I can't forget the face of someone who looked at me the way you did. Like I was nothing. Like you could do whatever you wanted to me, and I had to put up with it because I'm just a helpless little lady," she continued.

She laughed, her voice husky and enraged. "Now who's helpless? Certainly not me."

With her free hand, she held up the other clamping instrument. "This looks painful too, doesn't it?"

She clenched the handle, and the tool sprung open, then snapped shut with an audible twang.

"That's a valve-spring compressor," Bernard frowned. "Be careful with that. It can take off a finger, easily."

"Did you hear that, Mr. Rua?" Dessie purred, holding the compressor up to his face. "I should be *careful* with this. It'll take off a finger. Why, I wonder what else it might be able to take off."

Masso visibly paled and strained back.

Dessie put one knee up on his thigh, leaning her small body against his.

"Who has the upper hand now, huh?" she jeered, pressing her weight into him.

She paused, her eyes bored on him.

"I have to tell you the truth, Mr. Rua," she said, the scissors still pushed into his throat. "They might feel bad over torturing you, but I certainly don't. It's a funny thing, when you lose the only person that matters most to you. You become hard. Willing to do whatever you need to do, to get that person back."

Patrick jerked his head up in sudden comprehension. He glanced at me. "She loves Paz?" he mouthed. I nodded.

In the chair, Masso swallowed, his Adam's apple betraying his nerves. Dessie noticed.

"Scared, Mr. Rua?" she said coldly. "Good. You should be. Because I don't care what they think of me for doing this. I've never cared what anyone thought of me. And I'm sick and tired of men thinking they can do whatever they want to me—and take whoever they want from me—and not get in trouble for it."

She leaned in, her face inches from Masso. "You're scum. You prey on the weak and helpless. And by God, I'm going to make you *pay*. I'm going to make you bleed, and suffer horrifically, because you're a worthless sack of garbage that doesn't deserve to walk on this earth anymore."

We watched in horror as Dessie set the compressor in Masso's lap.

"I'll start with your fingers," she growled. "When I'm out of fingers, I'll move elsewhere."

"Dessie!" Hudson yelped, reaching for her.

She hit him hard in the mouth, and he stepped back, stunned.

"If any of you come near me, I swear on my mother's grave that I'll run him through right here and now," she said in an icy voice. She pressed the tinsnips deeper, and Masso uttered a strangled cry. She'd punctured the skin now, and blood trickled down his neck.

Hudson froze, blood trickling down his chin, too. She'd split his lip wide open.

Dessie turned back to Masso.

"You've taken away what mattered most to me, so I'm going to take away what matters most to you," she growled. "Maybe you'll bleed to death quickly, once I start cutting. Then again, maybe it'll take a while. Doesn't make any difference to me. I just hope you suffer."

"Dess, you can't be serious," Chito cried wildly. "Stop!"

She laughed cruelly. "What is it they say? 'An eye for an eye'? Maybe I'll use these tinsnips on that next."

Slowly, Dessie reached for Masso's hand. He panicked, and grunted through the shirt still lodged in his mouth.

"That's right. Take one last look," Dessie said savagely, picking up the valve-spring compressor.

Masso grunted again, louder, shaking his head. His good eye was rolling around wildly.

"Does he want to talk?" Patrick blurted out, stepping toward him. Masso stared at him, a helpless look on his face.

"Too late," Dessie said, clenching the compressor. It popped open with a snap.

Masso's face went white and he uttered a guttural cry through the gauze in his mouth.

# CHAPTER 63

"HOLD ON!" PATRICK SAID, throwing himself between Dessie and Masso.

He quickly untied the shirt sleeves holding Masso's gag in place and glared at him. "You don't scream, am I clear? If you do, I'll let her continue and I won't interrupt next time."

Masso nodded, his eye big with fright.

Patrick pulled the shirt out of Masso's mouth and he immediately started babbling, his Italian accent heavy as he exclaimed, "Fine, fine, I'll tell you what you want to know! Get her off me!"

"I'm not going anywhere until you spill it," Dessie said, the scissors still at his throat. "Tell us where you're hiding Paz. We know you know."

Masso sucked in a deep breath. "Fine. He's in Rome. In Stefano's old house."

"Who the hell is Stefano?" Dessie said, the scissors still at his throat. "Where in Rome?"

"Stefano! Stefano Crippa, one of the other men on our crew," Masso said frantically. "Put the scissors down, please! I'll tell you everything!"

"No," Dessie said, pushing them in suddenly. Masso squeaked in pain.

She glared. "Give us an address. We need actual information. Give us the information, and you'll walk out of here alive, relatively unharmed. If you don't, we'll make sure you suffer."

"I don't have an address!" he yelped, and Patrick slapped his hand over his mouth. Masso looked up at him, clearly frightened.

"Shut up!" Patrick said harshly. "I told you not to make any noise!"

Masso struggled against his bindings, looking up beseechingly at Patrick. Slowly, Patrick pulled his hand away.

"I don't have an address," Masso said as soon as Patrick's hand lifted, his voice lower. "I can tell you about where it is. Enzo doesn't let us write that kind of stuff down, anyway. He's—what do you say? He's paranoid."

"Why Rome?" Cap asked, stepping forward. "Explain the timeline to us. You attacked the Chinook Voyageurs, and then what?"

"Yes, fine," Masso said, his eye searching out Cap. "Tell her to get off me, please. The scissors, they hurt."

"Dessie, back off," Cap said, standing next to Patrick. "Hold onto the tinsnips, though. We might need to use them again."

"With pleasure," Dessie said, pulling them away slowly. The very ends were still slick with blood, and a drop landed on Dessie's skirt.

Masso stared fearfully at Dessie, then swiveled his good eye back to Cap and Patrick.

"We saw them in the bar that night, and the young one—the Spanish one—was going on and on about how rich they were, and how much money he had at home," he blurted. "He was such a little guy, and so drunk. We thought he'd be an easy mark. He blabbed all sorts of personal information, told us where you'd be headed next. I mean, he couldn't have made it easier for us."

Masso glanced again at Dessie, who sat on the edge of the bed across from him, still holding both instruments in her hands. She watched him like a hungry lion, ready to devour its kill.

"We hid out and waited for them to come. You know that part, I guess," Masso said, looking around at the Chinook crew. "I swear, it wasn't my idea. I didn't even participate. I was just there, with

Enzo and Stefano and Danilo. It was really Enzo who was the most responsible—"

"Liar," Dessie said hotly, rising to her feet and towering over him. "You're the one who hit Rollie and Willis in the back of the head! I saw the whole thing!"

Suddenly, I tasted bile. This was the man who'd nearly killed Rollie? I thought back to the endless hours I'd spent at Rollie's side in the hospital, looking at his grotesquely swollen face. Of watching his frustration grow as he couldn't speak, couldn't walk, couldn't lift his hands to feed himself. And this was the man who was responsible for all that?

In a flash, I understood Dessie's rage. I wanted to kill him myself now.

Willis roared with anger, jumping up. Chito caught him and held him back as he struggled, his fists flailing. He cursed angrily.

Marceau's face was red, too. He didn't stand up, but he was obviously agitated.

Without warning, Dessie slammed the tinsnips into Masso's shoulder. He screamed.

"Damn it!" Cap said, yanking the scissors out. Blood oozed down Masso's arm, and he howled in pain.

"Tell the truth!" Dessie roared, her eyes big. "I swear to you, I'll run it through your throat next time you lie to us!"

"Fine, fine, stop!" he said, jerking his head around. "The truth is that yes, I hit them. And I hurt some of you, and—and you, too," he said, nodding at Dessie. "We knew the little one, Paz, was the target, so we grabbed him. He was in the last car. I didn't think he'd be a fighter, but he was. But we subdued him, tied him up, threw him in our Ford, and took off."

"Where?" Cap said, face tight with fury.

"We hid in an old barn the first night, while Enzo rented a house a few villages away," he said. "We debated holding onto him in Switzerland, but we figured the police would be onto us because you were celebrities. So we decided to drive him over the border, to a location we knew would be secure. Far away from the actual operation, you know?"

"Stefano's house?" Patrick asked.

Masso nodded. "His parents are both dead. Left it to him in their will. He's an only child, and the house sits empty most of the time. It's a good-sized place. We've used it on jobs before."

"Where is it, exactly?" Cap said, reaching for a notepad from his pocket.

"Rome, on the north side of the city." He gave several names of roads, and a thorough description of the surrounding area and house itself. Cap scribbled it down.

"Who guards the house?" Patrick asked.

Masso shook his head. "No one. He has a neighbor woman who tends to the garden, on occasion, but otherwise, it's empty."

Cap looked up from his notes. "You do realize that if you're lying about any of this, we'll kill you?"

"I'm not lying," Masso insisted. "I've been there a few times now. We've used it before, with others that we've kidnapped. Been there for weeks at a time, no one bothers us. It's why we always go back to it."

"Is that why you didn't issue the ransom to his family until just the other day?" Hudson asked, his eyebrows knit together as he processed Masso's words. "Did you drive down to the house in Rome, dump Paz there, and then drive back here to Tarragona?"

"Yes," Masso replied. "We took our time, mostly driving at night. We didn't want anyone to see that we had someone tied up and bound in the back trunk, you know? Once we got to Stefano's place, we hid out there for a few days, and then made our way back up here to Spain."

"The timeline fits," Cap mused, staring down at Masso. "So what's your crew planning next? When were you going to collect the ransom money, and what were you going to do with Paz?"

Masso hesitated, staring up at him.

Dessie immediately snapped the compressor and Masso quickly started talking again.

"We gave the family forty-eight hours to get the money together. We asked for a hundred thousand—enough for an even four-way split. We've generally seen that two days is long enough for rich people to get the money together, but not plan anything else. Give them too long and they start trying to get creative, trying to mess around."

"Oh, you wouldn't want that," Marceau muttered angrily.

"How do you collect the money?" Hudson asked.

"We arrange a dead drop, and we—what's the word—we watch them? We are watching the family now, to make sure they have not contacted the police."

"Surveillance?" Hudson suggested.

"Yes, surveillance," Masso replied. "We take turns watching, in the days leading up. We ask them to put the money in bags and leave it in a set location. We already have our boys there, watching to make sure no one else is around. If we see a police man there, we leave. They've been told not to contact the police, not to bring them in. We don't pick up the money."

"And what do you do then with your victim?"

Masso looked up, pursing his lips.

"Spit it out," Hudson said. "What are you planning to do with Paz, when you get the ransom money?"

Masso grimaced. "We let them go. We have what we need. Why hold onto them?"

Patrick slammed his hand down hard on the desk.

"You're lying again!" he exclaimed angrily. "We have a whole file on you. We know you kill them, you son of a—"

"You warned him, Cap," Dessie interrupted, already on her feet and pushing Cap aside. "You said if he lied again we would kill him."

She held the tinsnips up, still stained red with his blood.

"No, hold on," Masso said desperately. "I don't participate. I've barely been on the crew, anyway. Enzo is the one who's the mastermind, not me!"

"Too bad. You still lied," Dessie replied, laying the sharp end of the tinsnips against the hollow spot above his collarbone. "I think maybe we should keep a tally going of all his lies, don't you, Cap? Carve it right here, so we can keep track?"

Cap hesitated, staring down at Masso. I gaped at him. He'd never allow someone to be tortured. Right?

# CHAPTER 64

THE MOMENT STRETCHED out, all of us frozen in breathless anticipation. Would Cap willingly allow Dessie to torture Masso?

*"No, he can't,"* I thought frantically, unable to draw a breath. *"Cap's honorable. He's disciplined. He would never!"*

Slowly, Cap nodded, not taking his eyes off of Masso.

Dessie didn't hesitate another moment. Wickedly, she carved into Masso's flesh and he cried out in shock and pain.

"Buon Dio, basta! Fa male!" he screamed in Italian, as a thin red line of blood bubbled out. "Stop!"

"Keep talking. We'll see how many more tallies you collect," Dessie cried, crossing her arms in front of her, the tinsnips still in her right hand.

I stared at Dessie and Cap in horror. I hadn't been sure that Dessie had the nerves to actually torture someone, and I certainly never thought Cap would let her do it. But here we were.

We'd crossed another line now.

"Yes, we have killed before," Masso confessed desperately, the words spilling out. "It's just too risky, after we get the money, to release the person. They've seen us and heard us talk to each other, using our names. They know where Stefano lives. We *have* to kill them. Don't you understand?"

Grimly, we all glared at him. He shook his head.

"I'm not saying I do it. It's Enzo. Not all of us are killers. I don't like it, personally. But in our business, it's necessary. We can't leave witnesses behind. We'll get caught."

"So you're saying that Enzo Trimboli is the only one who kills the victims you kidnap?" Hudson asked.

"Yes."

"How does he do it?"

Masso hesitated, looking up at Dessie. She stared down at him with a look of bloodlust in her face.

"He—he shoots them, usually," Masso admitted nervously. "We have to help dispose of the body. But he usually does the dirty work of killing them himself, without us."

Dessie bit her lip, inhaling a deep breath through her nose.

"It's quick," Masso added, looking up at her. "He doesn't make them suffer. He blindfolds them and takes them out back. One shot to the head."

Unable to control herself, Dessie pounced on him again. She slashed him with the tinsnips, swiping across the cut she'd just inflicted. Masso screamed as Cap slapped his hand over his mouth, trying to muffle him.

None of us tried to dissuade her from hurting him now. We were too upset at hearing the cold justification of the murder of multiple innocent souls.

"When are they going back down to Rome to kill Paz?" Cap asked, his face hard.

"As soon as they get the ransom money, they'll head back to Italy," Masso replied. "We have one guy there, a local kid, keeping an eye on Paz. He's not a part of the crew—he's just a small-time guy. Does odd jobs, here and there. He doesn't know the full scope of our operations."

"So he just guards the prisoners? He doesn't know you kill them?" Hudson asked, the veins in his neck bulging with his suppressed anger.

"Right," Masso nodded. "He's there, keeping an eye on the house and on Paz until we get back."

"And when will that be?" Cap asked, his forehead wrinkled.

"We're supposed to get the money tomorrow night, at eight o'clock," Masso replied. "We usually leave the next morning and head back to Rome. But I don't know, they might take off that night if they're worried about getting caught. They're already spooked by the car getting stolen and burned. And now I'm gone, too."

"Did you get a replacement car already?" Patrick asked.

Masso hesitated. "They're going to steal one. We've done it before. We need a car. We have to get back to Rome."

"And driving to Rome—you do it in one shot?"

"From here, it took us about four days," Masso admitted. "We stopped in hotels along the way from Rome to here. But I don't know, they might be in more of a hurry right now."

Cap's eyebrows lifted in concern. He turned around and faced the team. "I need to look at a map," he murmured. "I'm guessing Rome is at least a thousand kilometers away. We'd have to chart it out."

Patrick looked at Hudson. "We have a full confession now. We have the address of where they're hiding. Why don't we phone the police in Rome and have them handle it?"

"We'll talk about this outside," Cap stopped him. "Not in front of him."

I started to step out with Cap, Patrick, and Hudson, but Cap stopped me.

"We need you to keep an eye on Dessie," he said in a low voice, so she couldn't hear me. "I don't know if she actually would've done anything to him, but you're probably the only one who can stop her now if she tries."

"Fine," I said, stepping back. I sat down on the bed across from Masso and stared at him until he looked down.

Now what?

# CHAPTER 65

THE TEAM SAT APPREHENSIVELY in the hotel room with Masso as Patrick, Cap, and Hudson conferred outside.

It was evening now, and my stomach growled with hunger. They'd been talking for several minutes already. How much longer would they take to figure out what to do next?

A few minutes later, Hudson cracked open the door.

"Claude, Chito," he called, and they both got up and ducked outside, shutting the door softly behind them. The rest of us looked at each other.

"Maybe they're talking about supplies?" Leonce suggested in French.

We sat in silence again, lost in our own thoughts. If they were talking about supplies, that had to mean that they were considering us traveling to Rome, to Stefano's house.

I jiggled my foot nervously then stopped, realizing Masso was looking at me. I didn't want him to assume I was weak.

After several more minutes, Hudson stuck his head inside the room. "We're having a quick team conference in Bernard's room, down the hall. Willis and Dessie, stay here and keep an eye on Masso. The rest of you, get down there now."

Masso squirmed, watching everyone who got up to leave. I wondered if he was worried about getting stuck alone in a room with the two individuals who had lobbied hardest for his torture.

Then again, that was probably intentional. It smacked of Cap's planning, to cleverly wage psychological warfare against Masso Rua in this moment of vulnerability.

I followed everyone out. We walked down to Bernard and Chito's room, a few doors down. As soon as the door closed behind us, Cap started speaking quickly.

"We've talked this through pretty thoroughly, but we want to give everyone a chance to weigh in on it. But I'll warn you, we have to act fast," he said, glancing around the room. "We no longer have the luxury of time on our side. Does everyone understand that?"

We nodded. He squared his shoulders.

"And before I tell you what we think the best course of action is, I want you to understand that it's going to put a strain on the entire team," Cap said. "We know that. But it's what we have to do. We have to rise to the occasion, and work together—every one of us—to save Paz. Is everyone in agreement?"

Again, nods around the room. Hudson spoke up now.

"As Patrick pointed out, we know where Stefano's house is located. We have the names of the other men in Trimboli's gang. We know exactly what their plan of action is. That means we're several steps ahead of them, at this point. They still have to steal a car to replace the one we burned, don't forget. That will likely take some time."

He glanced at Cap, and continued. "We know they're going to get the money tomorrow night, at eight o'clock, and then immediately go back to Rome as soon as they steal an automobile. When they get to Rome, to their hideout where Paz is being guarded, they're going to kill him."

"Here's where we run into a big problem, though," Cap interjected. "Logic dictates that we go to the police, and tell them everything. We get the local police in Rome to bust in and rescue Paz, and the local police here to arrest Enzo Trimboli and his men. But we've burned that bridge with the police here in Tarragona."

He shook his head, continuing.

"In order for the police in Rome to work with us, we'd have to first work with the local Spanish force. Unfortunately, they won't work with us...and there's the little matter of the fact that we stole the file from them, in the first place, and they're sure to connect the dots now, if we go in talking about the same exact case. They'll look for the file, won't be able to find it, and piece together our conspicuous presence there and realize *we* stole it."

He paused, rubbing his face. "We'll go in trying to help Paz, and we'll end up all getting arrested. By the time they sort things out—assuming they even let us explain ourselves—Paz will already be dead."

"What if we try just going straight to the police in Rome, though?" Leonce suggested. "We could call them and tell them the whole story?"

"We discussed that," Cap replied. "But we already know the chain of command with these international cases, from working with the police in Switzerland and Spain. The process requires us to go first through the local police, who then hand the case off to another country's force. It's a no go."

Hudson jumped in. "Remember, Cap and I both went to the local government offices and our ambassadors, and even they were unwilling to break the chain of command. And who knows? The Italian police might already be on the take from the local mafia."

"So what are we possibly going to do?" I asked, feeling hopeless. We'd done so much to try to save Paz, and we now had the literal address of where we could find him—and we wouldn't be able to save him after all?

"We're going to beat Trimboli and his men to Rome," Cap replied.

"How?" Bernard asked, frowning. Cap looked at Chito and Claude.

"We've already discussed getting supplies and gassing up the Fords," he said. "We don't have a full supply of gasoline right now, so we can't leave tonight. The gas stations and stores are closed right now, because it's evening, but they'll go out first thing in the morning and get what we need. We'll send our team out in a fleet of cars, racing to get to Rome before Trimboli gets there."

He unfolded a large map and laid it out on the bed. We crowded around, shoulder-to-shoulder, looking down.

"We're here, in Tarragona," Cap pointed. He dragged his finger along the Mediterranean coast, showing us the route.

"Rome is here, in central Italy," he said. "It's about fifteen hundred kilometers from here to there. By my calculations, if we push the Fords as fast as they can go, without stopping, you could get there in just around twenty-three hours."

"Without stopping?" I asked, confused. "We need to sleep. And eat. And go to the bathroom."

Cap glanced up. "That's what I meant when I said it's going to put a strain on the entire team. You're going to have to drive straight through, with minimal stops. That means sleeping in the cars, taking turns while someone else drives. You'll travel day and night to get to Rome, not stopping at all unless it's to refuel or use the restroom."

"We've never done that before, and certainly not for so long," Bernard interrupted. "You're talking about pushing the Fords to their absolute limit. You heard Masso—it took four days to make this trip."

"Yes," Cap said. "That's why we're sending nearly the whole team. If one car breaks down, leave it. Let the others forge ahead. It's essential that we get someone there, as quickly as humanly possible. Just get to that house and get inside, get Paz out of there. Figure out a way."

We stared at each other, the mood uneasy.

"It's the only way we can save him," Hudson said quietly. "You heard Masso. They'll get the money tomorrow night, and head straight back to Rome to put a bullet in Paz's head."

"But how's this going to work?" Leonce frowned. "We're going to rotate drivers and just keep driving nonstop?"

"Yes."

Cap held up his journal. "We already have it mapped out. We'll send nine of you out, which means you'll always have several relief drivers at the ready. You'll have to figure out your own shifts, taking turns sleeping and eating. But it's entirely feasible."

"Wait, nine of us?" I asked, confused. "Who's staying back?"

Hudson and Cap looked at each other.

"The two of us," Cap replied.

# CHAPTER 66

CAP AND HUDSON FACED the group in silence.

"You can't stay back!" Patrick exclaimed, his shoulders tense. "What are you talking about? Why on earth would you stay back?"

"If anyone's responsible for facing the music here in Tarragona, it's the two of us," Hudson replied, shrugging his shoulders.

"What do you mean, face the music?" Chito asked.

Again, they glanced at each other.

"We can't hold onto Masso forever," Cap finally said. "We have to turn him in. Neither of us feel comfortable just letting him go—he's a dangerous criminal. But it's not our job to make him pay for what he's done, either. He belongs in the hands of the police."

"But you just said we burned that bridge, with the police in Tarragona?" Leonce asked.

"We have," Cap replied. "That's why only two of us are taking responsibility. We're your captains. It's our job to own up to our actions."

"So what exactly are you going to do?" I asked, concern in my voice.

"We're going to let you get a head start, first thing tomorrow—as soon as we have the vehicles ready to go—and then we're headed straight to the police," Cap answered quietly. "We'll confess the whole thing, and turn Masso in. And we'll pray that they understand why we took the actions we did, and be lenient with their consequences."

Around the room, there was a sharp inhale of breath. Cap and Hudson were going to turn themselves in?

"In case the police don't have any sympathy for us, though, we'll prepare letters for our ambassadors, explaining everything in detail. We'll appeal to them. If that doesn't work, well, there's always the possibility of appealing to the press later on," Hudson explained.

"But what if they don't listen to you?" Chito asked, concerned. "You won't be able to summon the press if you're sitting in jail cells."

"You'll already be a third of the way there, by the time Trimboli gets the ransom money tomorrow night," Cap replied. "You'll still be in the best position to save Paz. If the police in Tarragona *do* call the Roman police and request their help, you'll already be near enough to assist and then collect him after they go in and get him out. If the police *don't* call, and just throw us in jail, it'll be up to you to break into that house and save him."

"But you're both sure to be arrested!" I exclaimed. "There has to be some other option!"

Cap shook his head. "There isn't."

"But they'll throw you in jail! We committed so many crimes!"

"Oh, I always thought I'd look fetching in a prison uniform, anyway," Hudson joked.

I glared at him.

"Listen, I know it's upsetting. But we're the captains of these teams, and ultimately, we're the ones responsible for the actions everyone took," Cap said, his voice low. "It's our job to shoulder that responsibility, and that means dealing with whatever consequences our decisions may have. We knew the risks when we did all this stuff. We knew our decisions were against the law—doling out our own form of justice—and even though we did it for noble reasons, we have to do what's right now."

"But you'll go to prison!" I said, feeling close to tears. "We stole a car and committed arson! We kidnapped a man and tortured him!"

"We disabled a *criminal network*, and kidnapped a *murderer*," Cap replied evenly. "Hopefully they consider that, as they decide our punishment."

"So why don't we drive Masso out to the middle of the countryside and just drop him there?" Leonce suggested. "There has to be some other way!"

"Because we need the police's help, and there's no way around that," Cap replied. "We have to own up to our actions and accept the consequences. And more importantly, if it's what we need to do to get Trimboli and his boys off the streets and in prison, it's worth it. Without it, they go free. We can't have that. This is the right thing to do."

We stared at Hudson and Cap. My mind raced. *"If only we could redo the last few days,"* I thought desperately. But then again, what other options had we had? We'd made the best choices we felt we could make, at every corner.

And all those corners had led us here.

*"He's right,"* I thought, with a sinking heart. *"It's the best choice for us now, heading forward. Any other option will allow Trimboli and his men to get away and do this again, to someone else. Cap and Hudson are willing to risk their own freedom in order to put four dangerous criminals behind bars. No amount of argument is going to change their minds now. They're sacrificing themselves for us, and for all the other families who would be hurt with Trimboli's future crimes."*

I swallowed hard and accepted the reality that this was what we had to do. I resolved to step up and assume a leadership role that I knew would be missing, as Cap and Hudson wouldn't be with us anymore.

"Walk us through tomorrow, then," I said, my voice strong. "When do we leave?"

Cap looked at me, relief and pride and sadness mingled together in his face.

"It's going to take time to get the gas and supplies," he said. "Chito and Claude will go out immediately in the morning. They have their lists already. Bernard and Patrick and Marceau will need to check over the Fords and make sure they're ready for a grueling trip. We'll aim to have you hit the road as early as possible. We're racing against the clock."

I nodded. "We'll be ready."

Hudson patted me on the back. "We will be, too."

Cap glanced down at the map again. "I'll continue to work on the route and make the maps for each car. The rest of you, please prepare yourself for tomorrow's departure, pack, and go to bed. You'll need all the rest you can get tonight. The next few days are going to stretch all of you to your limit."

We nodded and started to file out of the room, heading back to our own respective hotel rooms. Patrick and I hung back.

"Cap? Hudson?" Patrick asked. They turned.

Patrick offered his hand. "I just wanted to thank you for being the best captains we could ever possibly have. I admire what you're doing. I know it wasn't an easy decision."

"Thank you," Cap replied, shaking.

"Come here," Hudson said, pulling Patrick into a quick hug. They slapped each other on the back. "Send me a letter or two when I'm in prison, will you?"

Patrick and Hudson let themselves out quietly, leaving Cap and me alone. Cap glanced at me. "I'm sorry. I have work to do with Hudson. We have a lot to write, for the police and our ambassadors. I can't talk."

"I know," I said, kissing him. "I just wanted to do that."

He smiled ruefully, pain in his eyes. "Don't wait up for me. Go to bed as soon as you can. Tomorrow's going to be a long day."

"I will," I said, heading toward the door. "Goodnight. And good luck."

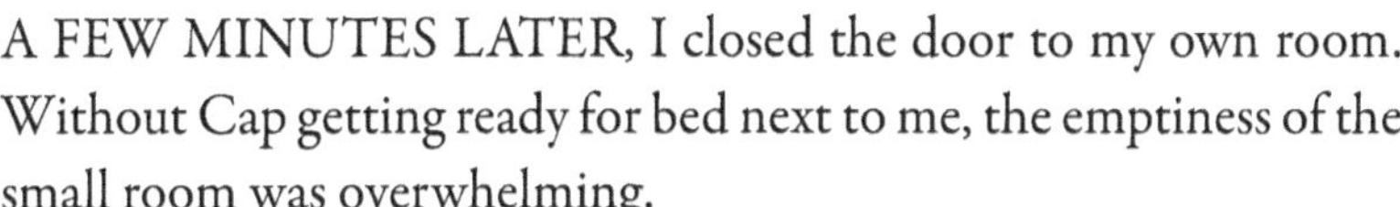

A FEW MINUTES LATER, I closed the door to my own room. Without Cap getting ready for bed next to me, the emptiness of the small room was overwhelming.

Would this be something I'd have to get used to, if Cap was thrown in prison? He could be there for years. We'd broken the law, in so many serious ways.

I laid down. There was nothing else I could do but sleep now. Even tears would be wasted.

I slept uneasily, and woke up when Cap tiptoed back into the room in the middle of the night. He quietly slid out of his boots and laid down on the bed next to me, still fully clothed. I rolled over and leaned against his chest.

"Cap," I whispered into the darkness. I felt his chest rise and fall as he sighed deeply.

"You need to sleep," he whispered back.

"But I don't want you to go to jail."

He sighed again. Gently, he ran his fingers through my hair. "It'll work out. But for now, sleep."

His fingers continued to stroke my head. Slowly, still in his arms, I drifted off. I felt his lips brush the top of my head tenderly, as I fell asleep.

# CHAPTER 67

CAP WOKE ME UP AS HE rolled out of bed at first light. He'd slept in his clothes, which were wrinkled, and yawned tiredly as he bent over, tying the laces on his boots.

"I'll change later," he said, glancing up at me as I reached for the clothes I'd set out the night before. "We have too much to do this morning."

"Cap, about you going to the police about all this—" I started, but he waved me off.

"I know you're worried, but it's the right thing to do. We need to own up to our actions. And we need Trimboli and his men to be locked away, for good."

"But they'll arrest you, too. You've broken the law."

"Then we'll face the consequences for our actions," Cap said, running his hands through his hair and pulling on a fedora.

"Don't tell them everything. Just lie."

"Even if we lie, Masso will tell them everything," Cap replied, lifting his hands, his gesture helpless. "We have no choice, Andi. We've lied too much already. I can hardly keep up with all the lies we've told."

"We won't be able to get married," I said desperately. "You're throwing away my future, too!"

He stared at me, his eyes pleading.

"Trust me, Andi," he said. "I have one last plan in mind. I think it'll all work out, in the end."

"But—"

"But you have to get going," Cap said, checking his pocket watch. "We're already late. Hopefully Chito and Claude are already out, getting what we need."

He rose and grabbed my packed bag as he hurried out the door. I finished putting my boots on behind him, and frowned as I closed the door.

Whatever vision I'd had of a private, romantic sendoff was dashed by his focus on getting the rest of the team on the road. It was the story of our relationship: always one adventure after another, never any time to slow down and just spend time together.

We reached the lobby, where Dessie and Patrick and Bernard hustled in and out, carrying boxes and bags to the Fords out front. In their hurry, they nodded, forgoing conversation.

Cap led me outside, where he tucked my bag into the Ford.

"The map's here," he said, pulling it out of his pocket. "You're lead car, to start off. Make sure you keep a tight hold on that map. I wrote the directions here, too, but you'll need to know where you are, especially as you drive through the night. Some of the roads will be easy to miss in the darkness."

Willis looked up from the back of the lead Ford, where he was tying down a box.

"You'll be pleased to hear that we're ahead of schedule, Cap," he reported. "Claude and Chito hit an early morning market, and just ducked out to get a few more things and refill the reserve gasoline supplies. We'll be ready to hit the road earlier than planned, I think."

"Good," Cap smiled. "I'll be inside for a few minutes, settling things with the hotel clerk. Keep up the packing."

I assisted Patrick with the last of the tie downs.

"You're lead car today," he told me as we worked. "I figured I could ride passenger, and maybe Leonce or Claude could hop in and rotate with you later?"

"Works for me," I said, pushing the hair out of my eyes. "I'll drive first, for a few hours, then? You'll have to navigate for me."

"Not a problem," he grinned. "I don't often get to sit back and relax. It'll be nice."

"Relax, huh?" I smirked. "Sounds more like you're planning to nap."

"Hey now, don't be jealous."

Suddenly, I heard a familiar voice behind me say, "Edith?"

That voice that shouldn't be here, though.

I turned, a sinking feeling in my stomach. I hadn't heard my real name in a year—maybe longer.

This couldn't be happening. Not now.

We were just about to leave. Another few minutes, and I would have missed him completely.

"What are you doing here?" I gasped, unable to drag my eyes away from him.

# CHAPTER 68

I FELT THE BLOOD DRAINING from my face as I froze, staring at him.

"Surprise!" he beamed, hugging me. "This timing is perfect, too! I didn't figure I'd get to see you in action, out here with the cars!"

My mouth hung open, my stomach lurching from panic. I felt faintly like I might throw up. He stared at me, concern flickering in his eyes. "Are you okay?"

"How?" I uttered, still shocked.

"We took the train in from Lyon, early, to surprise you," he replied, smiling. "Rollie just ducked inside to surprise the team. But it's incredible, really. He's all better now. I can't believe how rapidly he managed to recover."

He stood there, leaning casually against my car, more tanned than he was when I had last seen him many weeks ago. He was lean, his arms carved by the hours he spent outside around the farm. He was starting to get wrinkles around his eyes now, but they still held the same tiny gold flecks I remembered from years of staring into his face.

I tore myself away from his eyes. I tried to quench my growing panic. Why now? There was no time to explain this to Cap.

"You didn't send notice?" I gasped. "I told you to telegram or call when he was ready? You didn't even let me know. I told you to let me know! This is—I needed time to prepare for—for your arrival. And we can't, not right now! We're just about to leave!"

"You're not making sense," he replied slowly, his smile waning. "You know I don't have a telephone. And I *did* send a telegram. Didn't you get it?"

"No," I blurted, wondering if there was still time to rush him away from the cars before anyone else saw him. My heart thumped wildly, my brain racing. "I sent you a telegram telling you in no uncertain terms *not* to do this. Not to show up here—not like this!"

The smile disappeared from his face and was replaced with a look of confusion.

"I was trying to do you a favor," he replied, puzzled. "I didn't want you to have to drive all the way back. I thought it would help if I could instead bring Rollie to you. And besides, I thought it would be fun to see you in the middle of your new job, as a world explorer."

"No," I breathed again, panic swelling in my chest. He shook his head, his eyes now troubled.

"He was excited to come here and astonish you with his progress," he said slowly. "We both were. We thought you'd be happy about the surprise of it all."

The door to the hotel lobby opened and Rollie stepped out, a smile on his face.

"Hey, Andi," he said, grinning at me with his familiar boyish charm.

The leanness was finally gone, and the weight he'd lost laying in his hospital bed had come back. His cheeks were their familiar, hearty pink. He was wearing different clothes, simpler ones, but carrying a small bag that must contain his Chinook Voyageurs uniform.

Despite the terror I was experiencing at their unexpected arrival, I launched myself at him. "Rollie! How are you feeling?"

I smiled in spite of my lurching stomach as I felt his arms go around me to hug me, realizing that he could control them on his own at last.

"I feel great," he replied. "All that fresh air and good food, the time to sleep in and relax and do chores? I feel like a brand new man."

"You can talk normally again?" I cried, holding him at arm's length and studying his face. "You're fine? You're really okay?"

He grinned at me, the familiar action endearing. "It all came back. I can talk and move just fine. Like it never even happened. Hard to believe, isn't it?"

Impulsively, I threw my arms around him and hugged him again. "It's a miracle!"

Oh, how far Rollie had come. The last time I'd seen him, I'd had to help carry him from the car with Patrick. Now, he seemed back to his old self.

"How did you recover so fast?" I exclaimed. "You were a wreck when we dropped you off! It's only been a few weeks?"

"I had the will to heal, I guess," Rollie smiled. "You have no idea how frustrating it was laying in a bed, trying to speak and not being able to get the words out. You know I like to talk. It was torture. And seeing how much of a burden I was to everyone? I wanted nothing more than to get out of bed and keep trying to improve, every single moment."

"You weren't a burden to anyone," I shook my head. "You were attacked. Blindsided. No one blamed you for what happened. We prayed every day you'd wake up after being hit in the back of the head like that. Not everyone would've survived it, you know. You're lucky."

"Yeah, it was touch and go for a while, I hear," Rollie said, rubbing his face ruefully. "I'm just sorry you all had to wait with me so long. But I'm glad you did, Andi. You guys meant everything to me."

Rollie abruptly grinned wide, his whole face lighting up as he stared over my shoulder.

"Hey, look who's back!" he yelled, lifting his arms like a heavyweight boxer champion.

"Rollie!" I heard a clamor of excited voices cry out, rushing over to us.

"I *told* you it was a good surprise," Hudson's voice called out, above the clamor.

The Chinooks pounded him on the back, hugging him and babbling out dozens of questions. He was passed around again for a second round of hugs, as Hudson draped an arm around him and cheered.

"Roland!" he yelled, smiling. "You're one stubborn, strong-willed son of a gun, and I for one am grateful for that trait that brought you back here to us."

Marceau and Rollie hugged for a long moment, Rollie whispering something to Marceau. I smiled to see the heartfelt reunion between these two best friends.

Willis threw up his hands. "Drinks! We're going to toast to this moment, everyone. God knows we've had little to celebrate the last few months, so let's take advantage of this."

"We're just about to leave, though," Dessie exclaimed. "It's dawn, anyway."

"They're still loading the cars," Hudson said. "Chito only just returned, and we're still waiting on Claude to get back. Come on. It'll take a second. That's all. Then you guys can hit the road. It's our very last opportunity, as a team."

"I'll help get them," Chito said, following Willis into the lobby. Just then, Cap stepped out from the lobby, squinting in the early morning light. I saw him glance curiously at the man next to me.

Panic hit me with overwhelming force. Cap couldn't talk to him. I had to get him out of here, as quickly as possible.

I whirled around, quietly ushering him away from the cars, pushing him down the block. "Thank you for bringing him back here, but let's talk down the street."

I prayed that Cap wouldn't follow us.

"Of course," he replied, his French accent heavily coloring his words as he stared at me in confusion. "What's wrong?"

"I'll tell you down here," I said, pulling him toward a small bakery. "Follow me."

Patrick stepped into our path, blocking my quick exit.

"Good to see you again, my friend," he said, offering his hand. "Andi was right. You were the man for the job. We're so thankful for all you did to help Rollie."

"It was my pleasure," he replied, shaking Patrick's hand. "It was an honor to care for such a famous crew, to have a celebrity in my house. And it's sure nice to see a close-up view of what you all do. I'm glad we were able to catch you. It looks like you're just about to leave again?"

"We are," I said hastily. "I need to talk to you, just for a moment, and then I'm hitting the road."

"It was good seeing you again. And thank you for everything, really. We owe you a great deal," Patrick called out as I tried to usher him away. "Take care of yourself, Arnau!"

I winced as I heard Cap's stunned voice behind me.

*"What?"*

# CHAPTER 69

I TURNED TO SEE CAP staring, his jaw hanging open. He stared at Arnau, then dragged his gaze away from his face to mine, his blue eyes big.

"What did he just say?" Cap exclaimed.

Dread overtook me. These were the only two men on earth that I never wanted to have meet each other, yet here we were.

The secret fear I'd been carrying around for weeks had finally come to light. It had been Arnau, my childhood friend, that I'd gone to in Lyon and begged to take in Rollie.

Only Arnau wasn't just a friend—he had once asked me to marry him.

I'd refused, but had carried the lingering hope that we'd end up together even as I joined the Gallivanter Expedition. Cap had found out about Arnau in the first few months of our travels together, and I'd mislead my team into thinking that I *was* engaged to Arnau. I'd written to him nearly every day, for months, as I struggled through the early challenges of our expedition, before discovering that Arnau had fallen in love with someone else.

Instinctively, I knew that Cap would be upset that I'd turned to Arnau again in a time of trouble. Because of that, I had decided to keep it a secret from Cap that I'd taken Rollie to Arnau's home to recover, knowing he'd be livid once he found out. I didn't want one more thing to burden him—not with all the stress of the last few weeks piling up on his strained shoulders. I had planned to tell Cap at some point, but the timing never seemed right. Our situation had only become more desperate, by the day.

Apparently, the lie had finally caught up with me.

"You must be Captain Gallivanter!" Arnau smiled, stepping forward and offering his hand. "I've heard so much about you. It's an honor to finally meet you."

Cap reflexively shook his hand, staring hard at him. "You're *Arnau*?"

"Yes sir," he replied with a polite smile. "Arnau Deschamps."

Hudson drifted over and extended his hand. "Arnau, huh? Well, thank you, Arnau, for taking such good care of our Rollie. He's been telling me he stayed with you for the last few weeks. That you took good care of that rascal for us."

"It was our pleasure," Arnau replied. "Any friend of Edi's is a friend of mine. And I knew she must be desperate, if she came to me like she did."

"Hold on," Cap said, holding up his hand. He was rapidly piecing it together, frowning.

"You took Rollie to stay with *Arnau*?" he said, turning to me. "That's your friend in Lyon? It's been *Arnau* who cared for Rollie, all this time? That's who you've sent the telegrams to, to check in?"

"Yes," I said, hoping we'd be able to have a rational conversation about this in private. I watched as Cap's eyes blazed and he pursed his lips. He was angry.

Bernard saddled up next to Hudson. "You're the one who took care of Rollie?" he interrupted, oblivious to the tension between the four of us staring at each other.

"Yes sir," Arnau replied. "I'm Arnau Deschamps. It was a pleasure taking him in, really. No trouble. I'm glad I could help."

"Hold on now," Bernard said, squinting at him. "Did you say your name is Arnau?"

"Yes," he replied, glancing at me in confusion.

*"Dear God, smite Bernard down right now,"* I prayed. *"Don't let him say anything. Freeze his tongue, God. Don't let him speak. Don't let his mouth open."*

Even as I prayed feverishly, I heard Bernard blurt it out. "Wait—so that means you're the Arnau that Andi was going to marry?"

Silence descended on the group. I cringed as I stared between Cap and Arnau, squirming. Dear Lord, this couldn't possibly have gone any worse, could it? My cheeks flamed bright red.

"That was a long time ago, and we were very young," I said, wishing I could sink into the ground and never be seen again. "Obviously, things have changed. A lot has changed."

"Wait, you two were *engaged*?" Hudson asked, confused. "But what about Cap?"

Now Arnau turned to me, the question written all over his face. "Wait, you are engaged to someone?"

"Yes," I replied, nodding at Cap. "To Captain Gallivanter."

Cap and Arnau examined each other, holding each other's gaze, the two very different men who had loved me at two very different times in my life. I saw Arnau's eyes flicker as he studied Cap. Instantly, I recognized the competitive look that emerged in both of their faces—faces that I knew so well.

"Andi, what the hell is going on?" Cap finally said, breaking the gaze to glare at me. "Why is he here? Tell me you didn't go to him for help and then keep it a secret from me, all these weeks?"

"I can explain," I protested.

Cap took a step back. "You wouldn't really keep something like this from me, would you?"

"He was my only option. Rollie needed some place to stay. And I knew I could trust him. I knew he'd help me. So I went to him and asked for him to take Rollie in, watch over him—"

"But you didn't bother to tell me about it!" Cap interrupted. "You know I'm a man of truth, of integrity. You know I value honesty. And you *lied* to me about this? Why?"

"I didn't want you to worry—"

"You didn't want me to *worry*? So you went straight to the man you were planning to marry before you knew me, lied about seeing him, and expect me not to *worry*? Why not just tell me if you had nothing to hide, Andi?"

He breathed hard, trying to control his emotions. Abruptly, he turned to Arnau. "I'm sorry, sir. I appreciate all you've done to take care of Rollie and help him heal. I imagine it was a significant burden for you, and we are grateful for your efforts. I apologize for my anger. It's not directed at you."

"Right, but it's misplaced," Arnau replied, his face steely. "I don't understand why you're so upset with Edith. She explained it to me—how desperate their circumstances were. Surely you can find it in yourself to understand why she did what she did? Why she came to me? We're close, after all. She knew she could trust me."

I felt the breath go out of me. Arnau was standing up for me, against Cap? Good gravy—this was only going to make things worse.

The tension was thick as I watched Cap and Arnau glare at each other—two men who both cared deeply for me and clearly felt protective of me. Unfortunately, each man saw himself as my protector and the *other* as the adversary.

"That's our business," Cap retorted. "I'll thank you to keep your nose out of it."

Arnau turned to me and spoke in French, obviously trying to keep Cap from understanding him. "You are really engaged to this man? A man like *this*?"

"It's not like that," I responded quickly, in French. "He's a good man. He's just...upset right now. He's been under a lot of stress."

I realized with sudden guilt that Hudson could understand what we'd said, but Cap and Bernard were clueless. It would only add to Cap's feelings that I had gone around his back and purposely left him out.

Sure enough, Cap became angrier.

"Don't speak to her like that, in French," Cap glared at Arnau. "I understand that you and Andi have a history together. But it's in the past. You're not a part of this—not anymore. Please go home. We have work to do."

"Her real name is Edith," Arnau growled. "And maybe you don't know her as well as you think—maybe Edi's keeping things from you because you clearly can't control your temper—"

I winced at Cap's expression. I knew he'd exhibited remarkable self-control these last few weeks, trying to manage unthinkable strain and increasingly impossible circumstances. But Arnau had no clue about any of that. All he saw now was the proverbial straw that was breaking the camel's back, as Cap's last ounce of self-discipline dissolved right in front of us.

"Get lost," Cap snapped.

Now Arnau flushed.

"You can't tell me what to do," he responded angrily. "I'm not one of your employees. I just did a huge favor for you and your team these last few weeks. And for your information, I'm happily married and have no interest in Edi. Even though I can't help but question why the hell she's interested in *you*."

"Stop it!" I yelled, pushing between them. "This is my fault! Arnau, I'm grateful for your help. You were a saint to take Rollie in when we were desperate. Cap, whatever there was between Arnau and me, it was just friendship. You're right, it's in the past. I was a lonely kid, that's all."

"A lonely kid who is still apparently so close to her 'friend' that she turned to him in her most desperate hour, right?" Cap replied, his voice hard. "I can't believe you kept this from me."

I bit my lip, knowing that Cap was terribly sensitive to any hint of betrayal or deception. His first fiancée, Milly, had cheated on him with another man and lied to get Cap thrown in jail. Her unfaithfulness and duplicity had deeply wounded him.

*"He's lashing out because he's been hurt like this before, by someone else he thought he could trust,"* I thought. Still, his accusations stung.

"How can you say that?" I exclaimed. "I had no other choice! We couldn't leave Rollie in the hospital. He needed a safe place to go, a quiet place to recover for a few weeks. We couldn't bring him with us, he could barely even walk. The doctor said he needed a quiet place with low stimulation—"

"And Arnau was just at the forefront of your mind, apparently? His name was the first one that popped up?" Cap shot back.

The rest of the team now surrounded us and listened, mute spectators in the drama of my messy love life. My face was pink with humiliation.

"Yeah, it was," I replied, trying to control my anger. "He's my friend. A *good* friend. And like a good friend, he took Rollie in to help me. That's what friends do."

"Seems like a pretty damn close friendship," Cap replied, watching Arnau's face. "I can't believe you didn't tell me. Why would you lie to me about something like this? You know my job is to keep everyone safe. I'm responsible for an entire team, Andi. I need to know everything, in order to make the best decisions possible. What else have you not told me?"

Arnau jumped in before I had a chance to respond.

"Stop controlling her," he snapped, his French accent thick. "She doesn't need you to tell her what to do."

"I'm not controlling her, I'm controlling all of *this*," Cap shot back, pointing at the Fords. "See all those cars? All these people? I'm responsible for all of it—all of their lives. No, I'm not trying to control her—I'm trying to keep her *safe*. To keep all of us safe. And I can't do that when she's not telling me the whole story—"

"All I see, Captain, is you trying to control a strong woman who's supposed to be free," Arnau growled.

Cap turned to me. "Andiamo—"

"Andiamo," Arnau interrupted, with a wry laugh. "Has she ever even told you how she got that name? It's from me. *I* gave it to her."

Cap reeled back, his eyes blazing. His body reacted like he'd just been punched.

*"Oh, great, another thing I didn't ever tell Cap—this omission dating back to the earliest days of our expedition,"* I thought, biting my lip. He was sure to get even angrier, hearing that Arnau had been involved in picking the very name he called me. That I'd kept this from him, too.

I jumped in before the two of them could say anything more. "Listen, Cap, I was in charge and I had to make the call, in that moment. I was only trying to keep everyone safe, too, and spare you from stress. I should've told you, but I didn't want to make you angry—"

"Make me angry?" Cap retorted, taking a step away from me. "I can't believe you, Andi. I can't believe you kept this from me, all this time."

Arnau's face was flushed as he turned to me, shaking his head. In French, he spoke to me again, his words clipped with anger. "You cannot want to marry this man. You deserve better than this and you know it."

"It's stress," I responded, slipping into French as I pleaded with Arnau. "You don't know what else is going on. We're in a very difficult situation. Our crew—something bad happened to us, and we're trying to work it out. He's just under too much stress. He's not usually like this. He's usually calm and patient. Rational."

"What did I just say? Stop talking to her in French!" Cap cried, taking a step toward Arnau. Rollie stepped forward, laying his hand on Cap's arm.

"Cap, you need to calm down," he said sternly. "I can attest to what Andi is saying. You weren't there. You don't know what it was like. I just laid in that hospital bed, helpless, feeling like a worthless lump while they tried to figure out what to do with me. It was the best option, and I'm glad she made the call. Arnau and his wife were very kind and thoughtful, the entire time I was with them. They helped me. Andi made the right decision—the best decision she could've made, in that situation. She was the captain, and you need to respect her decisions. Just like we all respect *your* decisions, as captain."

"Right, like I'm going to trust what *you* say," Cap responded angrily, throwing Rollie's hand off his arm. "You had a thing for Andi, too—"

"Cap, stop!" I yelled. I'd never been so embarrassed.

Now Rollie was furious, as well.

"Listen, Captain Gallivanter," Rollie glared at him hotly. "Andi's a beautiful young woman, and she has a lot to offer. You'd have to be blind not to see how special she is. Clearly you did, because you snatched her up, didn't you? But this is your fault, too, for not telling anyone that you two are engaged. You're hiding her, demanding that she be yours and only yours, but she's her own person. You can't expect her to interact with a dozen other men who have no clue that you're together and then berate everyone when they show interest in her! Wake up! If anyone thinks she's possibly available, why wouldn't they go after her? I mean, *look* at her!"

I felt the heat creep up my face as I saw the eyes of everyone in the group swivel toward me.

Patrick cleared his throat. "Why don't we all take a break here? It's been a long couple of days, and I'm sure Rollie and Arnau are pretty stressed after their travel, too. Let's just calm down and relax for a few minutes—maybe you three can sit down and talk it out—"

"I'm not sitting down with either of these two," Cap exclaimed. "And Andi, of all the people on this planet, you know how much I value honesty—"

He stopped himself, biting his lip and running his hand through his hair. Exhaling, he shook his head.

"I'm going to prison, Andi," he said, his voice defeated. "Probably for a very long time. And in one fell swoop, the two other men in your life who have *also* loved you—the two men who have come closest to taking you away from me—just reentered your life. I have no idea what tomorrow will bring, but I'm certain of one thing: I'm going to be arrested. I won't be by your side anymore, but these two *will*. As I'm saying goodbye, they're saying hello again."

He whirled around and shoved through the group, heading toward the lobby door. He slammed it shut behind him, the sudden thud rattling loudly.

# CHAPTER 70

WE STARED AT EACH OTHER in silence for a moment, before Rollie spoke up.

"Well, at least he didn't hit me this time," he said, rubbing his jaw.

"He *hit* you?" Arnau exclaimed, his face clouding as he looked at Rollie. "Why?"

"You heard him," Rollie shrugged. "He thinks I have a thing for Andi."

Arnau shook his head. "I don't understand that word, 'thing'—what does it mean?"

"Love," Bernard said bluntly. "Rollie is in love with Andi, too."

"No, no," Rollie said quickly, his cheeks pink. "I didn't know she was engaged. You heard me. It's not my fault. And no, anyway."

"Oh," Arnau replied, glancing at Rollie. I wondered if they'd talked about me while Rollie stayed with Arnau and his wife, healing up. Apparently Rollie hadn't told Arnau about his feelings for me, at least.

"This is my nightmare," I muttered in a low voice, glancing at Chito.

He put his hand on my shoulder and squeezed. "It'll be alright," he murmured quietly, looking at Arnau with curiosity. I'd confided my feelings about Arnau to Chito months ago. I bet Chito never thought he'd get the chance to actually meet the man.

In my embarrassment, I just wanted to walk away. But I'd created this mess and I'd have to clean it up now. If Cap and Hudson could step up and shoulder the consequences of our actions, I could take responsibility for my mistakes, too.

I had to stop blushing and get over my humiliation. We had a life to save.

"I'm sorry, everyone," I spoke up, raising my voice to be heard by the whole group. "Rollie, I'm truly glad you're back. And I'm thankful that you've healed. Arnau—thank you for helping him. And please thank your wife too. You both are wonderful. But it's time we got going. We have a long day of travel ahead of us."

"I'll tell Sabine about what you said," Arnau said, nodding. "It was our pleasure. Rollie, you know you always have a home with us now, I hope."

"Only if you're not doing the cooking," Rollie grinned, slapping him on the back. "That rabbit stew? I can live without that for a while."

"Hey now," Arnau made a face. "It wasn't that bad."

I shoved my hands into my pockets. "I'm going to finish packing. Thanks, Arnau."

Arnau stepped to my side quickly, catching my arm.

"Hold on a moment," he said, speaking French again. "Clearly, we have some things we need to discuss before you leave. You can't just walk away right now—"

"They're French Canadian, you know," I interrupted, waving at the Chinook crew who stood around us, still listening. "They can understand everything you're saying in French. So if you're trying to keep things private, between us, they're *not*."

"Zut," Arnau exclaimed, pursing his lips. "I forgot. I knew Rollie was fluent, but I didn't realize about the rest. Why didn't you tell me sooner?"

"I didn't think you'd keep speaking in French. You shouldn't have. You did it just to get under Cap's skin. You knew it would make him mad."

"We'll let you two talk," Hudson said to the both of us in French, grinning. "We'll be in the lobby. But remember, we've got to get rolling. You have a few minutes, that's it. Just long enough that we can fill Rollie in on what's going on now. But you need to get going right away."

Chito stayed by my side as the rest of the team walked away. He searched my eyes, his face kind. "Do you want me to stay?"

"I need to do this on my own. Don't worry."

"I'm not worried about you," Chito replied, speaking quietly. "But honestly? I'm worried about your future with Cap. Be careful, Andi. You two need to work this out. You can't keep up this pattern of fighting and pulling away from each other—especially not with all of us under such immense stress. We both know that that's why Cap lost his temper here. But he has to know he can trust you, and that you respect him enough to be honest. And he has to do the same for you. The two of you are a team now. You need to act like it."

"I know, Chito," I nodded. "But I have things I need to talk about with Arnau. Privately. I owe him that. And if Cap can't trust that—a conversation between old friends, one of them married and one of them engaged—well, that's another issue. One that Cap and I will have to talk about together."

Chito started to respond, then stopped. He sighed, exhaling through his nose. "Fine. I'll be in the lobby."

Arnau and I watched him go, then turned to each other. I summoned my courage to speak first.

"I'm sorry," I replied. "I should have told them about Rollie staying with you. This is my fault."

"Why didn't you?" Arnau asked. "I didn't realize you were keeping me a secret in all of this. Why not just tell Cap the truth?"

"Why?" I repeated. "Why didn't I tell Cap about you? Come on, Arnau. You're a man. Figure this out. He worried about you. When I first started on this team, things were—complicated—between us. I knew he'd be livid that I went to you, of all people, for help. That he might assume that we're still *something*, if I turned to you in a moment of crisis. That it would appear as if I'd gone running straight back into your arms the second I left his side—"

Arnau shook his head, his curls flopping in the achingly familiar way that I remembered from all the years of boarding school, as we raced our horses around together every day. Those afternoons seemed so long ago, but standing here with him now, it was like they'd happened yesterday.

"I don't understand," he said, his voice soft. "What have you told them about me? Did you tell them we were engaged?"

I blushed again, cursing my face that couldn't hide my emotions.

"It was complicated," I explained, embarrassed. "I went away, after being kicked out of boarding school, and I had no one at my new school. And then I ended up on the Gallivanter team, and I thought Cap had feelings for someone else. It was maddening. I had feelings for him, and I foolishly assumed he didn't have feelings for me. I ended up pouring all my emotions into the friendship we had. You know, I had no real friends besides you and Clara at school. My team saw me writing letters to you and assumed you were my sweetheart, so I led them to believe that we were engaged. The lie just got away from me. I mean, it wasn't *that* far-fetched. You had proposed to me when we said goodbye—"

"I know," Arnau interrupted, his own cheeks flushed now. "I don't know what I was thinking. I was just overcome with emotion when you left. I didn't want you to go, you know. You were—and still are—so dear to me."

"I didn't want to go, either," I admitted. "But ever since then, I've been going. And going. All over the world. Leaving Lyon was just the first step."

"Apparently you were destined for a life of travel and adventure after all. Aren't you glad I bought you that geography book all those years ago? And you thought I was crazy for purchasing it."

"I did," I replied wistfully, remembering how he'd scraped together what little money he had, scrimping and saving for months to buy me a geography book. I'd nearly memorized that book, tracing the pages and pictures over and over again dozens of times. It was still in my travel bag, one of the few items I'd taken with me and not sent home to my mother.

We stood quietly for a moment, uncertain what to say to each other.

*"Be strong, Andi,"* I told myself. *"Speak your mind. It's no time to conceal things. Not anymore."*

I stared at Arnau, seeing his handsome face like I was a young, lonely little girl all over again. I remembered how immediately he'd offered friendship, how easy it had been to laugh with him. To escape together, from the confining bars of my cold Catholic school prison, and run away for a few hours every day and think of nothing but the sun on my face, the wind in my hair, and the companion by my side.

I'd been expelled from school for punching a bully. The headmistress had forced me to leave immediately. Arnau's friendship had been the biggest loss, as I was forced to move out of the city and go to another school across France.

"I missed you, Arnau," I said, my voice low. "When I left school and went to that new place? It was horrible. I missed you so much. And even when I went away and joined the Gallivanter team, I still missed you. You'd meant so much to me. You'd saved me, from that horrible place where no one else even looked twice at me. And somehow—it was silly—but I was holding onto hope for a long time. I thought there was more between us."

"There could have been—" Arnau blurted, then stopped abruptly. He bit his lip. "That's not what I mean to say."

I exhaled. "You got married. To Sabine."

Arnau stared down at his hands. "I know it hurt you," he confessed. "I love Sabine. She's a wonderful woman. But even if the two of us—it never would've worked out, you know."

"I know," I said quietly. "And somehow, I knew it then, when you first proposed. I think we both knew it, and just never could admit to each other that we both knew it."

Arnau shoved his hands into his pockets. He was uncomfortable. He paced away from me, shaking his head.

"Listen, now's the time to be honest with each other," I implored, holding out my hands. "This conversation is long overdue, Arnau. And clearly, I can't possibly be embarrassed any more than I have been today. I'm tired of lying and concealing. It's done nothing but get me in trouble lately. So let's be completely honest with each other, for once."

He laughed, but was still clearly uncomfortable.

"I feel stupid talking about all of this now," he confessed, staring across the road and avoiding my eyes. "But I've felt so guilty for so long. About how we left off. How the last thing I did was ask you to marry me, and then joked about it, not giving you a straight answer when you asked what I meant. I played with your heart, and I shouldn't have."

"You didn't play with my heart," I said gently. "We were too young to know what love really was, anyway."

"Were we?" Arnau asked, his face turned away from mine. I hesitated, but answered truthfully.

"I was," I replied. "I didn't know who I was yet. But all those letters I wrote to you, when I went away on the expedition...I know now it was your friendship I missed. And I *did* miss it. You kept me going through those first few months of my journey. Just like you kept me going, while I was at a school I hated, away from my family and without any other friends."

"No," Arnau interrupted. "It was the idea of me, maybe. The idea of friendship. But I had nothing to do with it—it's all you. It's who you are. You're a fighter, you know that? It's no coincidence you got thrown out of school for fighting. Come on."

I stared at Arnau's back as he paced away from me. The back of his neck was flushed, and he rubbed it uneasily. We'd always been so open with each other, teasing and laughing. What had happened between us?

"Arnau, I didn't even know who I was back then," I said. "We were so young. I treasure our friendship, but marriage? Thank God we didn't end up married. We're just not compatible. Not in that way."

He turned and looked at me. The simple white shirt he wore with the sleeves rolled up set off his tanned forearms.

"*I've* always known who you are," he replied. "Your spirit? Your courage? I've always admired it."

"You have?"

"I have. But I don't understand, though, why you're with these men," Arnau continued. "Especially not Cap. Is this really who you've become? He's angry. He seems dangerous."

"You don't understand," I replied, stepping toward him. "I can't tell you the full story, Arnau, even though I want to. You've walked into the middle of a tense situation. Everyone is under extreme stress. They're not acting as themselves."

"He's a loose cannon," Arnau pressed, ignoring me. "He punched Rollie? Over jealousy? How can you want to marry a man like that? He's not right for you."

I flushed. "You don't understand the whole story. There's good reason for it, I swear."

He stared at me. "And you don't trust me enough to tell it to me? Not even after you showed up at my farm, without notice, and begged me to take in one of your crew mates? I watched over Rollie for weeks, Edi. I brought him meals. I helped him walk. I took him on rides in my wagon, helped teach him to split wood and pitch hay bales to get his strength back. I taught him how to write again, practiced his words every day."

Arnau kicked at the tire of the Ford. He was angry.

"You're probably right, though," he added, his voice bitter. "You probably can't tell me. You can't trust me."

"Fine," I retorted, my patience gone. Cap and Hudson were going to prison, anyway. Why not tell one more person what was going on? I was sick of the lies. "Did Rollie tell you what happened to him?"

"No, not really," Arnau replied. "He said he was hit in the head and knocked unconscious. I assume it was some sort of accident with the automobiles?"

"Well, here's the truth," I said, leaning back against the car. "Their crew was attacked by criminals a few weeks ago. Rollie was hit from behind. Patrick was shot, Hudson had his hand fractured, and the others were beat up badly. Even Dessie was beat up."

"*What?*" Arnau replied, shocked. "When was this? Why didn't I hear about this in the newspapers?"

"Because we kept it from the newspapers on purpose," I said, lowering my voice. "It happened right before I brought Rollie to you. A bunch of them were in the hospital, but Rollie didn't recover as quickly as everyone else. We weren't sure if he would ever recover fully. We needed to move on, but we couldn't leave him behind. But he was too frail to take all the way here to Spain. His doctor said he needed some place quiet, not too far from Switzerland, where he could stay and heal. That's why I needed your help. He needed a safe place to recover while we all moved on.

And I needed someone I could trust—someone who wouldn't tell anyone else what was going on."

"I had no idea about all of the backstory," Arnau said, concern etched on his face. "I can't believe you didn't tell me when you first arrived at my farm. I could tell you were upset, but I wouldn't have guessed something like this was what you were facing. That's terrible."

"That's not even the worst of it," I replied. "They kidnapped Paz, one of our crew. His family is rich. He was bragging about their wealth at a bar one night, a few days before they got attacked in the middle of the country road, and the wrong people overheard him. Somehow, they traced the Chinook Voyageurs and were waiting for them. They pretended to have car trouble, and the Chinooks pulled over to help them. That's when they were attacked. And now they're holding Paz for ransom. They're going to kill him when they get the money. We haven't told anyone because we're racing to try to find him. To save him. The police haven't helped us at all, so we've had to handle it on our own. We've been at our breaking point for weeks—it's a race against the clock. You have no idea how stressful it's been—"

"This is impossible," Arnau sputtered, his dark eyebrows raised in utter disbelief. "You can't be mixed up in something like this. Not in real life. This doesn't happen to people like us."

"But it did."

He shook his head, overwhelmed.

"That's why I took Rollie to you. That's why I couldn't say more, when I left him with you. I know you had questions for me that I couldn't answer, when I saw you a few weeks ago," I confessed. "I'm sorry. I couldn't tell you the whole story then, but I am now."

Arnau blinked, his brown eyes filled with concern. "I understand. It makes sense why you were so quiet. So tense. Why Captain Gallivanter and Rollie just blew up back there."

"Rollie doesn't even know what's been going on here. After we dropped him off with you, we went in pursuit of the gang who kidnapped Paz," I continued, wrinkled my forehead. "Yesterday, we managed to capture one of the kidnappers, and we found out where they're hiding him. It's in Rome. We're headed there today, to get him out."

Even as I spoke, my mind reeled. Was it really only yesterday that we had kidnapped Masso and tortured him? This story sounded unbelievable, even as I uttered it.

"No one on earth besides our team—and now you—know about this," I added. "You can't tell anyone, Arnau. I'm trusting you with a huge secret. One that could get my entire team arrested."

Arnau stared at me blankly.

"I can't believe it," he said, finally finding his voice. "You want to be with these people? Doing this?"

"What?"

"You want to be with them? Your crew?" he repeated, his voice incredulous. "After all this? The danger? And all the terrible situations you've been in, the last year? And now, heading to Rome, into even more danger?"

"Wait," I frowned. "Have you been following the stories about me in the newspapers all year?"

"Of course I have!" he exclaimed. "I care about you! I worry about you!"

"Oh," I said, biting my lip. I'd written to him about our travels for many months, but I didn't realize that he'd been following along in the news, too.

We faced each other. I struggled for the right words to capture how I felt.

"I understand that they come across as angry, or reckless, or dangerous," I said slowly, trying to make him understand. "But you don't know this team like I do. You can't understand. The bonds that connect us are strong. We've lived together. Seen and experienced so much together. And no one but us can understand it. Only someone who's lived it. They're my family now, Arnau."

He stared at me.

"Is *this* the life you really want?" he blurted. "Not a house and a family of your own?"

"Yes," I smiled wryly. "I couldn't wake up in the same place, day after day, wondering about what I was missing out on. The world's a big place. I want to see it all."

"We're so different, Edi," Arnau said softly, shaking his head. We stared at each other, silent.

After a moment, he cleared his throat.

"Thank God we realized how different we are," he confessed. "I guess we should've had this conversation before you left, that last afternoon. At least we can clear the air now, after all this time."

I didn't know what to say. For so long, the elusive possibility of a future between us had lingered as we eluded honest conversation with each other. Now that we had spoken it aloud, the possibility had become impossible. The undefinable had been neatly defined, and it left a bittersweet wistfulness in its wake.

In a low voice, I replied, "I do appreciate all you've done to help us. Rollie's recovery is miraculous. I'm grateful."

"Anything for you, my Andiamo," Arnau quipped, using his old nickname for me.

I was well aware that he had been the one who came up with the nickname that I'd adopted as my stage name for the Gallivanter Expedition, even if I hadn't admitted it to Cap at the time I chose it for myself. In his own way, Arnau had influenced who I'd become.

*"He was right,"* I thought. *"He had known who I was, long before I knew it myself. The geography book? The nickname? The final push to go and live a new adventure?"*

Crossing his arms, Arnau interrupted my racing thoughts by adding, "But you're not really *my* Andiamo anymore, are you?"

I stood across from him, staring at him. My life had been turned upside down since I'd left him. Somehow, he was simultaneously a part of me and yet didn't even know me anymore.

I felt an odd sort of possessiveness about Arnau, like I wanted my childhood memories of him to remain unclouded and uncomplicated. He belonged in my past, not in my present. And yet here he was, his disapproval of my choices somehow chafing me. I wanted him to be proud of me, but—he wasn't. Not of what I was doing now, anyway. But it was *my* choice. *My* life. His approval didn't matter.

Not anymore.

For so long, I'd worshiped him from afar, holding him up as the man I might someday marry. And now, we both realized with finality that we never would've been compatible anyway.

He was still a wonderful man—just never the man for *me*.

"So, um," Arnau shuffled his feet, clearly embarrassed. "I thought maybe I could stay and catch up for a day or two, and get to know your team before I went back home. But I guess you're leaving now. Like, right now?"

"Yes. I'm sorry."

"Me too," he sighed, disappointment evident in his voice. "Well, I guess I'll head back to the station and get a ticket for the next train out."

"I'm sorry," I said again.

We stood staring at each other, neither of us sure how to end the conversation. Despite my fondness for my old friend, I was acutely aware that he'd caught me in an embarrassing moment with Cap and Rollie, and I still felt humiliated.

"I have to go," I said, finally breaking the silence between us. "I'm sorry. Really. I'm sorry for everything. But Arnau, thank you for being a dear friend and taking Rollie in like that. You're just the good, reliable man I always knew you'd become."

He smiled ruefully. I saw sadness and regret etched into his face alongside his pride and fondness for me.

"Be careful, Andiamo," he replied. "You're doing things I never dreamed you'd do. Especially now, headed into Rome. But I guess if anyone's capable of it, it'd be you."

Impulsively, I hugged him goodbye. For a moment, breathing in the familiar scent of his skin and hair, I was fifteen years old, laughing as we saddled up the horses in the barn after class. I was Edith again, free from the strain that pressed in on me every waking moment these last few weeks—free from the stress of desperately trying to save a man's life.

Then, the hug ended. The chapter of our lives we'd shared together closed.

I stood looking at him, back to being Andiamo Gallivanter, the world-famous adventurer and newly-minted vigilante on a mission.

Hudson stuck his head out of the lobby doors. "Sorry to interrupt, but Claude is back. Ready to roll?"

"Yes," I said, feeling guilty that I was relieved to be walking away from Arnau. I suspected that Hudson had been watching us from the hotel window, waiting for the opportunity to jump in.

Arnau tipped his hat at me and headed down the street, back toward the train station. I refused to look back at him, knowing Cap would be watching us, too.

# CHAPTER 71

I CROSSED THROUGH THE lobby doors to find the entire team circled around, talking. All eyes turned to me as I joined the group.

Across the circle, Chito lifted his eyebrows. I shrugged in response, pursing my lips. Cap was nowhere to be seen.

"We were just coming up with shift schedules for tonight," Patrick informed me, glancing my way. "Here's what we've written down so far."

He handed me the paper and I scanned it.

"Anything else before we get going?" Patrick asked, looking around the circle. We shook our heads. "Alright. Let's say our goodbyes to Hudson and Cap and hit the road. Remember, rest up and sleep when it's not your turn to drive. We're not stopping unless we absolutely need to."

The group disbanded, the Chinook Voyageurs immediately piling up around Hudson to say their goodbyes. I searched over their heads for a glimpse of Cap, but I didn't see his tall frame.

"Where's Cap?" I asked Bernard, after he shook Hudson's hand without comment and walked over to my side.

"I don't know."

*"He must be back up in our room,"* I thought, jogging toward the stairs. I had to see him before we left. We couldn't leave things like this. Not with the uncertainty we were facing.

I rushed up the stairs to our hallway and entered our room. He wasn't there.

Frowning, I checked down all the other hallways. At the sight of each empty corridor, my heart sank deeper.

He was gone.

*"Maybe he's back down in the lobby and I just missed him,"* I thought, heading downstairs. The team was still milling about, pulling on their goggles and helmets.

Dessie lifted her eyes to me as I crossed the room.

"Where's Cap?" she asked. "We didn't get the chance to say goodbye to him yet."

I inhaled, frustrated. "I don't know. I was hoping he was down here."

"Oh," she replied, searching my expression. Wisely, she held her tongue.

Patrick, Claude, and Rollie headed out to the cars, the others on their heels. Outside, I heard the sound of the engines rumbling as they started up. Only Chito and Dessie and Hudson remained in the lobby with me now.

"Where's Cap?" Hudson asked, looking around. "I thought he'd be here. You know him, he can never pass up an opportunity to boss people around."

"I don't know," I admitted, feeling my cheeks burn as my embarrassment deepened. I was his fiancée, for Pete's sake. We were headed out on a dangerous mission, and he was probably going to end up in prison when the dust settled. He couldn't even suspend his anger for a few minutes to say goodbye?

"You screwed up," Dessie shook her head. "You should've had him out there with you, when you and that Arnau character were talking to each other."

"Why would I do that?" I replied, rankled. "It was a private conversation. He should be able to trust me."

Dessie rolled her eyes. "You don't understand men. All he would've had to see is the body language between you and Arnau. You two were the most awkward people together. It's clear that there was never really anything romantic between you. If he would've been watching, he would've seen it."

"Wait, were *you* watching us that whole time?"

"Of course I was."

"You're ridiculous, Dessie."

Hudson looked at his watch. "Sorry, but you need to get going, ladies."

Chito put his arm around me. "You know how Cap is. He blows up and has to walk away, be by himself for a while. He runs hot and has to let some of that steam off on his own. And probably even more so right now, being under so much stress. Hudson will tell him you said goodbye. Right, Hudson?"

"Right," Hudson said sympathetically. "Sorry, Andi."

"But—what if I don't see him again?" I asked. How could Cap do this to me?

"Come on," Chito said, leading me out the front door. I squinted in the sun. He walked me to my car, where Patrick was already waiting. The others were still climbing in.

He opened the door for me and turned to face me.

"You're the strongest girl I know," he said quietly. "Yeah, you've made some mistakes. And maybe the way you handled things with Arnau was a big one. But you have the strength to learn from it and keep going. You can't beat yourself up over what's already been done. Right now, you need to focus on the task at hand. We need you, Andi. You need to help lead this team on to rescue Paz."

"I know," I sighed, squaring my shoulders. I inhaled, tasting the balmy air that was starting to heat up before a hot afternoon. Nodding to him, I climbed into the driver's seat and Patrick slid in next to me.

I waited until Chito was settled in the Ford behind me, and then turned to look at the convoy behind me.

"Everyone ready?" I shouted.

Horns honked and voices yelled, "Ready!"
"Let's go!" I hollered, pulling out.
We were on our way to Rome.

# CHAPTER 72

ONCE WE GOT OUT OF the city, clear of pedestrian traffic, I gunned the engine.

As lead driver, I knew I set the pace for the entire team behind me. It wasn't the first time we'd pushed the Fords to their limit, but it would be the longest we'd kept the Fords running at one time.

I prayed that Marceau and Bernard and Patrick could repair anything we might face over the next twenty-three hours of this madness.

Patrick said little to me, other than giving me a few directions until we got to a main road.

"I'm going to try to sleep now," he grunted, pulling his jacket over his face. "I don't know how I can. It's the middle of the morning. But I have to try."

"I'll wake you up if I need you."

Abruptly, Patrick slid the jacket down off his face and reached his long arm over to my shoulder. He squeezed it, sympathetic. "Hang in there, Andi."

I bit my lip and nodded. We didn't need words to communicate between us. Not anymore.

He pulled the jacket back up and curled up to sleep. Alone with my own thoughts now, I struggled not to worry about Cap. I was still angry that he hadn't come to say goodbye, to give me a chance to explain myself, but I was even more concerned about his plan to turn himself into the police.

*"You can't do anything about it,"* I told myself. *"They've made the decision. And you're stuck on the road, now. You can't even*

*communicate your thoughts to them anymore. You just have to trust that somehow, it'll work out."*

But my mind went again and again to Cap. Was our future over?

Hills and cliffs, lakes and streams and woods and farms and houses blurred by as I drove through without marveling at the changing scenery. Occasionally, I glanced down at the map to make sure we were still following the right roads, but when I looked up at the world around me, it was if I had blinders on.

My mind circled to Paz, then Cap, like water whirling down a drain. I couldn't shut it off.

We pushed on for hours, driving at full speed over the bumpy roads, until I needed to refill my gasoline tank. I raised my hand in the air, signaling to the automobiles behind me that I needed to pull over.

Skidding in the loose gravel on the side of the road, my car slowed to a stop. I turned it off and hopped to the back, retrieving a canister of fuel. We'd cut our supplies down to the bare essentials, leaving as much space as possible for gasoline. We only carried food, mechanic supplies, our medical kits, and almost literally, the clothes on our backs. I'd only brought one spare change of clothing. We'd left even the tents and tarps back at the hotel.

Patrick pulled the jacket off his face and yawned. He stood so I could pull the bench up to reach the gasoline tank. "Want to switch?"

"Probably should." I unscrewed the lid and tipped the canister in. The scent of gasoline stung my nostrils.

Behind me, the other cars filled their tanks. Marceau wandered up while I was pouring. "How are you guys doing?"

"Fine, what about you?" I asked.

"Tense," he admitted. "Even this feels like we're wasting time."

"I know."

"We're doing the best we can, to get there as quickly as possible. But still, I can't help but worry about him," Marceau said, rubbing his neck.

"I know. Me too."

"Well, better take advantage of the stop," he shrugged, walking toward a small wooded area several yards away. Having lived with men for a year now, I knew he was going to empty his bladder. All the other men had disappeared to the spot, their backs to us. Dessie and I would have to wait and go in there after them, discreetly, going deeper into the trees. We never had it as easy as they did while we traveled.

After we'd all taken care of our business and refueled, we climbed back in. This time, Patrick drove while I tried to nap. The rough road and sound of rocks pinging against the bottom of our automobile kept me up. A few times, I pulled my jacket off my head to look around at the scenery. The sun was setting, the pink and orange glow lighting up the sky, by the time I actually drifted off to sleep.

Patrick woke me up when it was pitch black outside, the stars sparkling bright in the sky above us.

"Hey, sleepy," he said, yawning. "I'm exhausted. I need to pull over and switch with someone else. And we probably need more gasoline, anyway."

"Sure," I said, stretching. My neck and back ached from the uncomfortable ball I'd wedged myself into, trying to sleep.

We pulled over again, grumbling about how tired we all were. I handed Chito the map, and he unfolded it, pinning it against the side of his Ford with one hand, while Marceau held a flashlight up so we could see.

"We've made it through Montpellier, France," Chito said, running his finger along the coast. "We're about halfway to

Aix-en-Provence now. From there, it's still nearly nine hundred more kilometers."

"We've been clipping along at just over sixty kilometers an hour, so we're looking at another fourteen hours or so," Rollie said, standing next to Chito and peering down at the map.

"Hey now, that's impressive," Chito replied, smiling at him. "You can still do math, huh?"

Rollie grinned. "I always had a head for numbers."

"We need to rotate drivers," Willis said, rubbing his eyes. "I'm wiped out. Who hasn't driven yet?"

"I can drive," Claude volunteered. Bernard and Marceau raised their hands, too, and Leonce volunteered to drive another leg though he'd started the earliest shift driving.

Racing through the darkness was a peculiar sort of exhilaration, we quickly discovered. With no one else in sight, we could push the engines as fast as possible. We never knew where road signs might be, however, and more than once we screeched to a halt when we saw the glimmer of animals' eyes on the road in front of us, darting away.

With the cool wind blowing in my hair and the moon waxing on the horizon, it felt like we were on another planet. We couldn't see any of the scenery, so time seemed to drag on endlessly.

The road here in France was smooth, but strewn with gravel that dinged hard against our car.

"I hate this," Bernard complained, driving carefully to avoid the rocks along the side while I sat in the passenger side, trying to sleep. "It'll completely ding up the Fords."

We followed behind Claude's car, which had taken the lead. Dessie was giving directions by flashlight, illuminating her torch every so often.

I dozed off lightly, still hearing the occasional pop of rocks bouncing against our car. Bernard swore under his breath every time we hit a big one. His terse words melted into the background of my brain as I drifted asleep.

Suddenly, I heard a pop and the tinkle of glass, and Dessie and Claude screamed.

# CHAPTER 73

I SAT UP ABRUPTLY, my eyes springing open.

Their automobile veered in the road in front of us, and Bernard frantically braked, skidding into the ditch to avoid crashing into the rear of their car.

Behind me, I heard Marceau swearing as he narrowly missed colliding with us.

"What's going on?" he yelled, as Rollie stood up to see into the cars in front of us. Willis was already out of his seat, jogging toward Dessie's car.

I wrenched my door open and darted forward to join him.

"Oh no," I gasped, as Dessie turned toward me. The headlights from our car illuminated the scene. Their windshield had shattered, broken pieces hanging haphazardly down from the metal frame. Broken glass was strewn all over the front seat, including bits all over Dessie and Claude.

"What do I do?" Dessie gasped, as blood trickled down her forehead and cheek. She appeared to be cut in dozens of places along her face and neck and hands.

I peered at Claude in the driver's seat, who stared down at the bleeding gashes all over his arms.

"I don't even know what happened," he said blankly, as blood dripped down and stained his pants. "Something must've hit the windshield just now."

"It had to be a rock," Dessie said, standing up slowly. Pieces of falling glass jangled together in a beautiful symphony, showering over her feet and the floor and bench seat of the Ford.

"Gloves," I uttered, sprinting back to the car.

"Don't touch them yet," I called, over my shoulder. I rummaged through our supply box, squinting in the darkness illuminated dully by the headlights of the cars, and pulled out a few pairs of leather gloves. I ran back to Willis and handed him a pair. We hurriedly pulled them on.

"Let's take it slowly here," I said, offering my hand to help Dessie step down from the car. She winced as she saw blood pooling on her clothes, down her pants.

"How bad is it?" she cried, touching her face and turning pale as she pulled her hand away and saw blood. In the darkness, it looked black.

"It's not bad," I replied, feverishly hoping that was true. I prayed there wasn't a piece embedded in one of them that had nicked a nerve or artery.

Dessie climbed out of the car, the small flecks of glass still caught in her clothes cascading onto the road at our feet. The cuts on her face were bleeding profusely, the blood staining the collar of her shirt a deep crimson.

Unwillingly, I flashed back to that moment I'd glimpsed Cap and Bernard after a rock slide had overturned their Ford as we traveled through a narrow gorge in French Sudan last year. Their car had flipped with the force of the rocks pummeling it, and we'd had to pull them out from the crumpled wreckage. They'd both had injuries so serious and lost so much blood that we'd initially thought they were dead.

Cap had barely survived. If I hadn't rushed him to a nearby hospital, he wouldn't be with us today.

I gritted my teeth and forced myself to concentrate on Dessie. "Do you feel pain anywhere else, other than your face and neck?"

I studied her body. She appeared to be bleeding from two deeper spots on her face, but the cuts all over her hands and neck looked shallow.

"I don't think so," she responded, her voice panicked. "I can't really tell. I feel like I hurt all over."

"This is why we all wear goggles when we drive," Willis said, as I unbuttoned Dessie's jacket. He helped me pull it off her arms, gently, and I laid it on the ground, several feet away. "Thank goodness you didn't get any glass in your eyes."

I glanced over at Claude, as Marceau and Patrick helped him out.

"How is Claude?" I asked, shaking Dessie's hair as little bits of glass fell out onto the dirt.

"He's fine, I think," Marceau responded, holding a piece of bandage up to Claude's face. "I think they're mostly minor cuts. Just a lot of them."

I held Dessie's thick blonde mane and suddenly froze. "Dessie, I need you to hold very still," I said, looking closely at her head.

A large shard of glass, about three inches long, was embedded in her scalp, on the crown of her head. It caught the light from our Ford, glimmering in the darkness.

*"She must've ducked her head when the rock hit the windshield,"* I thought, staring at it. It probably protected her face, but it was hard to tell how deeply this piece of glass was stuck. We'd have to remove it immediately.

"What? What is it?" Dessie exclaimed, her eyes wide under her goggles.

I spoke soothingly, trying to calm her fears. "You're going to be fine, but I need you to hold very still right now. Don't touch your head. There's a piece of glass stuck in there, and we need to remove it. If you reach for it, you'll risk shoving it in even farther."

"How deep is it in?" she cried, instinctively reaching toward the top of her head. I grabbed her hand.

"Don't touch it," I said. "You're going to need to sit down, on the ground, so I can reach it to pull it out."

Still holding her hand, I led her away from the glass outside her car and toward my car. I noticed that the blood dripping down her hands sprinkled the dirt as we walked. I helped her down to the ground, Willis following me.

Patrick now stood next to me, studying Dessie's wounds. He shone a flashlight down on her, revealing the extent of her cuts.

I walked around to the back of my car again, searching for our medical kit. Patrick followed me. "She got it worse than Claude. The windshield must've cracked on her side."

"I think so. She said she thinks it was a rock," I replied, tugging out our kit.

I pulled out the brown metal tin, unclasped it, and opened it up. Inside, we had several lengths of gauze bandage, burn emollient, cotton, scissors, a tourniquet, adhesive plaster, and paper drinking cups. The kit also contained spirit of ammonia for fainting, and mercurochrome and small wooden applicator sticks, for applying to wounds. A small first aid guide rested on top, with the content list printed inside the metal lid of the tin.

Inside another tin, we had a large collection of a new item called the band-aid. Cap had researched them, and bought us several packages. The small, self-sticking bandage was novel technology, a bit expensive but highly practical. They were handmade and had to be shipped over from the United States, but they stuck to our cuts better than the other bandages we had so we used them frequently.

I grabbed the tin of band-aids, several bandages, and the mercurochrome solution and walked back over to Dessie.

"Hold this," I said, handing the band-aid tin to Patrick. "Can you distract her while I pull this glass out of her head?"

"Sure," he said, kneeling down to face Dessie. He held the flashlight above her head, shining down on her crown. Willis stared down at her, next to me. "Let me know how I can help."

I pulled off my gloves and laid them next to me on the ground. I knelt down, too, to look Dessie in the eye.

"Listen to me, Dessie," I said, keeping my face calm even as I watched the blood ooze down her face and neck. Her collar was spotted with blood now, the bloom of saturated crimson now soaking down the front of her shirt. "I'm going to get this out, but you'll need to be still. I'm going to have Patrick hold your hands steady, so you don't reach for your head. When it's out, I'll apply some antiseptic to all your wounds and bandage you up."

"Okay," she replied nervously, staring at me. "Have you done this before?"

"Yes," I lied, knowing I couldn't tell her the truth.

Patrick leaned forward and smiled at Dessie as I stood up, handing Willis the bandages, the glass bottle of mercurochrome, and the applicators.

"Did you know that these first aid kits were first used to treat American railroad workers, in the 1880s?" Patrick said brightly. "And during the Spanish American War, they made them even smaller and more portable, so soldiers could carry them around?"

"That doesn't really matter to me right now," Dessie gasped in pain, as I attempted to gently pull the shard of glass out of her head. She bit her lip and tried to reach up. Patrick held her hands down.

"It hurts!" she shrieked, her head jerking back.

"I'm sorry," I responded grimly. "You need to hold still, though. I need to get it out."

"Then shut up and get it out!" Dessie cried.

"Those little bandages though, that she's going to put on you? They're new. Called band-aids. They were invented in America, too," Patrick continued. "Invented by a man who was tired of his wife burning and cutting herself while cooking. He created something that she could use to dress her own wounds, quickly and easily."

"Oh gosh, just shut up," Dessie groaned. "I don't care."

"How do you know all this, anyway?" Willis asked. "You sound just like—"

"Like Cap?" Patrick grinned. "Yeah, I know. He's the one who told me all this, when we drove together a few weeks ago. He's like a walking encyclopedia of knowledge, I swear."

I pulled again, this time successfully easing the glass chunk out of her head. Blood bubbled immediately, concealing the wound, as I tugged the shard clear.

"Got it!" I exclaimed, dropping it to the ground.

"Nice job. Thank God you have steady hands," Willis remarked, handing me a bandage. I pressed down, keeping my hand flat again Dessie's head. I could feel the blood welling up under the thin bandage, warm and wet.

"Dessie, put your hand up here and hold this in place," I said, coming around to study the cuts on her face. Carefully, I wiped each spot clean, and had Willis hold another bandage up to the deeper cut on her left cheek while I worked on a gash along her jawline that was dripping blood.

For several minutes, I worked quickly and quietly, applying pressure and wiping the blood up. I unstoppered the small glass bottle of mercurochrome and dabbed it on top of the cleaned wounds, gently, before placing several band-aids across the largest gashes on her jaw and cheek. Patrick held the flashlight while Willis helped me apply band-aids on several small cuts along her arms and neck.

Dessie still held the bandage up to the wound where the glass had been embedded in her scalp. I stood up, and gently lifted her hand, looking closely at the gash.

"It's still bleeding a bit, but I think we can apply some antiseptic now," I said, applying the mercurochrome and pressing a large, clean bandage into place. "This stuff is going to dye your skin, just so you know. You'll have patches of red from it, but it'll keep the infection out."

"We'll have to tie it on, I think," Willis said. Chito, newly arrived to our little medical party, fished through the medical kit to pull out a large strip of fabric.

"Oh, this is just wonderful," Dessie groaned, as Patrick held the bandage in place on her head and I deftly looped the fabric strip under her jaw, up along each side of her face, and tied it securely in place to hold the bandage. "I must look awful."

"You look like you're lucky you survived a windshield shattering in your face," Willis said. "You're damn lucky that you were both wearing goggles. And that you weren't going any faster than you were."

"It doesn't feel like luck," Dessie said, holding out her arms and studying the small bandages on them. "Can someone get the mirror out of my bag? I need to see my face."

Chito dug through her bag and found a small enamel compact, and brought it over. Dessie popped it open and grimaced.

"My face!" she moaned. "I look terrible!"

"It's not that bad," Willis and Patrick hastened to compliment her. I rolled my eyes, still cleaning Dessie's blood off my hands. It was crusted and dried under my fingernails now. Dessie studied herself with growing worry, and started to pull the bandages off the deep gash on her jawline.

"Stop that," Willis chided, pulling her hand away. "Andi just cleaned that up!"

"But I need to see how bad it is!" she protested, moving the tiny mirror around to get a better look. "How deep was the cut? Do you think it'll make a scar?"

"It's hard to say," Willis shrugged. "We're not doctors, doll."

Bernard held up his arms from where he was observing silently. "I have some scars from the car accident I was in, but they've healed pretty well. They're faint now."

Dessie stared at his arms, her disapproval evident in her face. "I can still see scars," she said dismissively, turning her attention back to her mirror. She pursed her lips as she turned her head and carefully examined the band-aids.

"Do you think this one will scar?" she asked me, pointing to her jaw. "It's in such a visible place!"

"I don't know," I responded. "But it could've been much worse. When those windshields crack, they can kill people pretty easily. There's a reason a lot of people wouldn't dare do what we're doing. These automobiles can be dangerous. We're all facing the possibility of getting hurt, maybe even seriously wounded, by driving them around everywhere. I mean, people get killed by shattered windshields just driving in between their house and their neighbor's house. That's why we have to be careful. And that's why Marceau and Bernard spend so much time inspecting the vehicles, to make sure we avoid any unnecessary accidents."

Dessie patted the bandage on her head, ignoring me. "How deep did this one look?"

I sighed and walked away without answering.

"Hey!" Dessie exclaimed behind my back. "Why do you just think you can walk away? I'm upset, Andi. I have every right to be."

I whirled around. "Dessie, we've all had misfortunes happen. Think of Rollie. And Cap. And Hudson and Patrick. We're in a dangerous profession. What did you think this would be? A fun little whirl on the merry-go-round? Sometimes you get hurt. Deal with it."

"But it's my face!" Dessie complained. "It's my best feature. It's the first thing men see when they look at me."

I glanced pointedly at her slender, curved body. "I think we both know that's not what men pay attention to when they're staring at you."

"Just because you have a man locked up already," Dessie pouted. "You don't get it. I need my beauty. It's all I have."

I threw back my head in frustration. "I'm sick of hearing this from you. It's not *all* you have. You have wit and strength. You can talk to anyone and convince anyone to give you what you want. That's your resourcefulness—your cleverness. Stop underselling yourself, Dessie. You're more than just a pretty girl."

"Of course I am," she snapped. "You don't have to tell me that."

"Then stop moaning about your injuries and get over it already," I replied. "By the way, maybe you'd like to thank me for spending the last half hour with your blood all over my hands, as I helped clean you up? It wasn't exactly fun, you know."

"You didn't give me a chance to thank you yet," Dessie glared at me. "But...thank you."

"You're welcome."

We stood glaring at each other. Willis read the tension as he put his arm around Dessie and led her back toward the group.

"You look wonderful, Dess," he soothed, smiling at her. "You'll heal up in no time. You'll be as good as new. As beautiful as ever. And it'll make a great story. I can just see it now, your face all over the papers again."

I breathed hard through my nose, trying to be understanding. I knew I'd be worried, too, if it'd been me in Dessie's position, all banged up.

But sakes alive, I certainly wouldn't act like *that*.

# CHAPTER 74

PATRICK AND I FINISHED bandaging up Claude's wounds and returned to the rest of group, who'd taken advantage of the stop to refill the gas tanks of each Ford.

"What are we going to do about their windshield?" Chito asked, wiping gasoline on his pants.

"Marceau said they'd have to remove all those broken shards and pull the whole frame out," Patrick responded. "He and Bernard are already working on it. We'll have to wait to repair it properly in a few days. For now, they'll just have to drive without a windshield. It'll be dangerous, but we have no choice."

"I guess Leonce and I should hand out a quick bite of food, then," Chito said, walking away to find him.

Patrick and I stood silently against my Ford, watching the others.

"Poor Dessie," he commented, watching her pout. Willis had his arm around her, rubbing her back.

I rolled my eyes. "She's fine. Trust me, she enjoys the attention."

Patrick gazed at me, a smile tugging on his cheeks. "You don't know the difference between you two, do you?"

"She's prettier. And shorter. And has everyone wrapped around her finger."

Patrick laughed. "First of all, she's not prettier. At the risk of sounding like a cad for saying this to another man's fiancée, you're both quite attractive girls."

"I am not—" I began, and Patrick shushed me with mock severity.

"Didn't your mother ever teach you not to interrupt a man when he's complimenting you, Miss Gallivanter?"

"Stop it," I grumbled. "I'm serious."

His smile faded. "You really don't get it?"

"No. Enlighten me."

He shrugged. "I thought it was obvious to you. What you see as disinterest, or dismissal, from the men here? It's respect. No one coddles you. Because they don't feel they have to. And that's because they respect you. As an equal."

"But Dessie gets so much attention. All the time."

"Right. Because no one thinks she can make it through these tough situations on her own. She exudes helplessness. *You* don't. Look at Claude. We patched him up, and nobody babied him. It's the same with you."

"It's still not fair," I muttered. My nerves felt raw, like I was about to snap at anyone and everyone.

*"It's the stress,"* I thought. *"You've been under tremendous stress, for weeks. This isn't you. This isn't how any of us really are."*

"I'd think that you being respected as an equal to every man here would make you happy," Patrick sighed. "Who cares about the attention she gets? Genuine, earned admiration is better than any exaggerated chivalry, massaged out of feigned vulnerability."

I rubbed my jacket, noticing for the first time that I had streaks of dried blood—Dessie's blood—all over the front of me.

"I don't dislike Dessie," I sighed. "She just gets on my nerves sometimes. And it bothers me that all the men treat her so differently than me. I understand why, and I get what you're saying. But it doesn't change my frustration."

Patrick nodded. "Just remember that you're not the same type of people, and that's not something you should hold against each other. Different experiences and different people have shaped you in different ways. You can't hate her because she's not like you.

Instead, you have to be fine with who you are—and just accept her for who she is."

"I know," I groaned. "Just do me a favor and don't go fawning over her like the rest of them do. She's perfectly capable of taking care of herself, you know. Clearly, as we saw when she had no problem carving into Masso, she's tougher than she looks."

"Yeah, I know," Patrick smiled. "Why do you think the two of us are such good friends? You don't pretend. I appreciate that you're honest and straightforward."

*"And yet not always honest and straightforward enough,"* I thought to myself, remembering Cap's face when he recognized Arnau that morning.

———◉———

BY THE TIME WE GOT the glass cleaned out of the car and the pieces of broken glass carefully removed from the now-empty windshield, it'd been nearly an hour.

The boys worked as fast as they could, the pressure of our tight schedule weighing on everyone's minds. The rest of us paced uneasily, covering our nervousness by cracking jokes.

A few of the men had made a quick fire, frantically brewing kettles of coffee and passing it around.

Chito had anticipated that we wouldn't have time to make coffee in our journey, and had instead packed small satchels of ground coffee beans in the front seat of every Ford. We snuck pinches of it into our mouths as we drove, sprinkling the grit directly on our tongues in an attempt to stay alert. A steady consumption of this, and now a mug of scalding coffee, worked along with my adrenaline to make me wired. I felt artificially bright, even though my body was heavy and sore.

I listened as the crew laughed together, trading barbs. It occurred to me that I never could've predicted this scene a few months ago. We'd fought each other publicly, in the newspapers, just a few months before. And now here we were, gabbing like best friends, trading stories and bringing up inside jokes.

What would we do if our expeditions ever resumed and we were both going after the same prize again?

A million dollar jackpot was on the line, offered to whichever crew made it through all the countries in the world the fastest. We had no timeline, but we'd already made it through twelve countries, nearly thirteen now.

I wasn't sure how many the Chinook team had made it through. Were they even still our competition?

I thought about Cap again. Assuming he got out of jail, I wondered if he'd ever want to continue traveling with the Chinook Voyageurs once we finally found Paz.

Knowing his stubborn independence and how he was close only to a few trusted people, I didn't imagine that he'd want to spend any time with them, after this. He was fiercely proud of our small crew of four.

It saddened me to think that our time with the Chinook crew would eventually end. Despite the terrifying, tense situation we'd been living through the last few weeks, we'd developed deep connections. The tragedy of losing someone that both teams cared about—ironically, the only person that both teams had known well—had bonded us.

Patrick nudged my boot with his, shaking me out of my taciturn reflection. We'd both unconsciously assumed the leadership positions for our teams, I realized, and had drawn closer than ever in our mutual roles.

"You're mighty quiet tonight," he asked, speaking indistinctly so only I could hear. "Is something wrong?"

"I'm just thinking," I replied. "Don't you ever stop and reflect about how strange this all is? That we're all traveling through these countries together, working to rescue Paz?"

Patrick shrugged. "We're on a mission."

"I know, but we're each other's competition. A few months ago, we hated each other so much that we were sabotaging each other in front of the whole world. But now we're working together. As friends. As one team."

"So? That's good."

"Yes, it *is* good," I sighed. "But what happens when this ends? Because you know it has to end. We can't go on together. The whole Million Dollar Wager competition thrives on the spirit of rivalry—multiple people vying for the same prize. So do we go back to being competitors, once we find Paz and get him back on your team?"

"I hadn't even thought that far ahead. I've only been thinking about the day-to-day. Each day has certainly had enough worry of its own lately."

"I know we don't have any idea what our plan for finding Paz is," I continued, swallowing back the growing doubts I had that we'd find him at all. Or that he would even be alive if we did finally find him. "But no one's talking about this. What's going to happen to all of us? Are we just going to split up again and never see each other after this?"

Patrick leaned against the car, thinking. "Be honest. Do you think Cap and Hudson could ever share the leadership of a team together, long-term?"

I considered his question. Cap was strong-willed and disciplined, a stickler for carefully researching and weighing all the options before we moved. He was charismatic in front of others, especially when he was on stage, but he could lose himself in quiet reflection when alone. He rarely let his guard down, and trusted only those closest to him.

Hudson shared many of those same qualities of discipline and charisma. He was rarely serious for long, leading his crew with a sort of lighthearted, carefree attitude that concealed the determination and dedication that marked him as their bold leader.

Right now, they were united with one common, simple objective: to find Paz.

But could they get along peacefully without that shared goal? I wasn't sure.

"I don't know," I replied. "I wish they would. But I'm not sure that when it came down to it if they could agree to supporting each other's decisions. They're two strong, independent men."

"Maybe I'll just leave and join your crew," Patrick joked.

"You wouldn't."

He sighed. "I couldn't. You're right. I couldn't ever do that to Hudson."

"What if we just stuck together long enough to travel through all the countries and finish the competition, and split the million dollar prize money together at the end?"

Patrick frowned. "A million dollars split four ways, between your crew—or nine ways for us—is pretty different than a million bucks split between thirteen people."

"Yeah, but we don't really need the money," I pointed out. "We had a ton of donations come in for us. Our bank account is full."

"But what happens when that money runs out? Or when Cap decides he wants to keep traveling, and you burn through a huge amount going on a new whirl somewhere else? Or when you have to pay for new cars or crew?" Patrick countered.

"I don't know."

"Besides, *we* need that million dollar jackpot. We don't have the donations pouring in like you do. And who knows? Maybe the

Odysseus Society would void the terms of our contracts if we don't proceed as two competing teams. Maybe neither of us would win, in the end."

I crossed my arms. "I guess we'll just have to enjoy the time we have together. I'm glad that we got to know each other, at least. Even for a brief time."

"We're ready to move again," Bernard finally called out, stretching his thin arms.

We quickly assembled, pulling our goggles back on and stretching, preparing for another long round of driving in the dark.

"Whoever is driving this car will need to be extremely careful now that we pulled the windshield out completely," Marceau told us, deep circles under his tired eyes. "I recommend you hang back, far behind the rest of the caravan, to avoid rocks getting kicked up. Keep those goggles and helmets in place as you drive."

"But look on the bright side—if we get in an accident, you'll fly right out the front and avoid crashing through the windshield," Willis cracked. "It'll be a quick death."

We climbed back into the cars, determined to keep going. We had no other choice.

"We're in it now, together, until the bitter and uncertain end," Patrick patted me on the shoulder. "See you at the next stop."

# CHAPTER 75

ALL NIGHT, THROUGH the inky darkness, we pushed ourselves and our Fords to exhaustion.

We crossed from southern France into northern Italy overnight, though it was impossible to see any scenery. When morning first started to color the sky with its soft pastels, Patrick motioned us from the lead car to pull over.

"Stretch your legs while we gas up," he groaned, his voice exhausted.

Chito and Leonce hurried to unpack food and hand items around. I tore into the soft tostada, recognizing the thick toast that had been often served to us with tomatoes, ham, and olive oil the last few weeks we'd been in Spain. Before I could finish the tostada, I was already back in the car and sitting behind the wheel, driving.

As we pressed on, urging the Fords to run at their limit, a tense sort of silence descended on the group.

Trees and hills, houses and farms and cities blurred past us as we kept going, refusing to stop until it was absolutely necessary to refuel.

Patrick and Chito and I studied the map as we stopped again, the others pouring gasoline into the fuel tanks. The sunshine was hot on the back of our necks. I already knew I was sunburned from spending all day yesterday and now today in the open-topped automobiles, but there was little we could do except drape scarves around our necks.

"We hit Pisa this morning and came down here, along the coast," I said, pointing. I consulted Cap's instructions. "We're right on track. Piombino is the last town we went through."

"So how much farther?" Chito asked, squinting. "Rome looks to be another two hundred, three hundred kilometers?"

I glanced at Cap's notes. "From Piombino, we keep heading straight south, down the coast, until we hit Santa Marinella. From there, we jog southeast, ending up in northern Rome. It looks like it's around two hundred seventy kilometers, give or take."

"That'll put us arriving in Rome around noon, then," Patrick said, wiping sweat off his brow. "We're close. Gosh."

"We haven't really talked through what we're going to do when we get there," I pointed out. "When do we have that conversation? And who makes the call?"

Patrick eyed me. "I think we all know who's already had some experience as captain of the crew."

"No way," I said, shaking my head. "That was just the three of us. This is different. There are nine of us now."

"So?"

"So? I'm no Cap or Hudson. I'm not a commander."

"But you're a leader. You've already been assuming the responsibility. And we need you."

"You're a leader too," I argued. "Why not you?"

He shook his head. "Why do you doubt your ability? No, you're no Cap. But leadership comes in different forms, at different times. Maybe we don't need an organized, meticulous person at the helm right now. Maybe we need to rally around someone with heart and courage at this moment."

I started to disagree, but stopped. He was right. We didn't have time to waste on dillydallying around.

"Fine," I replied. "But you're going to be my Hudson, then. We'll co-lead."

He grinned. "Oh, boy. Let's see, how to channel my inner Hudson Landry? Should I start by making inappropriate jokes at all the wrong times? Or by flirting with every girl I see, including those who are engaged to my co-captain?"

I rolled my eyes. "We'll drive the next leg together and figure out the plan when we get to Rome."

"Good," he said. He stretched his arms over his head, cracking his neck, and pocketed the map. I followed him to the car.

He tossed me the keys as we climbed in. "You're driving, though, Captain Gallivanter. That's *this* captain's orders."

# CHAPTER 76

AS I DROVE, WE PASSED lush ocean vistas of breathless beauty. Sunshine dappled trees and highlighted cliffs that dropped off into the ocean below, an endless blue horizon. Colorful buildings clung to the cliff sides and sprawled across the roadways we wound down.

Normally, I'd be gazing, enraptured, at the scenery. Instead, Patrick and I were strategizing.

"Do you think we should we head straight to the house where they're keeping Paz, or find a hotel for the team first?" Patrick asked. "I want to go straight to the house and do some surveillance. But my fear is that the team may be too exhausted to do anything today. We've pushed hard to get this far so quickly."

"Let's split the difference," I said, thinking. "We can send the team to find a hotel, and someone can circle back and tell us where. We pick an easy meeting spot, like the Colosseum. In the meantime, the two of us can quickly scout Stefano's house, then report back to the team. I'm hopeful we can take a quick nap and be refreshed and ready for action later."

"The hotel will have to be under fake names again," he pointed out, squinting at the trees we whizzed under.

"So we pretend to be old friends, reuniting in town for a wedding, like we did at the last place. It works. Explains our late hours and all the time together."

"We'll need to do surveillance on Stefano's place," Patrick replied. "Shifts, like we did with Trimboli's house."

"Right. But we have so little time. Everything needs to happen on an accelerated schedule."

He sighed. "We should've brought our disguises with us."

"I know. We were in such a rush, though. We can buy more, in Rome. Besides, it won't be as important—this kid doesn't know our faces like Trimboli and his men did."

"True."

"So what do we do about breaking into Stefano's house?" I asked.

"I don't know. We'll have to see what it looks like and figure it out."

"What about the police? Do we go to the local police?"

Patrick looked at me, shaking his head. "I've never appreciated Cap and Hudson more than I do right now, to tell you the truth. They have to deal with so many details—a thousand choices in front of them all the time. It's overwhelming."

"I know. I don't know how they manage to sort through this stuff and keep us all focused," I admitted. "But we have to do the best we can."

We tossed ideas out rapidly, thinking how we could approach the police without tipping our hands, and then fell silent. It was indeed overwhelming to have the responsibility of planning every step for every member of the crew, and know that they were trusting us to figure things out.

Patrick was quiet for a few minutes, looking out at the road.

Finally he said, "Do you think they're making the right decision, going to the police in Tarragona? They're going to be arrested, you know. There's no doubt about it. Even if we had good reason, they still broke the law. The law's black and white."

I remained silent. I didn't trust my tongue.

Truthfully, I was torn. Part of me was proud that Cap and Hudson were both honest men, willing to face the consequences of their decisions. The other part of me was angry and disappointed that they were turning themselves in and that they'd go to prison for the actions we all took together—especially Cap, who had tried hard to do the right thing, standing up against the others and bearing the brunt of their anger.

I just didn't feel like talking about the worry that had been swirling around in my brain nonstop.

Patrick glanced over at me, his look softening. "I'm sorry. I know it has to be hard on you. But I think you need to prepare yourself for the reality that they're going to be in prison for a very long time. Probably several years."

Grimly, I stared ahead at the road, clenching the steering wheel so hard my knuckles turned white. "I know."

We rode again in silence, Patrick wisely dropping the subject. I kept an eye on the mileage, and pulled over when it was time to refill the gasoline tanks.

"We've got to be pretty close now," Willis said, coming up to consult as Patrick held the map and tracked our progress.

"We are," Patrick replied. "Another hour or so. And when we get to Rome, we have a plan of action. Can you gather the team and have them come up here to get the rundown?"

"Will do, boss," Willis saluted, whistling to the others. "Hey! Get up here!"

In a few moments, the crew had gathered in a tight circle. I smiled in spite of myself, seeing Rollie join the group. It was good to have him back. I feared he'd never be able to join us again—he was a walking miracle. He met my eyes and grinned.

"Listen up, team," I said, filling them in on the plans Patrick and I had come up with. Heads nodded slowly around the circle.

"So you and Patrick are scouting the house first?" Chito clarified.

"Yes. We'll take the first look and report back to you. We'll drive the first rotation of surveillance teams over there and continue rotating through the day and night, like we did while we watched the gang's house in Tarragona. But we'll have to come up with a plan, and fast. We're on a much tighter schedule now."

"And you want to go to the police first thing?" Willis asked slowly.

"Yes," I nodded. "We have to try every possible avenue to help get Paz out of there. They'll have officers and resources that we don't have. Hopefully they'll agree to help us."

"Better take Patrick in with you and let him do all the talking, though," Willis replied, shooting me a hard look. "No offense, Andi. But you know how they are. They're a bunch of tough guys, a lot of them probably veterans of the Great War. They won't like a woman coming in and telling them what to do. Let Patty do the talking."

I bit my lip. He was probably right, but I still resented the reality. Patrick glanced at me and spoke up. "We'll handle it. You worry about the hotels and the surveillance. We'll deal with the police."

The team looked around, silent. Discouragement was written plainly on every face. We'd been driving now for over twenty-four hours straight, without stopping, through three different countries. We were exhausted and worried.

I blurted my thoughts aloud, instinctively.

"Listen, everyone, I know we're facing a lot of uncertainty right now. We're worried sick about Paz, we're worried that Cap and Hudson are in prison right now, as we speak, and we're worried about how we're going to pull off the next few days. We're tired, we're stretched too thin, and we're tense."

I looked around, making eye contact with all eight people in the little circle around me.

"I want to remind you that each one of you is on this team for a *reason*. You were handpicked—chosen—for your resiliency, your courage, and your resourcefulness. In the face of danger, when most people might freeze, you act. You persist. You find a way over and around obstacles."

Rollie gave me a small smile. It bolstered my courage.

"Over the last year of our expeditions around the world, we've faced incredible challenges," I continued. "Challenges that most people could never imagine. And we've survived every single step of the way. I promise you, we'll survive this, too. Look no farther than the faces around this circle. A few months ago, we hated each other. But now? Now, we're friends. No, we're more than that—we're family."

The group looked at each other, turning their heads as they met each other's eyes.

"We've each gone through hell and back the last few months, and we're still standing," I said, my voice low. "What's another day or two of stress? We've been shouldering it already, for weeks and months. Our shoulders are used to it now. We'll get through this. And in a week, we'll look back on this moment, too, with a sense of pride and purpose."

Intentionally, I sought each person's eyes, looking at my teammates.

"I trust each one of you in this group with my life," I said firmly. "And Paz is trusting us, too, with his life. We'll find him. We'll do whatever it takes to save him. By this time next week, we'll all be sitting around a bar, toasting our success. I promise you."

I finished up, the passion of my speech making my face pink with excitement. Breathlessly, I shut my mouth. The group stared at me, speechless.

"Damn, Andi," Willis finally said, with a grin. "I didn't know you could make speeches like that."

"That's my girl," Chito cried, as Dessie clapped for me.

"Even I thought that was good," Bernard admitted, nodding his head. "And honestly, I usually don't care to hear anyone's speeches. Or conversations."

"With those rousing words ringing in our ears, let's get back on the road," Patrick said. "Everyone knows what we're doing when we get to Rome, so let's get this done. We're nearly to the finish line, folks."

We walked back to the Ford, our boots crunching in the gravel. Patrick slapped me heartily on the back as we walked.

"And you didn't think you could lead this group?" Patrick grinned, looking sideways at me. "With speeches like that, you might put Cap and Hudson right out of a job."

# CHAPTER 77

THE TRAFFIC INCREASED as we drew near to Rome.

Other automobiles, horses and carriages, and people on bicycles trundled around the roads. Houses and neighborhoods, restaurants and schools and office buildings started to dominate the landscape, shifting from rolling fields and distant, hazy mountains to a bustling cityscape.

After the relative silence we'd had, speeding through the quiet night, the sounds of life felt foreign. Neighbors and children called to each other down the street, vendors chatted noisily from their market stalls and storefronts, and construction workers hammered and sawed high above our heads.

As we wound through the clogged streets into the heart of the city, I could scarcely tear my eyes away from the beautiful, ancient buildings. It seemed like every corner had a vast cathedral or set of imposing marble statues or ancient ruins, gleaming white and dusty pink and gray in the sunlight.

Except driving in Rome wasn't for the faint of heart. The roads were packed with vehicles, carriages, and pedestrians alike. It was mayhem. I gripped the steering wheel with white knuckles, trying desperately to control our Ford.

Ahead of us, the Colosseum towered with its grand arches, casting a shadow on the surrounding area. I'd seen pictures of it in books, but had never glimpsed it with my own eyes. It was staggering.

We had already determined this would be our meeting place in a few hours, once the team found a hotel and checked us in, and after Patrick and I scouted Stefano's house. We'd figured that such a famous destination in the heart of Rome would allow us a highly visible place to navigate to with ease.

"Good grief, it's huge," Patrick proclaimed. "It's crowded, too. We were right, we'll blend in with all the tourists. Perfect."

Patrick waved, signaling the cars behind us in the convoy. They beeped their horns in response, Willis navigating his Ford onto the road wrapping around the Colosseum and disappearing from sight. The others followed him.

"It's just you and me now," I said, glancing over at Patrick. "Get us to that house."

"Sure thing," he said, staring at the map. "We're heading out to the very outskirts of Rome, it appears."

The drive to Stefano's hideout took even longer than I expected, our journey slowed by the traffic and crowded streets of Rome.

Gradually, the crowds gave way as we wound through narrowing streets, old buildings and apartment complexes with chipped paint and grungy windows replacing the well-kept shops and homes in central Rome.

Silent faces watched out of doorframes and upstairs windows as we drove by. Homes and buildings slowly began to become more spaced apart, and overturned garbage cans and trash blowing through the street and abandoned, weed-infested lots added an air of depression to the area.

"Nice place to hide out," I commented.

"Or hide a body. You wouldn't even notice it in these streets."

Patrick guided me farther out into the countryside.

"We're close, I think. At least we know now Masso wasn't lying about the roads—the names he gave us all match," he said, peering up at larger homes, older and more solitary on acreage.

Tall hedges and ancient, gnarled trees protected most of the view of the road. "There. It's coming up," Patrick pointed. "That faded yellow one."

I slowed down as we drove past a sizable home, obviously aged but well-kept. It was surrounded on three sides with large trees and bushes. A carriage house draped its elegant arches across a wide cobblestone driveway.

*"Stefano's family must have had money,"* I thought to myself.

The windows were draped with dark curtains, shutting out the world. There was no sign of life whatsoever.

"That's it," Patrick said, staring as we drove. "Doesn't look like the hideout of a criminal mastermind, does it?"

"I'll keep going a bit farther down the road, and then turn back," I replied. "Do you think we could get out and poke around?"

"I don't know," Patrick mused. "There weren't any other vehicles around. But Masso said they have someone there guarding Paz, right? Some low-level kid?"

"Maybe he's gone for the day?" I asked, shrugging. "Maybe he's irresponsible and only shows up a few hours at a time?"

"So if he's not showing up regularly, maybe Paz is starving, or even sick. And he's stuck in there by himself, helpless. Oh, this is maddening," Patrick exhaled loudly. "We're so close. Should we just risk it?"

"We have to stick to the plan," I beseeched. "If we go in now, by ourselves, the others won't know what happened to us. Better to wait a few hours and have more of us here to help, rather than try to blaze in ourselves. I mean, what if we get taken hostage, too? Then the team will be trying to rescue three people."

"We could take him, Andi. You and me. You know we could."

I shook my head. "We have to stick to the plan. Logic our way through it."

"But shouldn't we at least check and see if he's in there?"

"How?" I exclaimed, frustrated. "We can't just go right up to the door and ask, 'Hey, is Paz de la Rosa here, by any chance?'"

"No, but we *can* pretend to be lost and ask for directions back to Rome. We're obviously not locals. It could work."

I wrinkled my forehead, thinking. He had a point. We could at least establish if anyone was at home.

"But if someone's there—this kid who's guarding Paz—and he sees our faces, then we're in trouble," I said. "The two of us won't be able to come back here at all. It'll be too suspicious."

"Fine, then let's make up a story about how we're thinking of buying a house that's for sale in the area, and we're lost," Patrick tried again. "If he sees us again, he'll think nothing of it. That we're just a nice American couple scoping out the area."

I nodded slowly. "Huh. That might actually work."

He held up the map. "We walk up with this, and make a show of being gregarious. You know, excited to meet our potential neighbors, ask a bunch of questions about the area, all that."

"Yes," I said, thinking. "We could even ask about his house, too. See if he lets us inside. You know, play dumb—how old is it, what's the furnace like, can we see the basement to check out the wiring?"

"He'll never let us in," Patrick shook his head. "He couldn't possibly be that dumb to let two strangers into the house where he's guarding a kidnapped victim."

We reached a turn, and I took advantage of the space to turn in and back the car up, reversing our course. I pointed the Ford back toward the house.

"We won't give him the option of refusing us," I said grimly, my mind made up. "We'll force our way in."

# CHAPTER 78

A FEW MINUTES LATER, I eased our car up the cobblestone driveway and under the cover of the carriage house. I took Patrick's arm as he smiled at me broadly, already playing the part.

"Let's meet our new neighbors, darling," he said, wrinkling his nose at me.

We walked arm-in-arm up the brick sidewalk to the front porch, our boots clacking against the old wood. The door was large and imposing, with a heavy brass knocker fixed in the middle of it. I glanced at the picture window next to the door, but it was blocked with heavy burgundy curtains.

Patrick knocked, already holding his map in his right hand, his left hand crooked so I could hang onto his arm.

"Seems no one's home," he said, as we listened carefully.

"Try again," I urged.

He knocked loudly, calling out, "Hello there, we're your new neighbors! We came to say hello!"

We stood silent for a moment, hearing nothing but the breeze scuttle dry leaves across the sidewalk.

"Let's go around back," I said, under my breath. "Maybe no one is home and we can sneak in."

I released his hand, and crept along the porch, sidling up to the oversized picture window. I leaned in, squinting to see if I could get a peek through the tiny crack in the curtains.

I bent over, my hands on my knees, my face up to the window. Suddenly, a dark eye stared back at me, inches away.

"Oh!" I shrieked, reeling back. "Someone's in there!"

A moment later, the door wrenched open. A short but powerfully built young man stood blocking the doorway, his face angry.

"Chi diavolo sei? Cosa stai facendo qui?" he called out, clearly upset with us.

I knew he was asking who we were and what we were doing on his porch, but I decided to play the part of a dumb American.

"Oh, honey, so nice to meet you!" I gushed, offering my hand. "We're your new neighbors, the Smiths. We're buying a house down the road, such a cute little place."

He glared at me, refusing to shake my hand. He shook his head, his dark eyes dangerous. As I studied him, I realized he was far younger than I initially thought. With his swarthy dark skin and features, he looked older at first glance but when he spoke, it was evident that he was only a teenager.

"Non puoi essere qui," he said sharply. "Esci."

I continued to babble, grabbing Patrick's hand.

"Baby, just look at the paint scheme they used here!" I said excitedly, letting my eyes travel all over the front of the house.

I smiled buoyantly at the Italian boy and explained, "We're going to redo our new place, and I just begged to come meet some of the neighbors and see what they've done with their own houses. Can we just pop in? I'm *dying* to see what you did with the living room."

The boy glared at me, his mouth pursed tightly.

"Non parlo inglese," he growled, then frowned as he stammered, "No English."

I knew our best chance was to keep playing dumb and hopefully confound him with the foreign language long enough to sneak a peek inside.

Patrick played along, jumping in.

"Say, fella, I'd love to see what you've done with the basement," he said amiably. "We're thinking of rewiring the electrical, and I think I may need a new furnace. Mind if I see what you have in the basement? I've been thinking about installing a wine room, too. It'd sure be swell to check out your downstairs so I can start dreaming myself."

"Oh, and I'd love to see the kitchen, too," I squealed, pretending to spot something over the Italian boy's shoulder.

Emboldened by the confused look on the boy's face, I pushed my way in, pressing up against him, talking animatedly the entire time.

"I love these old houses," I said, pretending to examine the window trim. "So much character, so much history—it's like I'm going back in time, just walking into one! This one's just beautiful, you've done so much with the place!"

Patrick squeezed in behind me, holding my hand.

"Women, you know?" he shrugged with a smile, as the boy stared at us in shock.

The Italian boy stood frozen for a split second, then started yelling. "No, no, vattene! Adesso!"

"Oh, 'adesso'—is that the word for kitchen? How quaint!" I asked with a smile, taking a step through the darkened living room to try to see beyond, knowing he was actually screaming at us to get out.

The boy rushed over and grabbed me by the elbow. Patrick took advantage of the boy's turned back and walked briskly toward a set of stairs down the hall.

*"The basement,"* I thought desperately, as the boy marched me forcefully toward the front door. *"Dear God, he's almost made it—Paz might be down there!"*

I had to keep the boy's attention on me.

"Say, what can you tell me about the garden?" I asked quickly, but it was too late. He'd noticed Patrick, and now screamed at him, too.

"Ti ucciderò! Esci subito!" he screamed, a panicked expression flitting across his face. He swiftly reached for something hidden in the small of his back, and I heard the cold click of metal.

I blanched and tried to hide it. He'd just told Patrick to get out or he'd kill him. His pistol was already cocked and in his hand.

My pistol was tucked in the small of my back, and I knew Patrick's was hidden there, too. But did we have time to draw it, or would the boy shoot us first? It would be two against one, but I had never handled a gun before. What if I screwed up? What if my gun jammed and he shot Patrick dead?

We had to get out of here.

"Sweetheart, let's go," I said, hoping my voice didn't betray the sudden fear I felt. "We have to get back and meet our agent. You know how he hates it if we're late."

"Coming," Patrick said, holding up his hands in surrender and walking swiftly toward the front door as the Italian boy held his hand behind his back, yelling at us.

Scowling, the boy yelled at us as he slammed the door in our faces. "Lasciami solo! Va via!"

I grabbed Patrick's arm as we hurried off the porch.

"What did he say?" Patrick asked in a low tone as we scrambled into the car. I backed up haphazardly, gravel spinning in the tires as I peeled out of the street and rushed away.

"Which part?" I asked, laughing nervously.

Patrick looked at me. "Why are you laughing right now? I think he was pulling a gun on me at the end there, you know."

"Yeah, I know," I couldn't help but giggle, though I knew it was completely inappropriate. My nerves were frayed. Maybe this was how Hudson felt. "He told us several times to get out. And when we didn't, he said he'd kill you."

"Cripes," Patrick uttered, recoiling in surprise. "So he got the gun out—because he said he'd kill me?"

I laughed again.

"I'm sorry," I confessed, still trying to suppress the fit of giggles. "I shouldn't be laughing. It's not funny. I don't know why I'm laughing."

"It's okay. He's probably still watching us, so we might as well stay in character now," Patrick said, staring at me under furrowed brows. "Get it out. But don't do this in front of the rest of the team, when we get back. We need to control ourselves, as their leaders."

I inhaled, trying desperately not to smile, but I grinned anyway.

"At least we didn't send me in as a cleaning lady again," I replied, wrinkling my nose. "That was a half-cocked idea in the first place. Looking back, I can't believe we actually did it. What a dumb ruse. I broke into the home of a criminal gang, alone, with the possibility of four murderous men finding me in there."

"It was a terrible plan," he agreed. "But real life is even more complicated than you realize. We can't always neatly plan it or predict it. Even the best laid plans are complicated by forces we can't control. All we can do is adapt and make the best decisions facing us at each moment, and try to keep moving forward."

I bit my lip, considering his words. They rang true. We'd spent hours, as a team, trying desperately to come up with the best plans at every juncture. Had they been foolproof? Not by a long shot.

But just like this, they'd been the best we could manage to come up with, at the time, under the circumstances.

"Perfection is the enemy of good," I replied slowly. "You're right. Not all of our plans will be perfect. Sometimes they're not even realistic. But we have to keep trying. Progress is progress."

We traveled down the road and Patrick navigated me back to Rome. I kept my mouth shut, willing myself to calm down and regain control. I had to remain logical, even in the face of tension. The entire team was looking to the two of us for guidance now. After a few minutes, I spoke again.

"What did you see in there?" I asked. "You must've gotten a look around."

"I was just thinking about that. I got a glimpse of the kitchen, and there was food out all over the counters. He must be hunkered down in there. But it was quiet. Too quiet. Where do you think Paz is? And how does the kid move around? Does he ever leave the house? There wasn't a car, but then again, a kid like that probably doesn't have a car."

"Maybe they dropped him off and made him park his car somewhere else, so it looks like the place is abandoned? Maybe he walked or rode a bicycle?"

"Maybe."

I drummed the steering wheel with one hand, thinking.

"So we have some idea where the basement steps are, at the very least," I said. "We know the kid's likely staying there, apparently by himself, potentially watching Paz twenty-four hours a day."

"Right," Patrick nodded. "I say we go to the police and share all of this. We give them a carefully edited version—just sticking to the basics. If they agree to help us, then we have allies. If not? We head straight here and break him out ourselves."

"You think it's worth wasting our time with the police again?"

"I think it's worth a shot," he replied. "Look at Hudson and Cap. They're going to jail for breaking the law. If we have any shot to do this legally, we have to try it. Our captains gave up their own freedom so we could stay out of jail. We can't carelessly throw that away by rushing to do something illegal."

"Maybe the police here will be different," I agreed. "We won't know until we ask. Okay. The two of us will go straight to the police after we meet up with the others and tell them about what we found. While we're at the police station, the rest of them can start working on a plan to break in, just in case the police refuse to help us."

Patrick's eyes met mine. In them, I read worry and tension mingled with exhaustion.

"We're strong," I reminded him. "We can do this."

"To the bitter end," he said, holding up his hand. "I'll be right here with you, Captain Gallivanter, come what may."

We shook hands, grim in our determination.

# CHAPTER 79

THE HUM OF THE CITY was starting to creep up on us again as we drove deeper into downtown Rome.

Old buildings and stately gardens filled our view as we drove toward the Colosseum, the afternoon light glinting off the white marble of the Forum.

As we drove, we ran through the story we could safely tell the Roman police.

"We're a crew traveling together and we received notice from Paz's father in Spain that he was kidnapped," Patrick practiced again, pretending I was a police officer taking his statement. "We have reason to think he's being held in this particular house, here in Rome, and we need help to get him out."

"But there are still too many holes in that," I groaned. "Why would his father contact us, and not the Spanish police? How did we find out about where he's being held? They'll ask questions we can't answer, Patty."

Patrick sighed. "This is Italy. The cops are notoriously on the take here, cooperating with the mafia. What if they've already been bribed by Trimboli and his men?"

"We have to try. Maybe there's a sympathetic detective who will be willing to help us."

"I don't know how we're going to possibly talk our way around the information we have, though. The edited version of our story barely makes sense."

I gritted my teeth. "We'll find a way."

The two of us zipped through the city, oblivious to the marble statues and fountains standing proudly on every corner, monuments to the ancient grandeur of Rome. I pulled up near the Colosseum, parking the Ford. We climbed out and started walking, looking for the rest of our team.

"I always wanted to visit this," I said, craning my neck to look at the massive, round amphitheater. Tourists flocked to the area, and an art class sat out in a small clearing, painting their plein air versions of the limestone monument. "I read about it in a book when I was just a kid."

"It's beautiful," Patrick said, gazing with me at the columns framing elegant rounded arches that gave us a glimpse of the interior arena.

We walked around the building, and I soon heard a shrill whistle. Turning my head, I saw the team standing together in a small clump.

"How'd it go?" Dessie asked anxiously, as we walked up. "Did you find the house? Was it like they said? Did you see any sign of him?"

"We found it, and yes, it's how Masso described it," Patrick said, pulling his hat down low on his head to keep the afternoon sun out of his eyes. "The house itself is out in the country, a remote area. It's all shut up, so Andi and I poked around a little bit, trying to see if anyone was home."

Quickly, he told them what we'd done.

"Long story short, there's an Italian kid there, guarding the house," I butted in. "Just like Masso said. But it looks like he's living there, which means it's going to be quite hard to break in. You'll see, when we send the groups out to do surveillance. Even finding a place to hide and observe the house will be tricky. I'm not sure we have the resources required."

"So you're sure we need to involve the police?" Chito asked, stroking his long beard. "How's that going to work?"

"Let's talk about it together back at the hotel," Patrick replied. "Andi and I need to change and freshen up if we're walking into a police station. We have a game plan. And then Andi and I can go in together to the local police, and hopefully get them on board."

"Hopefully," Dessie sighed, her shoulders slumped in disappointment.

We turned and headed back to the Fords. A long day, on the heels of what had already been a very long night, awaited us.

⸺⬦⸺

OVER COFFEE, WHICH we guzzled to keep ourselves alert, Patrick and I filled the others in on our plan.

"I don't know," Willis groaned. "It would be nine against one, if we just blast our way into that house and get Paz. Surely we have the upper hand?"

"But we can't reason with the kid," I reminded him. "He doesn't speak any English. And none of us speak Italian fluently. We won't be able to talk to him, and tell him to come out and give himself up. We won't be able to con him, either."

"She's right," Leonce sighed. "It'll end in a shootout, if we blaze in there. Some of us are bound to get hurt, even killed. The kid will likely be killed by one of us. Do we want to be responsible for that?"

"The police have the best shot at talking him down," Chito nodded. "He's young. According to Masso, he just guards their prisoners—he doesn't participate in any other crimes. He'd get off easy. And I'm sure they would tell him that, too."

"The clock is ticking," Dessie reminded us, her face pale under the bandages still plastered to her head. "We don't have time to reason through twenty different plans. We have to pick the best option and act. Trimboli and the others will be here any day. And we know what happens when they do."

The group went silent. Rollie spoke up.

"You don't have to convince me," he replied, his voice low. "I trust your judgment, Andi and Patrick."

"I do, too," Marceau said, lifting his chin. "Hudson and Cap are sure to be in jail by now. They're there because they chose to sacrifice their freedom for ours, and because it's the right thing to do. It's up to us now to do the right thing, too. And the right thing, in this moment, is to try to do it lawfully."

Willis made a small sound of disgust, but Bernard shot him a look.

"My vote is with Andi and Patrick, too," he declared. "Not all of us live our lives looking for the next opportunity to make a petrol bomb and destroy a Ford."

"Listen, we can't turn on each other now," I said, looking around the group. "We need each of you, working together, to pull this off. Don't let disagreements and petty squabbles distract us. Patrick and I will go to the police station, and it's up to the rest of you to come up with a plan to break into that house, if the police refuse to help us."

Chito stood up and put his hands on his hips.

"Let's do this," he said, looking around the group with determination. "We're one team. And we're going to find him, as one team. I'll go get another pot of coffee."

# CHAPTER 80

AROUND DINNERTIME, after our team meeting, Patrick and I walked into the police station in central Rome.

A huge wooden desk greeted us as we walked in the busy revolving doors, the two uniformed officers manning it looking newly minted, their posture erect and proud.

"Buongiorno, come posso aiutarti?" one of the young, dark-haired officer said, his white gloves interlocked, calmly, as he peered at me.

"I'm sorry, do you speak English?" Patrick asked politely. The officer tilted his head, and motioned his coworker over.

"Do either of you speak English?" Patrick repeated again, looking at the second officer.

"No inglese," the second officer said, as the first officer stood up and called across the room. "Abbiamo degli Americani qui!"

A lanky man in a suit wandered over, buttoning his jacket as he approached us. His eyes were dark but warm.

"Ah, yes, hello," he said, his thick Italian accent making the words sound musical. "I speak English. My name is ah, you would say, 'inspector,' yes? Inspector Baresi. How may we help you?"

"We have an urgent need to speak with your captain, sir," Patrick replied. "My name is Patrick Clark, and I'm the acting captain of the Chinook Voyageurs. You've probably heard of us—we've been traveling around the world in our Model T Fords?"

I shot a quick glance at Patrick. I'd lived with him for months and we'd grown especially close the last few weeks. I just now realized that I didn't know his last name until this very moment.

Inspector Baresi tapped his ear, staring at us. "Eh, no. I am so sorry, Mr. Clark. I have not heard of you." He shifted his attention to me, his dark eyes studying me. "You, though, I feel like I have seen your face before?"

I held out my hand. "Yes, Inspector. My name is Andiamo Gallivanter. I'm part of the Gallivanter team. We're also traveling around the world."

"Sì!" Baresi said, clapping his hands enthusiastically. "You have been in our newspapers many times, yes! The lady on the men's team! Now I see it! Signorina Gallivanter, how can we assist you?"

"Can we sit down, Inspector?" I asked, my eyebrows raised. "This is going to take some time to explain."

"Certainly, signorina," he said, loping through the busy bullpen where officers and detectives hustled around, smoking cigarettes and clacking furiously on typewriters. He pointed toward an empty desk in the middle of the chaos, snagging an extra chair as we walked over.

Patrick and I looked at each other.

"Actually, Inspector, is there any place we could chat that might be a bit more...quiet?" I asked, plastering a pretty smile on my face. *"What had Dessie always done?"* I thought desperately, suddenly remembering. *"Oh, eyelashes!"*

I did my best to lower my chin and batted my eyelashes.

Baresi wasn't even looking at me.

"We can duck into a private room, sì," he said, grabbing a notepad and a blank report form and a pen and walking us across the department. We turned and followed him down a long hallway, people talking and yelling in the alternating rooms that we passed.

"It's very busy here," Patrick commented.

"We are one of the single busiest police stations in the entire country," Baresi replied proudly. "We handle more crime here in a month than most stations handle all year, in all the other provinces."

I looked at Patrick darkly. It didn't bode well for us that this department was so busy. That meant they only took on legitimate cases, following strict protocol. They weren't likely to make time for a murky, half-baked case like ours.

"Inspector, are we able to speak directly to the captain?" I asked as Baresi stopped at a door, pulled it open, and noticed a detective and another man already inside. He apologized and closed the door, leading us farther down the hall.

"I am afraid not, Signorina Gallivanter," he replied. "We follow the chain of command religiously around here. You have to go through me first, then to the Sostituto Commissario Coordinatore—the senior chief inspector—in order to get to the captain."

"Very well," I said, shrugging at Patrick. He shook his head behind Baresi's back as the inspector tried another closed door.

"Perfetto!" Baresi exclaimed, finally finding an empty room. He held the door open and motioned us to sit.

We waited until he sat down, and Patrick spoke up. "Inspector, we're in quite a troubling situation," he began, laying his hands on the table. "You see, we—"

"Ah, one moment, please," Baresi said, squinting as he pulled a pair of spectacles out of his suit pocket. He carefully put them on, then frowned. Slowly, he pulled them off and polished them with his tie. "Much better."

Patrick tried again. "We're dealing with a terrible crime, and—"

Baresi swiftly held up his finger, like he was shushing a troublesome child. "Please. We must follow order here, Signor Clark."

He uncapped his fountain pen and leaned his head over the blank report, muttering under his breath in Italian as he filled out his own name and badge number, dating it and checking his watch to put the correct time.

Patrick and I watched him in silence. Finally, he glanced up. "And who should I put down as reporting the crime?"

"You can put both of us down," Patrick said quickly. "Patrick Clark and Andi Gallivanter."

"Wait, no," I replied, making a face. "If it's an official report, you better use my legal name. Edith Warren."

"Oh," Patrick exclaimed, recoiling. "*Edith*? You don't seem like an Edith..."

I shrugged.

"Honestly. I had no idea that was your real name," Patrick started to say, then stopped himself.

Inspector Baresi dutifully scratched our names in, his handwriting slow and labored.

"It's so important to write clearly," he said, pausing mid-word to look up at us with a smile. "You know, so many mistakes happen when we rush through things, especially on forms. Careful diligence makes all the difference, don't you think?"

"Yes," I agreed desperately, wanting nothing more than to rip the pen out of his hand and throw it against the wall. Advice about not rushing through things, in the very moment we were rushing through things, was terrible irony.

"So, Inspector," Patrick tried again, now bouncing his knee up and down frantically as he tried to control himself. "Here's the issue. Our friend—"

"Slow down, Mr. Clark," Baresi said, putting his pen down to hold up both hands. "I have some other details to write down first. As I mentioned, we are a workplace of order."

Patrick bit his lip so hard I thought he might bite right through it.

Baresi looked back down, craning his long neck over the form. "Mr. Clark, what is your occupation?"

"I'm acting captain of the Chinook Voyageurs Expedition," Patrick replied. For what seemed like an hour, the inspector crammed the tiny letters into the little box.

"And Miss Warren, what is your occupation?" he asked, looking at me over the rim of his glasses, which were perched on the very end of his large nose.

"I'm acting captain of the Gallivanter Expedition."

Inspector Baresi sat up straight, staring curiously at me. "You? A captain?"

"Yes," I said defiantly, already nettled.

"Hm," he replied, studying me. I felt my cheeks flush under his gaze. After a moment, Baresi bowed his head again and wrote neatly in the small box under my name, *"Capitana, Spedizione Gallivanter."*

"Good for you," he said softly, as he penned the last letter and looked up to meet my eyes. I blinked in surprise, but Baresi was already moving on. "Where did the crime occur?"

Patrick and I stared at each other. *"Now's the moment when we plead our case,"* I thought.

"Inspector Baresi, our teammate Paz de la Rosa has been kidnapped by a violent gang of criminals," I told him. "Our team was attacked and robbed, several of us hurt badly, by these criminals. You may already have notes on these men—Enzo Trimboli, he already has a long criminal history, as far as we know—and Massimiliano Rua. They kidnapped our friend, Paz, and tied him up and have been holding him, intending to receive a large ransom and then murder him, like they've done with others. Please, sir. We're desperate for your help. We believe we know where they're hiding him, and we need your help to save his life."

Baresi leaned forward. "Did the criminals already ask for a ransom? Who did they ask?"

"His family," Patrick replied. "They've asked for one hundred thousand dollars in cash. They were set to receive it last night. But we have reason to believe that this gang has a pattern of receiving the ransom money and then returning to their hideout and killing their victim—not returning them to their home like they promised. We suspect they've killed as many as seven men this way. Paz would be their eighth victim."

"Ah, yes, that is very common in ransom cases, unfortunately," the inspector replied sympathetically. "You said you think you know where they're hiding him?"

"Yes, it's a home here in Rome," Patrick said, fishing out the address and handing it over. Baresi nodded, tucking it into his file, and picked up his pen again.

"Excellent. That will be helpful. Let me see," he said, running his finger down the report. "Where did we leave off, where did we leave off...yes. Where did the crime occur?"

We couldn't dodge it forever. I had a dull feeling we were about to get the boot. "Originally, they were robbed in Zermatt, Switzerland," I replied cautiously.

Baresi wrote it down, then looked up. "And where does Mr. de la Rosa's family reside?"

"Tarragona, Spain."

"And where did the kidnappers ask for the ransom money to be handed off?" Baresi asked, his eyes narrowing behind his spectacles.

"Tarragona, Spain."

The inspector wrote it down, then capped his pen slowly. He reached up and pulled off his glasses, folded them, and set them on the table in front of him.

"Ah, now we run into a bit of a problem," he said, fixing his eyes on us. "Who exactly has been handling this particular case? The Swiss or Spanish police?"

Patrick spoke. "The Zermatt station transferred the case to the police department in Tarragona," he explained. "We've had some difficulty convincing them that this case merits their attention, to be perfectly honest. Please. We're desperate for your help. Paz is being held here in Rome, in your city."

Baresi shook his head. "I understand your concerns, and they are legitimate. However, our police department will be unable to assist you unless we have the authority of the Spanish police. The captain in Tarragona must release the case details to us first, and allow us to take over the case, in order for us to work on it. Otherwise, we can't do anything to help you."

"But they're not taking it seriously," I said, trying to keep my voice calm. "They have a very small department, and their resources are stretched thin already. We've already asked them, begged them. We need a police department like yours, a big one with officers to spare, who can assist us. Please! A man's life hangs in the balance!"

Inspector Baresi had a sympathetic look on his face. "I'm sorry. I know this is not the answer you want to hear, but we absolutely cannot move forward without them releasing the case to us. It's a matter of international protocol. You cannot ask me to operate outside of the law. It would be illegal."

"There must be something you can do?" Patrick tried. "What if we just slip you the address and lodge an anonymous complaint of illegal activity at the house? Wouldn't you be bound to go investigate it?"

"Ah, but you are not anonymous anymore, are you?" Baresi tapped the report. "I already know both your names, Mr. Clark. I know the real situation. It would be a lie. I am an officer of the law, and I do *not* lie."

"Please," I implored. "He's our dear friend. We love him. We have all the pieces of the puzzle to get a dangerous group of murderers and criminals off your streets, and save a man's life—can't we speak to the captain and discuss it with him?"

Baresi shook his head. "You will receive the same answer from anyone else, Signorina—ah, I apologize, *Captain* Gallivanter. As you have seen, we're very busy here in our office. Rome is a city of crime. We can only afford to put our resources and officers behind the cases that meet our strict criteria. This, unfortunately, does not."

"What can we do?" I asked desperately. "Do you want money? We have it—"

The inspector slapped his hand down on the table, the unexpected sound startling both of us.

"Do not go down that road," he commanded sternly. "I have been with this department for many years, and I've never once accepted a bribe. We are a place of integrity and honor, civil servants who uphold the law in all ways and even here, behind closed doors. No, Captain Gallivanter, we can do nothing for you."

"Please," Patrick implored. "We're begging. There must be some way you can help us?"

"I'm sorry," Inspector Baresi replied. "Not unless the police in Tarragona release the case to us."

He stood up, picking up his notepad and the report. "I'll hold onto this for now. And I do apologize. I know you're disappointed, but we have to uphold the law."

Patrick and I got to our feet, and dejectedly followed him down the hallway. He led us again through the busy bullpen, and out to the reception area.

"Good luck," he said, nodding. He pulled a small card from his interior jacket pocket.

"Here's the telephone number for this police station," he said, handing it to me. "If you require any additional assistance, or manage to convince the Spanish police to turn the case over to us, you may call that number."

With a polite nod, he turned on his heels and walked away.

I followed Patrick out through the revolving doors onto the sidewalk. Next door to the police station, a small cafe served dinner to patrons who laughed and chatted and read the newspaper at their tidy white tables.

"We're never going to convince the Tarragona police to hand over the case," I started, staring desperately at Patrick. "They don't—"

"I know. They don't even have the file," Patrick interrupted. "Because *we* stole it from them."

We gazed at each other for a moment.

"Well, we've really backed ourselves into quite a corner now, haven't we?" Patrick finally said.

I sighed. "Let's go tell the team. We'll have to hope they've figured something else out, somehow."

# CHAPTER 81

WHEN WE ARRIVED BACK at the hotel, the team was just sitting down to dinner in the hotel's small dining hall. Every face looked tired and haunted with worry.

They had two pots of coffee already on the table. Dessie looked up mid-pour as she served herself coffee, nearly pouring the hot liquid all over the table. "What'd they say?" she blurted.

Chito pulled out a chair for me and I sat down, while Patrick dragged a chair over from another table and squeezed in.

"It's not good," I replied. "They won't help us. They said they need the case handed over to them by the Tarragona police, before they can do anything at all."

"What?" Willis cried. "There must be something they can do!"

"Believe me, we tried every angle," Patrick explained, running through the whole story. The team listened, motionless, letting their meals get cold on their plates.

When he finished, Chito leaned back in his chair. "He didn't even finish writing the report. That alone speaks volumes."

I watched over Bernard's shoulder as two young waiters whispered to each other, staring openly at Dessie with stupid grins on their faces. She'd noticed, and smiled at them out of habit, tossing her long blonde hair over her shoulder.

"What if we come in with money in hand, and talk to someone else at the police station?" Claude suggested. "Maybe it's just that Inspector Baresi who's a stickler. Maybe someone else would be open to a bribe?"

"But how much will they want?" Chito replied. "We only have the cash we have on hand. Cap and Hudson are the only ones with access to the bank accounts, and they're undoubtedly in jail now."

Silence settled on the group. A sense of hopeless filled me. We were so close to saving Paz and yet unable to do so. Even as I sipped my coffee, I felt myself running out of steam.

"Has anyone actually heard from Hudson or Cap yet?" Rollie asked, as we all fiddled quietly with our cups of coffee and napkins.

"I checked in at the American and Canadian ambassador's offices this afternoon, after our meeting," Leonce offered. "That's where they agreed to send all their messages. But they hadn't received anything."

"Well, I assume that means they've been thrown in jail," Marceau sighed. "They were supposed to go to the police two days ago. And we haven't heard anything from them at all."

I pressed my lips together in a tight line. Could things get any worse?

One of the young waiters ambled over, grinning like an idiot as he kept his eyes fixed on Dessie.

"Excuse me, can I get you anything else?" he drawled, his English flawless even through his Italian accent. "Anything at all?"

"No, thank you," Chito said, waving him away.

"You're sure?" the waiter persisted, staring at Dessie with a smile on his face. "Signorina? Anything for you?"

"No thanks," she said, smiling sweetly. "We'll let you know if there's anything."

The waiter blushed as Dessie addressed him, and she deepened her smile. He turned scarlet and quickly hurried away, a grin plastered on his face. I watched him rush back to his coworker, and they indulged in excited gossip, their heads close together. Slowly, an idea unfolded in my mind.

"That's it," I exclaimed, studying Dessie through narrowed eyes.

"What?" she replied, confused.

"Look, why did both teams bring us girls on, in the first place?" I asked, looking around. The men eyed each other uncomfortably, shuffling their feet and clearing their throats. Each one carefully avoided my eyes.

"Come on," I urged. "Be honest. I know you know the answer."

"Fine, I'll say it, you wimps," Bernard spoke up. "We brought you on to get attention."

"Exactly!" I exclaimed. "You brought a woman onto an all-male team to get attention. To catch people's eyes. And it *worked.* That was before you even knew how capable we even were—you just needed to get people's eyes on your team. So let us attract that same attention now!"

"So you're saying what, exactly?" Leonce frowned.

"We hold a press conference," I said, hope growing within me as I spoke. "We put Dessie and me in front of the cameras, tell our story, make a passionate plea to the world for help. We let the press whip the public up into an indignant frenzy, hearing how the police haven't helped us."

I stared at the group, a smile playing on my lips. "You've seen how it is when we're on the front page of the newspapers—people rally around us. They mob us. We use that to our advantage, and direct them to petition the police, telephone them and send telegrams, maybe even riot. We use our fans to pressure the police into assisting us!"

"But we don't have time for that," Claude spoke up. "If we blast this story out to the world, the gang will just regroup somewhere else. Probably after killing Paz."

"But the gang isn't here yet," I countered. "We had double the drivers they have, so we could drive twice as fast to Rome, without stopping. And they had to steal a car, remember? Who knows how long that held them up? They're still at least a day or two behind us."

"So we still have at least one more shot to convince the police to help us," Rollie said slowly, thinking. "If our fans and the newspapers bombard them, it might be enough to prompt them to at least go out and check the house."

Marceau and Patrick and Willis were nodding, even before he finished speaking.

"By golly, you may be onto something," Chito said, crossing his arms and leaning back in his chair. "And you and Dessie being up there, leading the press conference—why, that itself will draw attention. Two women, doing a press conference all on their own? When has that ever been done? It'll raise eyebrows, for sure."

"Right," I said, glancing over at the two young waiters. They were still both sneaking looks at Dessie. I lowered my voice. "Dessie, you're going to get your wish. Your face will be on every newspaper all over the entire world, hopefully, by the end of this."

Instead of grinning, she frowned.

"No! I look terrible!" she exclaimed, touching the large bandage on her face. "I can't go on camera like this! Why, I still have stains from that nasty mercurochrome solution you put all over me!"

"All the better, to show how brave you've been in the face of such tragedy," I said. "Look at you. You're a beautiful girl who's been beat up, scarred in the race to save her teammate. All the more attention will be given to you *because* you're all cut up, Dess."

"Andi is exactly right," Patrick said, leaning in. "You're still gorgeous, but your very appearance right now underscores the seriousness of what we're facing. We couldn't have even planned it better, honestly."

"But I don't want my face to be all over the newspapers if I'm ugly," Dessie complained.

"We're talking about saving Paz's life," I exclaimed. "Who cares about your cuts?"

Dessie glared back at me, but her face softened. She pursed her lips, drawing her eyebrows together. "Fine. I hate to admit it, but it's a good idea."

"We'll start drafting it right now," I said, excitement in my voice. "Think how Cap and Hudson would do it—how they'd tug on people's heartstrings. Why, we can do that, Dessie! We're both good actresses!"

"True," Dessie nodded, hunching her delicate shoulders. "We should really play up the danger that we, as women, faced. It'll stir up the men, especially, with their protective instinct."

"How do you know that about us?" Willis started to ask, while Patrick shushed him.

"You'll have to be very careful what you say, though, about how we got the information about Paz," Patrick cautioned. "Being generic and vague is best. Don't take any questions at the end. We can't tip off that Hudson and Cap are in jail. We can't let anyone find out we stole a police file, or that we kidnapped Masso and tortured Paz's whereabouts out of him. If anyone finds out about any of that, we'll lose all public sympathy. And we'll be arrested, too."

"No, definitely no questions at the end. How about we just cry at the end instead, overwhelmed with emotion?" Dessie asked enthusiastically.

"I can't just cry on demand," I replied, leaning my head back in frustration. "You know that. You've asked me before."

"Fine. *I* can cry at the end," Dessie said. "Crying ladies always make men uncomfortable, too. They want to jump in and do something to stop the tears."

"How..." Willis said again, then stopped himself this time.

"You manipulate people," Bernard blurted, staring at Dessie. "You analyze all of us, don't you? You just sit on the information, waiting to use it somehow to get your way!"

"Yeah, aren't you glad I do?" she asked cheekily. "It sure comes in handy when we need it. I've always been a good read of people. Why not use it to my advantage?"

She glanced at Bernard and added, "Except you, doll. You're the only one I can't read. You're far too smart to fall for my tricks."

Bernard puffed up with pride, a satisfied grin on his wrinkled cheeks. I hid my own smile. I saw right through what she'd just done. I stood up.

"I'll get paper and pens from the reception desk right now," I said. "We'll work on it together, and Dessie and I will memorize a script. While we work, the rest of you can start looking up beat reporters. We'll need you to make telephone calls to every newspaper office, every reporter, and every cameraman you can manage to find."

Marceau raised his hand. "I can lead the charge on that," he volunteered. "Willis and Patrick and I have all served that role before, arranging press conferences for our team."

"Good," I said over my shoulder, hurrying to the reception desk and asking for supplies. When I came back to the table, the group was already brainstorming.

"I think we should be as honest as we can, without tipping our hand too much," Chito was saying as I sat back down in my seat and placed the paper in front of me. "We tell them the truth, that the Chinooks were attacked out in the country, after they were overheard by criminals at a bar. We share what they did to you, beating you all up, shooting you, Patrick—the more sensational, the better—in fact, we should have Rollie up there with you, too."

Rollie nodded eagerly. "I'll help. Whatever you need."

"We share that Dessie telephoned the Gallivanters and pleaded for our help," Chito continued, "That we immediately rushed to your aid, and sat with you in the hospital."

"So everything's clean until we get to the Tarragona police department," Willis interrupted. "How do we cover that? Everything we did after that was, um...*illegal.*"

"That's what we told you at the time," Chito replied hotly. "See why it wasn't the greatest idea to firebomb a car and torture someone we kidnapped, huh?"

"Stop," I said, holding up my hand. "We can't rehash the past. It's a waste of time to play the blame game. We have to keep moving forward, together. And it's going to take everyone on this team to pull this off. Don't pull us back into old arguments."

Dessie leaned forward. "I think I've got it," she said quietly, a confident look in her eyes. "Andi, start writing."

# CHAPTER 82

EARLY THE NEXT MORNING, I came down from my hotel room in my Gallivanter uniform. Following Dessie's urging, I borrowed her lipstick and applied it.

If there was ever a time to play up my femininity, it was now.

Marceau and Patrick and Willis had indeed pooled their talents together and called dozens of press agents to the hotel. The early hour underscored the unusual situation, and that itself attracted attention. I could hear the crowd from the second floor as I descended the stairs.

When I appeared, the crowd went wild, clapping and hollering. I smiled broadly, internally wondering what the boys had told them that had gotten them so riled up.

Or was it the fact that it had been so long since we'd last made an appearance for the press? Either way, we'd always had enthusiastic crowds—but not to this extent.

It was comforting to know that we could still draw a massive crowd at a moment's notice. We'd need all the attention we could muster up, in order to pull this off.

"Miss Gallivanter, we thought your team was in Romania!" one young reporter said, sidling up to me before I even made it down the steps. He already had a notepad in his hand, pen ready. "Isn't it true that just a few days ago, the newspaper in Bucharest carried a story about you visiting the city?"

I smiled. "We'll tell you everything in a moment."

Dessie breezed in behind me, looking like a movie starlet with her perfect body and expertly applied makeup. The men clapped and hooted for her, but as she drew closer and they saw the cuts and stains on her face, their applause turned to murmurs of concern. She scooted into place next to me.

Unexpectedly, she slid her arm through mine, squeezing my forearm.

"Showtime," she said under her breath, a smile already plastered on her beautiful face.

A translator stood next to us up front, helpfully ready to share our words with those who didn't speak English. He nodded, and turned to watch us.

"Gentlemen, thank you all for being here," I said, turning to the sea of people in front of me. Cameras started flashing and video cameras on their tripods started whirring. I used the little trick I'd learned from Cap long ago, staring slightly above the heads of the crowd in order to keep the flashing lights from blinding me and causing me to blink.

The translator murmured fluidly, his words musical over top of mine as I spoke.

"As I assume most of you know, I'm Andiamo Gallivanter, of the Gallivanter Expedition, hailing from the United States of America," I said. "My team and I have been traveling all over the world, and as you're aware, we've been partnering the last few months with the Chinook Voyageurs."

Dessie spoke up. "I'm Dessie Hickson, representing the Chinook Voyageurs, out of Canada," she smiled, flashing her mega-watt smile. I noticed several men smile back.

"You've seen our faces plastered all over the news, all over the world," I continued. "We've faced challenges and difficulties. We've persevered through troubles and trials. But today, we come to you facing what has become the biggest plight of all of our lives."

I paused for effect, lowering my eyes briefly so my face displayed my downcast spirit. Dessie patted my arm with her free hand. The cameras clicked, flashing, capturing the moment.

"I'm sorry, gentlemen," I said, forcing emotion into my voice. "To be honest, we've lied to you. We've lied to the world. And it's time for us to come clean about it. Because we're facing our most desperate days, as a team, and we've come to the end of our rope."

Reporters looked up from their notepads, still scribbling furiously, confusion evident on their faces. They were hanging on every word.

*"Good,"* I thought to myself. *"We have them right where we want them."*

"A few weeks ago, our teams amicably separated to travel different routes," I continued. "As they traveled through Switzerland, the Chinook Voyageurs crossed paths with a violent gang of criminals. Unbeknownst to them, this gang overheard them talking at a bar in Austria about their trip. They drove to an abandoned stretch of road that they knew the Chinooks would be traveling a few days later, and they lay in wait."

Cameras clicked furiously, echoing through the sudden silence in the room. I glanced over at Dessie and she looked at me.

"The Chinook Voyageurs were viciously attacked," I said, my voice rising in volume. "They pulled over to help what they thought was a stranded motorist. As they got out to look at his car—to help—they were waylaid by these evil men. They were beaten within an inch of their lives, then robbed."

Several members of the crowd gasped loudly. I could audibly hear the scribble of pens in notebooks as I paused.

I took a deep breath, and let it out slowly. "I'd like to ask Dessie to courageously share what happened to her, gentlemen. I warn you, it may not be easy to hear."

Dessie squared her shoulders, facing the crowd.

She took a deep breath. "We were driving in a remote part of Switzerland near dusk, a quiet road, and we came upon a car stalled out in the middle of the road. A man stood in front of us, waving us down. He appeared to be limping, and we assumed he was injured."

She tilted her chin up as she spoke, her cheeks starting to flush.

"What we didn't know was that it was the gang—the same men who had overheard us in Austria—and they were hiding in the woods, waiting for us to pull over and start helping. Two of my friends were already bent over, looking at the engine, when they were clubbed in the heads from behind. They went down immediately."

Dessie paused and pointed to Rollie, standing off in the front of the crowd.

"That's my friend Rollie, everyone," she said, breaking away from me to pull him to the front of the group.

"Look at him," she continued, her voice ringing through the room. "Rollie kindly went to help these evil men with their car. In return for his kindness, they hit him so hard he landed in the hospital for weeks and nearly died. His brain swelled up, and he had to relearn how to walk and talk and feed himself. It's a miracle he survived at all."

Rollie faced the reporters, his handsome round face shining with earnestness. He shrugged, embarrassed, and melted back into the crowd.

Whispers whipped through the room as Dessie paused, collecting herself. "After they attacked Rollie, our captain was immediately grabbed and held at gunpoint, while the other members of the gang rushed at the rest of us, still in our cars. I was in the back car. I saw the whole thing unfolding right in front of my eyes, like a nightmare I couldn't stop. I was helpless."

She shuddered involuntarily as the story poured out of her mouth.

"I had been driving with one of my teammates, and he quickly pulled his jacket off and shoved me under it, trying to hide me. He told me they'd hurt me if they found me, that I had to fight for my very life if they saw me."

I noticed that only some of the reporters in the room were still scribbling on their notepads. The others had stopped, pens poised above the paper, frozen as they listened to Dessie's words.

"From where I was hiding, I heard my teammates yelling and trying to fight the gang," she continued bravely. "I could hear them shoot one of my teammates. Patrick was shot in the leg. And then I heard them start screaming about me."

She stopped and lowered her eyes. Her face had gone from flushed to white, like the blood had drained completely from her body. A slight tremor went through her body, like she was about to faint.

After a long pause, Dessie sighed and continued. All eyes were on Dessie, a breathless anticipation in the room.

"I could hear Paz, my teammate, climb out of the car and try to reason with them," she continued. "He was trying to distract them from finding me, hidden in the back car. He gave them our money, pleaded with them to go away. But they recognized him from the bar, and started beating him mercilessly. I could hear him screaming, their fists landing on his body. He fought them, but there were too many of them. They beat him so long that eventually he stopped crying out. He went silent. I thought he was dead."

I put my arm around her and bowed my own head.

"They started asking my team where I was," Dessie said, her voice lower. "No one would tell them. I heard them attack each man, asking where I was—they called me vile names. They were beating them, hurting them, even as my team begged for mercy."

She paused. Every man in the room leaned forward, staring at her. Their visceral reaction was written plainly on their faces.

"I hid in that back car, under Paz's jacket, trying to control my breathing so they wouldn't hear me," she resumed. "All I could do was pray that they wouldn't look for me there. But suddenly, they ripped the jacket off me, and found me curled up on the floor. Two of them yanked me out, and tossed me on the ground painfully, laughing as they saw me land in the gravel."

Several of the reporters made a soft sound of disgust.

"One of the men yanked me back up to my feet, nearly dislocating my arm," Dessie said, pursing her lips. "He shoved me, and I head-butted him. Then he wrapped his big hands around my neck. He squeezed until I couldn't breathe. I thought he was going to kill me. Or worse."

I heard the sharp inhale of nearly every man in the room. I knew they were imagining, unwillingly, their own wives and sisters and daughters, faced with the same horrors. It was every man's greatest nightmare.

Dessie let their outrage and shock build, for a brief moment, while she closed her eyes. When she fluttered them open a few seconds later, she grimaced.

"He hit me, after he strangled me," she said, pointing to the faint shadow of a bruise on her cheek. "He was swearing, in Italian, and my teammates were screaming as they watched it all, begging and threatening him to stop hurting me. It was the most horrible, terrifying moment I've ever lived through. It haunts me, even now. I thought—I—"

She stumbled, fumbling over the words. We'd decided it was better to leave it here, to let the outraged reporters fill in their own speculation as to what happened next. Their anger was sure to explode across the pages of their articles and reports.

Sure enough, they visibly seethed, enraged. A low, furious murmur whipped through the crowd.

# CHAPTER 83

AS WE'D REHEARSED, I held up my hand, my arm still around Dessie's shoulders.

"Gentlemen, as you can see, simply recounting this story has been hard for my friend. We cannot ask her to continue and live through the horror again. Thank you, Dessie, for your courage."

She nodded, her eyes focused on the floor. I took up the rest of the story.

"After attacking a helpless young woman in such a brutal manner, they tied up Paz and kidnapped him, shoving him in their trunk. Before they drove away, leaving the Chinook Voyageurs bleeding and half dead on the road, they destroyed their cars, disabling them from going to get help. A few of the crew had to hobble to the nearest farm to get help, then beg for a ride to the hospital."

The reporters were again starting to take notes, hanging on our words.

"From the police station, Dessie tracked down the Gallivanters and called us, at our hotel," I pushed on. "The Gallivanters raced to the Chinook's side, as soon as we found out about this tragedy."

"While sitting in the hospital, unsure if some of the team would even survive their injuries, we deduced that the kidnappers would travel to Spain, to get the ransom from Paz's family, maybe even to rob them. We headed there as soon as we could, to help them. Sure enough, they were contacted for a ransom. An outrageous sum, too: one hundred thousand dollars, or they'd kill our friend, Paz."

*"Be calm, and remember your script,"* I thought, willing myself to slow down and take a breath to steady my nerves.

This next part would have to be word-for-word, or I risked blowing everything.

"As a team, we traveled to Spain. We went to where Paz's family was, a small seaside town near Barcelona, called Tarragona. As unbelievable as it sounds, we found a witness, someone who was familiar with this group of thugs, and who was able to provide us with several important details. He realized the enormity of what he'd done, and confessed everything that the gang was planning to do—everything."

There. I hadn't technically lied about anything. I'd just chosen my words very carefully.

I lowered my eyes, blinking, like I was fighting tears.

"He believed that they were planning to collect the ransom—that exorbitant sum, an amount that would bleed the family dry—and then kill Paz de la Rosa anyway."

Dessie clutched my waist and we paused for a moment, our heads bowed. After a beat, I lifted my head and met the breathless gaze of every single person in the room.

"The concerned citizen told us everything—where they're holding Paz captive, how they're planning to kill him, and when. And we bolted here to Rome from Spain, straight to the local police. But here's where it becomes tragic, my friends. I can scarcely believe I'm saying this. But you know the Gallivanters—if there's one thing we stand for, it's truth. Integrity. And in the spirit of that truthfulness, I must be honest."

I let my shoulders slump, an intentional posture of defeat. It wasn't as hard as I thought to fake these emotions, I realized. Though I was performing, I truly felt them.

"We met with an inspector, here in Rome. Yet to our great sadness, the police *refuse* to help us."

A shocked murmur went through the group. Reporters scribbled so quickly I thought they'd burn through their notepads. Cameras flashed again.

"Why would they refuse to help us?" I continued, shaking my head. "Over a technicality. The Spanish police station did not want to release the case to the Roman police. I understand, they have their rules. Their pride. But the Tarragona police have a very small force, and in their hands, the case is growing cold. They need to turn it over...and we need the police here in Rome to pursue it. Only they can save Paz's life. Only they can save an innocent man from a certain, horrific death at the hands of a ruthless gang of criminals. Only they can get these dangerous men off the streets, so they never put another family through this kind of pain."

Dessie broke in, her voice tremulous.

"Please," she begged. "We've traveled the world as ambassadors of good will, and now in our time of need, we are abandoned by the very people we need most."

She let a tear well up out of her eyes, trailing down her cheek slowly.

"We are desperate," she said, choking up. "Please. I need him."

I stared at her, surprised. She had added the last few words to our script. We hadn't rehearsed that. She was speaking from the heart, I realized.

As I glanced out at the sea of reporters, I saw that they were sympathetic. It tugged at their heartstrings to see a beautiful young girl like Dessie, an unfortunate victim of such barbaric violence, be in continued pain now over Paz.

*"Perfect. This is exactly what we need,"* I thought.

I let another beat pass, Dessie's crestfallen face commanding the eye of every man in the room, before I spoke again.

"Gentlemen, we are in desperate need of your help," I beseeched, holding out my hands. "We're out of time and out of options. Any day now, we expect the kidnappers to come back and murder our friend in cold blood. As soon as they arrive here from Spain, with their payoff, and get back to the house where they're holding him, we know they'll surely kill him. They've done it before, and they'll do it again now, according to the information we received."

I gazed out into the crowd, making eye contact with the men who watched me. Feverish whispers raced back and forth through the group.

I knew I had to make the plea personal now—put the burden of responsibility on them.

"You, and you only, can prevent them from putting a bullet in his head," I said. "We need you to do everything possible to blow this story up. Put it on the front page of every newspaper, get it on every radio station, plaster it around town and all over the world, any way you can. Call in every favor, share it with everyone you know. Please. We need the entire world's eyes on us to convince the police to take up the case and help us."

Dessie lifted her head and chimed in.

"Andi's right. We need the people of the world—all the good, wonderful people we know will care about this—to step up and make their voices heard. Together, with all our voices lifted in righteous outrage, we cannot be silenced. Together, we can make a difference. We can *save* him."

Lightbulbs flashed, but it was clear that the men were electrified by what we'd told them. Several of them stood motionless, animatedly taking notes as fast as they could.

A reporter from the front raised his hand. "Miss Gallivanter, where are the rest of your team members? We can't help but notice the glaring absence of Captain Gallivanter and Captain Landry. Where are they?"

"They're working behind the scenes, still tied up dealing with this whole situation," I replied swiftly. "As you can imagine, our team is desperate and trying every possible thing we can think of to try to save our friend's life. Dessie and I are doing what we can, in the hopes that each of you can assist us in our hour of need. That's all we have time for now, I'm afraid. Thank you all *so* much for coming. Please, do help us. However you can."

Another reporter spoke up from the middle of the crowd, as we tried to back away from the excited group.

"How exactly did it come about that someone came to you with such specific information?" he called out.

It was the question we'd dreaded someone asking. Dessie and I had rehearsed several possible answers, but the team couldn't agree on anything we came up with as a rebuttal. We'd decided instead to just refuse to answer any questions, pretending to be overcome with emotion.

But now, in the heat of the moment, Dessie stood her ground and met the man's gaze.

"I'm sorry, we don't have time for additional questions," I said again, taking Dessie's arm. "We—"

"The only thing that matters is what I have to say to you right now," Dessie said swiftly, cutting me off. Her cheeks were flushed and her voice was raised, clear above the low conversation of the crowd.

Instantly, the room froze. All heads swiveled to Dessie, who'd never looked more beautiful—or more fierce—than in this moment, as rage and desperation fueled her.

"We told you earlier that we stand for honesty, right?" Dessie said, her voice raised. "Well, let me be honest. I'll come clean. I'm standing right here, in front of you, a woman beyond desperation. I *love* Paz de la Rosa. If you won't do it for him, do it for me. For my happiness—a little bit of joy after the absolute hell I've just been through. If that's not a reason for you, then how dare you call yourself a man?"

She faced down the room, her passion crashing against the men like a tidal wave. They were swept away in its power, drowning in her words.

"My pride has been stripped from me," she said, her voice cracking with emotion. "My sense of safety and security, stripped away. They took so much away from me. All I have left is hope. Don't you dare strip *that* away from me, too."

With that, she whirled away, her blonde hair streaming out behind her. She grabbed my arm, her fingers digging in painfully, and rushed me out of sight, back up to Bernard's room, where we'd agreed to hide out until the crowd dispersed. We didn't want to encourage them to linger, but hoped they'd get right to work, sharing our desperate plea with the world.

Bernard had willingly agreed, of course, to hide out from the crowd and ferret us away as soon as we were done.

"That went well, don't you think?" Dessie grinned, as Bernard shut the door behind us.

"Yes, but that last part was unexpected," I remarked, rubbing my temples. "That wasn't part of our script."

Dessie shrugged.

"I read the room," she remarked airily, gliding to the small mirror above the desk and leaning forward to examine her lipstick. "Those men needed a bit of challenge. They needed to think it was personal for me."

I watched her as she popped her lips together, making a pouting face in the mirror.

"I think you actually meant it, though," I replied quietly, watching to see if her face changed. "He's the one for you, isn't he?"

Sure enough, she paused.

"We'll see, won't we?" she said, still gazing at herself in the mirror.

# CHAPTER 84

THE REST OF THE BOYS came back to the room half an hour later, beaming.

"Ladies, you're miracle workers!" Willis exclaimed. "I've never seen a group of people so fired up. Why, I must've had a half dozen of them promise you tomorrow's front page of the newspaper, on the spot!"

Patrick slapped me on the back and kissed Dessie on the cheek, whooping. "We need to get you two in front of the cameras more often! You're sensational spokeswomen!"

Just as we hoped, the story took the whole world by storm.

Within the hour, we started to receive a flurry of telegrams from people—first just citizens in Rome, but soon from people all over the world, sharing their indignant outrage and promises of prayer and support.

Because we'd held our press conference so early in the morning, several late editions of the newspaper picked up the story and ran it the same day. Every paper carried a photograph of Dessie and me, with our desperate message.

Private investigators stopped by the hotel in person, begging to help us. We took their contact information, but hoped the police would acquiesce.

Willis and Marceau had driven by the police station a few times that afternoon, and reported back that there was already an angry mob outside the station on the sidewalk.

"They were waving papers and everything, shouting in Italian," Willis said gleefully, when he returned. "Gosh, I'd hate to be the police. They're sure angry."

"Good," Dessie replied. "Let's just hope they're angry enough to do something about it."

"Who'd have ever thought all our fame would come in handy like this?" Chito wondered aloud, shaking his head. "Did you ever dream we could compel so many people to action, just with our words?"

We heard the telephone in the lobby ring, and listened as the clerk picked it up and responded in Italian.

"Have we heard yet from Cap or Hudson?" Rollie asked quietly, as we watched.

I shook my head. "Not yet."

I hoped no one noticed that I swallowed a lump after I answered. Their continued silence indicated that they were in serious trouble.

The clerk turned toward us, covering the mouthpiece with his hand. "Mr. Clark?" he called out. Patrick hurried over and took the call. The rest of us stared, waiting.

"This is Mr. Clark," Patrick spoke into the receiver, listening. After a moment, he nodded. "Yes, thank you. We'll be right there."

He hung up and walked toward us. "It's the police. Inspector Baresi, from the Rome office. Andi, they want to meet with the two of us."

"When?" I asked, my eyes widening.

"Right now," he said, pulling the keys out of his pocket. "We'll catch up with the rest of you later."

# CHAPTER 85

WE JOGGED TO THE CAR and made our way to the police station as quickly as we could.

Sure enough, there was a large group of men and women gathered on the sidewalk, clearly unsettled. Several reporters appeared to be in the mix, some with cameras. Officers patrolled the edge of the group, controlling the crowd. As we drove closer, we heard a boisterous cheer go up.

"Sono loro!" we heard several people gasp, through the cheers. A smattering of applause and whistles started as we climbed out of the Ford and made our way up to the door.

An older woman grabbed me, a delicate lace shawl covering her white hair.

"Vi hanno fatto un torto!" she exclaimed, gripping my arm with weak hands. "You've been wronged!"

"Erm, thank you," I smiled, peeling her hands off. Patrick and I stepped in the revolving doors, our eyes adjusting to the dark interior.

"It's a circus out there," Patrick muttered, as the door rotated closed behind us.

Inspector Baresi and a trim, muscular man with an unmistakable air of authority were already waiting at the reception desk of the police station when we walked in the doors. Both smiled pleasantly at us and offered their hands to shake, as the doors opened and the cameras flashed behind us, their officers struggling to contain the crowd on the sidewalk.

As soon as the doors closed, however, they both dropped their smiles and looked at us with pursed lips. Baresi nodded at us.

"Captain Clark, Captain Gallivanter, welcome back," he said politely. "This is our Sostituto Commissario Coordinatore, Senior Chief Inspector Albano."

Inspector Albano studied us both, his eyes narrowed. He was a good-looking older man, his dark hair gray above the temples. His suit looked expensive and was tailored impeccably, highlighting his powerful body. When he spoke, his English was flawless, his words well-placed. He gave off the instant impression of precision and intensity.

"Welcome back to our station," Albano said without any trace of warmth. I had the distinct impression that we were not, in fact, welcome at all. "We'll make our way back to my office, where we can speak in private."

Patrick and I followed Chief Inspector Albano to his office, Inspector Baresi trailing behind us. Inside the small office, he took his seat behind a large wooden desk, several stacks of papers and forms piled high atop it, pointing us toward two leather chairs sitting in front of his desk. Baresi closed the door, softly, and stood leaning against it, his arms crossed.

Albano lit a cigarette and took a long drag, leaning back slowly in his chair to gaze at us. The smoke wafted up above his head, curling toward the ceiling. I found his slowness maddening, considering our circumstances.

Patrick spoke up first. "Chief Inspector, we thank you for making time to meet with us. I assume this means you're willing to discuss taking on our case?"

Tipping his head back in his chair, Albano took another slow puff, watching us.

"I understand that Inspector Baresi already met with you and started the paperwork?" he replied, ignoring Patrick's question.

"That's correct," Patrick replied. "He told us he wouldn't be able to complete the forms until the Tarragona police department handed over the case. Has that happened yet?"

The chief inspector tilted his head back and exhaled a long, thin jet of smoke. "We talked, yes."

"And?"

"And they were willing to hand the case over."

"Oh, thank God," I exclaimed, putting my hand over my heart. "How soon then can you get moving?"

Inspector Albano narrowed his eyes and studied me with cool indifference. "Do you think you get to make that call, young lady? Do I look like the sort of man that takes orders from a woman?"

"I wasn't ordering you, sir," I began, but Albano interrupted me.

"Don't talk."

Inspector Baresi shifted uncomfortably in the door, clearing his throat in embarrassment. I remembered the way he'd apologized for addressing me as "miss" instead of "captain" when we'd met earlier. Perhaps he was more forward-thinking than his boss.

Rankled, I leaned forward before I could stop myself.

"Clearly, you need me telling you what to do, since you appear to be incapable of doing what's right. I guess you don't care that a man's life is at stake, do you?" I retorted. "So much for fairness and justice. We thought we could trust you to actually give a damn."

Albano glared. "Actually, Miss Gallivanter—"

"*Captain* Gallivanter," I corrected him, just to see his face twitch. He didn't disappoint.

"Actually, Captain Gallivanter," he said, the name clearly distasteful in his mouth, "We've already made some decisions regarding your friend's case."

Patrick and I glanced at each other, and leaned forward in our seats. "What?"

Instead of answering the question, Albano pulled out a pocket watch and glanced at it. He looked at Baresi and spoke rapidly in Italian. He responded quickly, his words coming so fast I had trouble trying to translate with my rudimentary knowledge of the language.

"Wait, what now?" Patrick blurted, looking back and forth between the two men. "Please. What's going on?"

Inspector Albano leaned back in his chair, tucking his watch into his pants. "We should have an update soon. You must be patient."

"Patient about what? What update?" I exclaimed, dangerously close to losing my temper. Didn't he understand that the clock was ticking? We were rapidly running out of time to save Paz's life, before Trimboli and the others returned and put a bullet in his head.

"Listen, how soon can you order your men to get into that house?" Patrick said, shooting to his feet and putting his hands flat on Albano's desk. "We gave you the address already. We told you everything we know!"

Behind us, Inspector Baresi finally spoke. "They're at the house now."

"What?" Patrick and I gasped in unison, talking over each other as questions spilled out of our mouths. "When? What happened? Is Paz there? Is he okay?"

Albano smoothed his expensive suit, looking at us smugly. "We already ordered a raid on the house where you claimed they were keeping your friend against his will. They should be reporting back to the station soon. We'll know more then. But I know my men, and I have full confidence in what they can accomplish. Of course—that depends on the accuracy of the information you gave us. We'll see."

I stared at him, my jaw hanging open in surprise. "Why didn't you just tell us that in the first place?"

The chief inspector stared back at me evenly, and merely shrugged.

*"Because I wanted to let you know who's really in control here,"* I filled in for him in my head.

It was unclear whether he'd given in because of the outrage in the media or the mob out front, but it was evident he resented us for it. We'd had the press conference only this morning, and already the city was whipped into a frenzy. It was only bound to intensify in the coming days. I knew he had to be angry that we'd made his department look so bad.

But our plan had worked, after all. *"I can't believe this,"* I thought feverishly.

Inspector Baresi cleared his throat after a moment, and replied, "Try to be patient. If your friend is alive, you should see him very soon here, once they bring him back to the station for processing."

I bit my lip and exchanged glances with Patrick. We both noticed that he used the phrase, *"if* your friend is alive."

"Why don't you follow me to the lobby?" Baresi suggested, opening the door. "That way, we can complete your report that I started the other day, and you can be the first to see the uh—what do you say—the *squad*, when they arrive back?"

We rose and nodded our thanks to the chief inspector, and Baresi shut the door behind us.

Like children, we followed him meekly back to the front lobby. He stopped at his desk to dig out our file—already buried beneath a pile of other manila folders—and walked over to two empty seats down the way from a crying older woman, who blew her nose into a sopping wet handkerchief.

Patrick and I sat wedged in next to each other. He jiggled his leg worriedly, jostling my leg in the process, the entire time the inspector asked us questions and laboriously scripted down our answers. Every time the door opened, we both swiveled to see who was entering. A steady stream of officers toting in drunks and distraught men and women came through the door, but not Paz.

Inspector Baresi finished his report and stood. "Si, grazie, Captain Clark, Captain Gallivanter."

Reflexively, Patrick stood and offered his hand. I followed suit. "Thank you, Inspector," I said, sitting back down. Patrick resumed jiggling his leg.

Baresi stood in front of us a moment longer, looking awkward.

"I—uh—I am very sorry this has happened to you," he said, his voice understanding. His expression was warm as he lowered his head and stared at us, under his brows. "Forgive me, but I did some checking up on all of you, after you came in the other day."

"Oh?" I asked, glancing up. I tried not to reveal any nervousness. What if he'd found out about something that we'd done?

"Si," Baresi replied. "From what I read, you're all very good people. Everyone, on both teams. It's a shame that you've run into such obstacles as you've tried to explore the world."

Patrick and I both stared up at him.

"Yes," Patrick replied. "It hasn't been easy."

"It's never easy when you are the first to do something," Baresi replied. "And besides, it's just never easy. But we continue on. Don't let this—what's the word? *Derail.* Don't let this derail you. It's easy to lose heart, when you face trouble. But you don't strike me as the type to give up easily."

"Thank you," I said, a wan smile on my face. I could tell he was trying to comfort us, in some small way.

He nodded and shuffled away. Patrick and I were left alone. I fiddled with my fingernails as Patrick's leg bounced. After a few moments of silence, I asked, "Should we call the team at the hotel?"

"I don't know," he admitted, staring at the tile floor. "What can they do? Wait with us here? What if..." he trailed off, abruptly closing his mouth.

"Yeah," I sighed. He didn't have to finish his thought.

*"What if they get in, and find that Paz is already dead? What if this was all for nothing? The theft, the arson, the break in, the kidnapping and torture—all for nothing? We couldn't even save him, after all of this?"* I reflected, finishing it for him.

We resumed waiting, suffering our purgatory in silence.

# CHAPTER 86

THE DOOR OPENED AGAIN and we sat up, sucking in our breath. It was two officers, carrying in a screaming man who spat a series of foul threats in Italian at everyone he laid eyes on.

I slumped in my seat again, my heart racing.

A few moments later, the lobby filled with a dozen men. *They must be coming in for a shift change,* I thought dully, watching as they smiled and slapped each other on the back, talking animatedly.

Two that walked nearest to us were speaking to each other quickly, laughing. I was only paying attention halfway when I heard the unmistakable words, "Chinook Voyageurs."

Instantly, I snapped to attention.

"Did you hear that?" I asked Patrick, digging my fingernails into his knee.

He was alert, nodding. He looked at me, his eyes wide.

The crowd of officers made their way into the lobby, and a short, slender figure emerged from the back of the group. He was wrapped in a gray wool blanket, moving slowly, but it was unmistakably him.

*It was Paz.*

As one, Patrick and I made our way to him, yelling joyfully. "Paz!"

"Andi? Patrick?" he spoke slowly, as we flung our arms around him. Even through the blanket, I could feel how thin he was. He smelled terrible, too.

"Dear Lord, you're alright!" I exclaimed, hugging him. "Are you okay? What happened to you? Did they hurt you? You're okay, right?"

Paz stiffened in my embrace. I drew back, concerned, searching his dark eyes. He stared at me, his expression unreadable.

"Paz?" I asked, taking a step back. "What's wrong?"

"Slow down," Patrick said, laying his hand on my shoulder. "Let's take this as slow as you need us to, buddy. We're here. We're not going anywhere."

Paz stared at Patrick now, his face blank. His normally tan, healthy complexion was pale, his cheekbones prominent in his gaunt face. He was unshaven, a dark beard and mustache covering his mouth and chin. From what I could see of his clothes under the blanket he clutched to himself, they were filthy and torn, marked with bloodstains.

"So what do you think?" he mumbled. His voice sounded dusty, like it hadn't been used much. I wondered if they'd kept him gagged the whole time.

"About what?" I asked cautiously, searching his eyes.

"About Cap and Hudson," he replied, staring back at me.

"What about them?" I asked, lifting my eyebrows.

Slowly, Paz smiled. "Do you think they'll keep making fun of me after this? Or have I earned a break, finally, from being the butt of their jokes?"

I laughed and threw myself at him again, hugging him tenderly. "We didn't give up on you. We weren't going to leave you behind. Never."

"I figured," he said, finally putting his arms around me. I felt the tension release in his body as we held each other. Without warning, my eyes welled. Patrick had stepped away, presumably to call the team at the hotel and share the happy news.

An officer tapped Paz on the shoulder, interrupting us. We dropped our embrace and Paz nodded.

"They still have to process me," he explained, starting to walk away. "They need to take my statement. They arrested the man who was holding me there, at the house. They told me my testimony is very important, to help ensure justice is served."

"We'll be here when you're done," I smiled, wiping the happy tears off of my face with the back of my hand.

"I know, Andi," he said, smiling over his shoulder. "I always knew you would be."

# CHAPTER 87

THE REST OF THE TEAM arrived within half an hour, bringing fresh clothes and food for Paz, which an officer helpfully carried back to him.

"It's going to take a while," the officer told us, his forehead wrinkled. "You might want to leave and come back later."

"We aren't going anywhere," Rollie spoke up. "We're a team. We don't abandon each other. We'll wait right here, as long as we need to."

I smiled, thinking of how we'd been there when Rollie woke up from his coma. He clearly treasured our loyalty, our unwillingness to leave him in his time of need.

With all nine of us crammed into the lobby together, there weren't enough seats for everyone. Willis and Patrick and Chito stood leaning against the wall while we waited.

Dessie was uncharacteristically quiet, chewing on her thumbnails. At one point, I glanced her way and remarked, "That's probably not good for you, to consume nail varnish like that."

She shot me a look so sour that I wisely closed my mouth and avoided her gaze.

We sat together for another hour, some of the team resorting to pacing around the reception area until an officer irritably told us we were free to go outside and wait there.

"Well, you don't have to tell me twice," Bernard said, already making his way to the revolving door. He and Chito and Patrick disappeared out the door, clumping up together outside the window. The rest of us sat, waiting.

Finally, we saw Paz being escorted down the hallway by two uniformed men. He moved slowly, painfully, taking short steps. We rose to our feet as he arrived to the lobby.

Willis whistled irreverently and we all clapped, grinning, as Paz laid eyes on us. En masse, we circled around him, cheering.

I watched Dessie, curious what she would do. She hung back, her cheeks flushed, as the rest of the group hugged him and chattered excitedly. When the group dispersed and he finally laid eyes on her, she stepped forward and embraced him.

Then, as I'd suspected she might do, she cupped his face with both hands and kissed him deeply.

"Well," Willis exclaimed, laughing, "That's hardly ladylike, is it, Dess? And in front of all these people?"

Dessie pulled away from Paz's surprised face long enough to retort, "Don't be jealous," before she swooped in and kissed him again.

When she let go of him, Paz's face was as white as a ghost.

"Am I dreaming?" he whispered, staring into Dessie's face. "This can't be real."

She grinned.

"It's real," she said, stroking his cheek. He blinked.

"Is it because of the beard?" he asked, a wide smile spreading across his face. "You like it?"

"No," Dessie replied, swatting him playfully. "It's because—I love you."

Paz blinked in shock, his mouth gaping open. He stared at her and started to open his mouth, but then frowned suddenly.

"What are those red stains on your skin?" he asked, peering at her face. "Are you hurt?"

"Let's give them a moment in private," Marceau said, smiling, as he ushered the rest of us toward the door. We all grinned like idiots. I looked over my shoulder as we ducked out the door and saw Paz take Dessie's hands, listening as she spoke to him in a low voice, looking up through her long eyelashes at him.

I stood on the sidewalk with my team, listening as they chatted with each other, exuberant. It was the first time in weeks I'd heard their voices happy, free of stress and worry.

As I watched their faces, glowing with happiness, I felt a twinge of worry over Cap. What was happening with him? We hadn't heard anything at all. Was he in prison already? How could we possibly get Hudson and him out? Was he still furious about Arnau?

As Dessie and Paz's relationship now blossomed, was mine doomed to wilt away entirely?

I pushed the worries from my head. For this moment, right now, it was enough that we'd accomplished our mission. It had taken all of us, together, and it had seemed impossible at times. But we'd done it.

*We'd saved Paz.*

# CHAPTER 88

ONCE PAZ AND DESSIE joined us out front on the sidewalk, their hands intertwined, we piled into the Fords to head back to the hotel.

"I'm sorry, but you need a hot bath and a lot of soap, pronto," Willis remarked, as Paz climbed up into the car next to him, Dessie squeezing into the back seat.

"What can I say? When you're held at gunpoint, you apparently don't get a change of clothing," Paz replied, sniffing. "At least my clothes are clean."

"Yeah, but you stink," Bernard blurted. "We're about the same size. I'll lend you more clothes, after your bath."

"Me too," Leonce said. "We'll get you back to the hotel and give you some time to clean up. Then we'll get dinner and celebrate."

"Dinner," Chito repeated, rubbing his face. "Gosh, I've even forgotten about eating the last few days, we've been so frantically busy."

I walked over to my car, which was parked down the street where Patrick and I had left it earlier this morning, before the rest of the team arrived. Rollie, Chito, and Patrick walked with me.

"I wonder what happened?" Rollie asked as we trudged to the automobiles. "If they ordered the raid today, that means they must have gotten permission from the Spanish police this morning, right? What do you think that means for Hudson and Cap?"

"I don't know," Chito admitted. "I'm guessing we'll have to make our way back to Tarragona and see what's going on with them. We'll likely have to find a way to get them out of jail now."

"And what's going on with Trimboli and the rest of the kidnappers, I wonder?" Patrick said, frown lines etched deeply in his forehead. "Do you figure the police in Tarragona arrested them? Or are they on their way here, to Stefano's house? Are we in danger now?"

"It'll be empty, if they do get there," I replied. "The police will be there, at the house, waiting for them. And at least Paz is safe."

"Right, but they deserve to rot behind bars," Patrick said grimly. "Our fight's not done yet."

We climbed into the Fords and drove to a new hotel. Out of an abundance of caution, we booked us into a new location, again under false names. We didn't want to deal with the crowds of reporters and fans that had appeared at our last hotel.

As I drove, I looked out at the people scurrying about their daily lives, carrying bags and chatting in the waning sunlight. It seemed strange that people could go about their day, carefree, when we'd dealt with such angst and terror the last several weeks.

The team waited in the lobby, relaxing, while Paz bathed and changed into fresh clothes. When he came down, his hair still wet but his clothes clean and unstained, I smiled.

He'd left the beard untouched.

"Ready to get something to eat?" Chito grinned, putting his arm around him and tousling his hair. "We've got to put some meat back on those bones."

"You can tell us everything over dinner," Rollie chimed in. Dessie was already at his side, tossing her hair and looking up at him with a smile on her beautiful face.

We walked together to a small restaurant, and asked the waiter to push two tables together so we could all sit facing each other. Wedged in, shoulder to shoulder, Leonce grinned.

"You'll love this place," he said, leaning forward. "You've probably never had anything like it before, though the owner told me his cousin just opened the same restaurant in New York City."

"What is it?" Marceau asked, sniffing the air. "It smells like spaghetti."

"Not quite," Leonce replied. "It's called pizza marinara. It's a flat sort of bread with tomato sauce and olive oil, some spices, and cheese on top. They bake it in an oven so it's nice and hot when it comes out. The bread gets all crispy and thin."

"Sounds good," Chito said eagerly, glancing at the wood burning oven in the corner of the candlelit restaurant, every table crowded with people. "I wonder how something like that will do in America?"

We ordered bottles of wine and pizzas for the group, then settled back with our drinks to listen to Paz share what the last few weeks had been like for him.

I found myself leaning forward, holding my breath, as he described their rough treatment. They had rushed him straight from where they attacked the Chinooks, shoved into their car and hidden under a blanket, to Stefano's house in Rome.

"Did you have any idea where you were?" Claude asked.

"None," Paz replied. "They kept me blindfolded. I was tied up in their trunk, covered by a tarp as they drove. We bounced along for hours each day, and they stopped to sleep. The first night, we stayed in a barn, but then we stayed in hotels after that."

"How on earth did they get you into a hotel?" Chito asked, his forehead wrinkled. "How does any desk clerk not notice a hostage?"

"They kept one of them out with me in the car, while the rest went in," Paz explained. "They'd wait until it was late, then sneak me in through a window. They only rented ground-floor rooms. Then, they'd slip me back out before dawn, and have a guard posted on me again. I tried to figure out a way to escape, but I knew they all had guns."

"Did they take care of you?" Dessie lifted his chin and studied him. We'd all noticed his thinness.

Paz hesitated, looking at her. "I got a bit of water. Some days, they gave me some bread. By the time they got me to their safe house in Rome, I got bread twice a day. One time, the kid even brought me some leftover beef stew."

Dessie bit her lip, her eyes angry.

"He kept me downstairs in the dark, the whole time," Paz continued. "I still don't know anything about the one who held me captive at the house. I tried speaking to him, every time, but he just replied to me in Italian and waved me off. The basement had obviously been used before, to hold other victims. There was a dirty mattress with no sheets, and a bucket for the facilities. But otherwise, it had no windows and a reinforced, soundproof door."

"So you were alone, in the darkness, for weeks?" Chito said, his face sympathetic. "Paz, I'm so sorry."

He nodded, lowering his eyes. After a moment, he spoke.

"I never could've imagined anything like this happening to me," he confessed. "I suppose you all know now what my family is like. You can imagine what my childhood was like. I was vain and pampered, waited on hand and foot from the moment I was born. But this? The days of monotony, this solitary confinement? Being alone with my thoughts, waiting, worrying? I don't know. It's chiseled me into something different now. I'm not the same man that I was."

We fell quiet, thinking. I wasn't the same either, after the last few weeks. None of us were.

Paz spoke up again. "Andi, did you somehow get into that house at some point? A few days ago?"

"You heard us?" I exclaimed.

He nodded, smiling. "I heard your voice. And a male voice—that was harder to place. But I recognized you. It was the first time I'd heard someone speaking English in weeks. I heard the sound of footsteps, and the boy yelling at you. He slammed the door hard."

"We thought you might be in there!" Patrick cried, thudding his fist down on the table. "Andi and I tried to make it to the basement at that house. We figured you were probably down there. He had supplies in the kitchen—it looked like he'd been holed up for weeks."

"I was there," Paz admitted. "I thought maybe I was dreaming it, at first. But I realized rather quickly that you'd found me. It gave me hope."

He looked over at Dessie and reached for her hand. "I needed hope, believe me. I worried they might kill me."

The rest of us looked down, fiddling with our napkins or taking sips of wine. No one wanted to tell Paz that we knew that Trimboli had been planning to put a bullet in his head when he returned.

*"He doesn't need to lay awake at night and imagine that that's how he would've died,"* I thought to myself, looking at his thin frame. *"He doesn't need to know that he was only hours from being savagely murdered."*

Wisely, no one brought it up as we shared our side of the story, filling him in about the last few weeks.

"No way!" Paz exclaimed with wide eyes, as we told him about how we hot-wired the gang's Ford and set it on fire. His mouth dropped open as he listened to us quietly tell him about how we'd snatched Masso from the liquor store and tortured the information out of him. As Patrick and Dessie and I told him about the press conference, he leaned back and smiled.

When I mentioned Dessie's passionate, unscripted plea at the end, Paz jolted up.

"Wait, you told people you loved me?" he cried, turning to Dessie.

She blushed, looking up at him with a guilty smile.

"Dess," Willis inhaled, his eyes wide. "I've never seen you blush before."

"Leave her alone," Chito grinned. "After what she's been through, she's allowed to blush as much as she wants."

Paz stared back at Dessie, adoration written plainly all over his face. He loved her, too. "So you told the world how you felt about me, before you even told me?" he questioned, tucking a strand of Dessie's hair behind her ear.

"Yes," she admitted.

"Oh, Dessie," he groaned happily. "You mean to tell me that all my friends and family back home have already seen your face and know that you've declared your love to me? They never would've believed that a girl like you would fall for me."

"Easy now," she teased, playfully swatting him on the shoulder. "I'm no trophy girlfriend. I'm an independent woman now. Just like Andi."

"Oh, gosh. I hope we're not that much alike," I blurted swiftly, as the rest of the team laughed.

Patrick raised his glass and grinned. "To a successful rescue operation, and the brilliant, unstoppable people around this table who wouldn't let anything get in their way. And to Paz, in his heroic efforts to save his team and live through hell and back. Let's savor this moment, my friends. We earned it."

We cheered, clinking our glasses together.

Unexpectedly, Bernard raised his glass and tinked it with a fork. All eyes turned to him, surprised. Undaunted by the sudden silence that descended on the group, Bernard looked around the table, meeting our eyes.

"You forgot one," he said, a smile splitting his wrinkled cheeks. "To family."

# CHAPTER 89

THAT NIGHT, I WENT to bed and slept through the night for the first time in weeks.

I had continued to have nightmares about Paz's death every few days for the last several weeks, but hopefully now that he was safely back with the team, sharing a room with Leonce, those nightmares would be behind me.

I awoke to a knock on my door. I sighed, cracking open my eyes. A dull headache from last night's celebratory wine already gripped my brain. I was still exhausted from the stress of the last few days.

"What?" I asked, pulling the covers higher.

"Hey, it's Chito," I heard him say from the other side of the door. "Can you open up?"

"What do you want?" I asked, groaning to myself. I didn't want to get out of bed yet.

"I need to talk to you."

I exhaled. "Can it wait? I just woke up."

He paused on the other side of the door. "It can't really wait, sorry."

Closing my eyes in frustration, I bit my lip. There was always something. Suddenly, I opened my eyes. What if it was news about Cap?

"Chito, is it an emergency?" I asked, fear slipping into my tone.

I heard silence on the other side of the door, and then Chito spoke again, his voice low. "I can't discuss it like this, through the door. I need to speak with you face-to-face."

A wordless terror gripped me. Oh, no. He must've heard bad news about Cap and Hudson.

I shot out of bed, wrapping the top blanket around my shoulders. *"It's not fair!"* I screamed in my head, frustrated. We'd just managed to celebrate the only good thing that had happened to any of us in weeks, with Paz's safe return, and that was going to be followed by more bad news? How could any of us bear this?

Quickly, I pulled open the door and faced Chito. "What?" I gasped, and reeled back in surprise.

Cap was standing next to him.

They were both grinning at me, an impish look in their eyes.

"Cap!" I yelled, throwing my arms around him. "What are you doing here? How are you even *here* right now? I thought—oh, Cap!"

"You thought I was in jail?" he finished for me. "I was. We just got here, actually."

"What happened? We thought we'd have to go back to Tarragona, and bail you both out somehow—wait, is Hudson out, too?"

"He's downstairs in the lobby, greeting his team," Chito butted in behind us. "Well, the ones who are awake already, anyway."

Cap pulled away from me unexpectedly, and glanced at Chito.

"We'll be down there in a minute," he said, his tone of voice swiftly changing, more serious. "I need to discuss something with Andi first. Alone."

Without another word, Chito raised his eyebrows and walked away.

As Chito disappeared down the hallway, Cap stepped into my doorway and closed the door softly behind us.

"We need to talk," he said quietly, staring at me below lowered brows. "I think we both know this has been coming for a while now."

Oh, no.

*"He's going to dump me,"* I realized suddenly. *"After all this time apart—after all we've faced—I thought he'd get over his anger. But he didn't. He's had time to think, sitting in jail. He's ending it."*

My mouth went dry. I knew he was still upset that I'd lied about Rollie and Arnau, but I never dreamed that it would be something he ended our engagement over. Couldn't he understand that I had no other choice? We had to find a safe place for Rollie to recover, and Arnau was our best option. Sure, I should've told him about it, but couldn't he understand the reasons why I didn't?

*"After all this,"* I thought. *"After everything we'd gone through, our desperate actions to save Paz, it came to this. I sacrificed my future with him. It's over."*

I felt the blood drain from my face as I stared at him.

In desperation, I remembered that he'd ended things with his previous fiancée, Milly, years before he met me. Maybe Cap had a habit of falling in love and then getting cold feet? Perhaps he just wasn't meant to settle down.

But even as I felt my spirit drop in dismay, the urge to fight bubbled swiftly to the surface.

I was Andiamo Gallivanter. I wasn't going to give up this easily. If I had to fight him, I would.

I wasn't about to leave anything unsaid anymore. I had realized just how fragile and unpredictable life was, and I wasn't going to leave important things unspoken from now on.

# CHAPTER 90

"I'M SORRY," I BLURTED quickly. "I know you're still angry about the fact that I lied to you about Arnau. I should have told you about it. But I was the captain, in that moment, in charge of making the calls. I made the decision I had to—and it was the right one. I stand behind it. But I knew you'd be mad that I went to Arnau. And I swear to you, he's just a friend. I was only trying to save you from added stress—I planned to tell you when the time was right, but our circumstances only grew more desperate. I could see the toll that all the stress was taking on you, Cap. I didn't want to add more to your shoulders."

He looked up at me, studying me in silence.

"Please, you have to believe me," I continued, biting my lip. "I don't even know where you've been, or what's been going on in your brain lately, but you need to hear me out. Just listen. The only one I've ever loved is you, Cap. I have no feelings for Arnau."

As I stared at Cap, a sudden rush of feeling came over me and my tongue loosened. For the first time in my life, I found myself sharing my emotions easily.

"Cap, I realize you love so fiercely that no one understands how deep your passion runs. You love more than you'll ever get, in return, and yet you continue to love, all the same," I said, hoping my words would get through to him somehow.

"It takes love to do what you do," I pressed on. "To guide our team, to bear the burden of leadership. I know you love each of us, and you show it in the unending acts of service you perform for us, day after day, with no recognition from anyone else. That's why you're the first one up and the last to sleep, as you shoulder the

485

burden of every detail for our team. You put up with the teasing about being the boring one, the bookworm, because you know what it takes to make this expedition happen—and you give yourself up to fill that role. You put yourself last, always. You willingly take on the jobs that no one else wants, so we can enjoy ourselves. And you never complain. It's your sacrifice—your act of love."

He bowed his head, sighing. I couldn't tell what he was feeling, but I had to tell him how *I* felt. He had to hear this.

"You're an incredible leader. It stuns me even more, now that I've had to fill your shoes for a while," I shook my head. "You're the most resilient, resourceful, committed man I've ever met. And you're the one I want to grow old with, Cap. And maybe our love story isn't as easy and romantic as others, but it's real. Because *we* are real."

I stared at him. His ears were pink.

"I'll never find the right words to tell you how I feel about you," I said desperately. "I'm not good with my words, anyway. I put my foot in my mouth all the time. But even if I never find the right words to tell you how I feel, I'll spend the rest of my life *trying* to tell you."

He pursed his lips, inhaling slowly.

"Even in the worst days of our lives, the most terrible fights, I'd still rather have you," I uttered, desperation edging into my voice. I didn't care.

"Even if it means facing another sandstorm, or a car accident, or another day being lost in the deepest, darkest jungle together, or even kidnapping someone together, I'd choose you. Even if it means settling down in a house with a white picket fence and giving up this life of travel."

Cap looked back at me, his expression unreadable. As my eyes lingered on him, I gazed at the unshaven stubble on his face, the deep shadows under his eyes. He looked tired.

"I'd rather go through the worst days of my life *together,* than experience an easy life by myself," I breathed out. "You're my soulmate, Cap. And in your love, I've found all the things I never thought I'd find anywhere. It's like you've always belonged in my life, and in my heart. It doesn't matter where I might end up in life—or what I might end up doing—but as long as it's by your side, I know it's where I'll want to be. Forever."

"Are you done?" Cap asked quietly.

I pressed my lips together, willing myself to keep my emotions inside. He was maddeningly calm.

"I'll take that as a yes," he said, pulling a folded white paper out of his pocket. Head bowed, he handed it to me.

I looked up wildly, afraid to read.

"No," I cried. "Tell me to my face! If you're going to do this to me, at least have the guts to say it to me, like a man!"

He shook his head and pushed the paper toward me. "Just read it."

I blinked, trying to clear the tears from my eyes. I couldn't read the words on the paper as they swam, wobbly with wetness.

Slowly, the words came into focus. They were handwritten, inked in Cap's own hand.

*"Ladies and gentlemen, thank you all for coming. As you know, the Gallivanter Expedition around the world has been temporarily suspended, pending some personal issues with our crew. Rest assured, we are all healthy and happy, and plan to resume our travels across the countries of the world soon.*

*We've always shared so much of our lives as a team with you, the public, and we appreciate the love and support you've shown us ever since we started our travels. We're delighted to finally announce news that we've held close to our own hearts for some time now, knowing that you will receive the happy news with great joy.*

*I, Captain Grant Gallivanter, and Miss Andiamo Gallivanter here have recently become engaged to be married. We are deeply in love, and despite the fact that we have worked hard to maintain a professional environment with our team, we can no longer deny the depth of feeling we have for each other. We want to share our love with the entire world.*

*Miss Gallivanter is my soulmate. She's the love of my life, and as long as my heart beats, I will love her. I pledge to adore her, care for her, lift her up and encourage her, and be her rock when times are difficult and her strength when her own courage ebbs. I know she's already done the same for me. In sickness, and in health, in good times and in bad, I will be by her side. I cannot wait to be her husband.*

*Andi, until the very end of time, and to the very ends of this vast earth, I will love you.*

*HOLD FOR APPLAUSE, THEN KISS IN FRONT OF THE CAMERAS."*

"Oh," I gasped, looking up from the paper. "What is—"

Cap was gone.

# CHAPTER 91

I LOWERED THE PAPER. Cap was down on one knee, holding a ring up to me.

"What?" I choked out, reeling back in confusion.

"I'm doing it properly this time," Cap proclaimed, a wide smile on his face.

"Wait, *what*?"

"No house and white picket fence necessary," he grinned. "Edith Warren—better known as Andi Gallivanter—will you marry me?"

"Wait, I thought—you're *proposing*? Again?" I cried, clasping my hands to my heart.

"And?" Cap pressed, still holding the ring up.

"Yes!" I yelled, grabbing his hands. "You already know that!"

Laughing, Cap slipped the ring onto my left hand. It glimmered, a plain gold band, catching the light.

"Cap!" I exclaimed, staring at the ring. "I don't even know what to say!"

"Good," he said, smiling as he stood up and pulled me against his chest. He grabbed my face and kissed me.

My head was spinning. I shook my head as we came up for air. "Wait. Slow down. What's going on? And where did this come from? I thought you were about to break off our engagement!"

He held me in his arms, his lips dangerously close to mine.

"Never," he murmured. "I love you. I couldn't live without you, Andi."

"But—but—you stormed off, after Rollie and Arnau came back," I faltered. "You were so angry. We didn't talk again, and—I don't even know what happened. And I understand why you were mad, I do. I never should've lied to you. But I thought you'd never forgive me."

He sighed, pressing his face into my hair and speaking in a muffled voice as he breathed through the strands.

"I can't lie, what you did hurt me. And yes, I was incredibly mad about it. But I overreacted," he said, holding me. "It was jealousy, of course, but mostly the tension of the weeks built up, overwhelming me. I was wrong to blow up and storm off like that, and I'm sorry. You're right—you were the captain, and you made the call to take Rollie to Arnau. And it was the right move, clearly."

"I was in charge. I did what I had to do. You know that, Cap. You have to know I was only trying to spare you from more stress."

"I do," he admitted. "And I should've respected your choice, like you respect my decisions. I can't put you in charge and then undercut you by making you justify every move you make. That was wrong of me. Honestly, once I got past the emotions—I realized that I was proud of you. I'm proud of the leadership it took to make that call, to guide that team to Spain. But the anger was there, over feeling like you didn't trust me enough to tell me—that came out first. And that wasn't fair to you."

"Why didn't you say goodbye to me before we left? You just disappeared. That hurt me."

He sighed deeply. "I should have come back to you and talked to you, but—I've been shouldering things by myself for a long time, I suppose. Even back to my childhood, I felt the burden of trying to provide, all on my own—taking care of my mother when she was sick, moving to America on my own as a teenager, creating this team...it's not an excuse, but it *is* a long-held habit. One that I need to work on. It's going to take time for me to shed my old habits and open up, to work through it together, instead of disappearing to deal with it on my own."

"You don't know how that made me feel," I murmured. "How the last few days have felt."

"I know," he groaned. "I'm so sorry. The stress just snapped me, I think. Even as I walked away from you, I realized that you're the one I always want to storm back to and argue with and kiss and make up with, no matter what we face. And if that's how I feel, in my moments of deepest anger, I know that you're the one for me."

"You were so upset, though."

"I was very upset," he admitted. "And Andi, I need to know—what Arnau said, about him giving you your name? Is that true?"

I cringed. "Arnau was the one who first called me 'Andiamo' so yes, it's true."

His eyes studied my face. "Why didn't you ever tell me that?"

I sighed. "He may have been the first one to call me that, but it's the name I chose for myself. The meaning behind it—*let's go*—is who I am, Cap. It wasn't a romantic ode to Arnau. It was an acceptance of who I am, adopting a nickname coined by someone who saw my character before I even realized it myself."

Cap's forehead wrinkled. "That's all?"

"That's all," I said softly. "Don't forget the last name I chose, too. Gallivanter. *Your* name. The name you chose for yourself, long ago."

His eyes stared into mine. "It cut me to the core to hear him say that. To realize I didn't know that about you. But Andi—*Andiamo*—I love all of you. Even the painful parts that shaped you, and the parts I don't yet know. The parts that we'll discover together."

"I feel the same way about you," I said quietly. "I know you've been hurt before. Terribly betrayed. And I'm sorry you endured that. But in its own way, that pain led you here. It brought us together. I'm thankful for that. I'm grateful for the crooked, broken path that led us to each other. Because now I know who'll be by my side as I walk down the rest of that path, in the future. And that's you, Cap."

Cap's lips gently pressed into my forehead. For a moment, we held each other without speaking.

"Life is a fragile thing," he finally said, his arms still wrapped securely around me. "What matters most is the people you're close to. The people who love you in your worst moments. The people who refuse to leave your side, even when things are unimaginably hard. Through all the chaos of the last few weeks, I was struck over and over again with that truth."

He lifted his head and smiled at me with his eyes, the little wrinkles crinkling as he stared at me.

"Sometimes love gets mad," he added. "But it doesn't change the fact that I love you. It will never change that fact."

"I was sure I'd ruined everything," I confessed. "I screwed up, even though I was just trying to protect you. I thought that we might be over."

Cap brushed a loose hair back behind my ear.

"Love is a choice," he said softly. "It's not just an emotion or a feeling. We have the choice to keep on loving someone, despite the headaches and frustrations and pain they cause us. And whenever two people are involved, there are *going* to be problems and hurt. But it's always going to be each of our choices to keep loving each other, in spite of the hurt we cause."

We stared at each other, our eyes locked.

"Feelings come and go, you know. But real love requires patience and understanding, and most of all, commitment," he continued. "And it's real love that I have for you, Andi. I vow to choose love, again and again, until the last breath escapes my body."

I smiled, glancing down once more at the paper in my hand. "Wait. That paper I just read? What is it?"

He grinned. I was so close to his eyes that I could see the reflection of my own bewildered face in them.

"That's the speech I'm giving at a press conference to announce our engagement," he laughed. "Thank God you said yes, again, or I'd have to sit down and write out an entirely new speech."

"Wait, you're actually planning to tell people now? We're going to announce it to the world?"

"Yes," he said, kissing me on the nose. "No more waiting until the perfect time. No more hiding and ducking away and trying to push down our feelings. We're coming clean about this, to everyone, all at once. Let the chips fall as they may. All that really matters is that I love you, and I will *always* love you, Andi. No matter what. We've put this off for far too long already. Let's take advantage of this fresh start and tell the world the truth from now on. No more lies—about anything, or to each other. It's not who we are."

I held up my left hand, staring at the thin band of gold. Cap looked at my face and wrinkled his nose.

"Sorry about the ring," he said apologetically. "I hope you know I wanted to get you a big diamond, but...uh...our circumstances have changed."

"You know I never cared about a flashy ring. This fits me better," I replied, meeting his eyes. "But what do you mean about our circumstances?"

"Well," Cap drawled, his forehead creasing. "We're kind of...broke."

"What?" I exclaimed, shocked. "How can that possibly be? We had a fortune in our account!"

"We did. Until about two days ago."

"What do you mean?"

"It's a bit of a long story, one that Hudson is no doubt telling the team downstairs right now," Cap replied. "But to make a long story short, we had to bribe our way out of prison. And it cost us pretty much every penny we had."

"Wait—*we?*"

Cap rubbed his jaw. "Yes. Hudson, too. The Gallivanter and Chinook crews are both regrettably dead broke."

"Hold on," I said, shaking my head. "But what does that mean for our crew? For our future?"

"Let's go downstairs and talk to the whole group, all at once," Cap suggested, putting his arm around my waist. "Besides, we have to share the happy news. And start scheduling our press conference."

# CHAPTER 92

WE MADE OUR WAY DOWNSTAIRS, where Hudson picked me up and twirled me around upon seeing the ring on my finger.

"It's about time!" he roared happily, as the team applauded and took turns hugging me. "Did that devil tell you he forced me to stop at the jewelry store with him and pick this ring up before we left Spain?"

I grinned. "He left that part out."

"You're marrying a stubborn man," he teased playfully. "I thought he might put a gun to my head when I suggested we just wait until we made it to Rome, and you could pick one out together."

"You know I wanted to surprise her," Cap complained. "Don't act like you hated it."

"Wait, what on earth happened with you guys, anyway?" Rollie asked, looking at Hudson and Cap. "How did you get here so fast?"

"Oh, we'll tell you the whole story," Hudson guffawed, slapping Rollie on the back. "And you tell us what happened with you, too. We only know what we saw in the papers in Spain, after Dessie and Andi's little show."

"Hold on a minute," Cap said, holding up his hand. "I have to say something first."

He searched out Paz in the group and crossed over to him, extending his hand.

"We never really resolved our differences after you left the Gallivanter team, but I want to clear the air," he said, shaking his hand. "I was hard on you when you left us in Kiffa. But I respect you, Paz. You've been through a hellish ordeal. And there's no need

495

to hash out old wounds, in light of what the last few weeks have been like for all of us. Let's let the past stay in the past, shall we?"

"Deal," Paz said gratefully. "I should've told you that I was leaving. And I regret the way I left all of you, really. I was too cowardly to take responsibility for my actions back then. But I'm a changed man now."

"I think we are all changed," Chito grinned, putting his arm around Paz's shoulders.

"If you would've told me my love life would've improved because I was held hostage, though, I might not have been so miserable the last few weeks," Paz added cheekily, winking at Dessie.

She rolled her eyes in response, but smiled.

"Let's crack open a bottle of wine and celebrate," Hudson said cheerfully, heading toward the dining room. "We'll trade war stories here."

"Oh, gosh," Willis groaned. "We did that last night, and I'm still paying for it this morning."

"Besides, it's still early," Patrick frowned. "You can't drink wine at this hour."

"We drove all night, though," Hudson groaned.

"Coffee then," Cap said, leading the way to the dining area.

"Fine," Hudson grumbled. Under his breath, he added, "I'll take mine with a drop of whiskey."

We followed him into the sun-drenched room, light glowing through the gauzy curtains in front of large arched windows, where we took over an entire corner of tables and chairs. Marceau and Chito dragged two tables together, and we crammed in as one group.

Over steaming mugs of coffee, we filled Cap and Hudson in on the last several days. Hudson whistled in admiration as we told him how Dessie and I had carried out the press conference.

"That was genius," he admitted proudly. "You know that's what got us sprung from the coop, right?"

"What?" I asked, looking at Cap. "It did?"

He nodded. "The police chief barged right into our cell with that morning's national newspaper. You and Dessie were the front page photograph. 'You called this station out by name!' he yelled at us, waving the paper in our faces. 'You made us a laughingstock in the eyes of the whole world!'"

"We hoped it would work out that way," Dessie admitted. "What'd you say back to him?"

"I told him that I could promise him two things," Cap responded. "That you two beautiful girls were smart as whips, and would continue to keep your faces on the front page of the newspapers as long as it took to get us released from prison. And that the media frenzy around us would only grow and cause more headaches for him."

"It was at that point that he agreed to see what he might be able to do," Hudson broke in, grinning. "They were desperate to save face, but they didn't want us to get off scott-free, either."

"He pulled us out of the cell, and put us into an interrogation room. When we started mentioning money—a hefty donation to his station, in particular—he sat up straight and started to listen to us more carefully."

Cap jumped in to clarify. "We encouraged them to think about how good it would look for them to get all the credit, and all the international attention for solving the case and getting a dangerous crime ring off the streets. We suggested maybe they deserved a big bonus, and that we might be able to help them out with that. After being embarrassed by you two in the newspapers, he liked our idea."

"We always suspected they were dirty," Willis interrupted. "Now we know for sure, huh?"

They nodded.

"So it was partly us, and partly a bribe?" Dessie said, her lips pursed. "How much did it cost?"

Hudson and Cap exchanged glances. They both sighed in perfect unison.

"Everything," Hudson admitted. "We tried to negotiate. But we'd committed some pretty serious crimes. Arson, grand theft, breaking and entering, kidnapping, assault—they had our backs up against the wall. We were forced to go higher and higher, and they cleaned us out in the end."

"Wait, how'd you afford my ring?" I asked, frowning. "If you had no money left, how could you spend money on this?"

Cap shrugged. "Don't worry about it."

Hudson cut him off. "He sold his pocket watch at a pawn shop."

I blushed, realizing the sacrifice he'd made for me. It made his gesture all the more endearing.

"Anyway, they arrested Trimboli and his men," Cap continued, clearing his throat. "They followed them after the ransom collection and caught them red-handed, depositing the bills in a small bank outside of Barcelona. Trimboli must've suspected something—he was hiding the money away for safekeeping. After that, they agreed to turn over permission to pursue the case to the Roman police."

"And they buried the story about our kidnapping and torture of Masso," Hudson added. "He's in jail with the rest of them now."

"Good riddance," Dessie breathed, her voice hard. "I hope he rots in there."

"I'll say, it's a damn good thing that we had a combined fortune," Hudson said. "Now that we're broke, let's try to be on our best behavior. We can't afford to screw up again. Literally, we *cannot* afford it. Willis, are you hearing me clearly?"

"And we better stay away from Spain, too," Cap added. "I can promise you, they do not like us there. Those police will never help us again."

The rest of us sat quietly, absorbing the news. I sipped my coffee, relieved that we were finally all back together and unharmed, but apprehensive about our future. Could we even continue on, without any funds?

"Well, we'll figure something out about where we go from here," Patrick finally said, interrupting the silence. "It'll be back to our penny-pinching early days, huh?"

"We'll have to start from scratch and fundraise our expeditions again," Cap sighed. "It took a few years, meeting with donors and convincing investors. We won't be able to admit to the world that we blew every penny on bailing ourselves out of prison, so we'll have to be more discreet than ever."

"Rice and beans for every meal again," Chito joked.

I looked around and spoke up. "Listen, if I've learned anything about this group over the last few weeks, it's that we're the most resourceful people on the planet. What matters most is that we're here, together. We've made it this far, surviving circumstances that most people could never imagine. And we're not going to give up now. We'll find a way."

Slow smiles and nods appeared around the group.

"You're getting a good one, Cap," Hudson grinned, shooting me an admiring glance. "Andi, are you sure you want to marry that ugly brute? I'm single, you know."

We erupted in laughter. It felt good.

"And don't forget, it's not all hopeless," Dessie added, smiling at me. "We have a wedding to plan now!"

"Yeah," Bernard grinned, sipping his coffee. "I hope you like rice and beans for your reception."

# CHAPTER 93

WE SPENT THE NEXT FEW days skipping around Rome together as a group, finally free from worry.

Together, we toured the Colosseum and the Forum, walking in the footsteps of emperors. Across town, we strode reverently through the massive St. Peter's cathedral and Sistine Chapel, our necks craned in admiration of the colorful ceiling.

Fans followed us around, excitedly greeting us at every corner. Newspaper reporters interviewed us and snapped photographs. We accommodated, grateful for their support. In our hour of need, they'd come through to help us.

"This is all good for us," Cap reminded us, as we signed autographs. "The Odysseus Society will be much more forgiving going forward, now, the more attention we get. And we certainly have some explaining to do, when we finally get the chance to talk to them."

Hudson and Cap finally issued a joint written statement for the newspapers, giving a brief and highly sanitized version of the last few weeks.

According to what they wrote, the Chinook Voyageurs had been attacked and Paz kidnapped. We'd worked together, with the police, to track down the kidnappers and discovered that they were a violent gang. But thankfully, they were off the streets, the injured Chinooks were completely healed up, and both teams would continue on their travels as soon as they could.

Cap had put out invitations far and wide for the press conference to announce our engagement. We were planning it for tomorrow.

Already, we anticipated a massive crowd of reporters. None of them knew what we planned to announce, only that the Gallivanter team would be making a "major announcement."

We were mobbed by people everywhere we went in Rome for the next few days, posing for photographs and shaking hands and signing autographs as we were recognized. The Italian people embraced us warmly, sharing their admiration for our courage as the media shared our story.

Even amidst all the excitement and the frenzy from the crowds, we were content. It was enough to be with each other, our little family of adventurers, exploring the city.

The thirteen of us lined up that evening along the edge of the Trevi Fountain, and tossed a coin into its bubbling waters for good luck.

"There it goes," Cap murmured in my ear as I flipped my coin. "Our honeymoon fund."

I laughed in spite of myself. "Well, we'll just have to keep traveling around the world with the crew, I guess, in lieu of a proper honeymoon."

"I don't know if we can even afford that anymore," he admitted. "But at least we got to live out the dream for the last year."

I heard the pain in his voice, even as he tried to make light of his casual comment. Cap had spent his entire life looking forward to this dream. He'd worked for years to prepare for the expedition. I reached for his hand, lacing my fingers through his.

"At least we got to do it together," I replied, my voice low. "This is where we've always belonged. Side by side, looking out at the wonders of the world."

For a few moments, we stood there together, silent, looking at the marble statues in front of us and listening to the crowd surrounding us. Finally, Chito leaned forward, fishing a coin out of his pocket.

"One more," he said, holding it up. "Make this last wish count, everyone."

I watched the coin arc through the air, catching the last remnant of sunlight as it flipped and broke through the surface of the water, settling on the bottom.

*"Just like my dreams of seeing the world,"* I thought wistfully, watching it disappear from sight, out of my reach.

# CHAPTER 94

THE NEXT MORNING, I readied for the press conference, dressing carefully. I smiled to myself as I slipped the gold ring onto my finger. At long last, my love wouldn't be a secret.

I'd finally mailed the letter to my mother yesterday, confessing my feelings for Cap and the fact that we were engaged.

We planned to telegram her that evening, and share the happy news in that brief form, before she opened the newspapers and saw it there. She'd have my letter in a few weeks to hear the whole story straight from me.

I heard a knock at my door, and knew it would be Cap coming to get me. I opened it, a smile already in place on my face.

Dessie stood in front of me, looking perky in her blue Chinook uniform. She looked like she could pose for a magazine cover, with her hair and makeup perfect despite the early morning hour.

"Just as I figured," she greeted me. "No lipstick."

"I don't have any," I rolled my eyes. "You know I hate that stuff."

"But you're going to be on camera!" she said, holding up a small metal tube. "Come on. Just a little. It's a special occasion."

"Will you leave me alone if I put it on?"

"Yes," she promised. "Come on. You're the woman everyone wants to be, on the arm of the man everyone wishes he could be. You're a bonafide celebrity. Dress the part."

"Fine," I said, cracking open the door to let her in. I realized she just wanted to contribute to my special day, in the only way she knew how. It was a peace offering. "Just a little, though."

Dessie carefully applied my lipstick as I sat in the desk chair in my room and pursed my lips.

"There," she said, squinting as she stepped back. "You look beautiful."

"Thanks," I said, meeting her eyes. It was the first time she'd ever genuinely complimented me, I realized. As I smiled at her, I noticed that the mercurochrome still left its faint reddish stain on the healing scars on her face. Even so, she was radiant.

"I'm happy for you," Dessie replied, her expression warm. "And I'm happy for me, too."

We grinned at each other.

"To think that only a few months ago, we were sniping at each other in the newspapers," she added.

I rolled my eyes. "You went after me first."

"Well, let's let bygones be bygones. It all worked out, in the end, didn't it?"

A knock sounded again from the hallway, and this time a voice accompanied it. "You ready?" Cap spoke through the closed door.

"Ready," Dessie said, bounding over to the door and wrenching it open.

"Oh, hey," he said absently, leaning past her to get a glimpse of my face. His eyes lit up as they landed on me. "You're ready, too?"

I beamed. "Let's do this."

Cap took my arm and led me down the hall, Dessie trailing behind us. We made our way down to the lobby, the sound of the boisterous crowd of reporters evident even from our upper staircase. As we walked down the stairs together, our arms linked, flashes from cameras went off, capturing us. The crowd buzzed with whispered comments.

As we strolled over in front of the crowd, I heard a shrill voice calling, "Captain Gallivanter! Sir! It's very important!"

I glanced over to see the hotel clerk waving his arms high above his head, frantically trying to get our attention. He held a telegram in his right hand, fluttering it like a white flag. I nudged Cap, and we walked over.

"Oh, Captain Gallivanter, grazie Dio," he groaned, clutching his chest dramatically. "This telegram just came a few minutes ago, sir, and it's urgent."

Cap and I exchanged concerned glances.

"Thank you," he said automatically, reaching for the telegram. I watched as he unfolded the paper and read, his eyes scanning back and forth across the page. He blinked in surprise, his mouth opening. His eyes darted across again, rereading.

"Dear Lord," he breathed, looking up at me.

"What?"

His eyes were big, the color draining from his face. He looked shell-shocked.

"What?" I repeated, worried. He shook his head numbly.

"Get the team," he said quietly, grabbing my shoulder. "The whole group. We have an urgent matter we need to attend to. Right now."

"But what—" I started to ask, while he waved me off and turned toward the clerk.

"Pardon me, can we use your back office for just a few moments?" he asked. "We need to have a quick conversation in private. Please."

"Certainly," the clerk stammered, moving aside.

"But—"

"The team, Andi," Cap repeated, giving me a little push. "Hurry."

I darted through the crowd, whispering the message to Rollie and Chito and Leonce, who spread it to the others. In a flash, everyone was huddled into the tiny back office. The space was small and cramped, and I squeezed painfully against a metal filing cabinet stacked high with receipts.

"What on earth?" Hudson asked, staring at Cap. "What's wrong?"

Cap held the telegram in his hands. "I don't know how to say this," he said, shaking his head in disbelief. "We have an offer."

"An offer for what?" Hudson asked, his brows knitting.

"An offer to stay together—permanently," Cap answered slowly. "They say the story is perfect. Two bitter rivals who turned into best friends, after secretly searching together for their kidnapped crew mate. They say the story will sell itself. And that they want to pay us to stay together and keep traveling the world. They want all our footage, and even more. They're willing to foot the bill for wherever we want to go next, and they want us to go *together*."

"You're not making sense!" Hudson frowned, snatching the letter away. "Let me read it."

His eyes ran over the page, a broad smile inching across his face. After a moment, he looked up.

"Well, it looks like the old expedition hasn't come to an end, after all," he grinned. "They've made us an offer we can't possibly refuse."

"*Who?*" our voices clamored, questioning.

"Hollywood," Cap said, finally finding his voice. "We're headed to Hollywood."

# AUTHOR'S NOTE

DID I EVER THINK I'D write a heist novel? No. But do I perhaps have a future, thinking like a criminal mastermind? Maybe.

This book continues the story of the Gallivanter Expedition in *The Gallivanter Saga*. Once again, as I did with the second book in the series, I simply finished one manuscript and started on the next one the following morning. It took me forty-nine days to finish writing this story, and I penned the last few chapters as the United States went into lockdown, at the start of the COVID pandemic. Its hopeful ending is more poignant as I remember the utter despair that consumed me, at that time.

Though this work is entirely fiction, born from my imagination, I was inspired by a real-life adventurer named Aloha Wanderwell Baker. In tribute to her courage, I sprinkled some real-life details about Aloha into my manuscript, but this story is my own. Though I remained as historically accurate as I could, I did write progressively about how women and various races and ethnicities were treated in the twentieth century.

Once again, I owe thanks to many people who helped me with this book.

My faithful readers have been unflagging in their appreciation of *The Gallivanter Saga*. Each review and comment delights me and brings a smile to my face, especially from my young fans. Thank you for loving the world I created—it means more than you'll ever know.

To Tyler, my husband—your love is a gift that keeps on blessing me every day. Thank you for the endless hours you spent helping me brainstorm the complicated twists and turns in this book's plot. Heaven help us if we ever decided to use our creativity for evil—we'd be unstoppable.

To my family and in-laws, your love and support in this journey has been monumental. Tracey and Grammie, especially, it's been a delight to hear your excitement over the Gallivanter adventures. Mom, your feedback has been invaluable as I wrote this series, and I'm so thankful for your whip-sharp brain and opinions.

I've been blessed to have worked with thousands of students over the course of my career, and their enthusiasm for this book series has been monumental. Thank you, guys, for cheering me on like you do.

To my many dear, wonderful friends—you're the best. One cannot write about such deep bonds of friendship without experiencing it herself. Thanks for being a part of my life.

Jon, a special shout out to you for asking me approximately nine hundred times about when "that heist book" was going to be out because you couldn't wait to read it. Eric, you *did* read the first draft of "that heist book" and in the way that only you can, your two words—"it's *good*"—was encouragement enough.

Chloe, Harry, Ludka, Pierre, Rena, and Luca, thanks for checking my foreign language accuracy. Mohammed, thank you for bringing the Gallivanter world to life with your cover art.

When I first began writing this book series, it was simply a creative outlet. I wasn't sure I'd ever share it with anyone, let alone the whole world. It took immense courage, effort, and will to bring *The Gallivanter Saga* to life—but boy, has the adventure been worth every second of the hard work.

Life is short. Do the brave thing. Go on the adventure. Have the conversation. Forgive. Move on. Grow. And never stop fighting to make *your* story a great one.

Soli Deo gloria.

# OTHER BOOKS IN *THE GALLIVANTER SAGA*

*The thrilling adventures of a ragtag team of world travelers, navigating danger and discovery in the Roaring Twenties.*

**Saving Andiamo**
Book One, *The Gallivanter Saga*

**A New Wild**
Book Two, *The Gallivanter Saga*

**Savage World**
Book Three, *The Gallivanter Saga*

**Uncharted Within**
Book Four, *The Gallivanter Saga*

**Audacia Always**
Book Five, *The Gallivanter Saga*

**A Dream Uninvited**
Book Six, *The Gallivanter Saga*

# About the Author

Cassie A. H. Moore is an author, speaker, educator, and consultant with over 15 years of experience working with young people.

She earned her master's degree in organizational leadership from the Townsend Institute at Concordia University in Irvine, California, has published non-fiction books, curriculum, and articles, and has taught and spoken to thousands of students and leaders all over North America.

As a lifelong student of culture, Moore weaves her interests in humanity, history, travel, and new experiences into her writing and speaking.

A travel enthusiast, Moore has enjoyed her own adventures traveling to 50 states, 21 countries, 10 islands, 6 Canadian provinces, and one erupting volcano. She and her husband live in Hood River, Oregon, with their two dogs, where they hike or kayak every chance they can get.

Learn more at cassieahmoore.com.

www.ingramcontent.com/pod-product-compliance
Lightning Source LLC
Chambersburg PA
CBHW022012300726

48970CB00003B/858